QEH
BI

DEAT

RUDI AND HANNA's search for the truth behind the corruption in their small village leads them to the Altdorf – capital city of the Empire. But as Rudi gets closer to the answers he desperately seeks, he realises that he must seek the aid of his bitter enemy, Gerhard the witch hunter. As the tension mounts and the final confrontation looms, Rudi must confront the darkness within him lest it consume him forever.

A WARHAMMER NOVEL

DEATH'S LEGACY

SANDY MITCHELL

For Katharine and Elspeth: remembered with love.

A BLACK LIBRARY PUBLICATION

First published in Great Britain in 2006 by
BL Publishing,
Games Workshop Ltd.,
Willow Road, Nottingham,
NG7 2WS, UK

10 9 8 7 6 5 4 3 2 1

Cover illustration by Wayne England.
Map by Nuala Kinrade.

A CIP record for this book is available from the British Library.

ISBN 13: 978 1 84416 392 2
ISBN 10: 1 84416 392 X

Distributed in the US by Simon & Schuster
1230 Avenue of the Americas, New York, NY 10020.

Printed and bound in Great Britain by
Bookmarque, Surrey, UK.

See the Black Library on the Internet at
www.blacklibrary.com

Find out more about Games Workshop
and the world of Warhammer at
www.games-workshop.com

THIS IS A DARK age, a bloody age, an age of daemons and of sorcery. It is an age of battle and death, and of the world's ending. Amidst all of the fire, flame and fury it is a time, too, of mighty heroes, of bold deeds and great courage.

AT THE HEART of the Old World sprawls the Empire, the largest and most powerful of the human realms. Known for its engineers, sorcerers, traders and soldiers, it is a land of great mountains, mighty rivers, dark forests and vast cities. And from his throne in Altdorf reigns the Emperor Karl-Franz, sacred descendant of the founder of these lands, Sigmar, and wielder of his magical warhammer.

BUT THESE ARE far from civilised times. Across the length and breadth of the Old World, from the knightly palaces of Bretonnia to ice-bound Kislev in the far north, come rumblings of war. In the towering World's Edge Mountains, the orc tribes are gathering for another assault. Bandits and renegades harry the wild southern lands of the Border Princes. There are rumours of rat-things, the skaven, emerging from the sewers and swamps across the land. And from the northern wildernesses there is the ever-present threat of Chaos, of daemons and beastmen corrupted by the foul powers of the Dark Gods. As the time of battle draws ever nearer, the Empire needs heroes like never before.

f Claus

North of Here Lie The
Dreaded Chaos Wastes.

Erengrad.

Here Be Trolls...

Praag.

Middle Mountains.

Kislev

Kislev.

enheim.

Wolfenburg.

Talabheim.

Alldorf.

The Empire

Karak Kad

Nuln.

The
Moot.

Sylvania.

Dracken
-hof.

Zhufbar.

Averheim.

Black
Water.

Karak
Norn.

Black fire Pass.

CHAPTER ONE

Rudi directed his stumbling footsteps away from the blazing ruins of the shantytown on the mudflats, the leaping flames behind the two fugitives seeming to turn the snowflakes flurrying around them into wisps of floating gold. Despite the way they blurred his vision, he found himself grateful for the presence of the drifting motes of ice. The cold they brought was intense, all the more so after the almost unbearable heat they'd so recently been exposed to, and the discomfort helped to keep him focused, and stop his mind from reeling under the strain of attempting to understand the events of the last few hours.

He glanced across at Hanna, who was still keeping pace with him despite the exhaustion that made her sway with every step. The price of the wild burst of uncontrolled magic, which had consumed the settlement of mutants and renegades, still blazed behind them.

'Are you all right?' he asked, realising how stupid the question was even as he asked it, but Hanna simply nodded.

'I'll live,' she said grimly.

'We both will,' Rudi assured her, sweeping his gaze across the ruins surrounding them, and adjusting his grip on the sword he hadn't bothered to sheath. The Doodkanal, he knew from personal experience, was no place to seem weak. Too many desperate and depraved individuals eked out a marginal existence there, and human predators lurked in every shadow. To his unspoken relief, however, he could detect none of the signs of stealthy movement which might betray the presence of any of the local denizens. No doubt the conflagration in the distance had them all spooked enough to stay well clear of the area, or the biting cold had driven them to seek whatever shelter they could find here, in the most derelict corner of Marienburg.

Rudi grinned, without humour. Anonymous footpads were the least of their worries. Gerhard and his band of mercenaries were no doubt still close at hand, although whether the witch hunter and his associates were in any fit state to fight after the battle they'd just been through was a debatable point. Rudi shook his head, dismissing the thought. He had too much respect for their martial abilities to dismiss them as a threat, despite the battering they'd taken. Besides, Krieger's sellswords were implacable foes on their own account, not just out of loyalty to the man who was paying them. At least Alwyn wouldn't be using her magic again this soon.

That brought his whirling thoughts back to Greta Reifenstahl. The witch had vanished again, as abruptly as she'd appeared to save them from the madman he'd once thought his friend. Despite Hanna's delight at discovering that her mother was still alive, Rudi felt a tremor of unease as he considered the sorceress's words to him: *'The fool was right about one thing, anyway. You do have a destiny.'* She clearly knew something of his origins, and the secret he'd hoped to uncover from Magnus von Blackenburg. Indeed, it now looked as if she'd been trying to protect him from the merchant, and the bizarre cult of disease and decay that he'd led, ever since his arrival in Marienburg. Equally clearly, she'd been touched by Chaos in some way herself; the horns on her forehead made that all too obvious.

In spite of himself he glanced across at Hanna, still plodding determinedly on at his shoulder, wondering for a brief, guilty instant if the taint her mother bore had somehow been passed on to her daughter, but that was ridiculous. After all they'd been through together, if he couldn't trust Hanna, he couldn't trust anyone.

'Wait,' he whispered, as they reached the mouth of an alleyway he recognised. Whirling snowflakes flickered against his face, the cobbles beneath his feet already slick with the first powdering of white. No footprints were visible apart from his and Hanna's, but that didn't mean much. Torches were flaring in the distance, and thin lines of light were visible around the shutters of some of the houses surrounding them. They'd already reached the more habitable margins of the Doodkanal, and a few more steps would lead them into the bustling streets of the Winkelmarkt.

He hesitated, trying to assess the risks. On the one hand, he knew almost every inch of that ward, as a result of having patrolled it for several months while working as a member of the city watch. He knew every bolthole, and every patch of concealing shadow that might help them to slip through unobserved. On the other hand, so did his erstwhile colleagues, who would undoubtedly be searching for both of them since he'd helped Hanna escape from the watch house earlier that evening.

'What's the matter?' Hanna asked, her face pinched in the diffuse illumination, huddling deeper inside the overlarge travelling cloak that she'd taken from the captain of the soldiers on the moors. She was shivering, and not just from the cold. She'd been severely debilitated by the effects of Gerhard's magic-nullifying talisman, which had been slowly sucking the life out of her ever since the fugitives had arrived in Marienburg, and the torrent of mystical energy that had flooded through her following its removal had taken its own toll. Clearly she couldn't stand much more of this strength-sapping chill.

'Just trying to work out the best route to the Suiddock,' Rudi told her, shading the truth a little. Dawn couldn't be far off, and the *Reikmaiden* was due to sail at first light. If they missed her, and he couldn't envisage Shenk delaying the departure of his vessel on their account, their last hope of escaping Marienburg would be gone. There simply wasn't time to take a more circuitous route.

'Don't take too long,' Hanna said, her teeth chattering, clearly having come to the same conclusion.

There was nothing else for it. Putting away the sword, which would have attracted too much attention in the populated streets, he offered the girl his other arm. He half expected her to spurn it, but Hanna was too far gone to stand on her dignity and took it gratefully, leaning against him for support. Once again, Rudi was astonished at how light she felt, but concealed his concern as best he could, angling his body to shield her from the wind as much as possible.

Luck seemed to be with them at first. As they slipped into the streets of the Winkelmarkt, Rudi's ears were assailed by the familiar sounds of the early risers going about their business, mingling with those of the last die-hard revellers lurching back to their beds. Shopkeepers were stirring, preparing their wares, and a few enterprising peddlers were firing up braziers in anticipation of doing good business with hot snacks to help keep out the cold. Though the streets were still comparatively empty, they were crowded enough to hold out the hope of concealment, as they blended into the throng of bustling people going about their everyday concerns.

Spotting a discarded wine bottle in the gutter, Rudi scooped it up, hoping that anyone noticing their dishevelled appearance, and Hanna's unsteady gait, would draw the obvious conclusion and dismiss them from their minds without looking too closely.

'Rudi?' someone called. He tensed, and kept moving, hoping that the hail was meant for someone else. He had a common enough name after all. Then the voice came again, familiar and insistent, accompanied by the unmistakable sound of running feet. 'Rudi, wait!' Cursing their luck, he turned, seeing the floppy black cap of a member of the city watch forging through the intervening citizens, its owner waving frantically in their direction.

'Gerrit,' Rudi said, half in greeting, half as a warning to Hanna. The two of them had met briefly, he remembered, when Hanna had visited him at the watch barracks. Gerrit was his best friend among the Caps, and had been unable to resist teasing him a little about the relationship he pretended to assume had existed between him and the girl. 'What are you doing up at this ungodly hour?' The two of them had rotated to the day shift the morning before, and weren't due on duty for some hours yet.

'Everyone's been called in,' Gerrit said slowly, his hand hovering near the hilt of his sword, but to Rudi's unspoken relief making no attempt to draw it yet. Despite trying to pretend he was simply engaged in a casual conversation, Rudi couldn't help glancing around as unobtrusively as he could, his old forester's instincts searching for the rest of Gerrit's patrol, but for some reason the young Cap seemed to be alone. Perhaps he hadn't heard the news of Rudi's treachery yet. 'But then you must have expected that.' The tone of voice in which this last comment was added put paid to that slender hope almost as soon as it had flared. Still, if anyone among the watch would be prepared to give him the benefit of the doubt, it would be Gerrit. Anyone else, he was sure, would have drawn steel and arrested them both by now. Perhaps he could still bluff it out.

'I've been a bit busy,' Rudi said, flourishing the bottle and blessing the gently falling snow for concealing Hanna's features even more effectively. She huddled deeper inside the enveloping cloak, the hood falling forward to conceal her features. The last time he'd seen Gerrit, on his way out of the barracks to rescue the girl, he'd contrived to give his friend the impression that he was meeting another young woman; maybe he could convince him that he'd been otherwise engaged all night, and that whatever he'd heard was some kind of mistake. 'That evening out lasted a bit longer than I expected.' Picking up the unspoken cue Hanna giggled, as if drunk, and leaned into him as if suddenly losing her footing.

'I remember.' Gerrit nodded. 'You said you were meeting Rauke van Stolke.' Of course he knew her too, slightly. She was a Cap herself, in the neighbouring Suiddock ward. He nodded affably to Hanna. 'Morning, Rauke.'

'Morning,' Hanna said, slurring her voice in an attempt to disguise it. She had no idea what the woman she was impersonating normally sounded like, but under the circumstances that probably wasn't important. Gerrit nodded again, as if something had just been confirmed, and drew his sword.

'Do you mind explaining how you got here from the Draainbrug watch house so fast?' he asked her. 'I only left you half an hour ago.' That at least explained why he was on his own, Rudi thought. He must have been on his way back from delivering a message to the Suiddock watch, warning them to be on the lookout for the pair of fugitives.

'Ger.' Rudi took a step back, as if startled and confused. 'I don't know what you've heard, but it's all a misunderstanding. There's no need for this.'

He flung the bottle at his friend. Gerrit ducked reflexively, wrong-footed for a moment, and Rudi dived at him, clamping a hand around the wrist of the young Cap's sword hand. Gerrit pivoted, trying to throw him, and Rudi countered, drawing on every street-brawling technique he'd learned as a law enforcer, keeping on his feet by a miracle.

'Hanna, run,' he shouted, and smashed his forehead into the other youth's face. Gerrit reeled back, blood gushing from his nose, and closed again, swinging his sword at Rudi's head. Rudi moved to evade it, his feet skidding on the carpet of fresh snow, and fell heavily. Gerrit loomed over him, his sword raised to strike.

'Witch-loving bastard,' he said, thrusting straight at Rudi's face. Before he could complete the movement, however, he staggered, an expression of surprise flitting briefly across his visage. The hilt of the dagger that Hanna habitually kept concealed in her bodice was projecting from his chest, and he fell heavily to his knees. It seemed that, despite her exhaustion, she'd lost none of the skill in knife throwing that she'd learned from Bruno while they'd been travelling with Krieger's mercenary band.

'Come on.' Hanna pulled Rudi to his feet, with a surprising surge of strength. She seemed sharper, more alert; although where the energy was coming from he had no idea. 'We have to run.'

'Help! Watch! Murder!' a nearby fishwife screeched, her wide eyes fixed on Gerrit's prostrate form. Hanna plucked her dagger from the young Cap's chest with a moist sucking sound. None of the passers-by seemed inclined to intervene – and Rudi couldn't blame them – but as he forced his legs into motion, his head spun with the enormity of what had just happened. With that amount of noise, the watch would be there in moments, he had no doubt, which might at least save Gerrit...

'Is he dead?' he asked. Hanna nodded jerkily.

'Should be, I aimed for the heart.' She dodged down an alleyway behind a fish-gutter's, the stench of old entrails still discernible despite the bitter chill. Rudi felt a shiver going through him at her words, which wasn't entirely due to the cold: Hanna was a healer, dedicated to preserving life, or at least she had been. Almost as if she could read his thoughts, she glanced back at him, her pale face framed by the hood of her cloak so that it seemed to be floating unsupported in a circle of darkness. 'I'm sorry about your friend, but it was him or us, and he died a lot easier than we will if they catch us.'

Rudi nodded, unable to argue with her. If they were caught, they'd be burned, there was no question about that. Hanna was a witch, a sorcereress, and her death was inevitable if she fell into the hands of the authorities. He was accused of heresy, targeted by a witch hunter, which was almost as bad. If they couldn't make it aboard the riverboat tonight, they were both as good as dead.

'This way,' he said, doubling through a courtyard in which lines of washing hung, stiff as tavern signs in the bitter cold. A low wall lay beyond it, behind which one of the innumerable back canals that threaded their way through the city lapped against its banks. Hanna glanced up and down the waterway, into which the drifting snowflakes vanished without a trace.

'It's a dead end!' she said.

Rudi shook his head. 'No it's not.' He clambered up on the wall, and held out a hand for her to join him. She took it, the skin of her palm feeling strangely warm against his, and bounded up beside him, all trace of her former exhaustion gone. He had no time to wonder about that now, though. 'It just looks that way.' A couple of planks bridged the gap, placed there by the residents of the sprawling rooming house that enclosed three sides of the courtyard, as a makeshift short cut to the boatyard on the other side where most of them worked. He edged across the frost-slick wood cautiously, trying not to look down at the scum-flecked water below, or let the snowflakes whirling about his face distract him too much. They flickered hypnotically across his field of vision, threatening to overwhelm him with vertigo at every step. Hanna, on the other hand, trotted in his wake as sure-footedly as if she was merely out for an afternoon stroll.

'Where are we?' she asked, as they hopped down a pile of lumber, evidently left as a makeshift staircase on the other side.

'Van der Decken's,' Rudi replied. The Winkelmarkt was well known for the quality of its boatyards, which produced most of the small craft that plied the waterways of Marienburg. The local residents knew the location of every one of them, but Hanna looked confused for a moment, and he remembered that she'd spent most of her stay in the city in the Templewijk. 'The slips are on the other side of the yard, near the fish docks.' Hanna nodded, orientated again, and Rudi became aware that her face seemed to be gently illuminated from below. It must be the stone she'd carried around her neck since taking it from the skaven they'd encountered in the wilderness all those months ago. It had glowed once before, he remembered, although Hanna had been at a loss to explain the phenomenon. Perhaps it was sustaining her in some fashion, lending her the energy she needed to get away.

'How are we going to get across the Bruynwater?' she asked. Rudi had been wondering the same thing. The *Reikmaiden* was berthed on the island of Luydenhoek, on the other side of the main shipping channel, and only one bridge, the Draainbrug, crossed the mighty waterway. After what Gerrit had told them, it was certain to be watched. Rudi shrugged.

'We're in a boatyard,' he said. Unfortunately that didn't help. The only vessels they found were in various states of assembly or repair, and none seemed river worthy to his inexperienced eyes, at least so far as he could tell in what fitful illumination was afforded by the lamps and torches in the nearby street. He began to wish that the baleful light of Morrslieb, the Chaos moon, was still visible instead of being hidden by the snow clouds. Sickly and necrotic as it was, even that would have been something of a help.

At length they gave it up as a bad job, and, moving cautiously, ventured out into the street again. Fortunately, none of the passers-by on this side of the water paid them any heed, apparently intent on nothing more than getting to their destinations and out of the snow as quickly as possible, and they made it through the rest of the Winkelmarkt without attracting any more unwelcome attention. There were a number of narrow squeaks, however: several times they were forced to take cover in the shadows or duck down a side passage to avoid watch patrols, grim-faced men that Rudi recognised and had once worked alongside, now determined to hunt him down.

A couple of times he thought about donning his own uniform hat, hiding behind the authority it gave him, and then dismissed the idea. His former colleagues would be on the lookout for him in any case, and there was no point in making himself even more visible. They'd be bound to hail another watchman, even if they didn't recognise his face at once, to exchange news and information, and all the other Caps he'd seen were in groups of two or three. Alone, he'd be far more noticeable than he would be just trying to blend in with the civilians surrounding them.

They passed into the Suiddock ward at last, and his steps became hesitant. He didn't know the streets here the way he did in the Winkelmarkt, just the main thoroughfares, and remaining concealed would be far more difficult. On the other hand, the crowds around them had grown as well, teamsters and stevedores hurrying to work, the bustle of the dock area never entirely still even at this pre-dawn hour. Indeed, several cargoes seemed to be on the move already. Taking Hanna by the elbow, he led her in among a tightly packed string of wagons heading for the Draainbrug. With a bit of luck they might be able to cross it, concealed by the surrounding traffic.

That hope was soon extinguished, however. Long before they could reach the marvel of dwarf engineering, the wagons stopped, blocked by a milling throng of pedestrians and other carts.

'What is it?' Hanna asked anxiously. 'What's going on?'

The carter on the wagon beside them glanced down, and gestured in the vague direction of the bridge.

Craning his neck, Rudi could just make out the huge tower in the middle of the river around which the mighty structure pivoted.

'The bridge is open,' the man said. He stood up on his seat for a better view, glancing left and right. 'That's funny. There doesn't seem to be a ship coming.' Rudi fought to keep his face neutral. Of course, he thought. The first thing the Suiddock watch would have done after getting Gerrit's message would be to open the bridge, trapping the fugitives in the southern half of the city. The disruption would be severe, of course, but the authorities would be prepared to tolerate it for a little while if it meant catching a couple of dangerous heretics.

'Come on.' He led Hanna through the growing, and increasingly restive, throng. Before long, some of the Suiddock Caps would be turning up to keep order, and they wouldn't be able to evade detection once that happened. The bridge was flanked by jetties where water coaches could usually be found, the Bruynwater being just as much an artery of commerce for the local communities that lined its banks as it was for the city as a whole, and if they were quick enough they ought to be able to hail one before too many of the people surrounding them had the same idea. 'Stick close.'

'Like a poultice,' the young witch assured him grimly. He'd been worried that her exhaustion would return, and that she wouldn't be in any condition to continue, but whatever preternatural energy was sustaining her seemed undiminished.

As they slipped through the crowd, he glanced back, and almost froze. A trio of Black Caps was forging its way through the crush towards the bridge, and a couple of them were carrying the unmistakable silhouettes of blunderbusses. That would have been worrying enough, but the third member of the group made the breath catch in his throat. Rauke van Stolke was clearing the way for her colleagues, none too gently with the flat of her sword, directing a bitter tirade back over her shoulder as she did so.

'Typical,' Rudi heard above the babble of the crowd. 'I finally meet someone who looks like he's halfway decent, and he turns out to be a witch-rutting Chaos worshipper.' She vented her anger by barging a halfling peddler out of the way with unnecessary vigour.

Rudi flushed. Woe betide any petty lawbreaker coming to her attention today, he thought. With a pang, he found himself remembering the pleasant meal they'd shared only the evening before, and the sense of wellbeing that had followed it. He'd enjoyed her company, and had been looking forward to experiencing more of it. He lowered his head, although from embarrassment at having hurt the woman's feelings or the more practical necessity of evading detection he couldn't have said.

'Keep moving,' Hanna urged him in an imperative undertone, and Rudi nodded, relieved at the distraction. The steps to the jetty were close at hand, and so far no one appeared to have noticed the two fugitives. As they descended the wooden steps, the snow closed in around them, cutting them off from the commotion at street level, and he glanced back for a final look around at the confusion above.

A knot of tension tightened itself in the pit of his stomach. The trio of Black Caps was unmistakably heading in their direction, and he cursed himself for his stupidity. Of course, they'd send someone to secure the jetties too. If he and Hanna couldn't find a boat in the next few minutes they'd just walked into a trap.

CHAPTER TWO

THE SNOW WAS falling more heavily than ever, obscuring the shipping channel in the darkness beyond, but to Rudi's relief the wooden jetty was illuminated by a couple of torches, hissing fitfully as the occasional snowflake drifted into the flames.

'Boats,' Hanna said, sudden hope colouring her voice.

Rudi nodded. 'Let's hope there's someone here who can sail one for us.' He had only ridden in one of the innumerable skiffs that plied for hire along the waterways of the city a handful of times, but that was enough for him to know that the intricacies of handling the sail would be far beyond him. He could probably manage the oars well enough, but that would be time consuming, and the sky was already taking on the first flush of grey, which warned that dawn was not far off. They'd stand a far better chance of making it to the candle wharf on Luydenhoek in time with a water coachman piloting the boat for them. Most, he knew, would still be at home, but there were usually a few about in the hours of darkness. Marienburg never completely slept, and there would be coin to be earned for those willing to put up with the inconvenience and occasional danger of providing transport during the night.

'I think we're in luck.' Hanna nudged his arm, and pointed. Beneath a sconce about halfway along the wooden walkway, a handful of men huddled around a brazier, their breath misting in the air as they talked among themselves. Their clothing and manner marked them out as watermen, and Rudi approached them briskly.

'I need passage to Luydenhoek,' he announced, as if that was a perfectly reasonable request at this hour. 'I'll pay two shillings to anyone who can get us there by dawn.'

'Two shillings?' One of the water coachmen looked at him narrowly, and noticing the suspicious expressions on the faces of the man's companions, Rudi cursed himself quietly under his breath. That was over four times the regular fare: hardly the best way to keep a low profile.

'That's right.' Rudi smiled, hoping to look like a late-returning reveller again, suddenly acutely conscious of the bow slung across his back, hardly a common sight in the streets of Marienburg. He indicated Hanna. 'The bridge is open, and if I don't get my girlfriend home before her father notices she's missing, she's going to be in real trouble.'

'I see,' the boatman said, probably more inclined to believe the two shillings than the story attached to it, if Rudi was any judge. He shrugged, smiling insincerely. 'Wish I could help you, laddie, but the Caps have said no sailing until further notice, and that's that.' He spat into the water. 'Typical. Some half-wit shouts, "witch" and the whole city grinds to a halt. Never mind our livelihoods.'

'Damn right,' somebody else said, and the little knot of boatmen aired their grievances among themselves for a moment, apparently forgetting their putative clients entirely.

'You have to help, please.' Hanna sounded tearful and frightened, her voice changing completely, as it had on the moors when she'd tried to bluff her way past Gerhard's soldiers. 'My father has such a temper. You've no idea what he'll do if he finds I sneaked out of the house.'

'Sorry, sweetheart.' The boatman's voice hardened. 'If we got caught, I'd be fined, couple of guilders at least. I could lose the boat over a debt like that.'

'Two guilders, fine.' Rudi dug the gold coins out of his purse, suddenly conscious of the stares of the men around him. He could hear their thoughts as clearly as if they'd been spoken aloud. *That's a lot of money. Wonder how much more there is in that purse. There's only one of him, and six of us.* He brushed the hilt of his sword casually as he returned the purse to his belt, and the moment passed. The boatman nodded.

'All right, but if we get caught you pay the fine, on top of this. Agreed?'

'Agreed,' Rudi said. The man gestured to a nearby boat.

'That's mine. Get in.' He watched while Rudi helped Hanna aboard, and unhitched the line securing the tiny craft to the dock. He turned to his companions. 'If the Caps come back and notice I'm missing, tell them I've gone to Gerda's to thaw out.'

'She can thaw me out any time,' one of the other boatmen said, to ribald laughter.

'Any time you've got sixpence in your purse,' the waterman said, jumping into the skiff. That provoked another round of laughter, but through it, Rudi was sure he could hear the clattering of feet on the steps leading up to the street above: the Caps. Without thinking, he glanced in that direction, catching sight of Rauke and her colleagues jogging down the wharf towards them, their outlines blurred by the flurrying snow.

'What's up?' the boatman asked, reading his expression, and glancing in the same direction. He must have taken in the sight of the approaching Caps almost at once, because he lunged at Rudi without warning, raising his voice to a shout. 'Help! They're stealing my boat!'

Under any other circumstances, the sheer effrontery of it would probably have taken Rudi completely by surprise, but after everything he'd already been through that night, he was ready for any eventuality. He blocked the man's clumsy rush without thinking, not even bothering to evade it, and punched him hard in the face. The boat rocked alarmingly. Hanna cried out and clung to the gunwales as freezing water slopped over the side, and Rudi sat down hard on the seat facing the stern.

The boatman wasn't so lucky. With an inarticulate cry, he lost his footing and pitched backwards over the side. A gout of foetid canal water broke over the boat, drenching the fugitives with its freezing spray, and the man surfaced, spluttering.

'Get them!' Rauke shouted, and the two gunners with her dropped to one knee, bringing their clumsy weapons up to fire. Clearly perceiving the danger he was in, the boatman struck out for the jetty, and the reaching arms of his friends, protesting loudly as he did so.

'Oi! That's my living! Don't you dare go blowing holes in it!'

Rudi cringed. He'd seen a blunderbuss discharged once before, during a raid on a weirdroot den. The cone of shot had blasted a thick wooden door off its hinges, and taken down the three would-be ambushers waiting behind it. Wallowing out here in the water, he and Hanna were sitting ducks. There was no way the watchmen could miss at this range.

'Who are they?' Rauke asked as the boatman floundered up onto the wharf, hauled to safety by his friends. Then her eyes nailed Rudi's. An expression of loathing and anger boiled up in them, following the spark of recognition. 'It's the witches!' she yelled. 'Fire!'

'Grab the oars,' Hanna said, her voice surprisingly calm. Rudi complied, although he knew it wouldn't make any difference. He dug the blades into the water, heaving with all his strength, trying to get the tiny craft moving. If he could just throw the gunners' aim off, and by some miracle they both missed, it would take them at least half a minute to reload, perhaps longer with cold-numbed fingers. By that time, he and Hanna would be well underway, obscured by the darkness and the flurrying snow, and the short-ranged weapons might not get time for another shot.

None of which actually mattered, of course, because the hail of hot metal would have shredded them both by then.

Rudi flinched at the sound of a double report from the wharf side, which echoed across the water in a curiously flat fashion, anticipating the agony of a dozen miniature musket balls ripping their way through his body, but the searing pain never came. He heaved at the oars, astonished at their good fortune.

Despite the urgency of their predicament, he was unable to resist glancing back at the wharf, trying to gauge how long they had left before the men reloaded, and almost froze with astonishment. Both gunners were down, thrashing about on the snow-covered planks like landed fish. Bright blood leaked through charred and blackened flesh, vivid against the backdrop of flurrying white.

'Keep rowing!' Hanna snapped.

Rudi did so, opening up the distance from the dock, heedless of the drama playing out behind them. Rauke was kneeling beside one of the downed gunners, apparently directing the boatmen to assist her fallen colleagues. She glanced in the fugitives' direction and shouted something, which perhaps fortunately was lost in the muffling snow, before returning her attention to the wounded.

'What happened?' Rudi asked. Hanna shrugged.

'They were carrying powder flasks. I'm a pyromancer, remember?' Rudi nodded grimly, recalling the way the oil lamps at the coaching inn on the Altdorf road had suddenly burst into flame while they were trying to escape the landlord who'd threatened to turn them over to the Roadwardens. It seemed that his companion was still able to use her abilities after all.

'How did you manage that?' he asked. 'I thought you were all in?'

Hanna shrugged. 'So did I,' she said, pulling the skaven's stone out from beneath her bodice. As Rudi had half expected, it was still glowing faintly. 'This seems to be helping me somehow.'

'Good.' Rudi hauled on the oars until he felt his back would break with the effort. 'Right now, we need all the help we can get.'

AT LEAST ONE of the gods must have been keeping an eye on them, Rudi thought, because they made it across the shipping channel without drowning or being swept out to sea. The tide was just on the turn, the water slack, and the realisation lent him renewed vigour. Shenk would want to make use of the surge of incoming seawater to help counteract the current of the Reik, making the going easier as the *Reikmaiden* began her long journey. The riverboat would be casting off any time now, just as soon as the water level in the canals began to rise.

Despite the surge of adrenaline the thought gave him, he began to slow down again after only a handful of minutes. Since waking around noon the previous day, he'd fought for his life more times than he could remember, become a fugitive again, and walked or run across what felt like half the city. Even the unusual reserves of strength he was somehow able to call on in times of stress weren't limitless. He was exhausted, and hard as he tried to force his body to do what was necessary with the clumsy oars, he misjudged his stroke several times, doing nothing more than flick a spray of freezing water into the boat. Each time he did it they wallowed, losing their way, and the prow of their tiny craft veered alarmingly.

'Move over.' Hanna reached out and took the oars briskly. Too numbed to protest, Rudi acquiesced, changing places with her, so that he was now facing forwards, towards the far bank. At least there was no chance of getting lost in the darkness, he thought. Despite the obscuring snow, still enclosing them in a pocket of chilling anonymity, the lights of Luydenhoek were clearly visible in the distance.

He fought down the memory of their frantic swim for the banks of the Reik, after Shenk had realised they were fugitives and became determined to collect whatever reward they were worth. Then they'd only made it to safety by luck, or so it had seemed at the time, the pitch darkness surrounding them and the chilling water robbing them of any sense of direction. Now they were trusting their lives to the riverboat captain again, a prospect he hardly relished, but at least this time he'd be on guard for any treachery, he thought.

That, at least, was a lesson he'd learned well since leaving Kohlstadt. No one could really be trusted, however benign they seemed to be.

'Can you manage?' he asked, although Hanna seemed to be rowing the boat with no difficulty at all, the strange energy imparted by the skaven's stone still evidently suffusing her body. He tried not to think about that either. Magic, he knew, always exacted a price for its use, and he hoped his friend wouldn't pay too dearly for the assistance she was getting.

'I'm fine,' Hanna assured him, her strokes deft and fluid, propelling the tiny craft faster and more efficiently across the water than he had. She grinned, with the closest thing to good humour he'd seen on her face for some time. 'I could do with the exercise. Helps warm me up.' Knowing that one of her talents was regulating the temperature of the air around her, Rudi doubted that, but tried to smile in response.

'I think there are some steps over there,' he said, craning his neck to see past her shoulder. Hanna turned the boat in the direction he'd suggested, as expertly as if she'd been on the water all her life, and made for the jetty he'd indicated. After a moment the wooden hull grated against stone, and he scrambled out, his feet slipping slightly on the weed-grown surface beneath his boot soles. Hanna followed nimbly, and turned to push the boat off again with her foot as soon as she'd gained the sanctuary of the steps. 'Why did you do that?'

'You told the boatman we were heading for Luydenhoek,' Hanna pointed out. 'Your little friend with the unbecoming hat will have had the bridge closed again as soon as she reported in, and messages sent to every watch house this side of the water.'

Rudi nodded. He knew enough of how the watch worked to know that this was true. If anything, the Suiddock Caps would have been relieved at the news that they'd stolen a boat. Closing the Draainbrug wouldn't be popular, and the last thing the watch needed was a large and restive crowd getting more angry and frustrated by the minute. Time was money in Marienburg, more literally than anywhere else in the known world, and they'd be under pressure from the mercantile guilds to get the lifeblood of commerce flowing again as soon as possible. 'No point making it obvious where we've come ashore.'

'Good point,' Rudi said, suspecting he ought to feel a little more sympathy for the boatman whose livelihood was beginning to drift slowly upstream with the swelling tide, but unable to summon any. Someone would probably find it and sell it back to him anyway. That was how things were in Marienburg. The abandoned craft was moving surprisingly quickly, and only a handful of the steps above them bore a thin coating of weeds and mud, indicating that they were still below the high water mark.

As he turned his head to watch the drifting boat he could see the first flush of red marking the sky beyond the rooftops of the Rijkspoort, the easternmost ward of the city, where the mighty river entered its precincts. The sight galvanised him: they had even less time to reach safety than he'd feared. 'We'd better get moving.'

'Right,' Hanna agreed. Cautiously, they made their way to the top of the steps, finding a row of warehouses facing the waterfront. Even at this hour several of them appeared to be busy, but none of the carters or stevedores spared them so much as a glance, engrossed as they were in their own concerns. 'Which way?'

'East,' Rudi said, as decisively as he could. His only previous trip to the candle wharf, where the *Reik-maiden* was berthed, had been the previous afternoon to arrange passage with Shenk, but he remembered enough about the layout of Luydenhoek to know that they were still too far to the west. Once they got closer, with any luck, he'd be able to recognise a landmark. He was still a skilled tracker, he reminded himself, even in an urban environment so different from the forest he'd grown up in, and his old instincts hadn't let him down yet.

He led the way through the bustling streets, trying not to worry about the way the crowds were thickening all the time, and how the thin grey light was growing brighter. It was hard to be sure beneath the snow clouds, but he had an uneasy feeling deep in his gut that the sun had risen already, and that the river-boat would be under way by now. He forced the thought away irritably. The last thing they needed was to be sapping their confidence with unfounded speculation.

'Down here.' With a thrill of relief, he recognised a tavern, the Mermaid, where he'd bargained with Shenk the previous afternoon. The wharf he sought was only a few streets away, and he hurried them along as best he could, trying not to slip on the freezing slush beneath their feet.

As they made their way through the growing press of bodies, packages, and barrows flowing into the streets, Rudi kept turning his head, looking out for the distinctive headgear of the Caps, but luck, or one of the gods, was still with them. The thoroughfares were almost as crowded as they were during the day, and the growing throng afforded them greater concealment than ever before. Despite his apprehension, he saw no sign of a floppy black hat, and no shouted challenge echoed from the walls around him.

They rounded the final corner onto the wharf itself, and he narrowed his eyes against a sudden flurry of wind-driven snow. He blinked his vision clear.

'She's still there!' He pointed. The familiar silhouette of the *Reikmaiden* was clearly visible between two other vessels about halfway along the wharf. Hanna nodded grimly.

'Not for long,' she said. With a thrill of horror, Rudi realised she was right. Pieter, the deckhand who'd befriended him the first time they'd sought refuge aboard, was loosening the hawser securing the riverboat to the dock. A moment later the thick rope splashed into the water, and Pieter began hauling it in, apparently heedless of the chill the icy water had imparted to it. Maybe his hands were numb already. The gangplank Rudi had boarded the boat by, the previous afternoon, was missing too, and even as he watched, the gap between the riverboat's hull and the wharf widened perceptibly.

'Hey! Wait!' Rudi called, breaking into a run, Hanna pacing him easily as he did so. Pieter's head came up, and he shouted something. A moment later, Shenk appeared at his shoulder, narrowing his eyes as he gazed at the approaching fugitives. As they got closer, Rudi could see the captain shrug. Clearly, returning to the wharf would be impossible, even if the *Reik-maiden's* master felt so inclined, and he seriously doubted that.

'Jump for it,' Hanna said, accelerating past him at a pace that left Rudi gaping, her cloak flapping like a banner in the wind from the river. Rudi ran as hard as he could, forcing his weary muscles into one final effort, ignoring the burning sensation in his chest as the freezing air gouged its way deep into his lungs. Hanna flung herself into the air, seeming to hang suspended for a moment above the chill grey water, and then crashed to the deck of the riverboat, where she lay unmoving. Almost before he realised it, Rudi's foot was thrusting against the edge of the dock, and he followed, willing himself to make it across the widening gap.

Time seemed to slow, as it had done the day before when he'd made his desperate leap from the jetty behind the lawyer's office to escape Theo and Bruno. With a strange sense of *déjà vu*, he took in Shenk's startled expression, uncannily similar to the one on the face of the bargee whose vessel he'd bounded across on his way to safety. Then, the breath was driven from his lungs as the rail of the *Reikmaiden* slammed into his midriff. He clutched at the worn wood, finding himself slipping on the powdering of snow that crested it, and began to topple backwards into the river.

'Welcome aboard.' To his surprise Shenk grabbed him just as his grip was about to fail, and yanked him over the rail. Rudi slithered onto the deck, retching and gasping. 'I see you decided to come this morning after all.' The captain's voice was mildly curious, but nothing more. When they'd spoken the previous day, Rudi had asked about passage the next time the boat put in at Marienburg, almost a month away.

'Things got complicated,' Rudi gasped, turning to look at Hanna. She was unconscious, her face pale, and a trickle of blood was running from her nose. To his relief, and complete lack of surprise, the chip of stone around her neck was no longer glowing, apparently as inert as the rock it resembled.

'Hmm.' Shenk nodded. 'I guessed that.' He turned to Pieter. 'Better get her below before she freezes.' He turned back to Rudi. 'You too. I've fished healthier-looking corpses out of this river, in my time.'

Too numbed to argue, Rudi simply nodded, but remained on his guard nevertheless. Shenk had seemed solicitous enough the last time he and Hanna had been aboard his boat, but he'd been ready to betray them at the first opportunity. Keeping his hand close to the hilt of his sword, he followed the deck-hand down into the warmth of the hold.

CHAPTER THREE

SOMEWHAT TO RUDI'S surprise, it seemed as if Shenk intended to go through with his end of the deal, at least for now. The captain had carried Hanna down to the hold himself, under Rudi's watchful eye, and waited while Pieter slung the hammocks that the two fugitives had slept in the last time they'd been aboard. At least, Rudi assumed they were the same ones; they certainly looked similar enough. Dropping his pack and his bow on one of the barrels beneath the arcs of cloth, he reached out to take his companion.

'Better let me do it,' Shenk advised. 'I'm more used to this sort of thing.' A fact he proved a moment later by hoisting the unconscious girl into the sailcloth cocoon with a swift economy of motion, which Rudi had to admit he could never have duplicated in his current condition. Noticing Rudi's expression, the captain smiled sardonically. 'Usually it's drunken deckhands,' he explained. 'Noisier, heavier, and...' his expression changed, 'actually, not a lot less fragrant. What have you been doing, rolling in a midden?'

'We got in a fight. We fell down,' Rudi said. The streets of Marienburg weren't exactly clean at the best of times, and the blighted quarter where they'd faced Magnus's mutants had been awash with filth. Only now did Rudi begin to appreciate quite how permeated with it he and Hanna had become. The smell was so familiar that he'd forgotten it was there. Reminded of it again, he found the sickly sweet stench of it almost comforting. Shenk nodded, as if that sounded reasonable.

'I'll get Pieter to bring you some water,' he said.

After the captain and the deckhand had departed, leaving behind them a bucket of chill water, a wash-cloth, and a plate of bread and cheese, Rudi stripped off his clothes and removed as much of the grime as he could before freezing. After donning a clean shirt and britches from his pack he felt warmer, and turned his attention to the food. He hesitated for a moment, wondering if it had been drugged, but it smelled no different from any other lump of slightly overripe cheese he'd ever eaten, and he wolfed it down eagerly. If anything, the slight hint of incipient putrefaction only sharpened his appetite. Shenk, he was sure, would be just as straightforward in any future betrayal as he'd been in the past, and starving himself wouldn't help anybody if his suspicions turned out to be correct.

Leaving part of the food uneaten, in case Hanna should wake, he clambered into his own hammock,

after a cursory glance at the sleeping girl. She looked
peaceful enough, as far as he could tell, although he
was only too aware that his knowledge of such things
was limited. Consoling himself with the notion that
the only cure for magical over-exertion he'd ever seen
was rest, and that both she and Alwyn had recovered
before, Rudi settled himself as best he could and tried
to sleep.

WHEN HE WOKE, the day was well advanced, judging by
the angle of the sunbeams slanting down into the
hold, and Rudi felt ravenous again. He rolled out of
his hammock, instinctively checking that his weapons
were where he'd left them. To his mingled surprise
and relief they were, although someone had clearly
been in the hold while he slept, because the bucket of
filthy water had been replaced by a fresh supply. His
purse was still inside his shirt, and the dagger he carried concealed in his boot nestled against his shin as
usual. Nevertheless, he felt a certain sense of relief
once his sword belt was buckled again. Sleeping with
it was impossible in the cramped confines of the hammock, as he'd discovered the hard way, but he'd
become so used to its presence that without it he felt
curiously incomplete.

Hanna was still sleeping, snoring gently, and he felt
reluctant to disturb her, but, struck by a pang of unexpected solicitude, he wrung out the washcloth and
tried to sponge the worst of the accumulated grime
from her face. He half hoped and half feared that he'd
wake her in the process, but she simply slept on, as
uncaring as an infant.

At length, feeling he could do nothing more for the young sorceress beyond letting her recover in her own time as best she could, Rudi ventured up the wooden stairs to the deck.

'Oh, you're up then.' The statement was flat, devoid of any concern, and Rudi was sure he could detect an undercurrent of barely-suppressed hostility in it. Rudi squinted his eyes against the afternoon sun, relishing the scent of fresh, clean air, the first he'd smelled since entering the city so many months before.

'Good afternoon, Herr Busch,' he replied. The first mate of the *Reikmaiden* was looking at him appraisingly. The last time they'd faced each other had been in a brutal brawl on the moonlit deck, and Rudi had come within a hair of killing the man, although Busch might not have realised that at the time.

Recalling that instant, he found it hard to believe the intensity of the dark desire to do harm that had so nearly overtaken him, but he had felt it on other occasions too, and had grown wary of it. He'd taken several lives since that night, both human and monstrous, and had learned to control the impulse to some extent. Generally, he used the energy that the surge of aggression gave him to win a fight, before overcoming the urge to finish his vanquished opponent by an act of will. Each time he did so, though, something deep inside him felt cheated, and on the occasions when he'd had no option but to strike the killing blow, the dark presence in the depths of his mind had exulted in the deed.

Rudi returned the man's stare, levelly. If Busch thought he could be intimidated, after all he'd seen and done in the last few months, he was sadly mistaken. Both he and Hanna were very different from the callow youths who'd fled the village of Kohlstadt last summer. Busch must have seen something of that change in Rudi's bearing, because rather than push the point, he simply nodded.

'Seen worse,' he allowed grudgingly, as if admitting as much was a huge concession. He'd take his lead from Shenk, Rudi knew, and so long as the captain was prepared to tolerate his unexpected guests the rest of the crew would accept their presence. 'Going far with us?'

'Altdorf,' Rudi replied, chafing inwardly at the stilted nature of the conversation.

Busch nodded, as if he hadn't already known. Shenk would have told everyone on board the nature of the deal he'd struck with Rudi, he was sure of that. Rudi had found him in a smuggler's den that the watch was raiding, and concealed his presence, more for the fear of being denounced as a fugitive from Imperial justice than anything else. Nevertheless, the captain seemed to feel that he was in his debt, and had agreed to provide safe passage to the Imperial capital in return. Assuming he wasn't just after the price on their heads again, of course, although that didn't seem all that likely. If he'd known the true nature of the charges against the two fugitives, Rudi was sure that he'd never have allowed them on board in the first place.

Rudi glanced around the deck. Pieter looked up from his work for a moment to smile a greeting that looked quite genuine, but for the most part, the rest of the crew ignored his presence. The only other exception was Ansbach, who'd also come off badly in the fight on the deck, and who glowered at him with unconcealed hostility.

'Is that where your cargo's for?'

'Most of it,' Busch said, 'apart from a stop-off in Carroburg.' He ran a hand through his close-cropped hair, a mannerism Rudi remembered from his last trip aboard the *Reikmaiden*. 'What's it to you?'

'Nothing,' Rudi assured him with a shrug. Given the circumstances of his unexpected meeting with Shenk back in Marienburg, which had led to their unlikely alliance, at least some of the cargo aboard the riverboat would no doubt have been of considerable interest to his erstwhile colleagues. That was none of his business, though, and he dismissed the matter from his mind. If anything, he was hoping that his suspicions were correct. If Shenk was up to something illegal he'd be as eager to avoid coming to the attention of the authorities as Hanna and himself. 'I just wondered if we'd be stopping much on the way, that's all.'

'Nowhere else you'd have heard of,' Busch assured him.

Rudi remembered there were innumerable landing stages along both banks of the river, serving hamlets barely large enough to deserve the name of villages. Boats like the *Reikmaiden* called at them frequently, bringing the necessities of life that were too bulky to transport economically in any other way. The coaching inn where he and Hanna had first met Krieger's mercenary band had been served by one such jetty, which was where their paths had first crossed Shenk's.

That thought was a sobering one. The news of Gerhard's arrest warrant, issued at the time he and Hanna had fled from Kohlstadt, would have had time to travel along the length of the coach road paralleling the southern bank of the river, and every stop they made on that side would carry the risk of discovery. Carroburg, he vaguely remembered, was on the northern bank of the Reik, so they wouldn't have so much to worry about there.

According to the tavern gossip he'd heard in Marienburg, it was still swamped with refugees from the recent wars in the north, so the chances of anyone noticing two more itinerants passing through would be minimal, even if news of the hunt for them had crossed the vast expanse of water separating the province of Middenland from the Reikland, where he'd spent the whole of his life apart from his handful of months in Marienburg.

Leaving the mate to his work, much to the man's visible relief, Rudi strode to the rail and looked out over the water. The snow had gone, replaced by the pale sunshine of early winter. As they moved up the Reik, away from the coast, Rudi knew, it would get a little warmer for a time, the biting westerly winds from the Sea of Claws mellowing a little as they met the bulk of the land.

The respite would only be a temporary one, however. He could still smell the frost on the breeze, and he knew, with all the assurance of a life spent outdoors, that the winter to come would be a hard one. The sunshine, though bright, carried little warmth with it. However, inured to the cold by a lifetime's experience, he found it exhilarating rather than debilitating.

Just as it had the first time he'd found himself aboard the riverboat, the sheer magnitude of the Reik left him almost breathless. Silver-flecked water surrounded the sturdy little vessel, stretching off in every direction almost as far as the eye could see. Upstream and down, nothing broke its gently undulating surface apart from the distant sails of boats like their own, too far off to make out any other details.

The far bank hovered almost at the limits of his vision, too distant to reveal anything other than faint irregularities of colour that hinted at variations in the terrain, hovering like a low cloudbank between the water and the sky. He strained his eyes nevertheless, trying to pick out any landmarks that he might have seen on the perilous journey towards the safety he and Hanna had hoped to find in the city they'd so precipitously fled. There was nothing, just the dull monotony of the moors and marshes that gave the Wasteland its name.

Orientated, he glanced back at the stern, failing to catch even a glimpse of Marienburg. He'd half expected to see the mighty span of the Hoogbrug, or the ramparts of the Vloedmuur still visible in the distance, but all he could see was the placid wake left by the *Reik-maiden* as she forged through the water. The widening 'V' disappeared to starboard, merging eventually with the ripples raised by the wind on the river and the passage of other boats. To his left a faint, continuous wave spent itself on the northern shoreline, panting behind the vessel that had created it, like a dog on a leash.

His interest piqued, Rudi leaned against the waist-high rail, the wood under his hand worn smooth by time and the elements, and took his first leisurely look at the lands north of the Reik as they slipped past, little more than a bowshot away. They didn't seem too different from the marshes and moorland that he and Hanna had struggled over on the opposite side of the river, although his spirits lifted a little at the thought of all the water that lay between the two territories.

So long as Shenk's business remained on the northern bank, he and Hanna should be relatively safe. If they showed any signs of veering over to the southern bank, they'd just have to stay below and hope for the best.

'Enjoying the view?' Shenk asked, appearing at his elbow. Aboard his vessel, he seemed more confident and businesslike, Rudi thought, a far cry from the nondescript little fellow he was when ashore. Even the faded blue coat he wore all the time, apparently as a mark of his authority, seemed to fit him a little better on deck. Determined to be courteous, Rudi nodded.

'It certainly beats walking,' he conceded. Shenk echoed the gesture.

'Or swimming,' he said. An awkward silence descended for a moment. 'I just wanted you to know that there won't be any need to jump ship this time around.'

'I'm sure there won't,' Rudi said, his hand resting casually against the hilt of his sword for a moment. Shenk nodded curtly, apparently genuinely insulted by his visible lack of trust.

'I told you, I owe you one, and I always make good on my debts. If I'm honest, I hope I never see either of you again once we get to Altdorf, but until we do, you've no call to be looking over your shoulder. Are we clear?'

'Clear as a spring,' Rudi assured him, his confidence somehow boosted by the man's bluntness, far more than it would have been by a show of strained politeness. Shenk seemed to relax a little too, as if reassured.

'Good.' He changed the subject. 'How's Hanna?'

'Still sleeping,' Rudi said, trying to sound casual. Shenk nodded sympathetically.

'Probably the best thing,' he said. 'She must be all in.' A faint air of wonderment tinted his voice. 'How she made that jump from the wharf, I'll never know. You either, come to that.'

'Well that makes two of us,' Rudi assured him, hoping to steer the conversation to safer ground. Shenk nodded again. Then he shrugged.

'We'll be putting in at Nocht's Landing tonight. They have a healer there. Nothing fancy, just a herbalist really, but I can get him to take a look at her if you like.'

Rudi fought to keep his face neutral. Hanna and her mother had been simple village healers back in Kohlstadt, at least so far as anybody knew, but they'd been hiding the secret of their magical abilities from all their friends and neighbours. What if this herbalist was the same, and had the gift of witchsight, like Hanna? He'd know her for what she was instantly, and if he was simply a healer after all, he might still recognise the cause of Hanna's malady. Either way, the risk was too great.

'Better to let her sleep, I think,' he said, trying to keep his tone light. 'She's also a healer, don't forget. I think they're a bit sensitive about being treated by someone else.'

'Well, you know her best,' Shenk conceded, 'but if she hasn't woken by nightfall you ought to think about it.'

'Perhaps I will,' Rudi said, hoping that nightfall was a long way off. His stomach growled suddenly, reminding him of how hungry he was, and he seized on the chance to change the subject gratefully. 'Do you have any food on board?' The question seemed to amuse Shenk.

'We've got a hold full of it,' he said, 'but you're not eating the cargo.' He pointed to a barrel on the deck, just forwards of the cabin, almost as large as the one Rudi had hidden in the first time he'd been carried aboard the boat. 'That's full of apples. Help yourself, that's what it's there for. You missed lunch, I'm afraid.'

Glad of the excuse to terminate the conversation, Rudi left the captain to go about his business and wandered over to the apple barrel. It was still full, and as he lifted the lid the sweet smell of autumnal fruit rose up around him, causing him to salivate. He plucked a couple out, finding them still firm and barely wrinkled, despite having been picked at least a month before. One thing Marienburgers were skilled at, he reflected, was the preservation of food, something essential in a maritime nation whose ships plied the waters of the world sometimes for months at a stretch. He bit into one, feeling the sweet juice flooding into his mouth, and almost bumped into

Ansbach, who had approached the barrel from the other side.

'Sorry. I didn't see you there.' He held out the second apple. Ansbach ignored it.

'I'll get my own.' The deckhand pushed past him, and selected a fruit from the barrel.

'Suit yourself,' Rudi said, stifling the impulse to let the lid fall on the man's fingers, and went to check on Hanna.

CHAPTER FOUR

To RUDI'S CAREFULLY concealed concern, Hanna still hadn't stirred by the time the *Reikmaiden* put into Nocht's Landing, which turned out to be pretty much as he'd expected. A wooden wharf, barely long enough for the sturdy little riverboat to lie alongside, projected out into the river. A couple of skiffs bobbed next to it, the fishing nets folded under their seats probably the only things that made life out here on the fringes of the Wasteland even marginally possible. Beyond the timber structure a handful of huts, too modest to be dignified with a label as grand as cottage, stood, clustered around a larger building that clearly served the tiny community as a meeting place. Although it couldn't have done enough business to qualify as a tavern, the smell of cooking food and the sound of chattering voices drifting from it were enough to inform Rudi that it was the next best thing, a mixture of social centre and communal dining room, like the ones he'd seen in the hamlets around Kohlstadt.

The scent of baking fish, tenuous as it was over the all-pervading odour of river mud and dung, which clung to the tiny settlement like a garment, hit him straight in the stomach, and began to remind him, in no uncertain terms, that he hadn't eaten a proper meal since his supper with Rauke the previous evening. The boat's cook had abandoned the galley, evidently intent on eating ashore with the rest of the crew, and if he didn't want to spend another night subsisting on apples he'd have no option but to join them.

That would mean abandoning Hanna, at least for a short while. He hesitated, assessing the risks. He'd been through enough to know that there was no such thing as safety to be found anywhere in the world, just a temporary approximation of it, but she should be secure enough sleeping in the hold of the boat. One of the crew would be left on watch, and could call him if she woke. It was hardly as if he'd be difficult to find in a hamlet this size. To his quiet relief the deckhand in question was Berta, the only other woman on board, who seemed to have joined the crew in Marienburg, and who wasn't regarding him with open suspicion like almost everyone else.

'I'll keep an eye on her,' she promised, tugging a woollen cap down over her cropped blonde hair. She was short and stocky, heavily muscled like a dwarf, and had evidently been around watercraft for a long

time, judging by the calluses on her hands from hauling ropes. Pieter and Ansbach seemed to get on all
right with her, and the cook, Yullis, probably did, at
least when he could be prised out of his galley to double up as a deckhand, which he did whenever
necessary. In his time as a watchman, Rudi had
become quite adept at reading people, particularly if
they were trying to conceal something, and Berta
seemed honest enough. She seemed a little reserved
around him, though, probably as a result of the stories she'd heard from the others.

'I appreciate that,' Rudi told her, with a friendly grin,
'and I'm sure Hanna will too, when I tell her how kind
you've been.'

'Yes, well, no need to ladle it on,' Berta said,
although she seemed pleased at the courtesy nevertheless. 'It's not as if I'll have much else to do.'

'Coming?' Shenk asked, pausing at Rudi's shoulder,
and he nodded.

'Might as well,' he agreed. Busch, Ansbach and Yullis
were already ashore, their silhouettes clearly visible in
the gathering dusk as they made their way through the
hamlet towards the community hall. Although he was
too distant to make out any conversation, they
seemed to be exchanging greetings with a few of the
local inhabitants as they went. 'I take it you've been
here before.'

'I've been a lot of places,' Shenk said, as they made
their way along the gangplank, 'but we put in here
every few months. Couple of other boats do too.'

Rudi looked at the motley collection of huts surrounding them, suddenly reminded of the one he'd

grown up in, in the woods outside Kohlstadt. He hadn't thought of it in a long time, he realised, and the notion was curiously depressing. Half a year ago, his world had been settled and secure, the most he'd had to worry about being whether his snares would be full and trying to master the bow his father had given him.

For a moment he considered asking Shenk what had happened to the weapon, which had been left behind along with everything else they'd owned when he and Hanna had fled the *Reikmaiden* a few months before, but decided not to bother. The captain would have sold or traded it at the first opportunity, and there was no point in bringing the matter up again. It was only a bow, after all, and he had another now. He didn't need a tangible reminder of his adoptive father to keep his memory fresh.

That prompted a flood of new memories, of the night Gunther Walder had died, struck down by a beastman, as the monstrous creatures had slaughtered their way through the participants of what he could no longer deny had been a Chaotic ritual of some kind. He shook his head, trying to clear it. The more he learned about his history, the more confused he became. Gunther had been a good man, he knew that, but he'd thought the same thing about Magnus until the horrors of the previous night had opened his eyes. Perhaps his father had been an innocent dupe, taken in by the man's charm and apparent goodwill.

'I'm surprised you find enough cargo in a place like this,' Rudi said, wrenching his thoughts back to the conversation, and hoping Shenk hadn't noticed his momentary distraction.

'You'd be surprised,' Pieter said, grinning. Then he shut his mouth as the captain shot him a warning look. Of course, Rudi thought, an isolated spot like this would be the ideal place to transfer illicit cargoes between riverboats.

'It's not a question of bulk,' Shenk explained. 'All these settlements would be completely cut off without the river. There are always letters or messages to pick up, small items to barter and sell.'

'Like lamp oil, that sort of thing,' said Rudi.

'Exactly,' Shenk said, although whether he recognised the reference to the barrels that Rudi and Hanna had been hiding in when they'd been brought on board before, or was simply being polite enough to pretend that he hadn't, Rudi couldn't tell. 'Putting in for the night's always better than sailing on in the dark. As we're here anyway, we might as well do a little business.'

The walk to the dining hall was a short one, but even so, Rudi had time to absorb his surroundings in some detail, aided by the frequent pauses that Shenk made to swap gossip with a few of the locals. Although small, the huts were all soundly built, presumably with timber shipped in along the river, since there were few trees to be seen apart from a handful of stunted specimens barely larger than bushes, and most had well-tended vegetable plots alongside them. A few even had chickens scratching about, although the other livestock, a handful of pigs and goats, seemed to have the run of the place, apparently left to

wander at will. There was little chance of them getting
lost, as the entire settlement was enclosed by a semi-
circular palisade, which probably accounted for the
scarcity of trees in the immediate vicinity. Anything
even remotely substantial had obviously been felled
to form part of the defences, which began and ended
abutting the river. Rudi was troubled for a moment by
a nagging sense of familiarity, until the memory of the
fortified stockade on the moors, where the Imperial
soldiers that Gerhard had been with had made their
camp, floated to the surface of his mind. The defen-
sive arrangements were strikingly similar, and he
mentioned as much.

'There are always dangers out here to be wary of,'
Pieter said, and Rudi nodded, noticing that most of
the men and several of the women appeared to be
armed. One of the locals, a tall man who seemed to be
some sort of leader among the little community,
broke off his conversation with Shenk to nod a confirmation.

'There is that,' he agreed. 'Mutants escaping from the
city, for one thing, and I've heard tell of worse.' He didn't
seem at all inclined to elaborate. Shenk nodded too.

'They say all sorts of things came down from the
north last year, and not all of them went home again.'
Rudi felt his scalp begin to prickle, in spite of his
instinctive cynicism. Tales he would have scoffed at in
the comfortable tap room of the Dancing Pirate could
seem all too plausible here, in the gathering dusk, surrounded by leagues of marsh and bog. He knew only
too well the sort of things that lurked in the wilderness. He had killed a skaven with his bare hands, and

seen a warband of beastmen far closer than most who'd lived to tell the tale.

'You're not taking any chances, I see,' he said, nodding at the spear the speaker carried. The man, whose name, he gathered from the half-overheard conversation he'd been having with Shenk, was Ranulph, fell into step beside them.

'Not at the moment,' he said. 'We lost someone this morning. Gofrey went out looking for herbs and didn't come back.'

'Could he just have gone further than usual?' Shenk asked. 'We were hoping to see him. There's a sick girl on the boat.'

'Then she'll just have to get better on her own,' Ranulph said. 'We couldn't find a trace of him, and it's coming on to dark. If he's not dead by now, he soon will be.'

'I'm a pretty good tracker,' Rudi said. The scent of the cooking fish called to him like one of the sirens the sailors of Marienburg prattled about in their traveller's tales, but the thought of someone lost out in the marshes, prey to the horrors he'd seen, overrode it. 'I might be able to find some trace of him, if we bring a couple of torches for light.'

'It's not quite dark yet,' Shenk said, surprising Rudi with his unexpected support. Ranulph glanced at the reddening sky, and nodded suddenly.

'Worth a try,' he said. He whistled, and a couple of the villagers trotted over, bows slung across their backs. 'This lad's a tracker, so he says, and he's willing to go after Gofrey. He'll need some help.' The two men glanced at one another, clearly uneasy. 'Get someone to go with you and carry a torch, and the minute the sun goes down you head back here. I'm not sending out another search party.'

'I'll go,' Pieter said unexpectedly. Everyone looked at him, and he shrugged. 'I like Gofrey. He cleared up that dose of the... you know.' Shenk nodded, with a trace of amusement. 'It was more than the leeches in Marienburg were able to do. I owe him one.'

'Fair enough.' Ranulph watched while Pieter selected a brand from one of the neighbouring fires, and held it above his head, casting a circle of warm light around the little party. 'See you later, I hope.'

ONCE THEY'D LEFT the warmth and light of the compound behind them, Rudi began to doubt the wisdom of his sudden impulse to help. The young men with them, who hadn't volunteered their names, kept arrows nocked, and looked around at the desolate marshes suspiciously. Thin tendrils of mist were beginning to rise from the boggy ground, making the going even more treacherous than it would otherwise have been, and Rudi placed his feet carefully, all too aware that a single misstep could have catastrophic consequences.

'He came this way,' one of the villagers volunteered. The light was greying, the floating patches of mist tinted gold by the westering sun, and Rudi was glad of the extra illumination afforded by the blazing torch that Pieter was carrying. It deepened the shadows of the tiny indentations in the ground left by the feet which had passed through ahead of them, and Rudi nodded.

'So did three other people, two men and a woman. They came back the same way. Your search party?'

'That's right,' the villager confirmed, visibly surprised. 'They couldn't find anything on the path, so they came back around noon.'

'No sign of the other one turning back,' Rudi said. To his relief the trail left by the missing herbalist was clear enough, his tracking skills having remained undiminished by his sojourn in the city. He pushed on as quickly as he dared, acutely conscious of the fading light around them. Conversation ebbed away as he kept his eyes on the ground ahead of him. Then he stopped, abruptly, confused.

'What is it?' Pieter asked.

'His footprints have disappeared,' Rudi said, stooping to examine the ground more closely. The marks left by the search party were still visible, both coming and going, and he wondered for a moment if they'd simply obliterated the ones he was interested in, but they were no more pronounced than before.

'You think he went under?' the other archer asked, exchanging a grim look with his companion. Rudi shook his head.

'There would have been more signs of disturbance in the mud if that had happened,' he explained. He moved back a few yards, until he'd found the prints he was looking for again, and cast around. To his relief the clear indentation of a booted heel was visible in a nearby tussock, a couple of feet from the track. He pointed. 'He went that way.'

'That's impossible,' the first bowman asserted. His companion nodded. 'There's no path there.'

'Nevertheless, it's the way he went.' Rudi hopped across the mud to the mound of grass. Even in the fading light, he could see a faint footprint in the next one. He jumped across to that one too, and then a third. He glanced behind. 'Come on, it's easy.'

'Not a chance.' The two villagers shook their heads vehemently, so quickly that Rudi couldn't tell which one had spoken. 'You miss your footing out there and you'll drown for sure.'

'He could be in real trouble,' Rudi urged. One of the bowmen shrugged.

'More fool him for leaving the path, then.' Their minds were clearly made up, and becoming aware of his position, Rudi couldn't altogether blame them for that. He gestured to Pieter.

'Coming?' The deckhand shook his head.

'I haven't got my land legs,' he said. 'I'd fall in for sure.'

'Fine, go back then.' Rudi felt a surge of anger rising up in him, although whether from unassuaged hunger or disgust at their apparent callousness, he couldn't be certain. The worst of it was that part of him agreed. If the herbalist remained missing he wouldn't be able to harm Hanna, even by accident. Forcing the thought away, he held out a hand for the torch. 'Just leave me the light.'

He thought for a moment that his companions would try to argue him out of it, but a quick glance at the sun, almost hidden by the horizon, was enough to settle their minds. Pieter leaned out over the stinking mud, just far enough for Rudi's groping fingers to grasp the torch, and then they were gone, heading back to Nocht's Landing as fast as they could before the light failed altogether.

Well, fine. It wasn't the first time Rudi had been left on his own, and somehow he doubted that it would be the last. Returning his attention to the quagmire in front of him, he found the next disturbed patch of grass, and jumped again.

The going was surprisingly easy, and he made good time, better than he would have done had his companions still been with him, he thought. The light from the torch was more than sufficient to pick out the marks he was following, although the flame was burning a little lower now. Once again he felt a brief pang of regret at his impulsiveness. If he didn't find the missing healer soon, he could be marooned out here himself, without light or a clue as to his direction back to the settlement. It was an almost certain death sentence.

He forced the thought away, along with the memory of his trek through a similar wilderness of mud with Hanna a few months before. They'd found firm ground then, but a nest of skaven too. Feeling the comforting weight of his sword at his hip, and wishing he hadn't left his bow behind, he hurried on as best he could, trying not to think about how close the dwindling flames were getting to his fingers.

The brand had almost burned down by the time the going underfoot became firmer, and he hurried forward onto solid ground with a sigh of relief. Almost as soon as he did so it scorched his hand, and he dropped it with a yelp of mingled pain and irritation. The light went out, hissing against the wet grass, and the darkness closed in around him.

Too experienced in the ways of the wilderness to panic, he stayed where he was, waiting for his night vision to adjust. Morrslieb was just visible over the horizon, the light it cast as sickly and ill-favoured as always, but even that was welcome. Rudi shivered as his surroundings came slowly into focus, the stars above adding their own modest increment of illumination, and took comfort from the familiar constellations above his head. They, at least, were unchanged, a reassuring presence.

The patch of dry ground he'd stumbled upon wasn't large, perhaps a score of yards across, but the far side of it was obscured by the first real trees he'd seen since entering the marshes. A small copse of them grew here, frail specimens compared to those he'd grown up surrounded by, but he took heart from their presence. A woodsman all his life, the improbable glade held out the promise of shelter and relative comfort for the night. As if to remind him just what a tenuous hope that was, his stomach growled again.

Well, at least he had his tinderbox, and he was sure he'd be able to kindle a fire. That would be something, and he wouldn't starve by the morning, he knew that much from experience. He just wasn't looking forward to the discomfort of another hungry night. He sniffed the air, catching the scent of a roasting rabbit. It seemed as if his mind was beginning to play tricks on him already, reminding him of what he was missing.

As he approached the stand of trees, however, he hesitated. Far from fading away as he'd expected, the scent of cooking meat was growing stronger, and an accompanying flicker of firelight was appearing intermittently between the trunks. Loosening his sword in its scabbard, he moved on, all his old forester's instincts coming into play, slipping stealthily from one patch of shadow to the next.

Concealing himself behind a trunk somewhat stouter than the rest, he peered cautiously into the open space at the centre of the copse. The trees grew in a ring, he realised, almost a perfect circle, and far too regular to be natural. Who had planted them, and why, he dismissed as fruitless speculation.

A fire had been kindled in the centre of the clearing, and a middle-aged man was warming his hands at it with every sign of comfort. Two coneys, expertly gutted and spitted, were sizzling over the flames, and Rudi's mouth watered at the smell of them. The fellow was dressed in rough but serviceable clothes, and carried a small shoulder bag like the one Hanna used on her herb-collecting forays.

'Herr Gofrey, I presume.' Further concealment would be pointless, Rudi decided. He stepped forwards into the circle of firelight, keeping his hands well away from his weapons. The herbalist must have assumed that he was completely alone out here, and there was no point in alarming him unnecessarily. To his surprise, though, the man seemed completely at ease with his sudden appearance, simply glancing up for a moment before returning his attention to the browning meat in front of him.

'That's right,' he said, sprinkling some shredded leaf across them, and sniffing appreciatively. Then he looked up again. 'You must be Rudi. I thought you'd be along about now.'

CHAPTER FIVE

'How DID you know that?' Rudi's hand went to the sword at his belt before he was even aware of the movement, and he checked himself in the act of beginning to draw it. The healer looked harmless enough, but he was only too aware of how deceptive appearances could be. On the other hand, there was no point in overreacting. Gofrey didn't seem at all put out by this sign of distrust, though, glancing away to check on the roasting rabbits as he smiled a welcome.

'Because somebody told me, of course.' He gestured towards the fire. 'Sit down and warm yourself. It's going to be a cold night. We might as well talk in comfort.'

Drawn as much by the scent of the food as by the man's show of friendliness, Rudi moved closer to the blaze. The warmth was indeed welcome.

'Who told you?' Rudi sat, and accepted a haunch of the sizzling meat. It was only as he began to chew it that the full extent of his hunger struck home, and it was all he could do to restrain himself from bolting the food down like a starving dog. Gofrey watched him eat for a moment with an air of quiet amusement, and then started in on the coney's other hind leg.

'News travels, even in the Wasteland,' he said around a mouthful of rabbit, leaning forward to sprinkle another pinch of herbs over the second one. As the first couple of mouthfuls eased his hunger, and he began to eat more slowly, Rudi began to appreciate the subtle flavour of his own portion. Clearly, Gofrey had a keen appreciation of herbs, which went far beyond the practicalities of his calling. 'Not all of it by the most conventional of routes.'

'You came here to meet someone,' Rudi said. He glanced around the clearing, looking for evidence of other footprints, but night was falling in earnest, and the fire didn't cast enough light to reveal them.

The healer nodded. 'I did. There are places like this all over the Empire, and far beyond it too, probably; anywhere there are people living in fear of the ignorant. People like me, and your friend Hanna.'

'What do you know about Hanna?' Rudi asked, suspicion flaring again. He glanced round at the encircling trees, half expecting Gerhard and his mercenaries to ooze out of the shadows.

Gofrey held out his hand. 'I know she can do this. Or something very like it.' A small flame, tinted a delicate blue like the skies of midsummer, burst into life in his upturned palm. Rudi watched it flicker for a moment, bemused, and then nodded slowly.

'You're a hedge wizard.'

Gofrey echoed the gesture, and closed his hand, extinguishing the magical flame.

'I see you've learned enough not to call me a witch, at any rate.' He held out another portion of rabbit. 'Thank you for that.'

'How do you know about Hanna?' Rudi asked, accepting the sizzling meat eagerly. 'Or me, for that matter.' He shivered, not entirely from the cold. 'Have you been watching us?' He wasn't sure how that was possible, but some mages, he knew, were able to see through other eyes, or cloak themselves in other foms.

The hedge-wizard laughed. 'Some of us stick together,' he said. 'We meet from time to time and pass on whatever information we have to share, especially about anyone the witch hunters are taking an interest in. The news about you left Marienburg almost as soon as you did, but it travelled a lot faster than a riverboat.'

'Can you help her?' Rudi asked.

Gofrey nodded. 'I can try, but it sounds as if all she needs is rest.'

Rudi shook his head. 'That's not what I meant. If you have friends, and they know about people like Hanna, they must be able to help keep her safe.'

The hedge wizard took another bite of rabbit before replying, clearly buying the time to order his thoughts.

'That's probably not such a good idea,' he said at last. 'Her best chance is to apply to one of the colleges in Altdorf. That's the only way anyone with the gift will ever be truly safe, and the colleges don't like us. They're almost as bad as the witch hunters.'

'You mean you think she'll betray you if they accept her,' Rudi said.

Gofrey smiled ruefully. 'I hope not, but I'll be moving on from here long before you get to Altdorf, just to be on the safe side. The rest of my friends in the Wheel wouldn't thank me for placing them in the same situation.'

'Hanna wouldn't do anything like that!' Rudi said hotly.

'We'll all do whatever it takes to survive, my young friend.' Gofrey shrugged. 'She might surprise you yet.'

Rudi tried not to think about the expression on Gerrit's face as he lay twitching in the snow, or the bloody ruins of the Black Cap gunners thrashing about on the jetty.

The mage continued. 'Besides, how much of a chance do you think she'll have of getting a college to accept her if they find out she's been consorting with witches? They'll burn her on the spot.'

'I suppose you're right,' Rudi said. There was much the man wasn't telling him, of that he was sure, but he didn't press the point. Instead, he stood, and approached the stand of trees. 'I'd better get some more wood. Like you said, it's going to be a cold night.'

DAWN CREPT SLOWLY through the curtain of trees, shrouded in mist. Rudi started awake, grateful for the residual heat of the fire, the embers of which still glowed warmly in their blanket of ash. He stretched, yawning, feeling surprisingly refreshed. He'd expected to be awake for most of the night, but the warmth of the fire and the food in his belly had combined to make him drowsy surprisingly fast. Or perhaps the herbs that Gofrey had used on the rabbits were for more than enhancing the flavour.

Struck by that thought, and the sudden memory of how Hanna had drugged the mercenaries the night they'd helped Fritz to escape, he sat upright, reaching for his sword again. Then he relaxed. The hedge wizard was snoring loudly, wrapped up in his cloak against the cold. Rudi clambered to his feet, feeling faintly foolish, and went to find a convenient tree.

Returning, with the pressure in his bladder comfortably relieved, he found Gofrey awake and pottering around the clearing.

'Ah, there you are.' The healer hailed him. 'I was beginning to think you'd fallen in the swamp.' He sat on a convenient tree branch, and started tying what looked like a lump of moss around his ankle. 'I'm afraid we'll have to put off breakfast until we get back to the landing.'

'I can wait,' Rudi assured him. Compared to the privations he and Hanna had endured on their journey to Marienburg, a late breakfast was barely worth considering. The mist was rising fast, and he would be able to set off and find his way back to the settlement without any danger fairly soon. As if to confirm the fact, a shaft of watery sunshine struck through the latticework of branches enclosing the glade, turning the frost-speckled grass into a rippling mirror. He nodded at the poultice. 'What's that for?'

'Sprained ankle,' Gofrey explained. 'Blackmoss makes the flesh swell up, and the skin look bruised. We'll need some excuse for staying out here all night.' He limped for a couple of paces, nodded in quiet satisfaction, and resumed his normal gait. 'I'll just need to hobble about a bit for a couple of days. Then the next boat to put in will bring an urgent letter from my cousin about a sick relative, I'll wave everyone here goodbye, and find somewhere else quiet and in need of a healer.'

Rudi nodded. It was clear that despite his assurances, Gofrey was still determined to move on. Well, he couldn't fault the man for being cautious. He'd obviously stayed ahead of the witch hunters for a long time, decades judging by his appearance. He tried to imagine what that must be like, never being able to settle anywhere or fully trust anyone, and smiled sourly. He didn't have to imagine it. He might not have mystical powers, but he was in almost exactly the same position as the hedge wizard.

Not quite, though. He still had a goal beyond simple survival, in a world that seemed to become more bewildering and threatening the more he discovered about it. The mystery of his origins continued to torment him, the questions buzzing around his head like flies around a midden; questions he hoped to find answers to in Altdorf. All he had to do was evade his enemies, track down some surviving member of the von Karien family, and...

Well, after that he wasn't sure. He supposed it would depend on the answers he got. Once Hanna was safe, he'd have to move on again, that much was certain, perhaps further upriver. There were vast tracts of woodland beyond Altdorf, he knew, and he had little doubt that he could live well in them. A lifelong forester, he should be able to elude any pursuers with little difficulty in such an environment. It would be a dubious haven at best, though. Bandits had fled to the forests for generations, and fouler things by far had always lurked in their deepest clearings: things grown more numerous and desperate than ever since the tide of war had turned in the Empire's favour, leaving the flotsam of the Chaos invasion stranded in isolated pockets wherever they could find places to hide.

Or perhaps they were closer at hand. As the sunlight strengthened, he began to see tracks in the floor of the glade, as he'd hoped to the previous night: his and Gofrey's, of course, but others too, entering and leaving from other directions. One set caught his eye at once, standing out from the rest because of their depth. Whoever made them was far larger and heavier than an ordinary man. There were other indentations too, just ahead of each step, which seemed to indicate that the feet were equipped with fearsome talons.

His mind racing, Rudi looked more closely at the prints. As he'd half expected, they were accompanied by a second pair, quite normal looking, left by a woman's shoe.

'Why didn't you tell me that Greta and Hans had been here?' he asked, as casually as he could. There could be no doubt in his mind. He'd followed the tracks left by the mutant, who had once been Hans Katzenjammer, into the woods outside Kohlstadt, and he'd seen them again in the offices of the lawyer in Marienburg, who had apparently been a part of Magnus's Chaos cult. These prints couldn't have been left by anyone, or anything, else. That meant that the woman who'd left her own alongside them must have been Greta Reifenstahl. Gofrey shrugged.

'Who?' His expression was open and ingenuous.

'The woman from Marienburg who told you about us. She's Hanna's mother.'

'Ah.' Gofrey nodded. 'We don't use names, or show faces either if we can avoid it. In case the witch hunters take one of us and put us to the question. We can't give up what we don't know.' The thought seemed to disturb him, as well it might. He shrugged. 'Why didn't you leave town with her?'

'We lost touch,' Rudi said shortly. Gofrey nodded. 'What about her... companion?'

'Big fellow, didn't say much. He kept to the shadows, bundled up in a cloak.' Gofrey shot him a challenging glance. 'Yes, he probably was a mutant. They're just people too, most of them, living ordinary lives, until suddenly they start changing through no fault of their own. If he's found someone to help him, good luck. Witch or mutant, it doesn't matter to me. We're all brands for the bonfire if we don't stick together.'

'I can't argue with that,' Rudi said. 'He's saved my life a couple of times, although Sigmar knows he's got no reason to. I'm just as dead as the rest of you if the authorities catch up with us.'

'Well then.' Gofrey shrugged. 'Shall we go?' He turned, and started towards the path leading back to

Nocht's Landing. Finding nothing else to say, Rudi followed.

AS THEY CAME in sight of the palisade, one of the villagers hailed them, waving frantically, and within moments of passing through the gates they were surrounded by a chattering mob, firing excited questions at them in a babble of overlapping voices, hardly pausing to draw breath or wait for an answer. Gofrey leaned against Rudi for greater effect, his assumed limp growing more exaggerated by the moment, and waved a tolerant hand at his friends and neighbours.

Struck by how glad they all were to see the friend they'd given up for dead, Rudi felt a pang of regret that his and Hanna's presence would soon force the man to depart. Perhaps this was a foreshadowing of his own future, he thought, forced to wander from one temporary refuge to another for the rest of his life. If Gofrey felt any regrets at being forced to leave, he gave no indication of it, just smiling happily in response to the chorus of greetings as if he didn't have a care in the world.

'It was my own fault,' he said cheerily. 'I saw some feverleaf growing a bit off the path, and hopped across to get it. Then I saw some spleenwort a bit further out. Before I knew it I was out of sight of the track, and twisted my ankle trying to jump back. If this lad hadn't come along, I'd have been swamp bait for sure.'

'Shallya must have sent him, right enough,' Ranulph agreed, slapping Rudi on the back and passing him a hunk of bread dripping with honey. 'They say she looks after the feeble-minded.' Gofrey bellowed with laughter.

'Then she'll have her work cut out around here.' He took a deep draught of the mug of mulled ale that someone had handed to him. 'Ah, that's better. It was a bit chilly out there in the dark.'

'Did you see any monsters?' a child asked, tugging at Rudi's trouser leg. Swallowing a mouthful of bread, he shook his head.

'Nothing we couldn't handle,' he assured the girl, with a wink at the assembled adults. 'They all ran off when they saw there were two of us.' The simple pleasures of conversation and goodwill were almost intoxicating. The morning was fine, growing brighter and clearer by the minute, and the food in his stomach seemed astonishingly reviving.

'So where's my patient?' Gofrey asked, pulling clear of the little knot of excited villagers. 'First things first.'

'On the boat.' Ranulph pointed to the wharf, where the *Reikmaiden* still lay. At the sight of her, Rudi let go a breath he hadn't been aware he was holding. Shenk would undoubtedly assume he was dead by now, and would have had no reason to delay his departure. As they walked slowly towards the gangplank, Rudi still supporting Gofrey for the sake of appearances, the captain himself appeared on deck.

'If you're going to leave it to the last minute to come aboard every time, you might not make it as far as Altdorf,' he said mildly. Rudi nodded.

'I brought the healer. How's Hanna?'

'Not much different,' Shenk said. 'She's stirring a bit, but she's still asleep.'

'I'd better take a look at her,' Gofrey said, 'since this young man seemed so keen to find me.' Rudi supported him up the gangplank, glancing around at the rest of the crew. Pieter waved a greeting, but Busch and Yullis could barely conceal their disappointment at his return. Ansbach wasn't even bothering to try, glaring at him as if his failure to drown in the swamp was a personal insult. Berta and Shenk's expressions remained neutral.

'She's been quiet all night,' the boatwoman volunteered. 'Then she started making these noises just after dawn.'

'What kind of noises?' Gofrey asked. Berta shrugged.

'Just noises,' she said. 'You know, like people do when they're asleep. I only noticed because she's been so still before.'

'That's a good sign,' the healer said, obviously reading Rudi's apprehension on his face. 'It means she's coming out of it.' He beckoned to Yullis. 'Can you get me some boiling water?'

'I suppose so.' The cook disappeared into the superstructure in the centre of the deck, and after a moment Rudi heard clattering noises coming from the galley.

'She's down here,' Rudi said, indicating the companionway that led to the hold. Gofrey nodded.

'Then if you wouldn't mind?' He held out a hand and let Rudi help him down the narrow flight of stairs, wincing a little every time he took his weight on the supposedly injured ankle. To Rudi's unspoken relief, everyone else remained on deck, dispersing to prepare the *Reikmaiden* for departure.

At first sight, Hanna looked exactly as she had when Rudi had gone ashore the previous evening, but as he stepped closer to the hammock he saw her stir fitfully as if dreaming. Her breathing seemed a little deeper too, and her face rather less pallid than he remembered. He mentioned as much to Gofrey.

'Good.' The healer nodded, his attention still fixed on the sleeping girl. 'She's definitely starting to recover. Anything else you can tell me?' Certain that they wouldn't be overheard, since the echoes of the footsteps on the deck above their heads let him know exactly where each of the crew was, Rudi nodded.

'She cast a spell, a big one. Then she just collapsed.'

'I see.' Gofrey bent over Hanna's recumbent form, examining her face minutely. Reminded of Gerhard's scrutiny, Rudi fought down the urge to drag him away. 'That would be after the witch hunter's mark was removed?'

'Yes,' Rudi confirmed. The healer nodded.

'Remarkable. You'd never know it had been there.'

'It was as if all the power it had been blocking suddenly burst out of her,' Rudi went on. Gofrey looked up at him, an expression of puzzlement on his face.

'That's what I don't understand,' he said. 'How could she possibly have survived for so long with that abomination in place?'

Rudi shrugged, unwilling to answer. The skaven's stone wasn't exactly a secret, but it was clearly a powerful charm of some kind, and Hanna had evidently bonded with it in some way. Perhaps Gofrey would want to take it if he found out about it, or if he touched it, it might harm Hanna by breaking the link.

Magic was a strange and capricious thing, he knew, and far beyond his comprehension.

'She's tougher than she looks,' he said truthfully, evading the issue. If Hanna thought that telling Gofrey about the stone was a good idea, she could do it herself when she woke.

'Evidently.' The healer pressed a hand to the girl's forehead, exactly where Gerhard's talisman had been, murmuring something under his breath. Alarmed, Rudi started forwards, but before he could intervene, Hanna sighed deeply, and her eyes flickered open.

'Who are you?' she asked, sounding puzzled rather than afraid. Rudi remembered she could recognise another magic user by sight. She sat up, awareness returning to her features, compensating for the rocking of the hammock with small, precise movements, and smiled at Rudi. 'We made it then.'

'This is Gofrey,' Rudi explained. No point telling her where they were, she'd obviously recognised the hold of the *Reikmaiden* instantly. 'He's a healer, like you.'

'Not quite,' Gofrey said. He nodded formally. 'My powers are far more limited than yours appear to be.' He turned to Rudi, and pulled some dried leaves from his bag. 'Could you take these to Yullis, and ask him to infuse them for me? He must have boiled the water by now.'

Torn between the desire to help and reluctance to leave Hanna again, Rudi hesitated. The girl nodded.

'I'll be fine,' she said. As he climbed up the companionway into the open air, the two mages began a hushed and urgent conversation behind him, none of which he could hear.

Rudi hurried through the errand as quickly as he could, but Yullis insisted on taking the time to infuse the leaves properly before they left his galley, and several minutes had passed before he was able to return to the hold. When he did, he was just in time to meet Gofrey emerging from the hatch.

'See that she drinks that,' the healer said. Turning away from Rudi, he waved at Shenk. 'Just going ashore,' he called. 'I'm sure I've delayed you quite long enough!'

'We'll make up the time,' Shenk assured him. With a final round of waving and shouted farewells, Gofrey hobbled down the gangplank, and Pieter and Ansbach began to unship the hawsers holding the riverboat in place. Having nothing better to do on deck, and anxious about Hanna, Rudi negotiated the narrow steps as best he could with a steaming mug in one hand and handed the drink to her.

'Thank you.' Hanna was out of the hammock, and sitting on one of the barrels stowed all through the hold. She sipped the fragrant brew carefully, and regarded Rudi through the steam with narrowed eyes.

'Did he tell you he'd seen Greta?' Rudi asked.

'Yes,' Hanna said, nodding, as if it wasn't really of any importance. Rudi felt a faint stirring of irritation.

'Did he say anything else?'

'We discussed my symptoms,' Hanna said, in a curiously flat tone that warned Rudi not to pursue the matter.

'I see.' Vaguely disconcerted, Rudi shrugged. 'Would you like some fresh air? We're just getting under way.'

'I'll join you on deck when I've finished this,' Hanna said. Taking the hint, Rudi climbed out of the hold again, leaving her to her thoughts.

The air outside was crisp, and the sun strong on the open water, but his spirits refused to lift. By the time he found himself able to relax again, the riverside settlement and its enigmatic healer were both long out of sight.

CHAPTER 5

CHAPTER SIX

THE NEXT WEEK or so passed without incident, the sturdy little riverboat forging its way upstream while the landscape beyond the rail changed slowly into something more familiar. The ever-present swamp and heathland began to be dotted with trees, isolated specimens at first, stunted and windswept for the most part, and then clustering into copses of gradually increasing size. After the first couple of days Rudi began to see patches of actual woodland, his spirits rising incrementally with each canopy of foliage to come into view. The leaves were turning the colours of autumn, evergreens mingled with browns, reds and yellows, so that from a distance some of the trees might have been pillars of frozen fire.

'It's beautiful,' Hanna said, as the *Reikmaiden* glided past a patch of forest that stretched down to the very banks of the river, making the water that reflected it appear to burn as it rippled with the wake of their passing. She seemed stronger, although she still hadn't recovered all her former vigour, and Rudi felt quietly encouraged by her words. Since Gofrey had woken her she'd seemed more thoughtful and with-drawn, although her underlying strength of character was just as evident, and she'd shown little inclination for small talk. 'Remind you of home?'

Taken by surprise at the question, Rudi could only nod. He could picture the scene under the trees all too vividly; almost smell the leaf mould, and feel the crispness of the frost-hardened leaves under his boots. That was where he belonged, he thought, in the tran-quillity of a forest glade, not chasing all over the Empire avoiding murderous lunatics. Reading his silence, Hanna squeezed his hand for a moment.

'Sorry,' she said, 'stupid question.'

'It's all right,' Rudi said, touched by her solicitude. This was almost like having the old Hanna back, but without the propensity to sarcasm and the hair-trigger temper. He tried not to think of it as an improvement. He'd changed too in the last few months, more than he would have believed possible, and he wondered for a moment what alterations she'd noticed in him.

'Any idea where we're putting in tonight?' he asked, hoping to cover the awkwardness. Hanna shrugged.

'I don't suppose it matters,' she said, 'they all seem pretty much the same.' Since leaving Nocht's Landing they'd spent most of the intervening nights at similar riverside settlements, and passed many more during the days, anonymous little islets of habitation that slipped past the railing and vanished as if they'd never been. Some undoubtedly had. He'd seen a couple of decayed jetties too, clearly long abandoned, although who'd built them and why they'd left he had no idea, and he hadn't felt much like asking any of the crew. On a couple of nights the boat had just kept sailing, forging through the dark, her running lights sketching her shape against the sky, but he knew that Shenk would rather lay up until the morning if he could. Gossip was the lifeblood of the river, and the news the captain gathered at these tiny settlements could be vital, and the steady stream of letters and messages the boat took on for forwarding at the next big town was a useful addition to her revenue.

'Wherever it is, we must be getting pretty close,' Rudi said, glancing back over the stern. The sun was low in the western sky, tinting the waters of the Reik the colour of molten gold, and he narrowed his eyes against the glare. 'It's almost dark.' Something seemed to be moving on the water behind the boat, but he couldn't be sure what it was, his vision dazzled by the dancing reflections.

'What is it?' Hanna asked, aware of the subtle changes in his body language that indicated tension.

'I'm not sure.' He shaded his eyes with a hand, and a dark silhouette resolved itself slowly, shimmering in the nimbus of light that surrounded it. 'It looks like a boat.' Whatever it was, it was moving fast, slipping through the water like a predator. The image rose unbidden in his mind, a warning from his subconscious. The tiller was only a few yards away, Ansbach leaning against it, ostentatiously unaware of their presence as he adjusted the ship's heading with small, precise movements. Rudi hailed him. 'Ansbach!'

'What do you want?' the steersman asked, his tone making it abundantly clear that he couldn't have cared less. Rudi gestured over the stern.

'There's a boat behind us, catching up fast. Should we be worried?' He'd half-expected some sarcastic rejoinder, the deckhand pretending to think he meant the small rowing boat that trailed in their wake at the end of a rope, but Ansbach simply turned, narrowing his eyes against the glare, and nodded grimly.

'Yes.' He filled his lungs, and bellowed, 'Stand to!'

The rest of the crew abandoned their jobs around the deck and ran to join them, Shenk emerging from his cabin, still fastening his coat.

'What is it?' the captain asked. Once again, Rudi marvelled at the transformation of the shabby little man, here in his natural habitat. He sounded crisp and incisive, every inch the leader that his crew evidently expected him to be.

'We've got company,' Ansbach reported, jerking a thumb in the direction of the stern. 'Your friend here spotted them.' The last was delivered in a grudging tone, it was true, but Rudi appreciated it nevertheless. Shenk nodded. The approaching vessel was clearly visible, slicing through the water at a speed the heavily laden riverboat couldn't hope to match. Its hull was lean and narrow, its sails rigged for speed, and it was closing fast.

'Typical pirate trick,' Shenk said, nodding his thanks to Rudi, 'coming out of the sun at dawn or dusk.' He turned, running back to his cabin, and vanished inside.

'Don't just stand there, arm yourselves!' Busch bellowed, and Berta, Yullis and Pieter scattered to find whatever makeshift weapons they could. That wouldn't be much, Rudi thought. Most people in the Empire carried a knife, for eating, odd jobs, and self-defence at a pinch, but the crew of the marauding vessel would be far better armed than that, he was sure.

'Better get below,' Rudi said to Hanna. He'd been expecting her to argue, but she simply nodded, tight-lipped. She might be well on the road to recovery, but she was still in no condition to fight. They both knew that. Her spell casting abilities could turn the tide of battle easily, of course, and he pictured a bolt of magical fire like the ones that had consumed the skaven and Magnus's mutants bursting on the deck of the approaching marauder with a sigh of regret. There was no way, however, that the young sorceress could use her abilities in front of the crew without betraying her secret, and if that happened, he had no doubt at all that Shenk would turn them in to the authorities, in spite of the debt he owed him. The captain wouldn't risk being burned for harbouring a witch, however grateful he might have been to Rudi for helping him evade arrest back in Marienburg.

'Good luck.' Hanna turned, and disappeared down the hatch to the hold. Relieved that she was safe, at least for the time being, Rudi turned his attention to the immediate threat.

The pirate vessel was close enough to have lost the protection of the westering sun, its sails blotting out the sinking ball of fire, and Rudi began to make out some of the details. A cluster of men stood on its deck, pointing and gesticulating, clearly getting ready for combat. Shafts of light from the setting sun glittered off the swords in their hands, turning the blades the colour of blood, and Rudi drew his own.

'Hadn't you better get a weapon too?' he asked Ansbach.

'I can't leave the tiller,' the deckhand said, with the weary patience of someone explaining the obvious. 'If we lose way, we're done for.' He was clearly unhappy about this, and Rudi could understand why. Standing at the stern, Ansbach was uncomfortably exposed, and would be unable to defend himself if he was attacked.

'I'll cover your back,' Rudi assured him. Ansbach didn't look as if he found that much of a comfort.

'Rudi!' Hanna's head and shoulders emerged from the hold, his bow and arrows held aloft. 'Here!'

'I'll take them. Get below!' Shenk grabbed the weapon and quiver in one hand, the other holding the cutlass he'd returned to his cabin for, and sprinted across the deck towards Rudi. Hanna ducked out of sight again. 'I hope you know how to use this.'

'I can use it all right on the land,' Rudi said. Needing both hands to draw the bow, he re-sheathed his sword, and shrugged the quiver into place across his shoulders. 'How good are you with that wood chopper?'

'Good as I have to be,' Shenk said, with more confidence than Rudi had expected. He turned to call out to his crew. 'Spread out, cover the deck. When they try to board, we'll take them.' He took a guard position, slightly stiffly to Rudi's practiced eye, but well enough to show him that the riverman actually knew how to use the weapon. The blade seemed to burn in the reddening light, picking out a few nicks along its length. That was reassuring too, Shenk had obviously used it successfully before.

'You sound confident at any rate.' Rudi nocked an arrow and drew back smoothly, seeking a target. He'd feared the faint rocking of the boat would throw off his aim, but he had his river legs, and found himself compensating for the motion as instinctively as all the other factors his conscious mind barely registered. Following the advice his adoptive father had tried so hard to instil in him, he drew and loosed in one fluid movement, leaving it to the arrow to find the target without trying too hard to aim.

The shot was a smooth one, and confident that it would find the mark, Rudi began reaching for another shaft even before the arrow buried itself in the chest of one of the pirates crowding the rail. The man fell back, choking, and Rudi drew the next arrow from his quiver, marvelling at the distance the marauding vessel had managed to close in so short a time. It had been well within range, and was coming closer with every passing moment. The sunset had been completely eclipsed by the pirates' boat, and he was able to pick out a surprising amount of detail, despite the mist that seemed to be shrouding its deck.

'Down!' he shouted, dropping the shaft he'd been about to nock, and crouching below the level of the rail. Ansbach hunkered down as best he could, looking confused and apprehensive, while Shenk dropped to the deck at once. He clearly trusted Rudi's instincts in this sort of situation.

'What's the...?' Ansbach started to ask, but the question was answered by a volley of overlapping reports that echoed flatly across the water. The thick wood of the boat's rail splintered under the impact of a hail of musket balls, and a few higher up whined across the deck.

'Mannan's bloody dolphins!' Shenk turned a panic-stricken face to Rudi. 'They've got guns!'

'Anyone hurt?' Rudi rose to his feet, nocking the arrow in his hand, and let fly again. One of the gunners pitched to the deck of the pirate vessel, still in the act of reloading. He found himself wishing that Hanna was here to do her trick with the powder flasks again, but she was out of sight in the hold, and there was no way to communicate with her.

'Pieter's down!' Berta's voice was shrill with panic, and Rudi glanced across to see the deckhand lying on the planking a few yards away, a pool of blood spreading around him. He was trying to sit up, looking dazed, and Rudi breathed a sigh of relief at the woman's next words. 'He took a bullet in the shoulder!'

'Get him below!' Shenk bawled. 'Hanna should know what to do!' He glanced at Rudi, and raised an eyebrow. 'Right?'

'Right,' Rudi agreed. The girl had been a healer all her life, and should be able to stem the bleeding without too much difficulty. Besides, with a casualty to tend to, she was less likely to do something rash. He wondered for a moment if Berta would be able to manage the job on her own, but the stocky woman was used to lugging heavy weights around, and hoisted Pieter to his feet with ease. A moment later, the pair of them disappeared below decks.

'Friends of yours?' Busch asked acidly. Rudi shook his head.

'Never seen them before in my life,' he replied. 'Why should they be?' Nevertheless, he'd found himself scanning the deck of the raiding vessel for the sight of a dwarf, or a red-haired sorceress, or some other member of Krieger's mercenary band. Busch shrugged.

'Never seen river rats with that kind of firepower before, that's all, and you did come aboard in something of a hurry.'

'Kurt. This isn't the time.' Shenk's voice was hard, and the first mate nodded.

'Right.' He gripped the belaying pin in his right hand convulsively, and tensed for combat. On the verge of nocking another arrow, Rudi changed his mind and dropped the bow, drawing his sword again. The pirates had clearly decided that there wouldn't be time for another volley, and were preparing to board. The raiding vessel was alongside, and with a sudden convulsive move of the tiller it swung about, ramming into the side of the *Reikmaiden*.

The sturdy little riverboat shuddered with the impact, timbers groaning as they distorted for a moment and sprang back into shape. With a wild yell, half a dozen armed marauders leapt the narrow gap, which was widening already as the helmsman of the raiders moved away again, no doubt fearful of breaching his own hull if he remained too close and gave

Ansbach the opportunity of returning the favour. There was no time to differentiate the assailants any further, and within an instant, Rudi was fighting for his life.

A huge fellow, bearded like a Norscan, swung a double-headed axe at Rudi's head with murderous intent. Rudi ducked and parried, feeling the impact jarring up his arm as he deflected the blade with the edge of his sword, and stepped in close, inside the axeman's reach. He knew from his time with the Black Caps that despite its intimidating appearance the weapon was a clumsy one, unsuited to fighting at close quarters. It needed room to be used effectively, and denied of it, the wielder would be at a serious disadvantage. He stamped down on the fellow's instep. The axeman gasped, losing his balance for a moment, and Rudi struck upwards, taking him in the throat with the hilt of his sword. Something gave, with a crunching sound, and the man fell heavily to the deck, his face contorting.

'Rudi!' Shenk called, and Rudi turned, leaving the axeman to expire: with a crushed larynx he couldn't last more than a moment or two. A bright sword thrust at his kidneys, and he evaded, the clash of his own blade against the one that had almost claimed his lif, echoing across the water.

'Thanks.' Rudi followed up the deflection with a thrust of his own, but the swordsman evaded it easily. Shenk made a cut at the man's back with his cutlass, but the raider was quick, Rudi had to admit, spinning round to engage the riverboat captain at once. Within seconds he was through Shenk's guard, and only a frantic leap back saved the mariner from disembowelment. Rudi cut at the duellist's leg, hoping to cripple him, but the man rallied again, and Rudi found himself being driven backwards across the deck.

Unable to look around for fear of giving his unexpectedly skilled opponent an opening, he saw the rest of the battle in snatches from his peripheral vision. Shenk tried to follow, but was immediately engaged by another of the pirates, a hard-faced young woman whose shirt was partially unbuttoned to reveal an impressive amount of cleavage. This was, no doubt, an effective distraction against most male opponents, but Shenk seemed too focused on saving his boat and his cargo to fall for that old trick. Busch was laying about himself with the belaying pin, heedless of the fact that the pirates' weapons were bladed.

Remembering the impact with which the improvised club had struck when he'd fought the mate himself, Rudi had no doubt of its effectiveness, an impression reinforced when a raider dropped his sword with a howl of agony and what sounded like the crack of shattering bone. With a cry of triumph, the mate swung the cylinder of wood a second time, up into the man's jaw, and he pitched over the rail with a splash.

That made two down already, Rudi thought. Yullis wasn't going to be much help, though. He was still swinging a meat cleaver from his galley with grim determination, but a self-evident lack of martial ability, when the remaining three unengaged pirates rushed him, knocked him off his feet, and left him gasping and winded on the deck. To Rudi's surprise they didn't stop to finish off the fallen cook, instead just pausing a moment to glance around as if orientating themselves.

'This way!' The young man in the middle of the trio appeared to be unarmed, Rudi saw, although he had something clutched tightly in his hand, which he seemed to be studying intently. The three of them turned, following his lead, and ran for the hatch leading down to the hold.

'Hanna!' Rudi tried to shout a warning, but his opponent made another cut at his belly, and all his attention returned to the fight. This one was good, he could tell, having faced a number of opponents of varying abilities during his brief career as a watchman: exceptionally good, in fact. He tried every trick he could think of, hoping to break through the man's guard, but nothing worked. The sliver of whirling steel was always there ahead of him, deflecting every blow, and licking out to threaten him with lazy deliberation. His opponent smiled.

'You're pretty good, river boy. It's a shame to have to kill you.'

'You haven't managed yet,' Rudi gasped, feeling the air beginning to labour in his lungs.

'I haven't really been trying.' A smile of lazy confidence appeared on the man's lips, and with a sudden chill, Rudi realised exactly what he was facing: a professional killer, who liked his work, and enjoyed tormenting his victims. That sudden moment of realisation probably saved his life, as it gave him an instant to prepare for the blizzard of stroke and counterstroke that would otherwise have swept him away, as the assassin began trying to dispatch him in earnest.

Then abruptly the duellist staggered, an expression of pain and surprise on his face. A wet, meaty thud echoed around the deck, and a belaying pin clattered to the planking at his feet. Busch had thrown the solid piece of timber with startling accuracy, catching the man in the side of the head. Rudi drove in, taking full advantage of the opening that his unexpected ally had just bought him, and thrust his blade straight through the assassin's heart with a sudden surge of vengeful rage. The over-confident duellist just had time to look surprised all over again before the light went out of his eyes, and he slumped to the deck.

'Thanks,' Rudi called. Then he frowned. 'That was pretty risky. How could you be sure you wouldn't hit me instead?'

'I wasn't.' Busch picked up the belaying pin, and went to check on Yullis, who was trying to rise to his feet despite looking dazed and disorientated. Shenk and the female pirate were still exchanging blows and invective, but the captain seemed to be holding his own, so Rudi hurried over to the hold.

'Hanna!' he yelled. 'Are you all right?'

'For the moment.' The sorceress's voice was grim, and Rudi leapt into the darkness of the hold without thought or care for his own safety. He landed on one of the boarders more by luck than judgement, driving the man to the deck with a loud grunt and the crack of breaking ribs. The impact of his fall broken, he rolled, feeling the quiver across his shoulders grinding into his back, and slashed at the legs of the man in front of him.

The fellow was quick, leaping over the sword blade, and striking down to deflect it with his own. Rudi rolled again, trying to get to his feet, and the marauder cut down at him, the heavy falchion slicing a fresh notch in the deck as it missed him by inches.

'Leave him alone!' Berta lifted a barrel the size of her own torso with an ease that Rudi would have found astonishing under most other circumstances, and threw it. Taken by surprise, the swordsman failed to evade the heavy container, and went crashing backwards into the neatly stowed cargo.

Rudi rolled to his feet, and glared around the confined space, looking for another target. The man he'd landed on lay limp and unmoving, and the bravo who'd just taken the barrel in the face didn't seem capable of doing much more than groaning quietly. Nevertheless, he kicked both their weapons well out of reach as he turned.

'Thanks,' he said, nodding to the boatwoman. She and Hanna were standing at one end of the hold, tending to Pieter, who was lying on a line of boxes hastily rearranged into a makeshift bed. His shoulder was bandaged, his shirt off, and he was stirring feebly, his expression dull and unfocused. Noticing Rudi's expression of puzzlement, Hanna shrugged.

'I gave him a sliver of manbane for the pain. I had to dig the ball out.' Rudi nodded, remembering the effect the powerful narcotic had had on Fritz when he'd been too badly beaten by Gerhard's thugs to stand without it. Hanna had her knife out, the regular one she carried at her waist rather than the dagger she normally kept concealed, and the blade of it was encrusted with fresh blood. In the half-light of the hold, she looked more like a bloody-handed priestess of Khaine than a healer. Startled by the image, Rudi fought down the vindictiveness that had threatened to consume him, shocked back to his senses by the thought that he was scarcely better than an acolyte of the dark god of murder himself at the moment.

'There was another one.' He glanced around the hold, seeking the young man who'd seemed to lead the raiding party. 'Where is he?'

'Over there,' Berta pointed, 'ransacking the cargo.' As the sailor spoke, Rudi found himself catching Hanna's eye. The sorceress seemed on the point of saying something else, but appeared to think better of it, and simply nodded.

'Seems like a lot of trouble to go to for a barrel or two of dried herring,' Rudi said, advancing on the young man, who backed away from him, clearly terrified. The speed with which his armed companions had been dispatched had evidently come as an unwelcome surprise. Rudi gestured towards the companionway with his sword. 'Up on deck.' He wasn't expecting any serious resistance, since the lad was obviously no fighter. He hadn't even drawn the dagger at his belt, his attention apparently still focused on the tiny object in the palm of his hand.

'Sure, fine.' The young man grinned insincerely. 'No problem.' His eyes flickered around the darkened hold, as if looking for something, but he began to move towards the hatch nevertheless. As his eyes began to adjust to the lower light levels down here, Rudi found he could see more clearly than before. Then he gasped. The thing in the young man's leather-gloved hand was glowing faintly, like Hanna's skaven stone, but with a duller, pulsating radiance like the beating of a heart. Rudi stared at it.

'Sorcery,' he said, unable to prevent the word from slipping out, and an edge of apprehension from colouring his voice.

The young man smiled lazily, evidently thinking he had some kind of advantage after all.

'That's right,' he said, his voice suddenly sounding more confident, 'and if you mess with it, or me, this boat's going straight to the bottom. Understood?' Rudi glanced across at Hanna, who stared back, her face blank. He'd been hoping for a lead from her, some hint as to whether the young man was bluffing or not, but she remained impassive. Berta was making the sign of the trident, her face white.

'Let him go, Rudi.' Hanna edged around the line of boxes, her expression growing grimmer by the moment. 'No telling what that thing might do.'

'Right.' Rudi stood aside, giving the young man a wide berth. His experience of sorcery had been limited so far, but he knew enough to realise that it could be extremely dangerous, and if Hanna thought there was a significant risk he wasn't about to take any chances.

'What's going on down there?' Busch's face appeared in the hatchway, framed by a rectangle of darkening sky, and Rudi glanced upwards.

'Everything's taken care of,' he said, trying to sound confident. 'This fellow's just climbing back up to the deck. Give him some room.'

'I'll give him a dent in his skull,' Busch said grimly. The young man held up the glowing talisman.

'That wouldn't be wise,' he said. As he edged nearer to the steep flight of steps leading up to the open air the light grew more intense, the pulsations faster, as if the heartbeat it so resembled was becoming panicky. Despite himself, the young man glanced around, catching sight of Hanna, and his eyes widened. 'It's you! You're–'

Before he could complete the sentence, Hanna stepped in, and drove her bloody knife up under his ribcage. The young man looked surprised for a moment, and then folded, his heels drumming on the deck.

'Merciful Shallya, you killed him!' Berta stared at the young healer in stupefied astonishment.

'Damn right I did.' Hanna threw a blooded scrap of Pieter's shirt over the glowing talisman, and wrapped it up carefully. 'There's no telling what he might have done with this.' Rudi suspected she knew perfectly well, but followed her lead anyway; she must have had good reason to act as she did.

'Better chuck it over the side,' he suggested.

'That's just what I'm going to do,' Hanna said.

'What about the other two?' Busch asked.

Hanna glanced at the pirate who'd broken Rudi's fall, still slumped beneath the open hatch.

'Dead,' she announced after a cursory inspection. 'Broken neck.' The man beneath the barrel stirred fitfully. 'And this one's in no state to fight. Can somebody bring him?'

'I'll do it,' Berta offered, hoisting the fellow none too gently across her shoulders. The man's incessant groaning intensified for a moment, and then choked off with a faint whimper of pain.

'Good.' Hanna clambered up on deck, and Rudi followed. From Busch's relatively relaxed demeanour, he assumed that the immediate danger had passed, an impression reinforced by a quick glance around the deck. Yullis was sitting against the cabin wall, still looking dazed, but otherwise none the worse for wear, and Shenk had clearly won his own fight; the female pirate was backed up against the rail, her sword on the deck, and the point of Shenk's cutlass at her throat.

'All right there, skipper?' Busch asked. Shenk nodded.

'I can manage.' The woman licked her lips, a little nervously.

'You wouldn't kill an unarmed woman, would you?' Shenk shrugged.

'That depends.'

'Depends on what?' the woman asked, shrugging too, in a manner designed to emphasise the goods on display in her abbreviated shirt. Shenk grinned.

'On whether you can swim,' he said, kicking her legs out from under her and shoving hard.

'You bas–' The rest of the sentence was cut off with a splash, and after a moment, the pirate surfaced, spluttering furiously.

'Oh, you can.' Shenk shrugged, as if the matter was only of academic interest.

'This one too, skip?' Berta asked, and the captain nodded.

'If you wouldn't mind, I like my decks kept clean.' The injured pirate followed his female companion over the side, and after a moment she stopped shouting abuse in favour of trying to keep his head above the water. 'Ah, that's a good sign.'

'What is?' Rudi asked.

'They don't leave their wounded. A lot of them do, but that means their boat will stop to pick them up.'

'That gives us a good head start,' Ansbach supplied helpfully. Rudi nodded. 'What about the others?'

'All dead,' Berta said. Shenk raised an eyebrow, and glanced at Rudi.

'Your handiwork, I take it?' He sounded impressed.

'Mostly,' Rudi admitted. In the distance, the pirate vessel had come about, and seemed to be engaged in recovering the last forlorn remnants of its boarding party.

'Hanna got one,' Berta supplied, 'and a good thing too. He was a witch, and he was summoning a daemon to sink us, and–'

'A witch?' Shenk's voice was disbelieving. 'I've seen a lot of strange things on the river over the years, but I've never known one of their kind turn pirate.'

'He had this,' Hanna said, holding out the bundle of rags in her hand at arms length, 'and it's definitely magical.' Even through its wrapping of bloodstained cloth, the light it emitted could still be seen, pulsing obscenely. Shenk nodded.

'Is it worth much?'

'Probably.' Hanna locked eyes with the captain for a moment. 'He said it could sink us too. If you want to keep it on board while you search for a buyer...'

'It's only a few more days to Altdorf, skipper,' Busch coughed nervously. 'You could probably find a wizard there who'd buy it.'

'Or a witch hunter who'd burn us just for having touched the damn thing.' Shenk recoiled from the bundle. 'I don't trust magic, never have, never will. Chuck it over the side.'

'With pleasure,' Hanna said, and did so. Rudi watched the little object sink, half expecting the sinister glow to follow them through the water, but it simply sank out of sight with a faint *plop!* as if it had been nothing more inimical than an ordinary pebble. As it hit the water, Rudi thought he heard Hanna sigh, as if with relief, but the gurgling of the water against the hull and the snap of the wind in the sails made it hard to be sure.

CHAPTER SEVEN

'WHAT WAS THAT thing?' Rudi asked, the first time he was sure that he and Hanna were alone and unlikely to be overheard. The *Reikmaiden* was tied up at another of the riverside settlements, on a wharf identical to most of the others he'd seen on their progress up the river, and the familiar huddle of huts surrounded it. The only difference was that this one was deep in the heart of the forest, its inhabitants apparently scratching a living by logging, and the presence of the trees so close at hand lifted his spirits more than he would have believed possible. Impatient to go ashore, he'd returned to their improvised quarters in the boat's hold to stow his bow and arrows, and found Hanna sitting pensively in her hammock, her legs swinging. She shrugged.

'A talisman: nothing special, just a basic enchantment on an old symbol of Mannan. You can buy something similar anywhere there are wizards with time on their hands and a hole in their purses. Crude, but they do the job they're made for.'

'What job is that?' Rudi asked again. Hanna hopped out of the hammock.

'There are all sorts. Ones like that detect the aura of magic,' she said. Rudi felt his blood run cold.

'You mean they were witch hunters?' That didn't make sense. There had been no sign of Gerhard or any of his associates on the vessel that had attacked them, and surely witch hunters would have ordered the *Reik-maiden* to heave to before boarding, relying on the authority of their office to enforce compliance, rather than simply attacking without warning. Hanna shook her head.

'I don't think so. They were looking for something hidden among the cargo.' She pointed. 'There's a hollow space in that bulkhead there, behind the fish barrels. There's something magical inside it; powerful, too.'

'How do you know?' Rudi asked, and Hanna looked at him scornfully.

'I've got the sight, remember?'

Rudi recalled how she'd been able to recognise Alwyn and Kris as fellow mages the first time she'd seen them, and read the marks on the enchanted cards in Tilman's gambling den. 'I noticed it as soon as I woke up in here.'

'So that's what Shenk's up to,' Rudi said. He'd been certain that the riverboat captain was smuggling something, ever since their encounter in the rooming house the Black Caps had been raiding back in Marienburg, and this seemed to confirm it. 'Do you think he knows his contraband is magical?'

'I doubt it.' Hanna shrugged. 'You saw how skittish he was with that gewgaw I threw over the side. He wouldn't go within a league of what's hidden back there if he knew how powerful it is.' Her tone became speculative. 'Unless he's being paid an enormous amount of money for shifting it, of course.'

'Maybe.' Rudi felt the good mood that the scent of the surrounding woodlands had kindled in him begin to evaporate, displaced by a formless sense of unease. Once again he was surrounded by secrets, which could get him killed without even knowing the reason why, or finding the answers to the questions that continued to plague him. He'd had enough of that back in Marienburg. 'I'll talk to him if I get the chance, see what I can find out.'

'Be careful,' Hanna counselled. 'You might not like what you uncover.'

Rudi nodded, certain that she was right.

'So it was just bad luck, the thing flaring up when you got close to it,' he said.

Hanna echoed the gesture. 'That's right. It picked up on my aura instead of that thing behind the barrels. Luckily, I was close enough to shut him up before he cried witch on me.'

'No one seems to have noticed, anyway,' Rudi said, while a small part of his mind watched appalled at the casual way they were both accepting the killing of another human being as a regrettable necessity. 'Pieter was well out of it the whole time, and Berta thinks you saved the boat from a hell-raising necromancer.'

'Good,' Hanna said. 'That avoids any more difficulties.'

Her matter-of-fact tone sent another shiver down Rudi's spine. Would she really have been willing to murder their friends to keep her secret if she'd had to? He forced the thought away. Life on the run was changing both of them, he knew, but he couldn't believe that Hanna would kill in cold blood simply because it was expedient. She looked at him, an odd expression on her face. 'Are you all right?'

'Fine,' Rudi assured her, hoping that it was true.

NIGHT HAD FALLEN completely by the time Rudi returned to the deck, and flaring torches lit the wharf, picking out golden highlights from the rippling darkness beneath the gangplank. It was the first time Rudi had seen such a display at any of the riverside settlements the boat had put in at, and after a moment's thought he recognised the resinous branches in the crudely-made sconces as by-products of the local timber trade.

'That's right,' Shenk confirmed when he voiced the thought aloud. 'Nothing gets wasted out here.' He glanced at Rudi. 'Finally put your toy away?' Rudi nodded. The pleasantry had been delivered in a tone, which, if no warmer than before, seemed a little more relaxed than Shenk had been around him hitherto.

'I don't think I'll be needing it now,' he said. Despite the fact that the pirates, if that was what they really were, had clearly been driven off, he'd kept his bow handy until the *Reikmaiden* was safely tied up at the quay. No one aboard had objected. After the ease with which he'd apparently dispatched the majority of their attackers, the crew had taken to watching him with wary respect, and even Busch and Ansbach spoke to him with a little more warmth in their voices. 'Not tonight, anyway.'

'We'll have seen the last of them,' Shenk said. 'Scum like that won't risk another savaging. They'll wait for an easier target to come along.'

'Maybe,' Rudi said, following the riverboat captain to the gangplank. 'If they really were pirates, of course.'

'What else would they be?' Shenk asked. Rudi shrugged.

'Fog Walkers?' he suggested, using the common nickname for the covert agents of the ruling council of Marienburg. He couldn't be sure in the guttering light cast by the torches on the wharf, but for a moment he thought a flicker of surprise and apprehension appeared on the captain's face. Then it was gone, and Shenk's expression became studiedly neutral.

'You've got an imagination, I'll say that,' he said. Rudi shrugged.

'If you say so. But if they were just ordinary pirates, why didn't we hear of them at any of the settlements we've put into? News like that travels fast.' Shenk shrugged.

'Maybe we were just the first boat they jumped,' he suggested.

'Perhaps we were.' Rudi led the way onto the gang-plank. As he gained the rough timbers of the wharf, his gait changed a little, his sense of balance thrown subtly off-kilter by the motionlessness of the solid footing. Shenk followed. 'Do river pirates usually have guns?'

'First time I've ever seen it,' Shenk admitted. Firearms were rare and precious, and to find so many in the hands of mere bandits would be almost unprecedented. He caught Rudi by the upper arm, and swung him round so the two of them were standing close together under the orange glow of a crudely made torch. In the sudden silence, Rudi could hear the hissing of it, and smell the unmistakable odour of burning resin. He tensed, wondering if Shenk was going to attack him, and then relaxed, dismissing the thought. After seeing his fighting abilities, that was the last thing the little man would do. The captain glanced around, certain that no one else was within earshot, and lowered his voice. 'Why would the Fog Walkers be interested in my boat?'

Rudi shrugged.

'I don't know, and I don't care,' he said honestly, 'so long as it doesn't stop Hanna and me from getting to Altdorf. I might take a guess, though.'

'I see.' Shenk nodded. 'And your guess would be?'

Rudi shrugged.

'I found you in a rooming house owned by a notorious smuggler, whose business had attracted a lot of official attention. Enough attention for the authorities to risk annoying the elves to close down, which they wouldn't do just to claw back a bit of evaded duty on a cargo of wine or cheese. The next thing I know, you're heading back upriver.'

'We go up and down the river all the time,' Shenk said. 'That's why they call it a river boat.'

'True,' Rudi said. 'But I was a Cap for long enough to develop a nasty suspicious mind, especially when there was an Imperial agent in town, who I know for a fact the Walkers were taking an interest in.'

'Do you now?' Shenk's voice was guarded. 'And how would a simple watchman know something like that?'

'A friend of mine works for him,' Rudi said, 'and Sam Warble asked me to find something out about what he was up to.' As he'd expected, Shenk nodded at the name of the halfling information broker. Everyone in Marienburg with a secret to sell or protect knew Sam.

'He told you he was working for the Fog Walkers,' Shenk said.

Rudi shrugged again. 'Not in so many words,' he said. 'But the way he didn't tell me was pretty convincing.'

'I see.' The riverboat captain's face and voice had turned grim. 'What conclusion does your nasty suspicious mind draw from all this?'

'That I don't want to draw any conclusions,' Rudi said. 'Boats like yours carry messages and packets all the time, don't they?'

'Yes.' Shenk nodded. 'And what's in them is none of my business.'

'Even if delivering them looks like getting you killed?' Rudi asked.

'Especially then,' Shenk said. He might have been about to say something else, but was interrupted by a hail from the gangplank. Ansbach and Berta were clattering onto the wharf, apparently in high spirits.

'Skipper, Rudi.' Ansbach looked at Rudi with more warmth than he'd ever done, albeit tempered with an air of wariness, like someone putting out a hand to pat a dog he thought might bite. 'We're off to the Floating Log for a celebration drink. Reckon we owe you at least one for this afternoon's work. Coming?'

'Thanks,' Rudi said, surprised almost as much by the man's relative affability as the news that the settlement was apparently prosperous enough to support an inn. 'This place has a real tavern?'

'Not as such,' Shenk said, clearly relieved at the change of subject. 'But they do have ale, and some stuff that'll make you go blind, but takes paint off really well.' He glanced back at the gangplank. 'Where's Kurt?'

'Staying on board with Yullis,' Berta said. 'He thought doubling the watches would be a good idea, at least as far as Carroburg.' Shenk nodded.

'Can't hurt,' he said, with a sideways glance at Rudi. Evidently the mate, at least, was also aware that the real target of the raid had been whatever lay hidden in the hold. 'Where's Hanna?'

'She's staying aboard too,' Rudi told him. 'She doesn't want to leave Pieter until she's sure he'll be all right.'

'That's good of her,' Shenk said. Then he nodded, relieved. 'Probably just as well, this isn't really the sort of place for a young lady.'

Berta snorted. 'Sounds like the right place for me, then,' she said.

* * *

ON CLOSER INSPECTION, Rudi had to concede that Shenk was right. The logging camp was populated almost entirely by men, and the few exceptions were clearly either there with a husband, or intent on making money from the lumberjacks in one of the traditional ancillary professions. From their manner of dress, or lack of it, most of the younger ones were evidently not cooks or laundresses. Hanna would undoubtedly have attracted unwelcome attention, and Rudi tried not to picture the likely consequences.

In contrast to the rude huts Rudi had been used to seeing in the settlements they'd stopped at before, the buildings seemed sturdier, constructed for the most part of logs or freshly-sawn timber. They seemed extravagantly large, too, until Shenk explained that most of them were communal dormitory blocks, or warehouses for the supplies that the flourishing community needed. Everything, it seemed, came in by boat, either casual visitors like the *Reikmaiden*, or the regularly-scheduled barges that arrived every week or so, laden with tools and food, and departed weighed down with timber.

'There's still a bit of room for some private enterprise, though,' Shenk assured Rudi.

Rudi wasn't surprised. He was beginning to suspect that the riverboat captain could find a profit pretty much anywhere.

'I think we're attracting some attention,' he said. Several of the men they'd passed were armed, carrying bows or spears, and most of them glanced in his direction, their expressions far from friendly. Shenk waved.

'It's your sword,' he explained. 'Most people around here don't carry one.'

Berta snorted with amusement. 'Why bother when you've got a big chopper to play with?' she said, sniggering at her own wit.

'Good point,' Rudi said, and studied the guards again with open curiosity. The wall enclosing the encampment was higher than the others he'd seen along the river, almost as large as the one that surrounded Kohlstadt, the village he'd grown up in, and a stout timber gate protected the stockade. 'So what are they carrying weapons for?'

Ansbach laughed. 'It's a forest out there,' he explained. 'Who knows what's lurking in it? Beastmen, goblins, covens of witches, you name it.'

'Trees?' Rudi suggested. 'Rabbits?' He grinned, draining the remark of any perceived belligerence. 'I grew up in a forest. It's not as bad as all that.'

'Not south of the river, maybe,' Ansbach conceded, with an obvious effort to be civil, 'but this side's Middenland. The greatest battle of the war was fought at Middenheim, and not all the Chaos scum went north again afterwards. Anything might have gone to ground in the Drakwald.'

'You're right about that.' Rudi nodded his agreement, and Ansbach looked surprised for a moment. 'We even saw beastmen in the Reikland last summer.' Suddenly conscious that he'd said too much about his past, and that Shenk was looking at him with a curiously speculative expression, he searched for a change of subject. A burst of raucous laughter attracted his attention at just the right moment, and he turned his head to look at the strange structure in the middle of the makeshift village. 'Is that it?'

'Looks like it to me,' Berta confirmed, picking up her pace. The tavern looked more like a tent than a building, although the floor was composed of planks, none of them were quite the same size or shape as any of its neighbours, and three of the walls were made of reasonably straight tree branches and off-cuts from the saw pits. Evidently, whoever owned it had scavenged whatever scrap timber they could to put the place together. The roof was a sheet of canvas, which could be extended to the ground on the open side to keep out the wind and rain.

Conscious of the way his breath misted in front of him, Rudi found himself wondering why it had been left open on a night that his woodsman's instincts told him would probably bring frost.

As the little party of mariners reached it, however, he had his answer. A blast of body heat, mingled with the smells of sweat, sour ale, old vomit and flatulence, rolled out over him, sparking incongruous memories of some of the less salubrious establishments of Marienburg he'd visited on official business. The ramshackle tavern was packed with men, for the most part muscular, and almost all drunk. The noise was almost as bad as the smell, and Ansbach had to raise his voice as he pushed his way to the bar and dropped a few coins onto it.

'Four ales!' he shouted, and turned back to Rudi and Shenk. An expression of puzzlement crossed his features. 'Where's Berta?'

'Over there.' Shenk pointed to a table in the middle of the throng, where his missing deckhand was joining in enthusiastically with some kind of drinking game. Ansbach shrugged.

'Oh well.' He drained one of the mugs in a couple of swallows, and distributed the other three. 'Pity to waste it.' After a cautious sip, Rudi decided he was right. It wasn't the best drink he'd ever tasted, but it was far more palatable than he'd feared. He swallowed appreciatively.

'Not bad,' he said. 'Thanks.'

Ansbach coloured a little, and took a swallow of his own drink. 'Well, I reckon I owed you,' he said awkwardly. 'We'd probably all have been fish bait if it hadn't been for you.' Rudi shrugged.

'Well, I couldn't let that happen. It's a long walk to Altdorf.' He grinned, pleasantly surprised to see a matching smile on Ansbach's face. 'Fancy another?'

'Thought you'd never ask.' Ansbach grinned a little more widely, and drained his tankard. 'Same again for you, skipper?'

'You two enjoy yourselves,' Shenk said, his eyes scanning the throng, and sparking with sudden recognition. 'I've got a bit of business to attend to.' He raised a hand in greeting, and slipped through the crowd of lumberjacks. A moment later Rudi saw him chatting to a man dressed rather better than the labourers, who he assumed must therefore be someone in authority.

'Looks like it's just us then,' Ansbach said.

To HIS VAGUE surprise, Rudi found the evening remarkably enjoyable. It had been a long time since he'd been able to savour the simple pleasures of socialising, and as the night wore on and the amount of ale they'd both consumed increased, Ansbach mellowed far more than he would have believed possible. The deckhand had a couple of acquaintances among the woodsmen, whose names Rudi never quite caught, but whose stories of life among the timber made him feel comfortably nostalgic for his former life in the woods around Kohlstadt, and who seemed gratifyingly pleased to have found a kindred spirit. Eventually, they went off to bed, and Rudi rose to his feet, swaying slightly, his head pleasantly clouded with the effects of the alcohol he'd drunk.

'We'd best be getting back too,' he suggested. Ansbach stood as well, a trifle unsteadily, and nodded.

'Reckon you're right,' he said at last. The makeshift taproom was much quieter now, most of the drinkers left snoring quietly to themselves, their heads pillowed on forearms folded neatly on the ale-puddled tabletops or vomit-puddled floor, and only a few diehards continuing to besiege the bar. Now that Rudi could see it more clearly, it turned out to be another assemblage of crudely nailed-together planking. 'Looks like it's just us left.'

'Looks like,' Rudi agreed. He glanced around, looking for their companions, but Shenk had long since disappeared, and Berta had vanished too, leaving most of the participants of her drinking game snoring quietly in a heap of tangled limbs. 'How do we get back to the wharf from here?'

'That's easy.' Ansbach led the way outside, and pointed. 'It's down that way.' He stepped into the shadows. 'Hang on a minute. Just need to make an offering to Mannan, if you know what I mean.' Stepping away from the relieved sigh and the sudden cloud of acrid-smelling steam that followed it, Rudi let his gaze wander around the logging camp. As he'd expected, the frost was hard, sharp pinpoints of starlight speckling the sky, and the silver disc of Mannslieb, the major moon, was crisply delineated like a hole in the sky. He amused himself for a moment looking for the shape of the rabbit in the softly glowing orb, as he had done as a child, and returned his gaze to the buildings surrounding them. Shards of frost glittered on every surface, painting the world silver, and he was able to see almost as well as he would have done in daylight. His breath puffed into little clouds that reflected the sheen of moonlight with every exhalation, and the bitter cold began to clear his head, although the alcohol he'd drunk insulated him from its worst effects.

As he waited for Ansbach to conclude his devotions, another glint of reflected moonlight caught his eye, and he turned, trying to find the source of it. For a moment he failed to see it again, and then there it was: a hard-edged glitter deep within the shadows cast by a nearby warehouse.

Something was moving, an indistinct mass, and then his night vision, which for so long had been muted by the ubiquitous lamps and torches of the city streets, reasserted itself. There had been no aids to vision growing up in the woods, and using them would surely have scared off the game he'd been after anyway, so for most of his life he'd been adept at distinguishing shapes in the darkness. This was a human figure, he was suddenly sure, wrapped in a cloak of some dark material. Why would anyone be hanging about outside on a freezing cold night like this?

His nascent suspicions flared up in earnest as a burst of raucous laughter echoed across the empty space, and the mysterious figure shrank back deeper into the shadows, as if fearful of discovery. Berta stumbled across the gap between two buildings, an arm each around the shoulders of a pair of lumberjacks, all three of them clearly in high spirits. A moment later, they disappeared, and the banging of a door cut off the second verse of a song about a goblin and a goat, which Rudi remembered being a perennial favourite among the drunk and disorderly cases he'd swept off the streets of Marienburg on a more or less nightly basis.

'Can you see that?' he asked, aware suddenly that Ansbach had just joined him. The deckhand shook his head, and tottered another pace forwards, unbalanced for a moment by the violent movement.

'See what?' he asked, and then his face cleared. 'Oh, you mean the skipper?' Shenk was walking down the middle of the thoroughfare leading back towards the wharf, with the air of a man whose business had just been satisfactorily concluded, and who was looking forward to reaching his bunk. The shadow moved again, the glitter of moonlight striking out from it once more, and Rudi had no doubt at all that what he was seeing was the reflection of an unsheathed blade.

'Shenk! Look out!' He began to run, his sword hissing from its scabbard as he did so. Ansbach stayed rooted to the spot for a moment, his expression one of stupefied bafflement. Then he stumbled in Rudi's wake, a good dozen paces behind the young forester, the gap widening with every misplaced step. He drew his knife from his belt regardless, flourishing it with drunken bravado, and a complete lack of comprehension.

'I'm right behind you!' he bellowed. 'Anyone messes with you, they mess with me!' Rudi was by no means sure that this was reassuring, but it seemed to give the lurker in the shadows pause. A hooded head snapped round in the direction of the commotion, rapidly assessed the relative positions of Rudi, Ansbach, and his intended target, and made a swift decision predicated entirely on self-preservation. There was a sudden blur of motion, and the shard of moonlight left his hand, hurtling straight for Rudi's chest.

As it had on so many previous occasions, time seemed to slow and stretch. Instinctively, without thinking, Rudi snapped his blade up into a guard position, parrying as if against a sword thrust, and the flung dagger rebounded into the darkness with a clang of clashing steel. He had what felt like several minutes to watch it spin away, shining like a silver comet, and to take in the assassin's panic-stricken reaction to the failure of his attack. He wondered if a second knife was about to follow the first, but the anonymous figure simply turned and ran.

'Oh no you don't!' Shenk tackled his would-be assailant with vigour and a degree of resolution that would have surprised Rudi before today, but the assassin was far more skilled in brawling than the riverboat captain. The black-clad figure slipped out of the boatman's grip easily, with a vicious backhanded strike to the face. Shenk went down, and the assassin turned, clearly intent on finishing him. Rudi was just within sword's reach of the man, and aimed a cut at his head, as intent on distracting him as on inflicting any actual damage, ripping through the cloth of the hood. It parted, revealing a glimpse of a nondescript face, indistinguishable at first sight from any of the lumberjacks inhabiting the settlement. Nevertheless, its owner turned away, continuing to conceal his identity as best he could.

'Hang on, skipper! We're coming!' Ansbach roared, and the assassin hesitated again. With what sounded to Rudi like a sigh of irritation, the man suddenly turned and bent over, lashing out with a booted foot, which connected solidly with the side of the young forester's head. Rudi staggered back, dazed and surprised by the unconventional attack. By the time he'd recovered, a second or two later, the black-clad figure was fleeing for the nearest patch of concealing shadow.

'That's right, run!' Ansbach bellowed, flushed with victory. Shenk staggered slowly to his feet, the blood streaming from his nose appearing black in the silvery moonlight.

'Are you all right?' he asked. Rudi nodded.

'Fine. I just wasn't expecting Bretonnian foot-boxing tricks.' Shenk raised an eyebrow, and pinched the bridge of his nose to stem the bleeding. 'I rousted a few cheese-breaths in the watch,' Rudi explained. 'First time I came across one who knew *savartay*, he nearly took my head off. How are you feeling?'

'I'll live.' The captain watched curiously as Rudi stared at the ground. 'What are you looking for?'

Rudi sighed in frustration. 'Tracks, but it's hopeless.' He'd been hoping the assassin had left enough traces to follow, but the frost-hardened ground was too solid to dent with fresh footprints, and the thin film of glistening rime had been disturbed by pretty much everybody in the settlement. After a few yards the scuffmarks in the glowing white surface vanished, swallowed by the maelstrom of footprints left by the bed-bound revellers from the Floating Log. 'What are you going to do now?' Shenk shrugged.

'Talk to Hanna, for a start,' he said, 'and think very hard about asking for a bonus when we get to Altdorf.'

CHAPTER EIGHT

BERTA RETURNED TO the *Reikmaiden* just after dawn, ambling up the gangplank with an air of self-satisfied lassitude, and a cheery wave to the brace of swains who had followed to see her off. Catching sight of Rudi and Shenk on deck, she allowed her grin to widen.

'You were right,' she told the captain. 'This is definitely no place for a lady. I might retire here.' Her expression changed slowly to one of puzzlement as she took in Shenk's bruised face and dishevelled appearance. 'What happened to you?'

'Someone went after my purse,' Shenk said shortly. 'Luckily, Rudi was there.' Ansbach, who looked a little pale, said nothing, but seemed a trifle disappointed that his own contribution to the affray had been overlooked. Shenk looked his errant deckhand up and down. 'If you've quite finished rutting your way through everything in britches, perhaps we could trouble you to do a little work? Help Ansbach get us under way.'

'Right, sorry Skipper, didn't mean to keep you waiting.' Colouring slightly, Berta began to unship the hawser securing the bow to the dock, while Ansbach let go the stern lines in an equally desultory fashion. Busch glared from one to the other as if their hangovers were a personal insult.

'Look lively, the pair of you! Let's try to get to Carroburg before we die of old age, shall we?'

'Yes, Herr Busch.' The two deckhands began to move a little more quickly, and within a few moments the strip of clear blue water between the wharf and the hull of the riverboat began to widen. Rudi watched the dock recede with wary eyes, trying to see anything out of the ordinary, refusing to relax until the *Reikmaiden* was at least a bowshot from the bank. Despite his trepidation, the mysterious assassin didn't try to prevent them from leaving, apparently content to blend back into the life of the logging camp. He wasn't sure that that was particularly reassuring, however. It meant that whoever he was, the Fog Walker was confident that another of his colleagues would be able to intercept the package that Shenk was carrying, further up the river. He said as much, and Shenk nodded.

'I know. But we should be in Carroburg tomorrow, and if we don't put in anywhere along the bank tonight they won't have another chance before we get there.'

'Unless they try boarding us again,' Rudi pointed out. Shenk shook his head.

'I doubt it. Their boat's fast enough to catch us, no doubt about that, but after the bloody nose they got last time, they'll think twice about trying it. I don't think they've got enough people left anyway, we took out nearly all of them.' Rudi nodded.

'What happens when we get to Carroburg?' he asked. Shenk shrugged.

'We offload our cargo, take on whatever we can, and put out again before dark. Then we run through the night till we get to Altdorf.' He sighed. 'I don't like doing it, but after last night, there's no telling how many more of them are waiting along the river.' He hesitated, as if wondering how much more to say, and then made a decision. Clearly he felt that Rudi had a right to know something of what was going on. 'Besides, we're supposed to meet our contact in Carroburg. With any luck he'll take the damn thing off my hands there, and we won't have to worry any more.'

'Let's hope so,' Rudi agreed.

IN THE EVENT, the journey to Carroburg passed without further incident, although Rudi spent most of the day, and the following night, on the deck, his bow to hand, scanning the river for any sign of pursuit or ambush. Hanna joined him at the rail shortly after sun-up, and handed him a steaming mug of one of her herbal infusions. Rudi took the aromatic drink gratefully, and warmed his hands around it before sipping a cautious mouthful, aware of the need to keep his fingers flexible enough to draw a bowstring.

'At least we'll be there a bit quicker than we expected,' she said. Rudi nodded, savouring the sensation of warmth that seemed to begin radiating outwards from his midriff as the drink began its work.

'Some time this morning, Shenk says.' As he spoke he found himself glancing forwards, looking for some sign of the city itself, although as yet the pale dawn glow showed nothing more than the endless forest, the few scattered settlements they passed still dark and apparently lifeless. There were no other boats to be seen on the water either, although several were still tied to the wharves on the bank. Running through the night was something most skippers would try to avoid if they could, if only because of the toll such a course would take on their crews.

Shenk had tried to minimise the strain, leaving only two hands on duty overnight, changing watches in the small hours and taking the tiller himself for most of the time. Watching him from his position by the rail, Rudi had had the distinct impression that the skipper had rather enjoyed the chance to take direct control of the sturdy little vessel. To everyone's surprise, Pieter had insisted on taking his turn on deck, standing watch alongside the captain, although he was still too incapacitated to do much heavy work. At one point, when the sails had needed trimming, he'd had to ask Rudi to haul on the ropes under his direction.

'The others need all the rest they can get,' he pointed out, when Rudi had asked if he was up to the task.

'They'll need to stow cargo tomorrow.' He gestured idly with the arm that Hanna had strapped up in a sling, 'and I can't lift boxes with this thing on. So, I might as well make myself useful while I can.'

Yullis had relieved him some time in the small hours, taking the tiller from Shenk, while Busch took charge of the *Reikmaiden* for the rest of the night. Neither of them had felt much like conversation, and Rudi had dozed for a while, sure that he'd be woken in the event of another attack.

'Are you going ashore when we get there?' Hanna asked. Rudi shrugged. He hadn't really considered the idea, although it did sound quite appealing now that Hanna suggested it.

'I might do,' he said. 'Stretch my legs a bit. Find something to eat.' The *Reikmaiden* would be in dock for several hours while her crew offloaded the portion of her cargo bound for Carroburg, and Shenk tried to find something else to fill the gap in her hold with for the final leg of their journey up to Altdorf. Remaining on board, he strongly suspected, would only result in her passengers getting in the way. 'How about you?'

'I think so,' Hanna said. 'I could do with some exercise.' She glanced down at her dress, from which energetic laundering had failed to completely remove the staining acquired in Marienburg. 'I might find something a little more respectable to wear. I'll need to make a good impression on the colleges when we get to Altdorf.'

'I've been wondering about that,' Rudi said. 'What are you going to do, exactly? You can't just walk in off the streets and ask to be admitted, can you?' For the first time since her recovery, he saw her façade of easy confidence begin to crumble.

'I'm not sure,' she conceded at last, 'but I still have my student's accreditation from Baron Hendryk's. I'm hoping that will be enough for one of them to take me seriously.'

'It's worth a try,' Rudi said. 'At least you can prove you were a licensed apprentice mage in Marienburg. That ought to count for something.'

'I hope so,' Hanna said. Then her mood lifted, with an obvious effort. 'Still, we won't be in Altdorf until tomorrow. There's time to worry about that when we get there.' She held out a hand. 'Finished with the mug?'

To his vague surprise, Rudi found that it was indeed empty, and that he felt more alert and energetic than he had any right to after such a long and relatively sleepless night. He nodded.

'Yes, thank you.' He handed it over, and watched her disappear into the galley, a troubled frown on his face. From what Shenk had said, Altdorf was full of witch hunters as well as licensed mages. If none of the colleges would offer her sanctuary, it was the most dangerous place in the whole Empire for Hanna to be heading for. Not that he would be particularly safe there either, having been condemned as a heretic, however unjustly.

Despite that thought, he felt a rising sense of excitement and anticipation that even his most pessimistic forebodings couldn't quite suppress. The answers he so desperately wanted lay in Altdorf, and he was only a day away from the place where his quest would end.

It was with an unexpectedly light heart that he resumed his position at the rail, alert for his first sight of Carroburg.

RUDI HADN'T BEEN sure what he was expecting to see when the city finally came into view, but his initial reaction was one of complete astonishment. Marienburg had been a low-lying metropolis, built on the chain of islands at the mouth of the Reik, and with a few exceptions, like the colossal span of the Hoogbrug, most of the rooflines had been more or less even. Carroburg, however, loomed over the river like a man-made mountain, sprawling back up the hillside that rose from the steep banks of the Reik, until its upper streets and houses became lost in the low-lying mist that wreathed the summits of the valley.

'Quite a sight, eh?' Pieter asked at his elbow, and Rudi nodded, lost for words. 'They say Middenheim makes it look like a pimple, but I wouldn't know.' He shrugged. 'Too far from the water, see?'

'I see.' Rudi nodded, taking in the scale of the place as the *Reikmaiden* forged through the water towards the docks, a bustling tangle of quays and wharves that, at least, seemed vaguely familiar. Dozens of other riverboats were visible, coming and going, or lying alongside, and innumerable smaller craft were scudding about on urgent business, or casting hopeful fishing nets into the choppy water. This at least was reminiscent of his sojourn in the maritime city, and he found the familiar bustle vaguely reassuring.

'The houses seem to get bigger towards the top,' Rudi said, and Pieter nodded.

'That's right. The richer you are, the higher up the hill you live.' He laughed. 'Riff-raff like us, we stick to the bottom. There're plenty of taverns around the docks anyway, so why work up a sweat looking for a drink?'

'Sound advice,' Rudi said. He pointed to a cluster of ramshackle huts clinging to the shoreline, and spreading back into the woods. The stumps of trees and the harsh white of newly cut timber showed that the clearings around the city wall were recent. 'Who lives there?'

'Refugees,' Pieter said. His voice took on a faintly pitying tone. 'Pretty much everything north of Middenheim's destroyed, they say, and what's left of it's crawling with Chaos scum. These are the lucky ones. They got out in time. Some of them talk about going home, but I can't see it happening any time soon.' He shook his head mournfully, and wandered off to attend to whatever duties Busch had decided he was still able to cope with.

Rudi watched the city grow, as the sturdy little riverboat drew closer and closer to it, until the rising tangle of streets and buildings completely filled his vision. Individual structures began to be distinguishable: large ornate houses looking down on the teeming masses below, the unmistakable bulk of temples and the wealthier guild houses, and, closer at hand, the warehouses around the docks.

'Impressive, isn't it?' Hanna asked dryly at his shoulder. Rudi shrugged.

'They might have a decent tavern or two,' he conceded, determined to seem no less cosmopolitan than

she did. After all, they were both experienced urban-
ites. Shenk ambled over to join them as Yullis and
Berta manhandled the gangplank into place.

'Going ashore?' he asked casually, unable to keep a
flicker of relief from his eyes as Rudi nodded in the
affirmative.

'We've got some errands to run,' Rudi assured him.
'We won't be cluttering up the deck while you're trying to move your cargo.'

'Glad to hear it,' Shenk said. 'Try to get back here
before we're about to sail this time, eh?'

'We'll do our best,' Hanna assured him and led the
way down the gangplank.

DESPITE THE BULK of the city looming above them like
a thundercloud of stone, Rudi felt surprisingly at
home in the cramped and narrow streets surrounding
the harbour. In all but scale, it reminded him of the
Suiddock back in Marienburg: the same air of purposeful activity, the ever-present carts and sweating
labourers transferring barrels and bundles from boat
holds to warehouses and back again, and through it
all, the never-ending flow of local citizens pursuing
their trades, honest or otherwise.

Surrounded by people again, he found his old
watchman's instincts surfacing, and amused himself picking out the local bawds and cutpurses from
the throng. Once, he saw a halfling pickpocket making off with the contents of a well-dressed
gentleman's purse, and had to suppress the impulse
to shout a challenge and give chase. Not his problem here, he reminded himself. The last thing he

and Hanna needed to do was draw unnecessary attention to themselves.

The halfling wasn't the only non-human he noticed as they made their way through the streets towards a local square that Pieter had assured him held enough clothier's shops to satisfy Hanna's most exacting requirements in a dress, and a couple of reasonable taverns besides, which Rudi would probably need after she'd completed her shopping. By the time they reached their destination, he'd seen a couple of dwarfs snoring loudly in a gutter outside a tavern while a third stood over them, swaying slightly, his negligently-hefted axe effectively deterring anyone from attempting to relieve them of their personal effects; a solitary elf; and almost a dozen halflings, who, for the most part, appeared to be vending foodstuffs of dubious palatability from small wheeled carts.

'Cosmopolitan, isn't it?' Hanna remarked, although Rudi wasn't sure how sarcastic she was being. He was saved from having to answer, as she stopped suddenly beside a market stall selling a wide variety of women's clothing. 'Ooh, this is nice. What do you think?' She held up a dress, which, to Rudi's eye, looked little different to the one she had on, apart from a lack of accumulated grime.

'It's your colour,' he hazarded, and Hanna laughed.

'Never mind.' She seemed to take his incomprehension for granted, and find it amusing. 'I've already got two blue ones.' Her only change of clothing, still back in her bag aboard the *Reikmaiden*, was almost identical to the dress she wore now, although even more patched and stained. They were almost the only things she still possessed that she'd brought with her from Kohlstadt. Rudi suspected that it was the only reason she hadn't discarded them.

'You're in luck, missy. I've got one just like that in green.' The stallholder, a ruddy-faced man with an easy manner, held up the garment in question. Hanna looked at it dubiously. 'Eighteen shillings to you, and cheap at half the price.'

'I don't know.' Hanna made a show of considering it. 'Green doesn't really go with my eyes, and besides, it's a spring colour. I want something warm for the winter.'

'Warm, you say?' The stallholder was clearly enjoying the game. 'How about this?' He held up a red dress, trimmed with yellow. 'Real Middenland wool, best in the Empire, and just the colour to warm the heart as well, eh laddie?' The last remark was directed at Rudi, who just nodded, unsure of how to respond. Hanna was holding the garment up in front of her, cocking a quizzical head at him, waiting for his response. Rudi nodded again, and swallowed the obstruction that had suddenly appeared in his throat.

'It, ah, suits you,' he said. 'It really does.' The yellow trim set off her blonde hair almost perfectly, and brighter colour seemed to infuse her with life and energy. 'But isn't it a bit, you know, draughty?'

'Low necklines are the fashion, laddie.' The stallholder grinned. 'Good thing too, I say.' He smiled at Hanna. 'If you've got it, flaunt it, that's what I say. Bring a bit of sunshine into the life of a sad old man like me.'

'I could always wear a shawl if it gets too cold,' Hanna said, smiling at Rudi's discomfiture. Of course, she could always shield herself from the chill by magical means, although saying so out loud would be foolish in the extreme. 'Eighteen shillings, you said?' The stallholder sighed regretfully, and shook his head.

'That was the plain one. This one's a crown two and six.' Hanna hesitated. 'Tell you what, we'll forget the sixpence, seeing as it looks so good on you, and I'll throw in a scarf to match.' He picked up a yellow headscarf, with a pattern of crimson thread worked into it. 'That's worth two shillings alone, if it's worth a farthing.'

'It's lovely,' Hanna said, running it between her fingers, the pattern in the fabric seeming to ripple like flames as she did so. She handed both garments back to the stallholder, who grinned happily as he began to fold them with expert precision, and took three coins from her purse. The stallholder frowned at the sight of the Marienburg guilder.

'Got any crowns? You never know with those foreign coins. If they haven't been clipped like a ewe they're probably counterfeit.'

'Sorry.' Hanna shook her head. 'We're straight off the boat from Marienburg. If you won't take guilders…' She began to turn away, as if about to leave.

'No, hang about. I'll risk it, seeing as you've got an honest face. Gold's gold, wherever it comes from.' He sighed, and bit the coin suspiciously. 'Seems all right, anyway.'

'Thank you.' Hanna smiled sweetly at the man, and accepted the package he held out.

'Well, that was easy.' Rudi watched while Hanna stowed the neat parcel in her shoulder bag, and started to look for a tavern. 'What do you want to do now?' Hanna shook her head.

'I haven't finished looking at clothes yet,' she explained, heading for the nearest shop. 'I could still do with another dress. That way I'll have something new to wash and one to wear, once we get to Altdorf. I can't go around looking respectable one day and like this the next.'

Rudi sighed, not seeing anything wrong with the way she looked now, and started after her. Clearly, it was going to be a long day.

Hanna was still glancing back over her shoulder to talk to him, and his attention was still on her, so neither noticed that the door to the shop was opening as they approached it. A couple emerged, chatting amiably.

'I'm not saying you don't look stunning in it,' the man said. 'I'm just wondering when you think you're ever going to get the chance to wear it.'

'I'll make the chance,' the woman said, flicking her head back to talk to her companion. 'It's not as if we're tramping around the wilderness all the time.' A flash of bright red hair accompanied the movement. Almost paralysed with astonishment, Rudi stopped dead in his tracks, and began reaching for his sword.

'Oops, sorry.' Before his horrified gaze, Hanna bumped into the couple, and began to turn towards them, an apologetic smile on her face.

'Don't mention it,' Alwyn said. Then recognition sparked between everyone present. 'Conrad, it's them!'

Even before she'd finished speaking, the two mercenaries had drawn their swords and moved in to attack.

CHAPTER NINE

'HANNA, DUCK!' RUDI yelled, fearing that Alwyn's blade would strike her in the face as it emerged from the scabbard, but Hanna had already moved, hurling herself at the other woman's waist. Too close to step away without making herself an easy target for the sword-wielding mage, she grappled with her assailant instead, hoping to remain inside her reach. It was a smart move, Rudi thought, exactly the right thing to do under the circumstances, although he would have followed up on the initial attack. Lacking his experience of street fighting, hard won in the back alleys of Marienburg during his days as a Black Cap, Hanna simply hung on grimly to her opponent, shrieking like a scalded cat, ducking under Alwyn's sword arm just in time to avoid a vicious downward blow from the hilt of the weapon.

Before Rudi could intervene, Conrad was on him, and he blocked a sword-cut to his leg before he even realised that his hand was in motion.

'You've improved,' Conrad said, his habitual easy-going tone sounding almost approving. He parried Rudi's counter strike, and gave ground a little.

I've got an advantage, Rudi thought, remembering that Gerhard's bounty on his head was conditional on bringing him in alive. He didn't want to kill the man he'd once thought of as a friend, but he was willing to do so if he had to, and that gave him the edge in the contest. At least until Conrad decided that his own life was worth more than the thirty crowns he'd lose by taking Rudi's.

'I've been practising,' he said, pressing home his attack. The crowd around them had scattered at the first clash of steel, to reform in a tightly packed ring of fascinated spectators at what most of them seemed to consider a safe distance. That ought to delay the watch a little at least, while they forced their way through the crush of onlookers, several of whom appeared to be placing bets on the outcome, although probably not for long. Pieter had told him that the influx of refugees had led to rising tensions within the city, and sporadic outbreaks of civil disorder, which meant that the local watch houses would be ready to respond to any reports of trouble at a moment's notice. He had to finish this quickly.

'Hanna.' He risked a glance at his companion. It only lasted an instant, but Conrad took advantage of it nevertheless. Disengaging from the melee, Conrad kicked out at a barrel that had been abandoned outside a nearby tavern by a carter, who was now shouting encouragement along with everyone else in the vicinity, although to which combatant Rudi couldn't tell. It rolled towards him, picking up speed on the downward slope. He saw it coming just in time, and hurdled it, landing in front of the astonished mercenary. Ignoring the yells of approbation from the baying crowd, he pressed home his advantage in a flurry of blows that Conrad was barely able to deflect in time. Behind them the barrel began to move faster, scattering spectators like skittles before smashing into the masonry frontage of a chapel of Mannan at the corner of the street leading down to the harbour, apparently set up for the spiritual refreshment of the riverboat crews heading into town for more earthly recreations.

'I'm fine,' Hanna assured him. Alwyn was trying to throw her over her hip with a wrestler's move, but the blonde girl had transferred her grip to the mercenary's sword hand and was clinging to it with even greater determination than before, remaining on her feet apparently by sheer willpower. Both women seemed too intent on their physical struggle to think of attempting to settle it by magical means, which was probably just as well, Rudi thought. In a city full of refugees from the ravages of the minions of Chaos, any display of sorcery would probably spark a riot. Giving up the attempt to throw Hanna or use her sword, Alwyn drew a dagger from her boot with her left hand and thrust it hard at Hanna's gut.

'You bitch!' Hanna stared at the hilt of the knife, protruding from the bulging satchel at her waist. 'I haven't even worn that yet!' Her teeth closed on Alwyn's wrist, and the mercenary's sword clattered to the cobbles with a shriek of outrage and pain.

Rudi stepped in towards Conrad, who'd half-turned towards his wife, clearly alarmed at her sudden scream, and struck at his head with the flat of his sword. The mercenary saw it coming and ducked, lashing out with his foot at Rudi's groin as he did so. Rudi flinched, riding the blow, and grinned as Conrad hopped backwards, favouring his uninjured foot – he'd spent the first week's wages he'd earned as a watchman on an armoured codpiece, and not for the first time, blessed his foresight. Pivoting, he returned the favour before Conrad could recover his balance, and watched the bounty hunter fold with an unmistakable sense of satisfaction.

'Hanna!' He leapt to intervene in the women's struggle, laying Alwyn out with the flat of the sword as he'd intended to do with her husband, and helped Hanna to her feet. Ignoring the faint sigh of disappointment from the crowd, which began to disperse about its interrupted business, now that the entertainment was over, the girl glared at the prostrate form of the red-headed mage, breathing hard, and then bent down to snatch the purse from her belt. 'Hanna! What in Taal's name do you think you're doing?'

'She owes me a new dress.' Hanna took a crown and a handful of silver out of the little bag, and dropped it carelessly back on top of its feebly-twitching owner. The mercer she'd dealt with before was returning to his stall, and watched warily while she rummaged through the stock, picking out a dress almost identical to the one she'd chosen before. 'This'll do. Same price as the other one?'

'Near enough,' the stallholder said, slipping the money out of sight with a quick glance at Alwyn, who was too busy trying to sit up to notice, and Conrad, who was still retching noisily in the gutter. He forced a grin. 'Even if it wasn't, I don't think I'd argue.' The grin stretched and became a little more sincere. 'You might talk like a pair of Reikland fops, but you've Middenland blood right enough.'

'Come on.' Hanna acknowledged the peculiar compliment with a tilt of her head, and turned away, the garment slung casually across her shoulder.

'I'm right behind you,' Rudi assured her. Conrad was still in no fit state to fight, if he was any judge, and seemed more interested in checking his wife's injuries now that he'd managed to regain his own feet in any case, but he had no desire to hang around any longer than they needed to. He had no doubt that both mercenaries would recover rapidly, and the watch would probably be there at any moment.

'I wonder where the others are?' Hanna said, as they jogged down the hill towards the docks. By way of an answer, Rudi pointed to the mouth of a nearby alleyway.

'Over there,' he said. Bodun the dwarf was trotting into the square, glancing around to talk to someone behind him, his axe held ready for use.

'Just because there's trouble in the direction they went off in, it doesn't have to mean they're mixed up in it,' Rudi heard, in the dwarf's familiar rumbling tone, before Bodun turned to face where he was going. His eyes widened with shock as he recognised Rudi, and then narrowed with all the pent-up anger of a dwarf with a grudge, and he bellowed a challenge that echoed from the surrounding buildings like a thunderclap. 'Stand and fight, skavenslayer!' He broke into a ponderous run, like a boulder beginning to roll down a mountainside, barging a couple of townsfolk out of the way as he did so. A moment later Theo and Bruno rounded the corner behind him, and charged, overtaking the short-legged warrior as they did so.

'It is him!' Bruno's eyes glittered with malice, his sword already drawn, and Rudi knew that the youth wouldn't think or care about the bounty, the way Conrad had. He clearly wanted blood, and mere money wouldn't satisfy his lust for vengeance. Theo Krieger drew his own blade, angling across the front of the impetuous youth, forestalling him from making the first attack. That was something at any rate, the captain of the mercenary band clearly still valued coin above retribution.

'Run!' Rudi shoved Hanna in the small of the back, impelling her towards the docks. 'I'll hold them off!'

'Still think you're Konrad from the ballads?' Hanna asked rhetorically, turning to face the charging mercenaries. Her gaze flickered past them, resting for a moment on their recently vanquished comrades as the crowd parted again, no one in their right minds wanting to be caught in the middle of what looked like becoming an ugly brawl. A few of the gamblers were exchanging coins once more, in anticipation of the sport to come, and a halfling sausage-seller seemed to be doing brisk business among the consolidating ring of putative spectators. 'Oh no you don't, you henna-haired sow.'

Alwyn was back on her feet, either supported by Conrad or holding him up, it was hard to be sure. Maybe they were supporting each other, Rudi thought. She was staring in their direction, her hand moving, although it was hard to focus on: the air around it seemed to be thickening, the sunlight glittering on sharp metallic points. Abruptly, they were moving, and Rudi became aware that a trio of daggers was hurtling through the air towards them.

One, at least, seemed to be missing the mark, expending itself harmlessly in the cover of the hot sausage cart, which was quickly abandoned by its diminutive owner with a shrill squeal of alarm. Then, to his horror, he saw the phantom knife shimmer in the air like summer heat haze as it passed clean through the obstacle and bore down on them as relentlessly as the other two. Somehow, he knew, they would be uncomfortably solid when they arrived at their target nevertheless.

'Party tricks,' Hanna said scornfully. 'Shield your eyes.' Before Rudi could react a wall of vivid yellow flame, almost exactly the same colour as her hair, erupted from nowhere in the space ahead of them. The phantom daggers hit it and vanished, as if they'd never been. The holiday mood among the onlookers evaporated, panic-stricken cries of 'Witchcraft!' beginning to rend the air, and the spectators scattered, running for whatever cover they could find.

Hanna's jaw tightened. 'If you want to play rough...'

The wall of flames seemed to shiver, contracting into a small, tight ball, and turning the same shade of hellish red as the blazing bolts that had dispatched the skaven and immolated Magnus's mutants. Before Rudi could protest, the tangled knot of fire hissed through the air towards Alwyn and Conrad, the shadow mage's eyes widening with shock. The air in front of them began to shimmer, like a summer heat haze, and the two spouses' outlines became indistinct. The fire bolt began to waver, and Rudi thought he could see the pair of shadowy figures begin to evade...

'Too late,' Hanna said, with vindictive satisfaction, and then the protective illusion vanished abruptly. Alwyn was down again, thrashing around on the cobbles like the victim of a fit. The fireball streaked over her head, missing Conrad by inches, and burst against the façade of the tavern behind them. The backwash of heat engulfed them both, and Conrad fell too, screaming as their clothes burst into flames.

'Rut this!' Theo said. 'We're not being paid enough to fight witches.' He turned, sprinting towards his fallen comrades, slicing down the awning of a market stall as he went with the blade of his sword. Clearly seeing what he had in mind, Bodun followed, seizing the other end of it. Between them, they swung the heavy canvas over Conrad and Alwyn, smothering the flames that surrounded their writhing forms.

'Oh dear,' Hanna said with heavy sarcasm. 'She fumbled it. That'll teach her to try doing magic with a headache.'

'If she lives,' Rudi said, sick with horror. Hanna shrugged.

'Speaking of which…' Bruno was still on the attack, bearing down on them regardless of the fate his friends had just suffered, brandishing his sword as he came. Not for the first time, Rudi found himself wondering just how sane the youth really was: not terribly, judging by his current demeanour. His face was contorted with hatred, and he was screaming incoherently, a peroration of malediction against every god Rudi had ever heard of and at least one he hadn't.

'You're going to die! Sigmar can't help you, Shallya can't help you, festering Tzeentch can't help you, Taal can't help you.' The crazed youth swung his sword wildly, without any trace of the precision or skill that Rudi remembered from previous battles. He blocked the clumsy stroke easily, and countered. Bruno parried, more by reflex than intent, Rudi thought, and he drove in past the attack, slashing down at the youth's unprotected leg.

Bruno howled as the blade laid the back of his calf open almost to the bone, and turned to face Rudi, his face still twisted. Rudi had expected him to fall, but the berserker rage kept him moving, and the torrent of blasphemy continued without respite. 'Rhya rolls in what Ursun leaves in the woods!'

'Run!' Rudi shouted to Hanna, fearful that she might resort to magic again. 'Before someone cries witch on you!' It was no idle fear. Faces were visible at the windows of the shops and taverns, where many of the bystanders had fled, and most wore expressions of shock and terror. He'd been expecting her to argue, but she clearly accepted the wisdom of retreat, merely turning and sprinting away.

'The gods only help themselves!' Bruno screamed, returning to the attack. Rudi had no idea what was possessing him, but simply blessed the fact that whatever it was had struck. A babble of voices in one of the alleys dragged his head round for a moment, and he caught a brief glimpse of sunlight reflecting from the heads of halberds above the knot of panic-stricken backs trying to shove their way out of the square. There was no sign of the bearers yet, but from the random motions of the shafts, they seemed to be mired in the crowd that was attempting to flee the other way.

It had to be the watch. He turned his head. Theo and Bodun were standing now, having done all they could for their fallen friends, and even at this distance Rudi could see the cold rage on their faces. Without Hanna to keep them scared off, they'd return to the fray at any moment, eager to claim the thirty crowns on his head. Weapons in hand, they started back towards him.

Rudi sighed with regret. He had no desire to kill, but he had to end this at once. Evading another clumsy rush, he struck Bruno's sword aside, and thrust his own blade deep into the youth's chest. Bruno's eyes widened in shock and pain, and Rudi raised a foot to push against his ribcage, withdrawing the blade. It came reluctantly, as if from thick mud, and the steel grated against Bruno's ribs. The youth fell, the light of madness dwindling in his eyes, to be replaced for a moment by astonishment. Then he fell to the ground, gurgling. Bloody froth gushed from his lips, and his heels drummed on the cobbles.

Taking his own advice, Rudi turned and ran, heading downhill towards the docks as fast as he could. Ahead of him, Hanna's blonde head shimmered and twisted through the crowd of ordinary citizens, going about their everyday business, blissfully unaware of the life and death drama that had just been enacted a couple of streets away, the crimson dress across her shoulder standing out like a beacon. Aware that the bloody sword in his hand was attracting unwelcome attention, Rudi wiped and sheathed it, still keeping up the best pace that he could. He risked a quick glance over his shoulder. Theo and Bodun were indeed in pursuit, a quartet of watchmen a few paces behind them.

'Rudi! Come on!' Hanna had stopped outside the hall of Mannan, just a few yards into the street leading back to the harbour.

'Keep going!' he yelled, unable to fathom why she would take such a chance.

'I intend to.' She fell into place at his shoulder, skirting the shattered barrel. A thin puddle of sweet-smelling liquid had spread across the width of the street, forming a wide pool as it flowed downhill. Hanna sniffed the air. 'Brandy. That'll do nicely.'

'Nicely for what?' Rudi panted. Hanna said nothing, but a moment later the volatile liquid burst into flames behind them, forming a blazing barrier across the street. 'Oh. I see.'

'I think we can slow down a bit,' Hanna said after a moment. The dock area was just ahead, the never-ending bustle of commerce swallowing them up and hiding them from observation. 'No need to draw attention to ourselves.'

'It's a shame you didn't think of that before,' Rudi said, a little shortly. Hanna shrugged.

'She started it. Luckily she got hit by Tzeentch's Curse before she could do too much damage.'

'By what?' Rudi looked at her in surprise. 'Bruno used that word too, while he was raving.' He frowned in even greater perplexity. 'What the hell was that all about anyway? I've never seen him like that before.'

'It's a sickness of the mind,' Hanna said. 'My mother told me about things like that, although there's not a lot a healer can do for it.' She shrugged. 'Given the life he'd led, and some of the things he'd seen and done, I'm not surprised he cracked. Toasting his friends was probably the final straw.'

'I see.' Rudi didn't quite, but maladies and their treatment were Hanna's area of expertise, and he was prepared to take her word for it. 'So what does that word mean?' Hanna glanced around, and led the way into a narrow gap between two warehouses, just wide enough to walk through in single file. It was evidently a well-used short cut, but no one was taking it at the moment, and she stopped halfway along, turning to face him, sure that they wouldn't be overheard. Nevertheless, her voice dropped so low that Rudi had to strain his ears to catch it.

'It's the name of one of the Dark Gods,' she whispered. Rudi felt his bowels turn to ice.

'How do you know that?' he asked, shocked to the core. Gerhard had accused Greta Reifenstahl of following one of the Chaos Gods, and although he hadn't wanted to believe her daughter was also a cultist, how else would she know of such things?

'They told us about his curse at the college in Marienburg,' Hanna said. The university there was the only place in the Old World other than the colleges of Altdorf where the study of magic was permitted, and Hanna had briefly enrolled as a student, before being forced to flee the city. 'That's what they call it when a spell goes wrong.' She shrugged. 'He's supposed to control change and mutation, so I suppose it's a sort of joke.'

'Not a very funny one,' Rudi said. Hanna shook her head.

'Not a safe one to talk about, either. If I were you, I'd forget you ever heard it, and the name.' Rudi nodded.

'So how do you suppose Bruno knew about it?' He remembered the story they'd been told of how the mercenary band had rescued him from a herd of beastmen while he was still a child, and shrugged. The youth had encountered the minions of Chaos at least once before, and that had probably only been the first time of many. 'Never mind. I don't suppose it's important.'

'Maybe not.' Hanna shrugged too, but her eyes remained troubled. 'Although, they say everything's significant to the Changer. Every coincidence has his hand in it.'

'Well, I don't think running into them was much of a coincidence,' Rudi said slowly. 'This is the only significant stopover on the river before we get to Altdorf. Gerhard probably sent them here to wait for us in case we were travelling by boat.'

Hanna considered it, and nodded, clearly much relieved.

'I suppose you're right,' she said. A troubled frown appeared on her face. 'Do you think he's waiting for us too?'

'I doubt it.' Rudi shook his head. 'We're only a day or so from Altdorf. He's probably gone back there to report or something.' That meant that every witch hunter in town would be keeping an eye out for them when they reached the capital. Hardly a comforting thought, but at least that was a problem for tomorrow. Squeezing past Hanna in the narrow passage, which was surprisingly pleasant despite the hard look she gave him, he peered cautiously out into the next thoroughfare.

The road was wide, with a wharf on the other side of it, and the keen wind carried the scent of the river. A couple of river boats similar in size to the *Reikmaiden* bobbed at anchor in the water, and beyond them a flat-bottomed barge was just putting in, sweating dock workers hauling in the lines.

'At least I know where we are,' he said, recognising the vessel as the ferry from the other side of the river. Pieter had pointed it out while they were entering the harbour. It connected with the coach road running between Altdorf and Marienburg on the south bank, and was presumably how the bounty hunters had managed to get to Carroburg ahead of them. Despite his assurances to Hanna, he was unable to resist glancing up and down the roadway, half expecting to see the black-clad figure of Gerhard waiting to pounce on them, but the shouted challenge never came. 'Come on, we're almost there.'

Hanna joined him, and they hurried along the dockside, dodging stevedores and handcarts as they did so. The *Reikmaiden* was only a few berths away, on the next wharf but one, and they should be there within moments. With any luck, Shenk would have concluded his business, and would be ready to get under way again. Certainly the news of a fight between two magicians would be all over the city by nightfall, and Rudi wanted to be well away before any of the crew had the chance to hear the story.

'Excuse me. Sorry.' They were passing the ferry dock, and the crush of disembarking passengers was beginning to spill out across the roadway, impeding their progress. Most of the new arrivals were on foot, but there were a handful of riders on horseback too, and even a couple of carts. Rudi and Hanna ducked around a wagon apparently loaded with turnips, and almost collided with an elegant young man in a neatly tailored doublet and cloak, his face hidden by a hat with a large floppy brim and an extravagant feather protruding from it. 'Oops, sorry.'

'Don't mention it.' The young man turned, eyes widening in surprise as he took in their faces. 'Sigmar's hammer, what are you two doing here?'

'Fritz?' Rudi shook his head in astonishment. 'I thought you were still in Marienburg.'

'Same here.' Fritz Katzenjammer shrugged, looking for a moment like the slow-witted yokel Rudi remembered growing up with in Kohlstadt, and then grinned widely. 'You'll have to tell me all about it over a meal and a drink, as soon as I've run a little errand for the boss.'

'What sort of errand?' Hanna asked suspiciously. Fritz worked for the Graf von Eckstein, an Imperial nobleman involved in some clandestine business back in Marienburg, the man that Sam Warble had asked Rudi to find some information about on behalf of the Fog Walkers. Fritz shrugged.

'I'm supposed to pick up a package and see that it gets to Altdorf.' He glanced around, taking in the scale of the harbour surrounding them with the air of vague bafflement, which Rudi remembered well. 'I don't suppose either of you have seen a boat called the *Reik-maiden* around here by any chance?'

CHAPTER TEN

'THE REIKMAIDEN?' RUDI repeated, exchanging a stunned glance with Hanna. For a moment, he wondered if their conversation about the Chaos god of coincidence had somehow invoked that baleful power, and a flood of irrational terror swept through him. A moment later, that was swept away in turn by a storm of hatred, welling up from somewhere deep in his mind, so strong and powerful that it left him physically trembling with the reaction.

'Yes,' Fritz confirmed, apparently oblivious of his friend's inner turmoil. 'I'm supposed to collect the package from her captain.'

'Then you're in luck,' Rudi told him, steadying his voice and forcing the unwelcome emotions away with the same effort of will that he used to overcome the rush of exultation in combat. As his rational mind took over and common sense began to reassert itself, he glanced across at Hanna again, wondering if she'd noticed anything, but her eyes were still on Fritz. 'That's the *Reikmaiden* over there. We've been sailing on her ourselves.'

He led the way towards the riverboat through the thinning crowd of ferry passengers, evading the bustling dockworkers as they went, pondering the implications of this unexpected turn of events. If the artefact that Shenk was smuggling really was for von Eckstein, that would explain the Fog Walkers' determination to intercept it. The attempted piracy and the attack on Shenk were all part of whatever covert power struggle was going on between Marienburg and the Empire, which he'd become peripherally involved in himself, and which he'd hoped had been left far behind them when they quit the city to begin their journey upstream.

Fritz's presence was equally explicable. His mission in Marienburg complete, von Eckstein would have wanted to return to Altdorf as quickly as possible, which would have meant travelling by the coach road. No doubt he had continued his journey along the south bank, after giving Fritz his instructions and seeing him off on the ferry to Carroburg.

'That's right,' Fritz confirmed, as soon as he'd put the thought into words. 'He and Mathilde are going on by coach, while I pick up the package and finish the journey by boat.' He grinned ingenuously. 'He thought anyone trying to get hold of it would think he had it himself, and concentrate on the road, while I slip into the city through the docks. Nobody in Altdorf knows I'm working for him, you see.'

'Neat idea,' Hanna said shortly, 'but it didn't work. His enemies have tried to steal it twice already.' She looked faintly surprised as Fritz stood aside to let her board the boat first, and Rudi suppressed a smile. Clearly, the lessons in etiquette that Rudi had noticed the effects of at their last meeting in Marienburg had extended to more than just table manners. Fritz looked concerned as he followed her up the gang-plank, his eyes narrowing as he looked behind them for signs of pursuit. Rudi followed, scanning the dock-side in case any more Fog Walkers were lurking among the stevedores, but if there were any, they were concealing themselves as well as the lumberjack in the logging camp had.

'Twice?' Fritz asked. Rudi nodded.

'They tried to board us a couple of days back. Then the night before last, they tried to kill Shenk after we put in at a riverside settlement.'

'Luckily, Rudi was around to see them off,' Hanna added. Fritz nodded, taking in the unwelcome news remarkably quickly.

'I suppose that would explain why no one tried to stop us along the coach road,' he said thoughtfully.

'I suppose it would,' Hanna said dryly.

Fritz frowned, the familiar puzzled expression on his face.

'I wonder how the Fog Walkers got on to us?' he mused, although without really expecting an answer. Rudi shrugged, feeling oddly embarrassed.

The information he'd cozened out of the simpleton over their last meal together hadn't included any travel plans, but he suspected that it might have

helped the agents of Marienburg to deduce them a little more easily.

'That's their job, isn't it?' he asked. 'To find out
things?'

'I suppose it is.' Fritz nodded, apparently satisfied
with that, and took a few steps towards Shenk, who
was talking to Busch on the far side of the deck. A scattering of boxes still lay on the planking, although
Berta and Yullis were taking them below with almost
exaggerated care, and Rudi was able to estimate that
the rest of the new cargo would be stowed within a
matter of minutes. So much the better, the sooner it
was done, the sooner they'd be away from here, and
from the unwelcome attention that Hanna's display of
sorcery had attracted.

As she began to descend the steep flight of steps to
the hold, Berta almost slipped, and the box on her
shoulder shifted alarmingly.

'Careful!' Shenk called, looking up in alarm. 'That's
pottery, not pickles! Break it and it comes out of your
wages!'

'I'm fine, thanks for asking.' The deckhand disappeared below, grumbling under her breath, and Shenk
caught sight of his visitor for the first time.

'Ah, here you are.' He took in the sight of Rudi and
Hanna accompanying the young bodyguard, and
sighed. 'And you too. Well at least you made it back
on board before we're ready to go this time. Interesting run ashore?'

'We passed the time,' Rudi said. 'Hanna bought a
new dress.' Shenk nodded at the garment, still slung
over the girl's shoulder, without interest.

'So I see, very becoming.' His tone became businesslike as he turned back to Fritz. 'I'll get it for you. I'm sure you're eager to get on with whatever you're doing, and we're in a hurry to leave for Altdorf.'

'Good.' Fritz sounded quite unlike his usual self, confident and incisive, his voice taking on the more rounded vowels of a gentleman to match the expensive clothes he wore. Von Eckstein's patronage seemed to be changing him in all sorts of unlikely ways. 'So am I. So, I'll be staying aboard until we get there. I take it that won't be a problem?' Even his posture had changed, conveying the automatic expectation that, as the representative of a nobleman, his wishes would be met without question or argument. Shenk nodded slowly.

'I think we can manage to find another hammock, if you can afford to pay your way. You'll have to share the hold with Rudi and Hanna, though.'

'That would be fine.' Fritz said, with every sign of genuine warmth. 'It wouldn't be the first time his snoring has kept me awake.'

'I don't snore!' Rudi protested. Fritz and Hanna looked at one another, and shared a knowing smile. 'Do I?'

'Like a pig,' Hanna assured him. Shenk sighed.

'I could ask how you all seem to know each other, but I don't think I want to know,' he said. Hanna nodded.

'Probably best,' she said.

IN SPITE OF the apprehension weighing heavily in Rudi's gut, the *Reikmaiden* sailed out onto the river again early that afternoon with no sign of either a witch-hunt or interference from Fog Walker agents intent on forestalling her departure. He was at a loss to explain their good luck, but as the sails filled and the sturdy little vessel began the final haul up the Reik towards their destination, Hanna pointed towards the shantytown outside the city walls. Smoke was rising from it in several places, and a cold chill rippled down his spine.

'They must have assumed we went to ground there,' she said.

'Either that, or we sparked another riot.' Rudi sighed. The refugees crowding the city, unwanted and resented by the native Carroburgers, would have become natural scapegoats for any rumours of witch-craft. Small wonder that the watch hadn't made it as far as the docks – they were probably too busy trying to rein in the lynch mobs and the looters.

'Maybe we did,' Hanna said, not seeming terribly concerned at the prospect. Fritz joined them at the rail.

'So, you're heading for Altdorf too,' he said.

Rudi nodded. 'I came across some papers in Marien-burg, which might have something to do with who my parents were.'

'Really?' Fritz looked at him in surprise. Like every-one else in Kohlstadt, he'd known that Rudi was a foundling, discovered deep in the woods by Gunther Walder, who had subsequently adopted him. 'I thought nobody knew where you came from.'

'So did I.' Rudi wondered how much to tell him. 'But I might be related to a family in Altdorf, the von Kariens.'

'Never heard of them,' Fritz said, 'but maybe the boss has. He seems to know everybody.' He shrugged. 'I'll ask him. It's the least he can do after you rescued his package from river pirates.'

'Thanks,' Rudi said awkwardly. 'I'd appreciate that.'

'What's inside it, anyway?' Hanna asked, clearly intent on deflecting questions about her own presence. Fritz glanced around the deck to make sure no one else was in earshot, and dropped his voice.

'Antiquities from Lustria, for the Emperor himself.'

'You're joking!' Hanna said, although her tone wasn't entirely disbelieving. Fritz shuffled his feet.

'Well, I don't suppose he'll actually collect them in person, but the boss is bringing them back on his behalf.'

'What for?' Rudi asked. Fritz shrugged, and looked a little uneasy.

'Well, I don't understand all the details.' Rudi could believe that readily enough. 'But it's all to do with the war, and the damage it caused. The northeastern provinces are barely clinging on. Ostland's the worst.'

'I know.' Rudi nodded. This was common tavern gossip even in Marienburg. 'But what's that got to do with Lustria?'

'Well…' Fritz hesitated again, although whether to order his thoughts or to think twice about the wisdom of discussing von Eckstein's business, Rudi couldn't be sure. It was evidently the former, though, because he went on happily enough after a moment. 'Years ago, someone had the idea that if you opened up a port on the northern coast you could bypass Marienburg, so the Empire could trade freely with the rest of the world, and cut out the middleman.'

Rudi nodded. He'd heard the same story from Sam Warble.

'It failed, though,' he said. 'The elves wouldn't cooperate.'

'True.' Fritz nodded. 'But times have changed, and one of the ports on the northern coast's the new capital of Ostland, at least until Wolfenberg gets back on its feet. If it becomes a major trading centre, it'll regenerate the entire north-east. That's what the boss thinks, anyway.'

'I see.' Rudi nodded too, his head reeling. He'd managed to pick up enough of the way commerce worked during his months in Marienburg to appreciate the magnitude of the gamble. If it worked, investment and capital would flood into the devastated province, and away from the Wasteland. 'No wonder the Fog Walkers are so desperate to stop it.'

'You still haven't explained what the antiquities are for,' Hanna said.

'Haven't I?' Fritz looked confused for a moment. 'Oh. Well I thought that was obvious: to show people that trade with the far reaches of the world is possible. It's one thing to ask a merchant or a noble to put his hand in his purse on a promise, and quite another to show them something that actually came from Lustria.'

'I see,' Hanna said. Then she grinned at him. 'Better make sure you don't lose the package, then.'

'No fear of that,' Fritz assured her, looking more serious than Rudi had ever seen him. His voice dropped even further. 'The Emperor himself is involved, they say. Nothing obvious, of course, but he's putting a lot of his own capital into this. If it fails, the best hope for the whole of the north falls with it.'

'Lucky they've got someone as reliable as you on the job,' Rudi said, vaguely surprised to find the remark lacking in sarcasm. Fritz nodded, with a trace of uncertainty.

'It's a big responsibility,' he admitted. 'I feel a lot happier about it, knowing you're on board to watch my back, though.'

'We'll try not to let you down,' Hanna said, although her eyes remained fixed on the columns of smoke in the distance long after the rest of Carroburg had vanished from sight.

'Is THAT IT?' Hanna asked, with some surprise. Shenk, still blissfully unaware that Hanna's witchsight had revealed the location of the hidden compartment in the bulkhead, had retrieved the package from its hiding place while his passengers had been eating their supper with most of the crew. Now, it was lying on the top of one of the crates of earthenware that had replaced the majority of the fish barrels in the hold. Food of any kind was at a premium in Carroburg these days, and Rudi suspected the only reason Shenk had kept any of it aboard at all was to fulfil a pre-existing contract. 'I was expecting something bigger.'

'Me too,' Rudi agreed, although he spoke mainly to distract himself from the irrational sense of dread that the oilskin packet evoked in him. Until now, he hadn't given the matter any real thought. It was roughly the size of a conventional belt pouch, like the one he used to keep his snare lines in back in his old life in the woods outside Kohlstadt. Hanna put out a cautious hand, prodding the wrapping carefully.

'There are several things in here,' she said. Indistinct lumps could be seen through the slick fabric, forming under the pressure of her probing fingers. She shot a glance at Fritz, trying to seem casual, but Rudi could tell she was desperate to find out what the magical item among them might be. 'Aren't you going to show us what we're supposed to be guarding?' To Rudi's silent relief, Fritz shook his head.

'The boss said to deliver it unopened,' he said. He turned the package over, to reveal the wax seal keeping the contents enshrouded. 'Sorry.'

'Probably just as well,' Rudi said, trying to keep the conversation light. 'I'd hate to drop something and break it. Lustria's a long way to go to get another one.'

'I suppose it is,' Hanna said, and yawned widely. She'd seemed tired ever since they'd got back to the boat, and Rudi supposed that the strange stone hadn't entirely sustained her during her magical duel with Alwyn, if she'd even had to draw on it at all. Her powers seemed to be growing again, and he wondered, not for the first time, just how much control she really had over them. 'Well, I think I'll turn in.'

'Me too,' Fritz said, stowing the package carefully inside his doublet. 'Coach travel isn't all it's cracked up to be. I may never get the feeling back in my arse again.'

'I think I'll get some air,' Rudi said, trying to wrest his attention away from the faint bulge in Fritz's impeccably cut jacket. The sensation of fear that he'd felt at the first sight of the package had diminished to an oppressive sense of unease, although he still couldn't understand why. Perhaps it was just because Hanna seemed so fascinated with it, although how it appeared to her magical senses he could barely imagine.

'All right.' Fritz rolled into the hammock that Pieter had slung for him, and pulled his cloak over his face. 'Yell if you see any pirates.'

'I'll do that,' Rudi assured him. The comment had been made purely in jest, he was sure, but now that it had been voiced, he found himself inclined to take it seriously. He picked up his bow, and ascended the steep flight of steps to the deck.

'Having trouble sleeping?' Shenk asked as he emerged, and raised an eyebrow at the sight of the weapon.

'A little,' Rudi said, letting the frosty air clear his head with a sense of exquisite relief. The stars shone down hard and sharp again tonight, their faint blue radiance limning the deck. Mannslieb was barely above the horizon, still too low to cast much light, and the baleful green glow of Morrslieb was nowhere to be seen. Out in the open, the sense of dread he'd felt at the sight of the package seemed irrational, and he let it go gratefully. 'You?'

'My watch,' the captain explained. 'We're running under a skeleton crew again.' He sighed. 'I'll be damned glad to get to Altdorf tomorrow. The sooner your friend and his parcel are off my boat, the happier I'll be.'

'That makes two of us,' Rudi said fervently. Shenk nodded at the bow.

'Expecting trouble?'

'Always,' Rudi said. Since leaving Kohlstadt, that was the one thing in life he'd found that he could constantly be sure of. 'If the Fog Walkers are going to try again before we get to Altdorf, it'll have to be tonight.' Shenk nodded.

'The same thought had occurred to me,' he admitted. Despite their mutual trepidation, however, the night wore on without incident, and after the watch changed and Ansbach replaced the skipper at the tiller, Rudi found a convenient corner and tried to get some sleep.

He was woken shortly before dawn by a faint splashing sound, which echoed in his ears long after the actual noise had vanished. Sitting up cautiously, he reached for his bow, and looked around, allowing his eyes to adjust to the meagre light levels. Mannslieb was higher in the sky, but the deck was still shrouded in shadows, made all the more deep and dark by the faint radiance it gave. He listened hard, stilling his breath, as he used to do in the woods when he was trying to locate game by the rustling in the foliage.

Just when he was beginning to convince himself that he'd imagined it, the sound came again. Nocking an arrow, he turned, moving as stealthily as he used to do in the forests he'd called home.

His instincts hadn't let him down: a patch of shadow moved by the rail, shimmering and indistinct. He gazed at it, trying to bring it into focus, but it refused to resolve itself. The hairs on the back of his neck began to prickle. Could this be sorcery?

There was only one way to find out. Trusting his archer's instincts, he drew back and let fly, without trying to distinguish a target. He was rewarded with a cry of pain, and suddenly the patch of concealing shadow was gone. A young man stood there, clad only in a pair of sodden britches, the arrow through his shoulder, dripping water and blood onto the deck. Both fluids looked equally black in the moonlight.

Having no doubt that he was indeed facing a wizard, with abilities similar to the ones he'd seen Alwyn display, Rudi drew another arrow from his quiver.

'Stand to!' Ansbach bellowed, but the warning hardly seemed necessary. Alerted by the intruder's scream, the crew of the *Reikmaiden* was piling out of the cabins onto the deck, clutching whatever makeshift weapons they could find. A moment later, Hanna and Fritz appeared too, Hanna's dagger in her hand, and Fritz flourishing his sword ready for use.

Rudi tensed, expecting the cornered mage to unleash a barrage of phantom knives, the way that Alwyn had done, but the intruder clearly felt that the odds against him were far too great to make a fight of it. Turning, he leapt over the side of the boat. Rudi expected him to fall, and wondered how he was hoping to swim with an arrow through his shoulder, but to his astonishment, the young mage kept rising, almost to the height of the mast, making an impossible leap across scores of yards of water to the bank.

Rudi tried to track him for a moment with the bow, drawing back the string as he did so, but decided against taking the shot. Whoever he was, the young man had been driven off, and there was no point injuring him any further; or wasting another perfectly good arrow, come to that. A moment later, he heard a crackling of vegetation from the bank, as the luckless wizard made it to dry land, and a muffled curse echoed across the water. Evidently, his landing hadn't been a comfortable one.

'What the hell was that?' Shenk asked, his face pale in the moonlight. Hanna shrugged.

'Shadowmancer,' she said. She shot a look of silent complicity at Rudi. 'He must have swum out to the boat, hoping to get aboard, hidden by magic.' Rudi nodded.

'We had one burgling houses like that when I was in the watch, back in Marienburg.' That happened to be true, although since the felon in question had confined his activities to the richer quarters on the other side of the river, he'd only heard about it through gossip with the other Black Caps from neighbouring wards. Apparently, the magician in question had disappeared without trace shortly after being taken into custody. Rudi had a sneaking suspicion that the Fog Walkers had known a useful recruit when they saw one and cut some kind of deal to keep him out of Rijker's Island, the vast stone fortress that dominated the mouth of the Reik, protecting the city from seaborne marauders and its own indigenous criminals alike.

'Well, there's one good thing,' Fritz said, 'it's nearly dawn. At least they won't have time for another try.'

'Not until we get to Altdorf, anyway,' Hanna pointed out.

CHAPTER ELEVEN

RUDI'S FIRST SIGHT of Altdorf was a massive stone wall, looming up on both banks of the river and stretching away into the distance on either side, diminishing with the perspective as it went. From this far away, the effect was uncannily like a single vast building, into which the mighty Reik disappeared as if it was nothing more than an irrigation ditch, or the sewage outflow of a palisaded village. He couldn't help but be reminded of the Vloedmuur, which surrounded Marienburg, however, this barrier was clearly built to resist armies rather than the elements, squat and monolithic compared to the coastal defences that kept the sea from swamping the mighty coastal port, at least for most of the time.

The pressures of commerce and a growing population had pushed a few buildings out beyond the walls, but unlike the ragged shanty town clinging to the skirts of Carroburg, the structures he could see were mainly constructed of solid stone, clearly meant to last. Almost since sunrise, and for the first time since the travellers had left the Wasteland behind, the trees that had fringed the riverbanks for most of the journey had receded into the distance. In their place, fields had appeared, scattered farmsteads at first, and then modest agricultural villages that reminded him all too vividly of Kohlstadt.

'You wouldn't think it,' Fritz remarked at his elbow, 'but that's all part of the city's defences. They cleared the trees from around the walls so the enemy couldn't sneak up on them, and the farmers just kept on felling them to get more growing space.'

'What enemy?' Rudi asked, unable to imagine any foe foolish enough to lay siege to these mighty walls. They reduced the riverboats entering and leaving the city to the scale of toys, like the chips of bark he'd sent gurgling down the forest streams as a child, and nothing he could conceive of would be capable of breaching them.

'The vampire counts – from Sylvania,' Fritz said. 'They tried to take the city twice, oh, hundreds of years ago now.' He shrugged. 'Although they're believed to have fought against the Chaos hordes in the north last year, so who knows what their true agenda is.'

'When did you start taking an interest in history?' Hanna asked, her voice tinged with surprise.

Fritz coloured a little.

'Mathilde's been filling me in. She said that if I'm going to live here I ought to know a bit about the place.'

'Well, that's more than we do,' Rudi admitted. They were passing through the wall, and he caught a glimpse of batteries of cannon poised to pour thundering death down on any river-borne malefactor foolish enough to try running the gap. Giant windlasses were also visible on both banks, heavily protected by the massive stone fortifications, and he realised that if necessary the river could be blocked by heavy chains. Marienburg had taken similar precautions at the mouth of the Reik, although there he suspected the intention had been to prevent smugglers from departing rather than to guard the city from waterborne invasion.

His first impression of the city proper was that it seemed almost like Marienburg in some respects, although in others it was disconcertingly different. It hardly resembled Carroburg at all, although he had to admit that his acquaintance with that particular city had been cursory at best.

As in Marienburg, the houses fought for space within the encircling walls, building upwards rather than outwards to make as much use of the limited land at their disposal as possible. Not one of the buildings he could see was less than four storeys in height, and most were even taller, rising in some cases to six or seven. Unlike the bustling port, however, there had been room to expand outwards to some extent, and the relatively open farmlands beyond the city had been able to take some of the pressure from inside the fortifications, so they seemed squatter and more solid than those he was used to.

'Well, it's less soggy than Marienburg,' Hanna said. Instead of the intricate network of bridges and canals that had stitched the islands of the Reikmouth together, Altdorf was a city of roads, although many of the streets he could see on the bank barely qualified for the term, being closer to alleyways, or possibly open sewers. Rudi took a deep breath, and almost gagged.

'It smells even worse, though. I didn't think that was possible.'

'They don't call it the Great Reek for nothing,' Shenk said, wandering past. They were approaching the docks, at the confluence of the Reik and the Talabec, and the river traffic was growing denser. More riverboats than Rudi could count were scudding out on the water, riding low with the cargoes they were bringing in or had just taken on board, and smaller craft wove between them with casual indifference to the threat of collision. He hadn't seen such a dense concentration of watercraft since leaving Marienburg.

'Cosmopolitan sort of place,' he commented casually, spotting an ungainly Kislevite barge and an elegant vessel crewed by elves within moments of each other. He thought briefly of drawing Fritz's attention to the latter, with some good-natured reminder of his excitement at his first sight of an elf vessel entering the harbour as they'd first approached Marienburg, but before he could speak, his voice was drowned out by an unearthly shriek that echoed across the water and left his ears ringing. 'Sigmar preserve us, what the hell's that?' It looked like a boat of some kind, but it was thrashing through the water without any sign of a sail, churning up a thick white soup of froth in its wake. Choking black smoke poured from a stovepipe in the superstructure, and a crew of grimy dwarfs ran back and forth on its deck, growling at one another in their incomprehensible tongue.

'A steamboat.' Shenk's voice was suffused with disgust. 'Don't often see them this far downriver. The hairbarrels seem to like them well enough, but you wouldn't get a real sailor aboard one at any price.'

'It's made of metal,' Fritz said, his voice tinged with awe. 'Why doesn't it sink?'

'Probably too pig-headed to,' Shenk said, 'like its crew. Bullying your way through the water instead of using the wind and the tide might be all right for stumpies, but it's no way for a human to travel.'

Rudi was inclined to agree. The strange vessel was like nothing he'd ever seen before. He watched it go, heading upstream with a cavalier disregard for everything else on the water, and braced himself against the rail as the backwash threw the *Reik-maiden* through a series of vertiginous lurches. As it diminished in the distance, trailed by the profanity of the crews left bobbing in its wake, he blinked his eyes clear of the acrid smoke that had drifted across the deck. The dockside loomed up through it, surprisingly close, and he hefted his pack, feeling it settle into place across his back with a welcome sense of familiarity.

'Got everything?' he asked. Beside him, Hanna nodded. She was wearing her new dress, and the headscarf she'd purchased in Carroburg, everything else she owned stuffed into the satchel she habitually carried.

The bright colours made her look different, Rudi thought, harder and more assertive, if that was possible. He tried to keep his attention on her face, instead of letting it drift lower to the expanse of cleavage that the dress exposed, and ignore the disturbing memories of the night on the banks of the Reik last summer that the sight evoked. Meeting his gaze, she grinned, as if she could read his thoughts, and he flushed despite himself.

'If this frock has the effect on the wizards that it seems to have on you, it was money well spent,' she said. Rudi was by no means sure that the senior mages of the Colleges of Magic would be swayed by something so simple, but if it increased her confidence it was no bad thing. He shrugged.

'Assuming you can find any,' he said.

'I don't think I'll have too much trouble,' Hanna said, and anyone who knew her less well than Rudi did would probably have thought she was as confident as she sounded. 'The city's supposed to be crawling with mages, remember?'

'Well, here we are,' Shenk said. 'Altdorf, as promised. Good luck.' He stood aside as the three travellers filed up the gangplank, and turned away before Rudi could say a farewell. 'Look alive for Mannan's sake, I want those pots unloaded before a week next Koenigstag!'

'Well,' Rudi said, as his boots hit the cobbles, 'where to?' The bustle of the docks was almost comforting in its familiarity, but daunting nevertheless. It was beginning to dawn on him that, once again, he and his companions were alone in a huge and unknown city. At least in Marienburg they'd had Artemus as a guide, and had found food and shelter for the night. Here they had no one...

A piercing whistle interrupted his gloomy thoughts, and Fritz looked up in response to it, reminding Rudi incongruously for a moment of an eager puppy. A cheery grin spread across the simpleton's face, and he waved a greeting in response.

'There you are. About time too, I've been freezing hanging about here waiting for you.' Mathilde wove her way through the hurrying dockhands, and kissed him affectionately on the cheek. 'Let's find somewhere with good food and some halfway decent ale, and thaw ourselves out for an hour or two. I can always tell the boss the tide was out or something.' Fritz blushed, pulling away, and for the first time the red-haired woman noticed that her fellow bodyguard wasn't alone. The insouciant grin Rudi remembered so vividly quirked her mouth as she took in his and Hanna's presence. 'Well, this is a surprise.'

'I could say the same,' Hanna said, raising an eyebrow. 'I see you and Fritz are still getting along all right.'

'You could say that,' Mathilde agreed. 'Are you planning to stay in Altdorf long?'

Hanna nodded. 'I hope so,' she said.

Mathilde's expression softened. 'Good. We could do with some more guests at the wedding.'

'Who's getting married?' Rudi asked, before the penny dropped, and he stared at Fritz in astonishment. The muscular youth blushed even more furiously than before.

'Who do you think?' he said, a little defensively.

Noting Rudi's dumbfounded expression, Hanna stepped into the breach. 'Congratulations,' she said. 'When did this happen?'

'It sort of snuck up on us,' Mathilde said happily. 'We spend most of our time together anyway, and it just occurred to me one evening that he scrubbed up pretty well for a yokel from the back of beyond. One thing just sort of led to another.'

Fritz shrugged, looking oddly embarrassed.

'You'd had a lot to drink, though,' he said. Mathilde punched him affectionately on the arm.

'You hadn't, though, which I suppose was just as well.' She raised an eyebrow at Hanna. 'So you see how desperate I am, flinging myself at the sort of lowlife who'd take advantage of a helpless young maiden in her cups.'

'Scandalous,' Hanna agreed, keeping a straight face with difficulty.

'You're about as helpless as an orc,' Fritz riposted, clearly playing a long-established game, 'and what sort of heartless harridan would toy with the affections of an innocent country lad in the first place?'

'I can see you were made for each other,' Rudi said, while the two lovers grinned inanely. He wondered if Conrad and Alwyn had been like that at first, and whether they were alive at all now. Such speculation was fruitless, though, so he forced the thought away, and tried to be happy for his friends.

'Come on,' Mathilde said, linking her arm with Fritz's and leading the way out of the docks. 'I'm cold and hungry, and the boss won't wait for ever.' Rudi and Hanna fell in behind them, exchanging glances of amused perplexity.

'Well,' Rudi said, 'Altdorf is certainly full of surprises.'

'You haven't seen anything yet,' Mathilde assured him, glancing back to speak to them over her shoulder. Rudi could well believe it. As they left the waterfront and entered the city, he could see several men and women dressed in the clothing of lands far from the Empire, a common enough sight in the great port of Marienburg, but one he'd hardly expected to see this far inland. Kislevite and Tilean mercenaries were common enough everywhere, of course, but within a score of paces he'd seen the robes of Araby and heard a couple of passers-by arguing loudly in Bretonnian. Several times they passed dwarfs and halflings.

'Stick close,' Mathilde advised. 'If you lose your way in Altdorf, you might never find it again.'

Rudi eyed the narrow strip of sky visible far above them, and nodded. With nothing familiar to go on, and even the sun out of sight, his innate sense of direction would be of little help. At least in Marienburg there had been the occasional break between the buildings, usually where the street crossed one of the innumerable waterways, but here, it seemed, there was no such respite from the masonry that loomed on every side.

'I can believe that,' he said. Mathilde shook her head.

'No, I mean that literally. The Colleges of Magic bend the world around themselves. Streets don't always go where they should, at least in some quarters, and sometimes they don't go to the same place twice.' She shrugged. 'You get used to it. The trick's just to go where you're going, and not worry too much about how you got there.'

'I see.' Rudi didn't, quite, but he thought he should try to stay positive. 'And you've been here long enough to pick up the trick?'

'I should hope so.' Mathilde shot another grin over her shoulder. 'I'm a 'dorfer, born and bred. I can find my way anywhere.'

'Would that include one of the colleges?' Hanna asked. Mathilde shrugged.

'Anywhere I'd want to go, that is.' Her voice became elaborately casual. 'You won't find anything interesting there.'

Hanna looked as if she was about to argue the point, but subsided, looking grim.

'Seen any wizards yet?' Rudi asked her, lowering his voice.

Hanna nodded, looking a trifle unhappy.

'Plenty.' She indicated a couple of passers-by. 'Those two, and that man over there.' They all looked surprisingly ordinary to Rudi, who had been expecting mages to wear the robes of their college or display some overt symbol of power, but he trusted Hanna's gift of perception. As he began to take more notice of the people thronging the streets around them, he noticed several glancing at Hanna in a faintly guarded manner. Others with the gift of witchsight, he supposed. 'There's one in that alley up ahead, too, but he doesn't seem to be moving.' She indicated the mouth of the thoroughfare that Fritz and Mathilde were just beginning to turn down.

'Are you sure?' Moved by an impulse he couldn't quite explain, Rudi dropped his hand to his sword hilt. Hanna nodded, and they followed their friends into the narrow side street.

At first, he thought his suspicions were unfounded. Then he noticed the small knot of people standing casually in the middle of the thoroughfare, apparently talking to one another. They were spaced just a little too evenly. Mathilde had obviously noticed them too. She detached her arm from her fiancé's, and shifted her weight on to the balls of her feet.

'Ah, there he is.' Hanna glanced behind them. A shadowy figure stepped out of the doorway of a ramshackle tenement, shrouded in a cloak. 'Remind you of anyone?'

Rudi nodded. The man's arm was strapped up beneath the cloak, hanging awkwardly. This just had to be the wizard he'd shot the previous night. A moment later, the man confirmed it.

'You should have let me take it without waking you,' he said, in an unmistakable Marienburg accent. 'Now we'll just have to do this the hard way.'

CHAPTER TWELVE

'THE HARD WAY's fine by me,' Mathilde said, drawing her sword. She took a step towards the young wizard, who raised his uninjured arm in what was clearly intended to be a threatening gesture. Rudi flinched, expecting an onslaught of phantom knives, like the ones Alwyn had unleashed, or the cobbles to vanish beneath his feet, but it seemed that the shadow mage had something else in mind. Mathilde's charge faltered suddenly, a dazed expression entering her eyes, and she looked at her surroundings with an air of vague bewilderment. 'Sorry, what was the other thing?'

'Protect Fritz!' Rudi yelled, hoping that her feelings for the simpleton would overcome whatever sorcery was befuddling her mind. He realised, too late, that he'd just revealed who was carrying the package of artefacts. The wizard would know anyway, of course, because he'd be able to see the mystical energy it gave off in the same way that Hanna had done, but the thugs bearing down on them wouldn't have had a clue who their target was, and would probably have split up to tackle everyone in the party individually. As it was, they all targeted the young bodyguard, running towards him with murder in their eyes. Cursing under his breath, Rudi leapt to intervene.

As the sword left his scabbard, he found the street fighting instincts he'd learned as a city watchman kicking in, and assessed their assailants with a cool-headed detachment that vaguely surprised him. There were five of them, all rough-looking fellows, armed for the most part with clubs and daggers. Only one carried a sword, and he seemed to be the leader of the rag-tag band.

Despite the odds against them, Rudi felt confident. He knew the type: a local gang of petty criminals recruited in a hurry with the promise of quick and easy cash. The Fog Walkers must be getting desperate, he thought to himself, recruiting street scum like this to do their dirty work, but no doubt most of their more competent operatives had been left at the bottom of the Reik after their ill-fated venture into piracy, leaving them no option but to take whatever help they could get.

Fritz had his sword out too, and the two erstwhile enemies stood shoulder to shoulder, facing the onrushing thugs. Rudi had hoped that the sight of drawn steel would make them think twice, but they came on regardless. No doubt they were counting on their superior numbers, and were more afraid of losing face in front of their friends than they were of anything Rudi and Fritz might do. Rudi smiled grimly to himself. That could be the last mistake some of them would ever make.

He struck out at the first man on his right, ducking under a descending club, and opening up an ugly gash along the fellow's leg. The man screamed, trying to hop backwards, and Rudi followed up, spinning around to smash the hilt of his sword into the thug's face. The man went down hard, howling as he clapped a hand to the wreckage of his nose.

Once again, Rudi's old street brawling skills had served him well. By targeting the man at the end of the line, he'd opened up a significant gap in their ranks, keeping the fellow with the club between him and the rest of the mob, so he could pick off his chosen target at leisure without having to worry about interference from the others.

Stepping into the space he'd created, he turned, finding himself behind the main group, and hoping that Fritz had had the common sense to duplicate the move on their other flank. No such luck, of course. True to form, Fritz had simply charged at the nearest foe, and was now surrounded. He was giving a good account of himself, though, Rudi had to admit. The dagger-wielding bandit he'd tackled was kneeling on the filthy cobbles, hugging his belly, fresh blood seeping from beneath his arms, and the young bodyguard was engaged in a furious duel with the swordsman apparently leading the ragged band. Stepping in again to engage another bandit, whose knife was flashing towards Fritz's kidneys, Rudi glanced up over the milling heads to see what was happening to Hanna and Mathilde.

'Snap out of it!' Hanna said, slapping the swordswoman hard around the face. The vacant look fled from Mathilde's eyes, and her muscles twitched as she overrode the instinctive counterblow that she'd been about to launch. Comprehension dawned across her visage.

'He's using magic,' she said, as if such a thing was both an everyday occurrence and the direst form of personal insult, and raised her sword as if to attack the shadow mage again.

'I know.' Hanna pushed the red-headed woman towards the melee. 'Go and help the boys. I'll take care of this jumped-up little sneak thief.'

Mathilde opened her mouth as if she was about to argue the point, and then caught sight of the blade lunging at Fritz's unprotected back. Rudi tried to complete the blocking movement he'd already begun, but stumbled as his shins met the ruffian he'd just downed. The man clutched at his leg, trying to trip him, and Rudi cut down again with his sword, not even bothering to look. There was a meaty thud somewhere around knee height, and the grip around his calf was abruptly released.

Prevented from parrying the blow aimed at Fritz, he watched Mathilde leap towards the knifeman, time slowing and stretching, as it so often seemed to in combat. He even had time to notice that the bustling streets had quieted, a few of the passers-by pausing to watch the spectacle as they had in Carroburg, although most of them continued to go about their business regardless of the fracas, giving it little more than a cursory glance.

'Look out!' Mathilde called, but Fritz's attention was wholly on the fight he was having with the swordsman, and he barely acknowledged her warning shout. Before Rudi's horrified gaze, the dagger struck squarely home, and then rebounded, the point snapping off with a faint metallic ring. A gleam of metal became visible beneath the ragged new tear in Fritz's immaculate jacket, and with a sigh of relief, Rudi recalled the concealed mail shirt that Mathilde had been wearing during the brawl in the gambling den when they'd first met her and von Eckstein. Obviously, the nobleman believed in equipping his employees with a little discreet protection as a matter of course.

Before the knifeman could recover, Mathilde was on him, striking him down with a furious blow that cleaved deep into his shoulder. As the wounded man tried to crawl away, she kicked him hard in the face, her expression murderously vengeful.

'Not so tough face-to-face, are you, you backstabbing little runt.' Her blade rose and fell again, and the thug expired with a single choked-off scream of mortal terror.

Rudi turned to face the last ruffian, who was already backing away, and took a step towards him, raising his blade. That was enough. The man turned and fled, weaving through the growing crowd of onlookers at an impressive turn of speed. His comrade with the belly wound followed, rather more slowly and

erratically, leaving a trail of spattered blood behind
him. Unless he found a healer or a chirurgeon pretty
soon, Rudi thought, he wasn't going very far. Fritz
seemed to be gaining the upper hand against their
leader, although his handling of the sword still
seemed a little less elegant and instinctive than
Mathilde's or Rudi's own, so Rudi left him to it while
he hurdled the body of his fallen opponent and
turned towards Hanna again.

'You talk a good fight for a hedge wizard,' the
shadow mage said, 'but you're in way over your head,
little girl. You've got no idea what you're dealing with.'

'Neither have you,' Hanna said. Before Rudi could
intervene, a ball of seething red flame winked into
existence in the air ahead of her, and streaked towards
the black-clad wizard. Before he could react it struck
him full in the chest, and he went down shrieking, a
neat, charred hole punched almost the whole way
through his torso. For a moment Rudi thought he
could see the man's spine from the wrong side, and
shuddered with instinctive revulsion. Then the fellow
expired in a miasma of burning flesh and smouldering cloth.

'Hanna!' he gasped in horror, anticipating an out-
break of hysteria among the crowd like the one they'd
fled from in Carroburg. To his astonishment, however,
none of the passers-by reacted at all, other than to step
around the gently smoking corpse with carefully composed expressions of fastidious distaste. Hanna
shrugged.

'He didn't leave me any choice,' she said, her tone
making it perfectly clear that any doubts Rudi might

have harboured on that score would be best kept to himself.

'Come on.' He looked around grimly, prepared to fight his way clear of the inevitable lynch mob, but the crowd remained strangely passive. For a moment, he found himself wondering if they were all under some kind of enchantment.

'You got that thing off your head, then,' Fritz said, taking advantage of his opponent's momentary distraction to get in under his guard. There was a brief scraping of metal on metal, and the gang leader's sword clattered to the ordure-slick cobbles underfoot. Fritz rested the tip of his blade against the man's throat. 'Leave. Now,' he said, slowly and distinctly. With a squeak of relief, and the sudden smell of soiled britches, the would-be assassin complied. Fritz sheathed his sword, and beamed happily at Mathilde. 'How did I do?' he asked proudly.

'Not too bad,' the woman said. 'You're still dropping your point a little, but you're definitely getting the hang of that disarming move.'

'Which way?' Rudi asked urgently. He glanced around at the curiously passive crowd, eager to be gone before they came to their senses. None of them seemed remotely interested in what had just happened, except for an enterprising halfling who was already removing the dead wizard's purse from his belt. 'We have to get out of here. The last time Hanna did something like that, we nearly got lynched.'

'Calm down,' Mathilde said, with evident amusement, although she was covertly eyeing Hanna with a faintly wary air. 'This is Altdorf, not some scabby village in the middle of nowhere. There's a lot of wizards round here.' Rudi felt his jaw go slack.

'I suppose we'd better get on, though,' Fritz conceded, clearly determined to follow his girlfriend's lead. 'Like you said, we can't keep the boss waiting forever.' He linked arms with Mathilde again, and shot a slightly forced grin at Rudi. 'Close your mouth, Rudi, you look like a provincial.' Nettled, Rudi snapped his jaw shut, his temper hardly improved by Hanna's barely stifled giggle. 'I thought you were used to Hanna doing magic stuff.'

'Oh, that's right. You were studying at the college in Marienburg, weren't you?' Mathilde said, the barest trace of relief seeping into her voice. 'Fritz told me he'd seen you there a couple of times.' She began to lead the way through the maze of streets with all the assurance she'd shown before, and Rudi began to relax. Before more than a few moments had passed, the street where the slain wizard still lay had passed from sight, and he truly felt he couldn't have found his way back to it if he'd tried. Hanna nodded.

'That's right.' Her hand crept towards her satchel, without her apparently having been aware of the gesture. 'I've got my papers here with me.'

'Just as well,' Mathilde said. 'Altdorf is crawling with witch hunters as well as wizards. You'd be surprised how many witches think they can hide here, by blending in with the college-trained wizards.'

'And can they?' Rudi asked, trying to sound casual. Mathilde shrugged.

'I doubt it. If the witch hunters don't get them, the Knights Panther probably do. They both seem pretty busy, anyway.' She shrugged again. 'On the other hand, the only ones we ever hear about are the ones that get burned. For all I know, there are dozens of them running loose in the streets.'

'So why have you come all this way?' Fritz asked. 'I'd have thought you'd want to stay put in Marienburg, at least till you got properly trained by Baron Hendryk.'

'I thought I'd do better with one of the colleges here,' Hanna said shortly. By this time, to Rudi's great and unspoken relief, they'd left the maze of narrow streets behind them and emerged onto a wider thoroughfare, so they could all walk abreast. The buildings around them didn't seem all that different, though, being the same mixture of shops and houses that had closed in on them the moment they'd left the docks. Fritz glanced longingly at a few of the more expensive-looking taverns as they passed, but the brawl in the alleyway had clearly focused Mathilde's mind on the errand at hand, and she kept walking with an evident air of purpose. Fritz nodded sympathetically, as if he understood, and voiced his thoughts with his usual lack of tact.

'Things not work out with Kris, then? Shame, I kind of liked him.' Hanna's jaw tightened. Parting from the young Marienburger had been a severe blow for her, perhaps almost as bad as being forced to take her chances with the witch hunters again, and Rudi squeezed her hand sympathetically. To his pleased surprise, she returned the pressure for a moment before pulling away from his grip.

'Kris is fine, thank you. I'll be writing to him as soon as I'm settled here.'

'Oh, good,' Fritz said, with every sign of sincerity, and Rudi tried not to acknowledge the pang of disappointment he felt at the girl's words.

'Here we are,' Mathilde said suddenly, turning down an alleyway between two shops. One seemed to be selling nothing but hats, while the one on the adjacent plot had a display of well-crafted furniture in a variety of different woods. Like all the other businesses they'd passed, the upper storeys of the buildings appeared to be given over to living accommodation.

As he turned the corner, Rudi's scalp began to prickle. The alleyway was reasonably wide, just wide enough so as to accommodate a horse-drawn cart, but it came to an abrupt end a few yards ahead of them in a pair of stout timber gates that barred any further progress. They were walking into a confined space, which his instincts told him felt like a trap, and he began to reach surreptitiously for the hilt of his sword. True, he had no reason to anticipate treachery from Fritz or Mathilde, but Magnus had appeared to be a friend too, right up to the moment he'd revealed himself to be an insane Chaos cultist with designs on his life.

Mathilde just kept on walking, however, and a moment later, his hand fell away from the weapon again. A small door, just large enough for a single person to walk through, stood in the middle of one of the stout timber gates. As she approached it, the red-headed bodyguard reached out to rap loudly on the wood with the hilt of her dagger.

'Who's there?' Within seconds, a tiny panel had opened at head height, and a face appeared behind a metal grille. Rudi could see very little of the man from where he stood, but then he hadn't needed to in order to pick up on the note of suspicion in the gatekeeper's voice.

'It's me, Oderic.' Mathilde sighed, and stepped back a pace to allow the sentry to get a good look at her. She gestured to her fiancé. 'And this is Fritz, the one I've been telling you about.'

'Ah.' The guard seemed unimpressed. 'What about them others? I wasn't told you'd be bringing others.'

'That's Rudi and Hanna. The boss knows them from Marienburg. They were on the same boat as Fritz.'

Fritz nodded.

'Thank Sigmar they were, too, otherwise the boss's package wouldn't have got here at all.'

'So stop fiddling about and open the gate,' Mathilde finished, 'before the Fog Walkers catch up with us and have another go.' The hatch banged shut, and a moment later Rudi heard the clatter of bolts being drawn.

Despite the evident solidity of the timberwork, the small wicket opened smoothly and silently. Rudi tensed, but the gatekeeper made no overtly threatening move, and after a moment, he followed Mathilde and Fritz through the narrow gap. He half turned as he entered the space beyond, to make sure that Hanna was following safely. By doing so, he was unaware of his surroundings until the gate had banged shut behind them, and the girl had stepped forward to join the rest of the group. As her eyes moved past him, they widened in astonishment, and he turned to see what had surprised her so much.

'I had no idea places like this existed in a city,' she said. Mathilde looked smug.

'They don't in Marienburg. They haven't got the space, but there are one or two in Altdorf.' Rudi felt the breath catch in his throat.

In truth, he thought, as his initial impression of a vast open space receded, to be replaced by a more sober assessment of the wide formal garden in front of him, von Eckstein's estate wasn't that large. It was no more than an acre or so, but here, surrounded by buildings in a city where space was at a premium, it exuded an air of wealth and power so strong that he could almost taste it.

Wide lawns, still dusted with frost in places where the sun had yet to fall, led the eye naturally through artfully-placed flowerbeds and shrubberies, for the most part denuded of foliage by the early winter chill, towards the house that occupied the centre of this peculiar clearing among the forest of stone surrounding it. A handful of mature trees offered the promise of shade in the summer, and Rudi's lifelong affinity for wooded spaces told him that they were spaced a little too precisely to have grown there naturally. They were as much a crafted feature of the hidden parkland as the small ornamental structures scattered around the place, and he marvelled at the patience of whoever had first planted them. They'd clearly had an eye for future generations, never expecting to see the full effect of their work in their own lifetime.

Tiny figures in the distance pottered about, tending to the few winter-flowering plants in the beds, raking the gravel paths smooth, and trimming the open lawns with scythes.

'The gardeners,' Mathilde explained, following the direction of his gaze. 'There are about a dozen of them, I think.'

'You think?' Hanna echoed, sounding faintly incredulous. Mathilde shrugged. 'They come and go. Halflings mostly, so they all look alike to me.' She laughed. 'From this distance, anyway.'

'You should see it in the summer,' Oderic volunteered. The gatekeeper had turned out to be a white-haired man in late middle age, with a faintly perceptible limp and an ugly scar across his face, which someone or something had evidently laid open with a sword many years back. He wore a mail shirt and carried a loaded crossbow with a casual air that showed he knew how to use it, and Rudi had no doubt that he would be equally adept with the sword hanging from his belt. Now that they were inside, he seemed more comfortable with the unexpected visitors, although he didn't put the weapon down. 'Come the spring, you'll really see something. It doesn't start to come into its own until mid-year turn.'

'Later than that, surely,' Rudi said. He'd spent all his life in the open air, and had never seen real spring growth until the following month of ploughtide. After all, that was why the festival that separated the months was known as 'Startgrowth'. Oderic smiled, an expression that Rudi was beginning to associate with Altdorfers proclaiming the wonders of their city to a country bumpkin.

'The gardeners round here have a little help,' he said. Mathilde nodded.

'The boss has friends in the Jade College.'

'He knows a senior wizard?' Hanna asked hopefully. Mathilde nodded again.

'The boss knows pretty much everyone worth knowing. He's got contacts in several of the colleges.' She shrugged. 'I guess he owes you a favour. Maybe he can give you an introduction.' The expression on Hanna's face pierced Rudi like a sword thrust: hope, joy, and the falling away of a burden that he sensed she'd been carrying since their fateful meeting with Gerhard on the moors of the Wasteland. For a moment, the impulse to take her in his arms and reassure her that everything was going to turn out all right was almost irresistible. He fought it down nevertheless. She would resent what she'd take as a patronising gesture, he knew, and besides, it was obviously still Kris that she wanted, not him. To distract himself, he pointed towards the house, which stood squarely in the distance at the end of an immaculate gravel drive.

'I bet that view impresses his visitors whatever time of the year it is,' he said.

Oderic and Mathilde exchanged amused glances.

'Visitors come in at the front,' Oderic said. 'This is just the servants' gate.'

CHAPTER THIRTEEN

SURE ENOUGH, THE drive ended in a courtyard surrounded by kitchens and stable blocks, artfully concealed behind a tall evergreen hedge. The walk took several minutes, the small group of travellers loitering a little as they made their way up to the house, and Rudi was able to take in his unexpected surroundings in greater detail.

It was, not unnaturally, the house that took up most of his attention, as tall as most of the others he'd seen since his arrival in Altdorf, towering four storeys above the sprawling gardens that surrounded it. Constructed of warm red brick, over which climbing plants grew in a pleasing profusion that artfully mimicked the random patterns of nature, its roof line was punctuated by dormer windows that hinted at a fifth layer of rooms within. Seeing the direction of his gaze, Mathilde nodded.

'Servants' quarters,' she said, and looked at Fritz. 'Don't worry. We've got a suite on the second floor, next to the boss's. No point trying to watch his back if it's going to take us ten minutes to find it.'

'So, who's looking after him now?' Rudi asked, trying not to sound too sarcastic. 'Or do you think he's safe enough in his own home?'

To his surprise, Mathilde laughed.

'You don't think we're the only guards he's got, do you?' She pointed to a couple of the gardeners, who now Rudi's attention had been drawn to them, seemed to be taking a surreptitious interest in the party walking up the driveway rather than the bush they were supposed to be pruning. 'We're just the ones he wants people to notice.'

'Except when you're collecting valuable packages, presumably,' Hanna said dryly.

Mathilde nodded, clearly enjoying some kind of private joke.

'That's right,' she said, with a wink at Fritz.

'I thought so.' Hanna nodded too, as if sharing the joke. 'Is that why Fritz left it behind on the boat?'

'What?' Mathilde stopped moving, and stared at her, showing the first signs of surprise that Rudi had seen her display since they left the docks. 'How do you know that?'

'How do you think?' Hanna asked, a trifle smugly. Clearly, the novelty of being able to reveal her abilities openly was proving more than a little seductive. Determined not to seem impressed, in the manner

Rudi was beginning to suspect was something of a citywide affectation, Mathilde shrugged.

'Oh, that.' She linked arms with Fritz again, and resumed her stroll towards the house. 'Well, it worked, didn't it? The creep in the cape was fooled.'

'Very clever,' Rudi said, trying not to resent the way he'd apparently been used as a decoy. 'But supposing we'd all been killed?'

'The boss can always hire another bodyguard,' Mathilde said, as if the answer to that one was obvious. 'Plenty more like me in the 'dorf.'

That wasn't what Rudi had meant, but he let the matter drop, in favour of taking in as much as he could of the garden before they moved inside. He wasn't sure how much longer he was going to be in Altdorf, but he doubted that he was going to see anything so pleasant for a long time to come. Even the ever-present stench of the streets had receded, along with the endless clamour of voices, so that here it was almost possible to forget that you were surrounded by thousands and thousands of people. The high walls surrounding the estate obliterated them as if they had never existed. Even where other buildings backed directly on to von Eckstein's private preserve, as they did by the gateway, their windows had been bricked up to ensure the nobleman's privacy.

'Through here,' Mathilde said, leading the way though the profusion of outbuildings towards a small door in the main house. Here, there were more servants to be seen, men and women in matching livery, or plain garments protected by aprons. Rudi began to smell food, and was abruptly reminded of how long it had been since his last meal.

The trio of outcasts from Kohlstadt followed her inside, and as they did so, Rudi was shaken by the presentiment that their paths were diverging again. Fritz followed his fiancé with calm assurance, despite never having been here before. He clearly felt that he belonged, and had no doubts or qualms about his future. Hanna would be following the route laid down by her mystical talents, wherever it led. The only thing he could be sure of was that it was somewhere he couldn't follow, and his own quest was nearing completion. If von Eckstein could really help him find the von Kariens, he would at last find out where he came from, and what Greta Reifenstahl had meant by her mysterious words: *You do have a destiny.*

Absorbed in his thoughts, he paid scant attention to where they were going, and soon found himself lost in a bewildering maze of corridors.

Mathilde seemed to know where they were, though, and Fritz seemed indifferent, content to trust her. Hanna looked around, taking in their simple surroundings, looking a trifle disappointed.

'I thought it was going to be a bit more opulent than this,' she said. The corridors were narrow, just wide enough for three people to walk abreast, and their walls were plain whitewashed plaster, pierced at intervals by well-crafted but unornamented wooden doors. Even Magnus's house in Kohlstadt had been grander than this, although it was a little larger than a peasant's cottage in comparison. Rudi wasn't quite sure what he'd been expecting to find inside the nobleman's mansion, but it certainly wasn't anything as austere as this.

As the little group moved on they encountered a steady flow of servants travelling in both directions, apparently in accordance with some kind of protocol governing who gave way to whom. So far as Rudi could tell, the servants in livery generally took precedence over those without, and among those in uniform, the ones whose attire was more elaborate clearly expected the others to stand aside. Regardless of their ranking among themselves, all of the domestic staff gave way to Mathilde, with good grace, sullen resentment, or, in a few cases, unmistakable trepidation.

'These are just the servants' corridors,' Mathilde explained, with a trace of amusement. 'We can use the main ones if we like, but this way's quicker.' Rudi surmised that her position was somehow different to that of the household servants, despite being just as much an employee as they were, but the distinction was beyond him. 'Through here.'

She slipped through one of the plain narrow doors, indistinguishable to Rudi's eyes from any of the others, which led into a long, sunlit passageway. The contrast to the area they'd just left was extraordinary. In place of plain wood and neatly polished floorboards, there was a gallery wide enough and high enough for two horsemen to have ridden down side by side. The floor was gleaming oak, against which their boot soles echoed, with a strip of carpet two yards wide down the centre, woven into an intricate pattern of interlocking triangles in muted shades of red. Items of furniture stood against the wood-panelled walls, dressers and settles for the most part, with a few delicate china vases on carved occasional tables of exquisite workmanship. On the side of the room they'd entered, these were interspersed with imposing portraits of aristocratic-looking men and women that Rudi assumed were von Eckstein's forebears, easily the full size of their original sitters, even those that included a mount of some kind. On the other, windows of leaded glass stretched almost to ceiling height, providing restful views of the garden outside.

'This is the short gallery,' Mathilde explained. 'It runs along the edge of the wing.'

'Now that's impressive,' Hanna conceded. Looking as if she'd just won a hand of cards, Mathilde led the way through a pair of double doors at the far end, which seemed, to Rudi's astonished eyes to be scarcely smaller than the gates they'd entered the estate by, and into a wide hall. Doors led off in several directions, all panelled in a strange dark wood that he failed to recognise, and the furniture and portraits seemed more functional and muted, blending subtly into their background. This was clearly not a space in which anyone was expected to linger. Their boots rang on polished marble, and the temperature of the air dropped a little, sharp with the chill of the stone.

Without hesitating, Mathilde led the way up a wide, curving staircase, the treads of which were covered with a rich blue carpet in which stars and comets had been worked in yellow thread. Every fourth or fifth comet had a second tail, although whether that was an attempt to invoke the blessing of Sigmar on the household, or simply a matter of aesthetics, Rudi had no idea.

'You get used to it,' Mathilde said, her voice echoing from the dome above the stairwell. Craning his head to look up the four-storey abyss, Rudi felt a momentary twinge of vertigo. The concavity had been painted the deep, dark blue of the midnight sky, and tiny pinpoints of light seemed to dance up there, picking out the familiar outlines of the constellations.

'That's right,' Fritz agreed, apparently as indifferent to the splendour of their surroundings as his companion, but then he'd been in the nobleman's employ for some months, long enough to become inured to the signs of wealth that left Rudi's head reeling. Before he could think of a reply, Mathilde led the way down a short corridor, paused at the threshold of a door, indistinguishable to Rudi's eye from any of the others, and knocked with a degree of restraint that quite surprised him.

'Enter,' a voice called, in the same easy-going tone that Rudi recalled from a single encounter in Marienburg, and he wasn't particularly surprised to see von Eckstein looking up from an exquisitely inlaid desk of polished walnut wood as Mathilde pushed open the door. He set down the sheaf of papers in his hand. 'Ah, that was quick. Did you have any trouble?'

'No more than we expected,' Mathilde said, ushering Rudi and Hanna into the room ahead of her, 'but we must have had a leak somewhere in Marienburg. The Fog Walkers made a play for the boat before Fritz even joined it.'

'I take it from your relaxed attitude to the news that they didn't get what they were after,' von Eckstein said, rising to greet his unexpected guests. 'Rudi and Hanna, isn't it?' He bowed to Hanna, the faint tilt of his head precisely calculated to balance the good manners due to a lady with the clear and vast gulf between their relative social positions. 'I'm pleased to see you recovered.' After a moment's confusion, Rudi remembered that von Eckstein's last sight of the girl had been as he carried her unconscious form back to the tavern they were staying in. The stress of the fight in the gambling den where they'd met had triggered another magical seizure, as the power that Gerhard's talisman had dammed up in her had fought for instinctive release.

'Quite recovered, thank you.' Hanna answered mechanically, her attention apparently directed elsewhere in the room, although Rudi's remained fixed on the nobleman whose privacy they'd so abruptly invaded. He couldn't imagine what had caught her interest so completely. One of the many curios littering the warm and well-appointed chamber, he supposed. Either that, or the shelves of books lining the walls. There were dozens of them; more titles than he would have believed existed, although their spines were too far away for him to read what they might contain.

'Good.' The graf raised a quizzical eyebrow in Fritz's direction. 'I assume you have a good reason to be holding your reunion with your friends in my study, rather than your own quarters?' Fritz nodded.

'Yes, sir. They were travelling on the *Reikmaiden.* If it wasn't for them, the Walkers would have snatched the packet. Twice.'

'So we thought you might want to talk to them,' Mathilde added. 'See if they know anything useful.'

'I see.' Von Eckstein nodded, and turned to a seat in the corner. For the first time, Rudi became aware that he already had another guest in his study, and a strange sense of foreboding washed over him. 'If you'll excuse me, Magister Hollobach, this sounds as if I ought to give it some attention.'

'By all means.' The man stood, in a single fluid movement, and Rudi felt the hairs on his scalp begin to stir. His skin was pale, almost translucent in the bright winter sunshine falling through the windows, and the thin frosting of stubble on his shaved head wasn't so much white as simply devoid of colour. This, and the fact that his seat had been in the middle of a shaft of sunlight falling into the room, had been enough to fool the eye, making his clothing appear simply as an abstract shape draped over the chair. Only in retrospect did it fill out into a well-cut robe of a purple so deep that it was nearly black, nestled around a body almost skeletal in its thinness. The clasps were a curious yellowish white, and carefully carved into the shape of an hourglass leaning against a skull.

Despite the thrill of horror the thought sparked in him, Rudi couldn't quite shake the idea that they had been made from human bone. 'Our business was concluded in any case. My only reason for delaying was the pleasure of your company.' He smiled, the pale visage acquiring an expression of self-deprecatory good humour. 'No doubt you'd far rather spend time with these lively young people than a fusty old

Amethyst magister reeking of grave dust. I'm sure I would in your position.'

'Nonsense.' Von Eckstein shook his head, smiling affably. 'Where else am I going to find another chess player of your calibre?'

'One you can beat, you mean?' The cadaverous wizard nodded a greeting to the newcomers, and started for the door. 'I'll be waiting for your message with interest.'

'Wait.' To Rudi's amazement, and, so far as he could tell that of everyone else in the room, Hanna took a step forwards to impede his progress. 'I need to talk to you.'

'Are you sure?' the wizard asked, with an air of faint surprise. 'I can assure you, young lady, my order is most definitely not for you.'

Ignoring the looks of astonishment on the faces of everyone else in the room, he and Hanna continued their conversation as if no one else was present.

Hanna dug a sheaf of parchment out of her satchel. Rudi recognised the seal on it as that of Baron Hendryk's College of Navigation and Sea Magics, the great university in Marienburg that, Wastelanders at least believed, rivalled the more famous centres of learning in Altdorf and Nuln.

'I was a student of magic in Marienburg,' Hanna said, waving the papers in front of the wizard's face, 'and I've come all the way to Altdorf to study at the Imperial Colleges.' For a moment, a flicker of desperation appeared in her eyes. 'Please, I need to find a refuge. I've already escaped the witch hunters once, and I might not be so lucky next time.'

'Well, you've certainly made a courageous decision.' The Amethyst mage nodded encouragingly. 'A wise one, too, despite the risks you took in coming here. The training you'd get in Marienburg would be flawed at best. Little more use than hedge magic. Of course, the witch hunters wouldn't recognise a licence issued by anyone other than an Imperial College in any case.' That meant that Kris wouldn't be coming to Altdorf any time soon, Rudi realised, and then felt ashamed at the brief flare of exultation that had accompanied the thought.

'That's why I need someone to help me,' Hanna said earnestly, something of her old volatile nature threatening to break through. The pale-eyed wizard watched her fight down the impulse to raise her voice with detached interest. After a moment, Hanna unclenched her fists. 'I need to find a college that will take me, before the witch hunters track me down.'

'You do have a strand of death in your aura,' Hollobach said, 'but other winds blow far more strongly around you.' For a moment, Rudi thought he detected an air of uncertainty in the mage's voice, although his intonation was so dry that it was hard to be sure. 'My advice would be to seek out the Bright College. If anyone can help you, it would be them.'

'Thank you.' Hanna said, her whole face radiating relief. 'Where can I find it?'

'On the eastern edge of the city, although if you're really suited, it might be truer to say that the college will find you.' The mage stepped past her, and paused in the doorway, with a final nod at von Eckstein. 'Until later.'

'I'll send word,' the nobleman promised. He looked quizzically at Hanna, as if evaluating a new addition to his collection of art. 'So, you're a hedge witch.'

'So they tell me,' Hanna said shortly.

'Just as well,' Fritz put in. 'The Fog Walkers sent a shadow mage after us, and she took him down without breaking sweat.'

'A shadow mage?' Von Eckstein shook his head. 'I seriously doubt that, the shadowmancers' loyalty to the Emperor is unparalleled. One of their home-grown dabblers from Baron Hendryk's, with a few spells copied or stolen from the Grey College, I would imagine.' He returned to his desk, and gestured to the chairs scattered around the room. 'I'd be very interested to hear about it, though, and the other attacks you mentioned.' Rudi and Hanna seated themselves, followed a moment later by Mathilde and Fritz. No one, Rudi noted, seemed particularly keen to claim the chair so recently occupied by Magister Hollobach. Von Eckstein lifted a small silver bell from beside his inkstand, and rang it. 'It sounds like a long story, so I think perhaps a little refreshment before we begin.'

CHAPTER FOURTEEN

THE AFTERNOON WAS well advanced by the time that Rudi and Hanna had finished a suitably abridged account of their journey up the Reik, and Rudi was grateful for the food that von Eckstein had ordered before they began. The meal itself had been simple enough, a platter of bread, cheese and fruit, accompanied by a flagon of wine, which von Eckstein had discreetly avoided in favour of the contents of a carafe already sitting inconspicuously on a side table, but the flavours and textures had been of a quality that Rudi had never before experienced.

Hanna had accepted the wine dubiously, waiting until Rudi had taken a mouthful of his own before sipping cautiously at it. Having tried the drink before, during his meal with Fritz in Marienburg, Rudi had felt no such reservations. The vintage was a little fruitier than the bottle he'd shared with the simpleton at the Gull and Trident, but just as refreshing, and it complemented the food perfectly.

'It seems Fritz was right,' von Eckstein said at last. 'We were lucky you decided to leave Marienburg when you did.' Though he was undoubtedly astute enough to have realised there was much they were leaving out of their account, to Rudi's relief the nobleman didn't press the point, preferring to concentrate his questioning on their encounters with the agents of Marienburg. Instead, he looked at Hanna. 'I hope you fare well enough at the Bright College to feel that the rigours of the journey were worth enduring.' Encouraged by his matter-of-fact acceptance of her gifts, the young sorceress had been uncharacteristically forthcoming about her part in the events that had brought them there, even though there was still much she'd glossed over.

'So do I,' Hanna said, trying to sound casual, but failing to conceal her nervousness at the prospect. Before she could say more, they were interrupted by a knock on the study door.

'Enter,' von Eckstein called. Rudi assumed at first that the servant who stepped into the room was there to clear the dishes, but the man ignored the scattered remains of the meal they'd shared, crossing the room to address the nobleman instead, in hushed and urgent tones. Unlike the girl who had brought the food to the study, he was dressed in full livery, the elaborate heraldry embroidered on it clearly indicating that he was someone of consequence among the household staff.

'There's a carter downstairs with a box, my lord, insisting that you be informed at once of his arrival. I told him you were busy, but he claims that those were his express instructions from your personal representative.' As he spoke the last words, he glanced at Fritz, his expression studiously neutral. The nobleman nodded.

'They were. Thank you, Albrecht. If you would be so good, relieve the fellow of his burden, and arrange for someone to bring it up here right away?'

'At once, my lord.' Keeping whatever opinions he might have about the matter to himself, Albrecht departed, with a faintly curious look at Rudi and Hanna. No doubt he was used to his master's covert activities on behalf of the Empire, bringing all kinds of apparently incongruous people into his inner sanctum, and knew better than to speculate or ask.

'Good.' Von Eckstein cleared some papers from the surface of his desk, and waited impatiently until a couple of footmen had heaved a large wooden box into the room and departed. 'I've been waiting for this.' He gestured to the roughly nailed crate, which seemed somehow vaguely familiar, although Rudi couldn't quite put his finger on where he might have seen it before. 'Fritz, if I could prevail on your strong right arm?'

'Right away, sir.' The muscular youth drew the knife from his belt and levered for a moment at the raw planking. With a splintering of wood and the squeaking of nails, the lid came free.

'Excellent.' Von Eckstein burrowed in the crate, displacing a copious amount of straw, which he scattered across the immaculate Arabyan rug without a moment's thought for the mess it created. 'Ah, here we are – quite hideous.' He pulled out a heavy-lidded baking dish of crudely glazed earthenware, the sort of thing that Rudi was accustomed to seeing in taverns. In these refined surroundings it looked utterly misplaced. 'This is the one?'

'I think so,' Fritz said. 'There were two or three in there, but that's the one nearest the top.'

Rudi nodded, understanding at last. This must be one of the boxes of pottery that Shenk had taken aboard the *Reikmaiden* in Carroburg. Fritz had obviously concealed the package inside it, replacing the lid afterwards, and instructed the captain to dispatch it directly to von Eckstein's house. While the Fog Walkers followed the visible messengers, Mathilde having no doubt used her chilly wait on the quayside to make sure their attention was on her, the precious contraband had been conveyed through the streets unnoticed.

'Well, let's take a look at it.' Von Eckstein removed the lid and upended the pot, catching the familiar oilskin package in his hand as it fell out into his upturned palm. He placed the dish back in the crate, and laid the package carefully on the surface of his desk before stepping back. 'Fritz, if you would?'

Without a word, Fritz stepped forwards, slitting the seal with the point of his dagger, and returning the weapon to his belt. He stood aside to make room for his master. Von Eckstein gestured for Rudi and Hanna to join him at the table.

'I'm sure you're both eager to see what you've been risking your lives to protect,' he said. Rudi was by no means sure that he was. The sense of dread he'd felt before at the sight of the oilskin packet was back again, and the thought of seeing what was inside it started his gut churning with apprehension. Nevertheless, he forced himself to step forwards, ignoring the sweat that broke out on the palms of his hands, and the spasms in his belly. For a moment he was sure that everyone else in the room was aware of his agitation, but with one exception, their attention was fixed on the package, because so much seemed to depend on it.

'I've already seen it,' Mathilde said, moving to guard the door with barely a glance at the table. This, above all, impressed Rudi with the gravity of the situation, and the magnitude of the trust von Eckstein seemed ready to place in them. If his bodyguard felt the need to take precautions here, of all places, the contraband must be valuable indeed.

Ignoring her, von Eckstein folded back the weather-proof cloth, and spread its contents out on the polished wooden surface. Hanna's breath stilled, her eyes widening with astonishment, while Rudi fought the impulse to turn and run, a blast of terror stronger than anything he could ever recall almost sweeping his legs out from under him. Trying to slow his hammering heart, he forced himself to look at the wonders laid out before his eyes.

In all, there were around half a dozen different items. Rudi's eyes skipped quickly over a couple of gems of almost impossible brilliance and depth of colour, and a series of small statuettes no bigger than his thumb, depicting creatures like none he'd ever seen before, all bearing marks of a script he didn't recognise. They had the soft, refulgent gleam of solid gold, and under any other circumstances would have attracted his undivided attention. This time, however, he barely noticed them. In the middle of the table lay two other objects: a flat disc of polished stone, about the size of a crown piece, so black and lustrous that the light in the room seemed to fall into it and be lost entirely, and a curious tangle of cords, knotted in dozens of places with a precision he instinctively knew must carry a wealth of meaning.

'What's that?' Hanna asked, stretching out a hand towards the peculiar stone, and then clearly thinking better of it.

Von Eckstein shrugged. 'I've no idea, but Hollobach seems eager to get his hands on it.' To Rudi's intense relief, he rewrapped the bundle of marvels from the ends of the world, and as the mysterious objects disappeared from sight, the feeling of dread they'd conjured up in him began to diminish.

'Where did they come from?' Hanna asked, clearly awestruck. Rudi couldn't even imagine how they'd looked to her magical senses. Von Eckstein shrugged again.

'Southern Lustria,' he said, 'one of the lost cities the reptile folk abandoned centuries ago. There was a temple there, full of stuff like this, apparently.'

'Apparently?' Hanna asked.

Von Eckstein sighed. 'The lizards take a dim view of tomb robbing. Not much more than this made it back, and whatever else there was, the elves kept. Under the circumstances, I felt it best not to press the matter. There's enough here to get the merchants' guilds salivating, and it doesn't hurt to keep Silvershine happy at the moment. We need him and his clan, and he knows it.'

'I'm surprised he didn't want that magic thing,' Hanna said. 'It must be worth a fortune.'

'Not to an elf,' said von Eckstein. 'Their mages have a different perspective on such things, but it certainly doesn't hurt to have something that the colleges here in Altdorf want.' He didn't elaborate, but Rudi was beginning to realise that, far from being remote bastions of intellectual endeavour, the Colleges of Magic were as bound up in the politics of the Empire as any other institution.

To his unspoken relief, the nobleman placed the packet of treasures in a drawer and locked it. As the small package disappeared from sight, Rudi felt the tension drain out of his body, leaving him feeling weak and enervated.

'Talking of which,' Hanna said, with a glance through the window at the lengthening shadows. 'I'd better get moving if I'm going to find the Bright College before dark.'

'I suppose you had,' von Eckstein said guardedly.

'Where are you going to be staying?' Fritz asked ingenuously. 'Have you found a room anywhere yet?' Hanna shrugged.

'If they take me in, that won't be a problem,' she said. Von Eckstein nodded.

'That's true. All the colleges prefer to keep their apprentices on the premises. At least until they're sure they're not a danger to themselves or anyone else.'

'What if they turn you down?' Fritz persisted. Hanna's jaw tightened.

'Then you'll be far better off not knowing where I am,' she said. Fritz continued to look puzzled, although everyone else present nodded sombrely. If the colleges refused her sanctuary, the girl would continue to be a target for every witch hunter in the Empire.

'What about you?' Mathilde asked Rudi. He shrugged, taken by surprise. Carried along by the flow of events, he hadn't really thought about it until now.

'I'm looking for some relatives in Altdorf,' he said. 'At least, I think they might be related.' He hesitated. Now he was so close to his goal, the practicalities of trying to find somewhere to eat and sleep seemed almost irrelevant. 'Maybe I can find something close to them.' That sounded feeble even to him. In his heart, he knew, he had hoped to find some kind of acceptance from the von Kariens, whoever they might turn out to be, perhaps even to be taken in by them. He was forced to concede now that it was an idle dream, even more desperate and tenuous than Hanna's.

'There's a place near here that's not too bad,' Mathilde said. 'The Cordwainer's Last. I drink in there sometimes. Full of 'prentices and burghers on the make, but the ale's all right, and the rooms are clean.'

'How do you know about the rooms?' Fritz asked. Mathilde grinned.

'Some things I don't want to bring home, if you know what I mean.' She shot a look at her fiancé, in which embarrassment and reassurance mingled awkwardly. 'Didn't, that is. I mean, I hadn't even met you the last time I was here.' She turned back to Rudi, seizing on the change of subject like a drowning sailor suddenly noticing a passing log. 'So, who are these relatives of yours anyway?'

'If they are relatives,' Rudi said. He'd skated over his reasons for leaving Marienburg in his account of their voyage up the Reik, contriving to give the impression that he was accompanying Hanna out of concern for her safety, which was true enough, and only alluding to his own business in Altdorf in passing. More interested in whatever shreds of information they could recall about their encounters with the Fog Walkers, von Eckstein hadn't pressed the point. Now that he was on the point of putting Fritz's assurances of the nobleman's assistance to the test, he found himself hesitating. 'Does the name von Karien mean anything to you?'

'Von Karien?' Despite years of experience in the art of diplomatic evasion, von Eckstein couldn't keep a trace of surprise from his voice. 'Are you sure that's the right name?'

Rudi nodded. 'Reasonably sure. There was a lawyer in Marienburg, who had some papers mentioning them.'

'I see.' von Eckstein nodded slowly. 'Well, I've met Osric von Karien a couple of times. He's the current graf, as you probably know.' His voice remained tinged with doubt. 'But so far as I was aware, he's the last surviving member of his family.'

'I know.' Rudi nodded gravely. 'I heard he inherited the title from his cousin, after the old graf was executed.' As he spoke, it occurred to him for the first time that he had no idea of the name of the man who, if his suspicions were right, had been his father.

'Not just executed,' von Eckstein said, 'burned for heresy, along with his entire family.' He looked narrowly at Rudi. 'If you really are related to them, it might be wiser not to pursue the matter any further.'

Rudi shook his head. 'I've come too far to turn back,' he said, 'and besides, this Osric must have been proved innocent, whatever his cousin did, or he would have been burned too, wouldn't he?'

Von Eckstein nodded, conceding the point. 'His innocence was generally felt to be beyond doubt,' he said, 'and his actions since would appear to confirm it, but the family name remains indelibly tainted. No doubt it's best that it dies with him.'

'He might be happy to find that he's not alone in the world after all,' Rudi said.

Von Eckstein rubbed his chin thoughtfully, clearly not convinced of that, but tacitly conceding that Rudi wouldn't be deterred by anything else he might say on the subject.

The nobleman sighed. 'I would advise you most strongly against pursuing this,' he said heavily, 'but if I can't convince you to drop the matter, at least allow me to write you a letter of introduction. Osric von Karien is not a man to take the news that someone is making enquiries about him idly, and would certainly be moved to take action as soon as he heard you were doing so. At least if you approach him openly, he won't be unnecessarily antagonised.'

'Thank you,' Rudi said, trying to absorb the implications of this. It sounded as if von Karien was some kind of recluse, trying to live down the legacy of his cousin's heretical activities as best he could, but still retaining some measure of influence.

'Don't thank me until you've met the man,' von Eckstein said dryly, and Mathilde nodded in agreement, clearly sharing his opinion. Nevertheless, Rudi couldn't shake a rising sense of euphoria as the nobleman dipped a quill into his inkpot and wrote rapidly on a sheet of thick paper. 'Can you read?'

'Yes,' Rudi said proudly. Von Eckstein nodded, folded the letter, and pressed his ring into the blob of molten wax that he'd dripped across the join. Satisfied that the wax had hardened, he picked up the quill again, and scribbled a few lines across the outside of the message.

'Good. Here are directions from the Bright College. It's a well-known landmark, so you shouldn't have too much trouble finding the house from there.' He glanced across the room at Hanna. 'I assume you've no objection to Rudi accompanying you that far?'

'None at all,' Hanna said, looking much happier all of a sudden. 'I'd be glad of the company.'

'I could show you the way,' Mathilde offered, and looked at von Eckstein for permission.

The nobleman shook his head. 'I need you to take a message in the opposite direction. The sooner Hollobach takes possession of that little trinket the happier I'll be.' He glanced involuntarily at the desk drawer as he spoke, and his bodyguard echoed the gesture. 'Take Fritz with you. The sooner he begins to find his way around the city the better.'

'That thing's magic?' Fritz asked, looking surprised.

Von Eckstein nodded. 'And powerful,' he said, 'so they tell me.'

'You have no idea,' Hanna confirmed.

CHAPTER FIFTEEN

As RUDI AND Hanna left the sanctuary of von Eckstein's estate, the gate they'd entered the hidden house and gardens by closing behind them with a solid-sounding *thunk!*, the noise and stench of the city rushed in upon them again like a breaking wave. After the haven of tranquillity they'd just experienced, the shock was disorientating, even inured to the sights and sounds of the city as they'd become after their months of urban living in Marienburg.

'Where to?' Rudi asked, hesitating on the verge of immersing himself in the stream of hurrying figures channelled between the tall, narrow buildings he was beginning to associate with the capital city of the Empire. Hanna shrugged.

'East, apparently,' she said. Mathilde had given them slightly more precise directions before bidding them farewell, although they were still as vague as most instructions for finding somewhere specific in the city seemed to be. 'If we can find the Koenigsplatz, we should be all right from there.'

'I guess so,' Rudi said, trying to keep a taint of doubt from his voice. After all, if the Bright College, or to be more precise the site of it, was distinctive enough to be a major landmark, it couldn't be that hard to find. The uncomfortable thought came to him that if he was wrong, he might never find von Karien's house either. The peculiar way the magical auras surrounding the various colleges affected the topography of the city meant that directions to anywhere always started from a particular fixed point, and would be all but useless if the landmark in question couldn't be found.

Luckily, they were able to locate the Koenigsplatz without too much difficulty. After several minutes of shoving and sidestepping through the ever-present crush of bodies, Rudi at last caught sight of the famous statue over the heads of the crowd. The Emperor was mounted on a griffon, his sword held aloft in a suitably heroic pose, which would probably have pitched him over the creature's neck to the ground if he'd ever been incautious enough to try it while airborne. Rudi pointed.

'This way!' With Hanna at his heels, he forced his way into the wide open space, finding a few square feet of relative calm in the lee of the massive plinth. He glanced up, hoping to read the inscription, but the sinking sun struck hard from the gilded lettering, rendering it unintelligible. He wasn't even sure if this was supposed to be Karl Franz himself, or his father Luit-pold. Or Magnus the Pious, come to that, whose foresight had established the Colleges of Magic in the first place. That reminded him. 'Where to now?'

'That way.' Hanna pointed, following the direction indicated by the shadow of the statue, as if it was a compass needle. At first, Rudi thought she must be mistaken. The main routes in and out of the Koenigsplatz were on the north side, leading to the main gate of the city, and the south, after the thor-oughfare had split in two to flow around the gigantic sculpture, as if it was a tree root in a stream. The streets in the direction Hanna had indicated seemed small by comparison, little more than alleyways, but the girl seemed sure of herself, so Rudi simply nodded, and launched himself into the milling crowds again. To his battered senses, it seemed as if half of the Empire, if not the entire Old World, had congregated there, hawking wares of dubious provenance, arguing in tongues he hadn't heard even in Marienburg, and in one or two cases picking the pockets of the unwary.

'Fresh pies! Rumster's Originals! Get 'em while they're hot!' A halfling-sized pushcart rammed into his shins, its owner apparently so busy scanning the forest of knees surrounding him for potential cus-tomers that he'd forgotten to watch where he was going. 'Oops, sorry sir, my fault I'm sure.'

'Don't mention it.' Rudi shot out a hand without looking, finding to his complete lack of surprise that a second halfling was attempting to lift the flap of his belt pouch. Grasping the tiny wrist, he dragged the miscreant around and into view. 'You need to get another routine, lads. Distract and lift was old when Sigmar was in swaddling.'

'I dunno what you're talking about,' the pie vendor said, in tones of aggrieved innocence. 'I've never seen this ruffian before in my life, have I, Ned?'

'No,' his confederate confirmed, wriggling in Rudi's grasp. 'You're a witness, Peasemold. This great lummox just assaulted me for no reason at all. Be off with you, or I'll call a watchman!'

'He *is* a watchman,' Hanna said, with a trace of amusement.

Ned stopped squirming, and Peasemold's jaw went slack.

'I'm sure we can sort this out,' the pie vendor said, back peddling hastily. 'Just a little misunderstanding, that's all. Have a pie, on me, your lady friend too.'

'Thanks, but no.' Rudi put Ned down, and the would-be pickpocket scurried behind his friend, keeping the cart between himself and the possibility of further retribution. 'If I did, I'd have to take you in for attempted poisoning too, most likely.' He shrugged, content to have kept his money and made his point. 'Just don't let me catch you at it again.'

'No sir. Thank you, sir. Ranald bless you.' The halflings knuckled their forelocks and scurried off, vanishing into the crowd. A moment later, Rudi heard 'Oops, sorry, madam. My fault I'm sure,' echoing through the intervening bodies.

'Maybe you could join the watch here,' Hanna said. 'You were a good Cap in Marienburg.'

'Maybe I could,' Rudi said. He supposed he'd have to find some way of earning a living while he was in

Altdorf, but had no real desire to linger there once his
business in the city was concluded. Hanna would be
safe from the witch hunters as soon as a college took
her in, but Gerhard would still be after him, of that
much he was certain. Once again, he felt the woods
and forests of the Empire calling him, and resolved to
find refuge in the wilderness as soon as he could.

As they drew nearer to the street that Hanna had
selected, he realised that the sheer scale of the
Koenigsplatz had fooled him. The thoroughfare was
as wide as many of the ones he'd been familiar with
in Marienburg. They were just as crowded as the other
streets he'd seen in Altdorf, and just as cosmopolitan.
Within a hundred yards, they passed a shop selling
exotic rugs and tapestries, and a dark-skinned merchant pedalled pungent spices, the odour of which
endured even through the all-pervading street stench
of stale perspiration and ordure, and before which
Hanna paused with an expression of deep interest.
Further along was a blacksmith's forge in which a
sweat-slicked dwarf, stripped to the waist to reveal a
plethora of peculiar tattoos, hammered at a lump of
glowing iron with an expression of deep concentration.

'I suppose we must be getting nearer,' Hanna said
after a while. The streets had narrowed, the businesses
becoming more mundane, and the houses thinner,
though no less tall. Mindful of their progress from the
docks, Rudi kept an eye out for passers-by who
seemed to know Hanna for what she was, and noted
an increasing number of people who turned to look at
her with controlled and unobtrusive movements.

More of the ones he noticed seemed to be in red or orange robes, and he began to wonder if her choice of dress was entirely coincidental. She certainly looked the part, he thought, even if she wasn't actually a fire mage yet.

'Look.' Hanna paused in the middle of a wide stone bridge. Unlike the ones Rudi had grown used to in Marienburg, it was edged for the most part with a simple parapet, rather than being choked by buildings. She leaned on the balustrade, and pointed. Beneath them, a broad stretch of river flowed, confined by stone embankments, but still wide enough for two riverboats to pass one another unimpeded with room to spare. 'Shenk didn't waste much time, did he?' Sure enough, the *Reikmaiden* was making her way slowly upstream, navigating cautiously between the piers of the bridges obstructing the route.

'Evidently not,' Rudi said, quietly sympathising with the skipper's desire to get out of town as quickly as possible. He shrugged. 'Can't really blame him though, can you? If I was him, I'd want to put as much distance as I could between myself and the Fog Walkers for a while, just to be on the safe side.'

'Guess that's why he's heading up the Talabec,' Hanna said, waving. One of the figures on deck glanced up and returned the greeting, grinning with delighted recognition. It was Pieter, his arm still strapped up. Whether he was about to point their former passengers out to anyone else on board, Rudi would never know. As the deckhand turned to speak to someone, the *Reikmaiden* passed majestically between the pillars of the next bridge along, which, rather more conventionally, supported a townhouse or two, and vanished from sight. 'By the time he's been up to Kislev and back they'll have forgotten all about him.' Rudi rather doubted that, but it wasn't his problem, so he simply shrugged.

'We'd better get moving,' he said. The shadows had lengthened noticeably, and the air was growing chill. He retrieved his woollen cap from his pack, and pulled it down over his ears gratefully. It was going to be cold tonight, he could tell, discerning the tang of frost in the air even over the reek of the sewage in the gutters.

'I suppose so,' Hanna said, and began walking again. If he hadn't known her so well, Rudi would probably have missed the faint hesitation in her voice, and the nervousness it betrayed.

'You'll be fine,' he said, reaching out to squeeze her hand for a moment. It felt warm to the touch, a little more so than he might have expected given the chill in the air, and he assumed she must be using her abilities to keep herself comfortable despite her relatively immodest attire. Perhaps it was intentional, a visible demonstration of her powers, he thought, or perhaps the trick had simply become so much second nature that she barely realised she was doing it. 'They're bound to see how talented you are.'

'You're right, of course,' Hanna said, returning the pressure for a moment before retrieving her hand. She seemed encouraged by his words, striding out a little more confidently, but her tone was still uncertain.

This side of the Talabec, the streets had grown even narrower, the shops replaced mainly by taverns or

rooming houses, and the few that remained stocking
little more than staple foodstuffs and other items of
basic utility. Orange robes were still prevalent among
the passers-by, so Rudi remained confident that they
hadn't strayed from the route that they ought to be
following.

'It can't be much further,' he said, and then stopped,
staring ahead in sudden disbelief. For the last few
minutes the ever-present crowd around them had
been thinning out, but preoccupied as he was the sig-
nificance of that hadn't really registered, other than as
a vague sense of relief that he didn't have to keep
using his elbows to make a reasonable amount of
headway. A few yards in front of him, the street had
simply ended. Instead of cobbles and buildings, a vast
open space, carpeted with ash and littered with the
remains of burned-out structures, stretched away in
front of them. Far in the distance, the jumble of
houses and businesses resumed, and beyond them,
the city wall loomed, but in between, and stretching
for hundreds of yards in every direction, there was
nothing but desolation.

'I think we've arrived,' Hanna said dryly, leading the
way confidently into the gently smouldering ruins.
Her feet left deep prints in the carpet of ash, and as he
followed her, Rudi felt his boots sinking almost to his
ankles with every step, but when he turned to check
his bearings, the thick grey blanket lay pristine and
unmarked behind them. He felt the hairs on the back
of his neck beginning to stir.

'Well it *was* here,' Rudi said hesitantly. He glanced
around, uncomfortably reminded of the burning farm

cottage that he'd stumbled across outside Kohlstadt. Some of the beams of the collapsed houses around them still smoked lazily, as if they hadn't quite been extinguished, and little pockets of glowing embers rippled the air around them like dancing phantoms, testament to their residual heat. 'Do you think it's been destroyed?'

'No,' Hanna said decisively. 'Come on, this way.' The deeper they ventured into the zone of desolation, the more confident she seemed to become. At a loss for anything else to do, Rudi followed on behind her, beginning to wonder what he was doing here at all. What little he'd seen of sorcery so far left him inclined to avoid it, not head straight towards one of the biggest concentrations of mystical energy in the whole of the Empire. If it hadn't been for the loyalty he felt to Hanna, and the desire to see her safe, he would probably have turned and run. 'There you are. What did I tell you?'

Hanna's voice was triumphant, and for a moment, Rudi couldn't understand her euphoria. Then he took another step himself, and suddenly the College was right there in front of them, shimmering into existence like a solidifying heat haze.

'Sigmar preserve us,' he whispered. The building was vast, larger than almost anything he'd ever seen in his life. Perhaps the façade of Baron Hendryk's College in Marienburg, or the staadholder's palace there, rivalled it in size, but in form, it exuded a simplicity and power that made them both look like peasants' huts. Huge towers rose into the smoke-blackened sky, vivid roaring flames apparently bursting from their summits to tint the whole area around the college the colour of perpetual sunset. A wall of stone, the colour of the iron the dwarf had been hammering, soared overhead, at least to the height of the ramparts protecting the city itself, and a gate of dully-glowing metal stood squarely in the centre of it. 'What do we do now?'

'Ask to see someone,' Hanna said, striding forwards, her confidence apparently growing with every step. Rudi followed, feeling the heat beating back at him from the vast portal in the wall ahead. 'Do you think we should knock?'

'There's no point in disturbing the gatekeeper unnecessarily,' a new voice said. A man stepped out from behind a tumbled heap of masonry, which had presumably once been a house. He was dressed in red and orange robes, and his hair and beard were both the colour of flickering flames. 'I happened to be on my way into the city when I noticed your approach. State your business.'

'I want to study with the Bright College,' Hanna said. 'I was a licensed student of magic in Marienburg, and…'

'I see.' The Bright wizard took a step forward, and stared at the girl intently. Determined not to seem intimidated, Hanna gazed levelly back, although Rudi was sure the mage was studying her with something more than normal sight. After a moment, the man shook his head. 'I'm afraid not. Application denied.'

'Now wait just a minute!' Hanna said, her voice rising. 'I've travelled all the way from Marienburg for this. If you think I'm just going to turn around and take my chances with the witch hunters because you can't be bothered to wake up your porter, you've got another think coming! I demand to see someone in authority!'

'I *am* in authority,' the wizard said. 'Like all magisters, I'm empowered to speak for the order to which I belong, and I would be grossly derelict in my duty if I let a Chaos-tainted witch set foot inside the college.' Hanna's fists clenched, and her jaw tightened.

'I'm not a witch!' she said, her voice tight with anger, clearly fighting the impulse to shout. 'I'm a pyromancer like you! I need training to control my gift, that's all!'

The wizard shook his head, a trace of regret entering his voice for the first time.

'The red wind blows strongly around you, that's true, but so does something else. I can quite clearly see the stain of *dhar* in your aura, and it's gone far too deep to control or eradicate.'

'You can see what?' Rudi asked, more in the hope of keeping the conversation reasonable than because he expected an answer he could hope to understand. Hollobach had implied that this was the only college that Hanna might be qualified for, and if they refused to take her, she was surely doomed. If she lost her temper now, it would all be over. The fire mage looked at him curiously, as if he'd only just registered his presence. Perhaps he had.

'The dark wind of magic.' The man's voice softened a little more. 'Your friend has a strong natural affinity for pyromancy, it's true, and to anyone with the sight from a different college, the strength of the red wind around her would tend to obscure anything else, but for one of the Bright Order, it's all too obvious.' He turned back to Hanna. 'If you'd come to us earlier, we might have been able to help you, but I'm afraid the taint goes too deep for that now.'

'I see.' Hanna nodded tightly. Rudi expected her to argue, grow angry, and even threaten the man. The old Hanna might have done, but the changes that the last few months had wrought in her evidently went further than he suspected. 'I'm sorry to have wasted your time.' She turned. 'Come on, Rudi, we're going.'

'I'm afraid I can't allow that,' the wizard said. His posture shifted subtly, and Rudi felt the hairs on the back of his head begin to rise, his scalp tingling as if a thunderstorm was imminent.

'You can't stop me,' Hanna replied, her voice level. To Rudi's horror, a seething ball of red flame appeared in the air in front of her, hissing and spitting as it hovered in the space between them and the mage.

The wizard's expression hardened.

'You dare to call on the power of the Changer here? You're more corrupted than I thought.' He muttered something under his breath, and the flames vanished. A moment later, a sword materialised in his hand, apparently composed of fire itself, and he took a step towards Hanna, raising the supernatural weapon.

'Leave her alone!' Rudi shouted, drawing his own sword by reflex. A part of his mind watched in wonderment as he interposed himself between the mage and the girl, feeling the heat of the blazing blade against his skin. An expression of irritated surprise crossed the wizard's face.

'Out of the way, boy.' He struck, a lazy blow, clearly not expecting Rudi to stand his ground. Rudi countered reflexively, expecting the flames to sweep around the thin strip of steel and across him, but the parry connected with something that felt physical, redirecting the strike in the nick of time. A blast of heat seared past his face, and he kicked out, taking the wizard in the back of the knee as he stepped around him to avoid the blow. With a bellow of hurt surprise, the man fell, the impact raising a cloud of ash that hung in the air between them, coating Rudi's throat, and leaving his eyes stinging from the choking grit.

'Hanna, run!' He turned, expecting the girl to have taken advantage of the momentary distraction to escape, but she was holding her ground, her face tense. The bronze gate was opening, and, in the distance, other orange-robed figures could be seen running through the ashes towards them, bobbing and weaving like living flames. Clearly, despite her jibe to the magister, the gatekeeper hadn't been neglecting his duty after all.

'I've done with running,' she said flatly. Rudi took a step back to stand by her shoulder, his blade raised to fend off the wizard, who was clambering to his feet. The man's face was contorted with rage, his robes mottled with grey powder, and his insubstantial sword hissed gently as he brought it up to a guard position. He clearly knew something of swordplay, and wasn't about to make the mistake of underestimating Rudi for a second time.

'Then die where you stand, witch.' He moved into the attack again, a little more warily, but sure of the support of his approaching colleagues.

Hanna screamed something incomprehensible, which seemed to vibrate through every bone in Rudi's skeleton, and he was barely able to deflect the blazing weapon once more. Had it not been for his extensive experience of street fighting, which allowed instinct to take over, he knew he wouldn't have made it at all. Exploiting the opening he'd made, he kicked out again, driving the wizard back with a boot to the midriff.

Abruptly, the man was enveloped in a nimbus of emerald fire. Rudi flinched, expecting him to immolate, like the skaven that Hanna had killed, or the soldiers that Greta had struck down on the moors, but the wizard seemed completely unharmed. It appeared that Bright wizards were immune to pyromancy, which now he came to think about it wasn't all that surprising. With a nervous glance at the approaching mages, who seemed to have closed the distance far more quickly than he would have thought possible, he shifted his stance, and prepared for his opponent's next onslaught.

'Get out of here. I'll hold them off.' To Rudi's astonishment, the wizard turned to face his approaching colleagues. The flaming sword vanished as abruptly as it had appeared, and a sheet of flame burst into existence, cutting off the reinforcements from the college, snapping and twisting like a banner in the wind.

'Thanks,' Hanna said, with a feral grin. She grabbed Rudi's arm, and tugged him into motion. 'Come on, we haven't got much time.' His head reeling, Rudi began to run back the way they'd come.

'What did you do?' he asked. For a moment, Hanna looked confused.

'I'm not really sure,' she said at last, their footfalls stumbling through the carpet of ash. 'It was like when the skaven attacked us, and I found I could do the fireball spell. It just appeared in my head, and I knew I could cast it. I've affected his mind, so he thinks his friends are enemies, and we're on his side.'

'I see.' Rudi stole a glance back behind them. From the flashes in the distance, the deluded mage was still making a fight of it. 'Will it last long?'

'I don't know,' Hanna said, as their footsteps began to clatter on cobbles again. Somehow, in the handful of minutes that Rudi could have sworn was all they'd spent in the wilderness of ash, night had fallen, the streets in the distance illuminated by flaring sconces, and the slivers of light leaking around the edges of doors and shutters. She shrugged, a malicious smile appearing on her face. 'I don't suppose he will, though.'

'What will you do now?' Rudi asked, slowing their pace to a more normal one as they approached the inhabited area again, hoping to blend into the ever-present crowd. Raucous laughter drifted from a couple of nearby taverns, mocking the ruination of Hanna's hopes. He could barely imagine the disappointment that the girl must be feeling. Instead of a refuge, she had only found more enemies. 'Where will you go?'

'I'll be fine,' Hanna said, with a resolution that surprised him. 'I pretty much expected this to happen anyway.'

'You did?' Rudi fought to keep the astonishment from his voice. Hanna nodded.

'I spoke to Gofrey on the boat. He warned me that the colleges might be afraid of anyone showing real talent. They want dutiful little apprentices who do what they're told, not powerful mages with minds of their own.'

'What did he suggest you do?' Rudi asked. 'He seemed to be part of a group of some kind, but he didn't want to say much about it.'

'In case he was wrong. I know.' Hanna nodded again. 'But he did say that the college would be watched. If something like this happened, the Silver Wheel would know, and take steps to help me.'

'What kind of steps?' Rudi asked. Hanna shrugged, looking slightly nonplussed.

'I don't know. Send someone to get in touch, I suppose.'

'I see.' Rudi nodded, scanning the sea of faces around them for any sign of recognition or complicity. 'Any idea how we're supposed to recognise them?'

'I don't think you'll have much trouble with that,' a new voice said quietly from the shadows of an alley mouth. It was soft and feminine, and vaguely familiar. Turning, his hand already on his sword hilt, Rudi struggled to identify it.

Hanna had no such difficulty, breaking into a run towards the half-obscured figure, wrapped in a hooded cloak against the evening chill. As Rudi followed, the lurking woman was briefly illuminated by a shaft of light that burst momentarily from an opening door. It only lasted an instant, but that was all it took. Then the alley mouth plunged back into darkness, obscuring the familiar face of Greta Reifenstahl once again.

CHAPTER SIXTEEN

'MOTHER!' HANNA FLUNG herself into Greta's arms, and the two women embraced one another fervently. Feeling uncomfortably intrusive, Rudi turned away from their emotional reunion, preferring to remain a few paces closer to the mouth of the alley where he could keep watch more easily. While Hanna and Greta continued their conversation in a hushed and excited undertone he scanned the street for any signs of unusual activity, fearing that if they lingered much longer they'd attract the attention of their enemies. After all, if the Silver Wheel, whoever they were, could keep a discreet eye on the Bright College without any-one noticing, then so might the witch hunters, eager to pounce on disappointed applicants like Hanna.

His jaw knotted at the thought. Even now, he couldn't quite believe the casual arrogance with which the magister they'd met had turned her away, without even giving her the chance to prove herself.

'Hanna, my love.' After a few moments Greta stepped away from her daughter's encircling arms, and smiled at her fondly. 'You're looking well.'

'I feel well.' A new strength seemed to be flowing through the girl. Her posture was relaxed and confident, despite the renewed threat to her life that was hanging over her, without even the hope of a reprieve. Rudi watched her as unobtrusively as he could, concerned that the effort of casting the mysterious spell that had turned the wizard against his own colleagues had fatigued her as much as the previous eruptions of spontaneous magic seemed to have done, but this time she seemed completely unaffected by the experience. She didn't even seem breathless after fleeing from the wilderness of ash. 'I'm growing more powerful by the day.'

Her voice seemed different too, Rudi thought. It had always sounded mellifluous enough to him, but it seemed richer now, with textures and harmonies in it that he couldn't really distinguish individually, but which were undeniably there. Greta nodded, with more than a trace of maternal pride.

'I could tell that. Precious few natural talents could best a college magister in a contest of power.'

'You saw that?' Rudi asked. He wasn't sure why he was so surprised. Greta had been turning up from time to time ever since the fugitives had left Kohlstadt, usually accompanied by the hulking mutant, Hans Katzenjammer. Every time she did so she helped them in some way, before vanishing again, usually leaving a pile of dead enemies behind her. Greta nodded in response. 'Then why didn't you do something to help?'

'There was no need,' the witch said. 'I knew Hanna was going to beat the arrogant fool. The Changer is the source of all magic. He's scarcely going to allow it to harm his chosen servants, is he?'

'Then Gerhard was right.' Rudi felt a sickening lurch in the pit of his stomach, unable to tear his eyes away from the horned sorceress. Part of him didn't even want to, that would mean looking at Hanna again, his friend and companion for the last few months, the one person in the world on whom he'd felt able to rely. 'You really are agents of Chaos.'

'Gerhard knows a lot less than he thinks he does,' Greta countered. 'You've seen him murder and terrorise, just on the suspicion that someone might have glimpsed a little of the truth he tries so hard to suppress. Have you forgotten what he did to Hans's mother?'

Rudi hadn't. The image of Frau Katzenjammer, eyes wide with shock, still trying to comprehend what had happened to her son, even as Gerhard slit her throat, rose up vividly in his mind. He shook his head, trying to dispel the unsettling vision.

'Of course not, but...' He could scarcely force the words out. He took a step deeper into the darkness of the alleyway, and lowered his voice, afraid of being overheard by the distant revellers, whose innocent merriment seemed so ironic a counterpoint to the maelstrom of horror that he felt sweeping over him. 'You worship the Dark Gods!'

'Only one of them,' Greta said, 'and whatever you've been told, unlike the others, Tzeentch is essentially benign.'

'Tell that to the Ostlanders!' Rudi snapped. 'He didn't seem all that benign to them when his armies were slaughtering their way across the Empire!'

For the first time, Greta's face clouded a little. 'Not all change is subtle or peaceful,' she said, 'but the real damage was done by the servants of the other three. They truly do deserve the execration heaped on their names throughout the world.'

'You really are an acolyte of the Changer?' Hanna asked, doubt entering her voice for the first time. She stared at her mother in what seemed to Rudi to be honest perplexity.

Greta nodded. 'Of course I am. His greatest adversary is the Lord of Decay. How could I call myself a real healer if I didn't do all I could to confound the machinations of the bringers of disease? The more I called upon his aid, the more powerful I became, and the better able I was to help people. How can there possibly be anything wrong in that?'

Rudi's head spun, and he felt sick to his stomach. So much he hadn't wanted to acknowledge, had all but wilfully closed his mind to, began to make sense at last. Somehow, he knew, she was twisting things, cloaking her actions in a semblance of reason. It was the same kind of blindness that Gerhard had shown, he thought, an unassailable conviction that there was only one path to follow, and that any action was justified in the name of the greater good they claimed to be serving.

'That's why you tried to kill Magnus in Marienburg,' he said. 'He'd been spreading the plague in Kohlstadt, hadn't he? Those other people in the woods with him, you led the beastmen to them!' Despite himself, his voice was beginning to rise, and he fought it back to a whisper. 'You killed my father!'

'Your father died a long time ago, a long way from Kohlstadt,' Greta said calmly. 'As for Gunther, he was a decent man, snared by the lies of Nurgle, just as Magnus and the others were. If they'd been permitted to finish their ritual, something far worse than disease would have been unleashed, believe me.'

'I don't understand,' Hanna said. 'You mean Magnus really was the leader of a Chaos cult, just like Gerhard said?' Greta nodded. 'Rudi's fath... Gunther Walder was a member?'

'As I said, he was ensnared by the lies he was told.' Greta sighed, sadly. 'Nurgle promises his followers much. The more diseased they become, the stronger they feel. It's a seductive delusion.' She looked at a mangy cat that looked up from scavenging in the gutter just long enough to stare at them with cool disdain, before scuttling off into the shadows. 'You must have realised that, after seeing what Magnus had become in Marienburg.'

Rudi nodded, remembering the preternatural strength of the madman's ravaged body, and the degenerate creatures that had served him. There was something else: his adopted father's dogged insistence that he'd felt better and stronger than ever before, despite the clear signs of infection spreading from his injured arm.

'You realised what he was, and what he was doing?' Rudi asked.

'I suspected as much,' said Greta. 'I knew something was going on, and that he had secrets he didn't want revealed. Come to that, he never bothered to conceal the fact that he harboured doubts about me, but suspicion isn't proof, whatever Gerhard might think. The two of us circled one another for months, waiting for the other to slip up in some way and reveal their true allegiance. If I'd only had the courage to act sooner.' She sighed regretfully.

'You were right, he did think you knew something.' Rudi remembered the enigmatic note from Magnus that he'd discovered in the lawyer's office. 'I found a letter among van Crackenmeer's papers, one you missed when you searched the place after Hans had killed him.' He hesitated, waiting for the sorceress to confirm or deny it, but she said nothing. He tried to look her in the eye, but found he couldn't. The more intently he tried to focus on her face, the more it seemed to shimmer, remaining at the edges of his vision. When he went on, he couldn't quite keep the air of desperation from his voice. 'Do you know? Am I the von Karien heir?'

'You'll have to ask them that when you find them,' Greta said. 'The Changer maps everyone's path, but we all have to walk it alone. You'll know your destination when you reach it, but I can't show you any short cuts, I'm afraid.' She turned to her daughter. 'Come , my daughter. We have friends who can help us not far from here, and it wouldn't be polite to keep them waiting.'

As she turned away to follow her mother, Hanna hesitated, and Rudi caught her eye.

'Hanna, wait!'

The girl looked back at him, her expression a curious amalgam of doubt and hope. 'You can't go off with her just like that! You heard what she said. She's a Chaos worshipper, for Taal's sake!'

'She's my mother!' Hanna said fiercely. 'And she's kept us safe so far, in case you've forgotten.' For a moment, the flicker of uncertainty was back in her voice, and she forced it away with an obvious effort. 'Besides, where else can I go? The witch hunters will kill me on sight.'

'I don't think so, child.' Greta smiled maternally at her daughter. 'Your powers are growing all the time. Tzeentch gifted you with extra powers just when you needed them, and after what I saw in Marienburg, I suspect it's not the first time that's happened.' Remembering how Hanna had suddenly discovered the ability to throw fireballs when the skaven attacked them, Rudi felt she was probably right. 'The Changer has marked you already, and he protects his own. You'll soon be so powerful that you need never fear anyone again, and I can help you to walk that path.' The pride was back in her voice, along with a faintly rueful air. 'At least until you leave me behind.'

'I'll never do that.' Hanna's voice was decisive, and she linked arms with her mother. 'Where are we going?'

'Away from here,' Greta said. She turned to look at Rudi, who remained stupefied in the mouth of the alley, trying to assimilate all that he'd heard. 'I'm afraid you're better off not knowing where. You'll understand why soon enough.'

'Hanna!' Rudi shook off the paralysis that had him in its grip, and took a step forwards, reaching out a hand to hold her back. Before his fingers could close, he stumbled, his shins meeting something soft and yielding, which let out an unearthly screech as it shot away down the darkness of the alleyway. Cursing the cat that had tripped him, he regained his balance and looked around, but the momentary distraction had been enough. Hanna and her mother were gone.

SEARCHING FOR THE two women would be pointless, Rudi knew, but he still cast around the reeking alleyways for several minutes before accepting the inevitable and giving up. At length, and conscious that he was beginning to attract the attention of the local residents, he made his way back to the main street and, with his back to the wilderness of ash, studied the directions that von Eckstein had scribbled for him by the light of a guttering torch, clearly meant to illuminate the sign of a nearby tavern. They seemed simple enough, and after orientating himself with respect to the burned-out wasteland behind him, he set off, more or less retracing the route that he and Hanna had taken to get there.

At first, shaken by what had so recently happened, Rudi had to force himself to concentrate on finding the way. His thoughts kept returning to the girl, wondering if she was all right, and fearful for her safety. Soon, however, as he felt himself getting nearer to his destination and the answers he craved, a growing excitement took hold of him, and his pace quickened.

'Third on the left,' he reminded himself. None of the streets he passed had name plaques visible, but then most of the residents around here probably wouldn't have been able to make use of them anyway. Many of the people he passed wore patched and ragged garments, and the smell of excrement in the gutters seemed unusually strong. As it had on a few previous occasions, though, far from making him gag as he might reasonably have expected, the stench seemed almost pleasant, an effect, he assumed, of his growing hunger and the series of shocks he'd experienced since leaving the riverboat such a short time before.

Stepping around the contents of a chamber pot, which someone had flung from an upper window and which had missed him by inches, he started down the side street that he'd been looking for with renewed determination.

At first, Rudi thought he must have missed his way after all. The houses here were narrower and more cramped than any he'd yet seen, and crowded with people who spilled from windows and doors as if forcibly expelled by the pressure of their fellows within. Even at this hour, many of them were abroad, and all stared at him with barely concealed hostility. Clearly, strangers were a rarity here, although his muscular build and visible weapons were all the passport he needed to walk the length of the street without any overt challenge.

Scanning the buildings on either side in search of a clue as to their ownership, he found himself making eye contact with a woman loitering in front of one of the seething tenements. Even before she spoke, her dress, or lack of it, was enough to tell him what she was doing out there on a night as cold as this.

'Wanting a good time, dearie?' Even from this distance, Rudi could tell that her face was deeply lined beneath her thickly applied makeup, and she was missing a couple of teeth.

'I'm looking for someone,' he said diplomatically. The woman laughed, her years of practice almost managing to stifle the insincerity of it.

'Aren't we all, dear? Anyone in particular, or will Maggi do? You won't do better for tuppence round here, I guarantee.'

'Osric von Karien,' Rudi said. 'I was told he lives somewhere nearby?'

He read his answer in the ageing doxy's eyes even before she spoke, the pretence of friendliness vanishing like dew on a hot summer morning. Withdrawing a pace, she pointed to a house about twenty yards down the road.

'That one there.' She stared at him warily, and Rudi was suddenly reminded of the crone who'd thrown a brick at him when he tried to ask directions to Magnus's house in the Doodkanal. No one in the vicinity seemed quite that hostile, at any rate, but the brief conversation had clearly been overheard. The space around him suddenly seemed much greater, even in the narrow, crowded street, and as he looked around, gazes were suddenly and unobtrusively averted. It seemed that the family was indeed shunned, even in so unprepossessing a quarter as this; hardly the sort of place Rudi had expected to find the sole surviving member of a noble family, however minor their lineage.

'Thank you.' He dug a penny out of his purse. 'You've been very helpful.' He flicked the coin into the air, expecting the woman to catch it, but she flinched back, letting the metal disc fall unheeded into the filth choking the gutter between them. Feeling vaguely disconcerted, Rudi walked away, conscious of eyes upon him, and studied the house she'd indicated.

At first sight it was little different from any of its neighbours, looking somehow as if it had been jammed into a space too small for it, although as he approached the building Rudi became aware that it stood out from the others surrounding it in one significant respect at least. All the other houses he could see were seething with life, lamplight leaking from behind every shutter, accompanied by the sounds of human habitation: shouting, laughter, the crying of infants and the chatter of children. Von Karien's house, by comparison, was dark, deserted and desolate. Its shutters were firmly fastened, and its front door was thick and solid looking, in marked contrast to the flimsy timberwork visible along the rest of the street.

Forcing down the sudden stab of apprehension that the house was indeed empty, and that he'd made the journey here for nothing, Rudi walked up to the forbidding portal. It opened directly onto the street, and as he stood there in front of it the local inhabitants kept stepping around him as if he was cocooned inside an invisible barrier, instead of jostling past him as he might have expected.

A large, ornate knocker, in the shape of Sigmar's hammer, was mounted in the middle of the door. The workmanship was impressive, the decoration intricate, and it felt very solid in Rudi's hand. Taking a deep breath he lifted it, rapping several times. The noise it produced was surprisingly loud, audible even over the babble of the street, booming away into the depths of the dark, shuttered house.

Rudi waited for what seemed like a long time, but which was probably no more than a handful of minutes. Gradually, his stomach sinking slowly with the weight of disappointment, he began to accept that his initial impression had been the right one, and that the house was as deserted as it had first appeared. He was on the verge of turning away, and had just decided to knock again to make absolutely sure the place was empty, when the sound of a lock being turned arrested his attention.

'Yes?' The door opened, just wide enough to reveal a man, standing a pace or two inside the entrance hall. Rudi could make out little of the house's interior, as the hall itself was in darkness. A faint glow in the distance suggested lamplight, as if an interior door had been left ajar, but that was scarcely sufficient to see by. Even the man who'd answered his summons was indistinct, blending into the shadows within. Rudi could just make out the shape of a plain white shirt, dark trousers, and a pale face surmounted by closely cropped blond hair.

'I want to see Osric von Karien,' Rudi said, as decisively as he could, suddenly aware of how he must look in his battered and travel-stained clothes. The man smiled sardonically.

'Well, you've seen him.' He made as if to close the door. Before he was even aware of what he was doing, Rudi stepped forwards, blocking the doorway with his foot, and held out the letter addressed to von Karien, angling it so that von Eckstein's seal was clearly visible.

'I've a letter of introduction from the Graf von Eckstein,' he said, hardly able to believe that the man he was talking to wasn't a servant as he'd at first assumed. Aristocrats didn't answer their own front doors, did they? Von Karien, if that was who he really was, glanced at the missive.

'Run across something unexpected in one of his little plots again, has he?' The shadowy figure stood aside, and for the first time Rudi became aware that he'd been holding a dagger behind the door. 'You'd better come in, then. It's too dark to read out here anyway.' The empty hand gestured towards the glow of lamplight. 'After you.'

CHAPTER SEVENTEEN

THE HEAVY DOOR boomed closed behind them, echoes reverberating along the narrow passageway, and von Karien gestured towards the faint glow of light in the distance. Used to life in the forest, stalking and trapping game by moonlight, Rudi found his eyes adjusting quickly to the darkness, making out the shape of his strange host's shirt and pale face apparently floating in the gloom like a gigantic moth.

'This way.' Von Karien waited for Rudi to start moving ahead of him, the knife in his hand still held ready, as if anticipating treachery of some kind. After a moment's hesitation Rudi started walking, opening the distance between them instinctively to one where he would be able to turn and defend himself if he had to. This, he was suddenly sure, had been noted by the taciturn man behind him, but whether it would relieve or accentuate his manifest suspicion he couldn't tell.

The corridor was plain and unfurnished, in stark contrast to the opulence that he'd seen in von Eckstein's palatial residence. Even the entrance hall of Magnus's house in Kohlstadt, which had seemed lavish enough when the village was all he'd known of the world, had contained more furniture than this. The only thing breaking the monotony of the whitewashed wall was another symbol of Sigmar, a twin-tailed comet this time, almost exactly opposite the bottom tread of the narrow stairway, leading up into an unseen hallway choked with hovering shadows. Skirting it, Rudi pushed open the door ahead of him, limned by the soft glow of candlelight, and stepped into the room beyond.

This, too, was a complete surprise. He'd been expecting a parlour of some kind, like the one Magnus had used to receive his guests and conduct business in, but instead he found himself being ushered into a warm, well-lit kitchen. A worn wooden table stood in the middle of the room, three chairs drawn up to it, and a fourth pushed away, evidently the one von Karien had been occupying when he'd knocked on the door. A pewter plate, containing the remains of a stew, stood next to it, alongside a mug of ale and a chunk of bread. The aroma of food hit him at once, flooding his mouth with saliva, and his stomach growled softly.

'You've come quite a way.' Von Karien resumed his seat, and cut a piece off the loaf with his knife, while he looked at Rudi appraisingly.

'From Marienburg. I arrived in the city this morning,' said Rudi. Despite his desperate desire to find the answers he sought, which might only be minutes away, he couldn't help glancing at the pot on the stove. Von Karien jerked a perfunctory head at it.

'Help yourself.' He slit the seal on von Eckstein's letter, and skimmed the contents, while Rudi rummaged around looking for another plate. 'The cupboard behind you.'

'Thank you.' Rudi found another of the metal plates, and a spoon. There was more in the pot on the stove than he'd expected, and he ladled out a generous portion, surprised by how hungry he felt, and returned to the table. Von Karien pushed one of the chairs out with his foot, wordlessly inviting him to sit. It was the one next to his right hand, Rudi noted, which still held the knife. Placing the food carefully on the worn wooden surface, he slipped the bow, quiver and pack off his back, and propped them up against the nearest table leg.

'It says here that you want to see me on personal business,' von Karien said. He turned the paper over, his eyes narrowing. 'And he's directed you from the fire wizards' den. Did you have personal business with them too?' Rudi shook his head.

'He just seemed to think it was the best landmark around here to aim for, as I don't know the city. It's pretty hard to miss.' He took a mouthful of the stew as he spoke, hoping to mask any unease that he might have betrayed in his answer. The food was underdone, the lumps of meat chewy and the vegetables almost raw, but there was still a faint aftertaste of burning, where the pan had been left for too long without stirring. Nonetheless, it was warm and filling, and he found himself wolfing it down regardless. Von Karien regarded him with an expression of faint curiosity.

'That's true enough,' he conceded. If he noticed Rudi's evasion, he gave no sign of it. 'Walk here from the Wasteland, did you?' Rudi shook his head, his mouth full.

'I came up the Reik,' he said, indistinctly, 'on a boat. Why do you ask?' The pale-faced man shrugged.

'I'm not used to anyone eating my cooking with such obvious enthusiasm,' he said dryly.

'I've had worse,' Rudi assured him.

Von Karien regarded him appraisingly. 'I can believe it. You're obviously used to surviving outdoors.'

Surprised, Rudi looked up at him. 'How can you tell?'

'You're dressed like a forester, and you walk like someone used to stalking game.' The nobleman nodded at Rudi's pack. 'That's a symbol of Taal on the clasp there. Not something you see many city people with.'

'That's right.' Rudi was vaguely surprised at how easy conversation with the man seemed to be. Perhaps they really were related, he thought, with rising elation. Perhaps that accounted for it. 'I grew up in the woods, near a village called Kohlstadt, on the border of the Wasteland.' He watched von Karien's face carefully as he said the name, hoping to see a spark of recognition. None came. The pale face just stared at him intently, waiting for him to go on, and he was uncomfortably reminded of the expression on the face of the wizard who'd asked Hanna the nature of her business with the Bright Order.

'Never heard of it,' von Karien said, after the silence had lengthened between them. 'I take it that's why you moved on to Marienburg?'

'Sort of,' Rudi said, wondering how best to lead up to the purpose of his visit. 'My father died in a beast-man attack.'

'Beastmen?' A flicker of interest animated von Karien's face at last. 'You've actually seen them?'

'I've fought them,' Rudi said. 'Skaven too, if you know what they are.'

'I've spent some time in the wilderness myself,' said von Karien. 'I've few illusions left about the true state of the world.' That probably accounted for the number of religious symbols scattered around the house, Rudi thought. Now that his hunger had been assuaged enough for him to take a little more notice of his surroundings, he could see another hammerhead, hanging on the wall behind his host, and the candle-light gleamed from a chain around von Karien's neck. Something was concealed beneath his shirt, and Rudi would have bet most of the contents of his purse that it was another of the ubiquitous talismans. 'The min-ions of Chaos are everywhere, not just marching in the armies of the north.'

'I know.' Rudi nodded. 'I've fought them several times. Before he died, my father... although he wasn't my father really...' He hesitated, not quite sure how to proceed. Von Karien nodded encouragingly.

'Not your father? Then who was he?'

'He was a forester. He found me wandering in the woods when I was just a child, and took me in. No one ever knew who my real parents were, or what had happened to them. Except…' The memory of Gunther's last words, gasped out despite the terrible wounds he'd endured, rose up in his mind, making him hesitate, overwhelmed for a moment with a renewed sense of loss. With an effort of will he forced himself to go on. 'As he died, he told me there was someone in Marienburg who might know who my parents were.'

'So you went to Marienburg to find out.' Von Karien's expression was appraising again. 'Something of a shock to a country lad, I would have thought.'

'I got by,' Rudi said. 'I managed to get a job fairly quickly, so that helped.'

'Really?' Von Karien's voice took on a tinge of scepticism. 'I wouldn't have thought there was much call for woodcraft in Marienburg.'

'I was a Black Cap.' Rudi corrected himself, realising that his host was unlikely to be familiar with the Marienburg slang term. 'A member of the city watch.'

'I see.' Von Karien nodded slowly. 'Which is where you learned to stay out of reach of a knife so readily. I wondered about that.'

'You pick these things up,' Rudi said casually.

'You do if you're prudent. Did you find who you went there to look for?' asked von Karien.

'Sort of,' Rudi said, 'but he was completely insane. He tried to kill me.'

'Really?' The slate grey eyes were appraising him again, searching for any obvious untruths. Von

Karien's voice took on a tinge of scepticism. 'Why would he want to do a thing like that?'

'Sigmar alone knows,' Rudi said without thinking, before realising that the man sitting next to him was evidently exceptionally pious, which was hardly surprising, he supposed, given his family history. Fortunately, von Karien didn't seem to have taken offence at the casual use of the name of his patron deity. 'So far as I could tell, he was the ringleader of a Chaos cult, which probably had something to do with it. A visiting witch hunter managed to get to him before he had the chance to finish me off, though.'

'How very fortunate,' von Karien said.

Rudi shuddered at the memory. Much as he hated the man, he had to admit that Gerhard's intervention could hardly have come at a more propitious moment.

'It was,' he admitted, somewhat reluctantly. 'But before that, I did find some evidence that Magnus – the cult leader – might have known the von Karien family years before.'

'I see.' Rudi hadn't been sure how he expected von Karien to react to this, but the man's air of calmness was all the more unnerving for clearly being the result of an act of considerable willpower. 'So, you've come running to me in the hope that my cousin's twisted legacy still lives on?' He was holding the knife again, his knuckles white on the hilt.

'Sigmar preserve us, no!' Rudi protested. 'If you'd seen what Magnus was, what he'd become, you'd never ask that!' His sincerity seemed to be obvious, and after a moment von Karien nodded slowly, relaxing back into his seat, and loosening his grip on the weapon. It remained in his hand, however.

'So why did you come all the way to Altdorf, if not for that?' he asked. Rudi hesitated.

'Your cousin had a son, didn't he?' he responded at last. 'A child who was never found, when the witch hunters raided his estate?' Von Karien nodded, clearly understanding the import of the question, but waiting for Rudi to commit himself. Stumbling a little, he went on. 'The papers I found mentioned the von Karien heir. He was about the same age as me, and Magnus lived in Kohlstadt, at least part of the time, so I wondered if possibly...' His voice trailed away.

'You thought you might be the missing boy.' Von Karien nodded slowly, studying his face intently. 'It's possible, I suppose. There does seem to be a bit of a family resemblance.' He stood abruptly. 'But we need to be sure. Fortunately, I have a friend who might be able to resolve the matter.'

'You do?' Rudi felt a wild flare of hope.

'I do,' said von Karien. 'Although for your sake, I sincerely hope that you're wrong. Ours is a tainted name, and I wouldn't wish our legacy on another.' He shot another appraising look at Rudi. 'Surely von Eckstein told you that?'

'He did.' Rudi pushed his empty plate away, and accepted the mug of ale his host passed across the table towards him. The dagger, he noted with some relief, was now lying on the tabletop again, apparently forgotten. 'He wasn't the first one, either.'

'I don't doubt it.' Von Karien poured another drink for himself, and relaxed back into his chair. 'Our notoriety seems to have spread far beyond Altdorf. How do you come to be so well connected, by the way? I wouldn't have thought a city watchman makes friends with a nobleman all that frequently, even in Marienburg.'

'A friend of mine works for him,' Rudi said, 'and I happened to be around to help defend something his enemies tried to steal from the boat I was travelling on. He felt he owed me something for that, so he wrote me the letter.'

'I see.' Von Karien smiled sardonically. 'Although I suppose, if your suspicions are correct, you're of noble blood yourself.' He waved vaguely at the kitchen around them, presumably meaning to encompass the whole of the house. 'And all this magnificence is yours by right.'

'I hadn't thought of that,' Rudi said, his astonishment at the idea so evident in his voice that von Karien seemed convinced of his sincerity at once.

The pale-faced man's smile grew a little warmer.

'Then you should consider it now,' he said, 'although there's precious little left of your birthright, I'm afraid.'

'What happened to it?' Rudi asked. His gaze swept the cluttered room. 'I have to admit this wasn't quite what I expected. I thought you'd be living–'

'Like some perfume-sodden fop?' von Karien asked. The idea seemed to amuse him. 'Even when the family had money and influence, that wasn't the life for me. I followed the colours, boy, determined to defend the Empire from its enemies.' His eyes clouded, suddenly. 'I should have been looking a lot closer to home.'

'You were a soldier?' Rudi asked. That explained a great deal, he thought.

Von Karien shook his head. 'More than that: a crusader. I rode to Kislev with the Knights Panther, eager to honour our ancient obligations, and to battle the minions of Chaos face-to-face. Three years I was there, raiding into the Northern Wastes, and I saw things I doubt you'd believe. Saw them, and killed them all.' Pride and sorrow mingled in his voice. 'All the time I was hunting beastmen, and far fouler things, Manfred and Gertrude were nurturing their corruption right here, in the heart of the Empire.'

'Manfred and Gertrude?' Rudi asked, sure he already knew the import of the unfamiliar names.

'Your parents, if you really are who you think you are,' said Von Karien. 'I'm afraid I can't show you a portrait of either of them. I had them all burned.'

'I can understand that,' Rudi said. It didn't matter, he told himself, despite the sudden pang of disappointment. The face of Gunther Walder was still vivid in his memory, and that was the only image of a father he'd ever needed. 'After all, they were executed as heretics.' Burned like their portraits, he thought, and forced the uncomfortable notion away as quickly as he could. He gazed at von Karien, trying to read his expression, but the nobleman's face was neutral. 'I suppose there was no doubt of their guilt?'

'None whatsoever.' Von Karien shook his head. 'They were taken in the very act of performing some blasphemous ritual. Fortunately, we were able to intervene before they could complete it.'

'You were there?' Rudi asked, stunned at the revelation.

'Of course I was,' said von Karien. 'It was my duty as a member of a knightly order. I knew the estate, and co-ordinated the assault on it.' He sighed, and replaced his tankard on the table. 'You might as well know the rest now, as hear it from someone else later. It was me who denounced Manfred to the witch hunters in the first place.' He watched Rudi intently, clearly wondering how he was going to take this latest surprise.

'I see,' Rudi said levelly. He took another gulp of the thin, sour ale, more to help order his thoughts than because he wanted it. 'Can you tell me why you did that?' He kept expecting some flare of violent emotion to shake him, but nothing came. Manfred and Gertrude were just names to him, whatever their blood relationship had been, and he couldn't bring himself to care for them, or their hideous fate, at least not yet.

'I had no choice,' von Karien said. 'My duty demanded it, to the Empire, and to civilisation itself. How could I put family feeling ahead of that? The damage they were doing to everything I swore to pro-tect...' He shook his head. 'How they were ensnared in the first place, I don't know. By the time they were taken, neither was in a fit state to answer questions. Neither were most of their acolytes. They all put up quite a fight.' He shook his head again, clearly moved by the memory. 'There were sorcerers among them too. Those we burned first, of course.'

'I see.' Rudi nodded. 'And did anyone manage to escape?'

'At least one, we assumed.' Von Karien's eyes were fixed on the past, reliving the traumatic events of a decade and a half ago. 'After all, someone must have spirited the boy away, although how and why we had no idea.' He shrugged. 'I'd always assumed he was long dead, sacrificed to the blasphemous thing they worshipped.' His eyes fell on Rudi again, cold and appraising. 'Then you turned up tonight on my doorstep, stirring up memories I'd rather leave buried.'

'I can understand that,' Rudi said sincerely. He took another mouthful of ale that he didn't really want. 'What made you suspect your cousin in the first place?'

Von Karien sighed. 'I'd spent more time among the minions of Chaos than any sane man would care to. By the time I returned to civilisation, I knew the signs of their presence. Even the ones most people would miss.' He emptied his tankard. 'I tried to dismiss my suspicions at first, telling myself I'd become so used to looking out for the taint of the Dark Powers that I was seeing their traces where none truly existed, but after a month or two, I could no longer deny the evidence of my own eyes. I returned to Altdorf, and sought the advice of the Templars of Sigmar.'

'That must have been difficult for you,' Rudi said tactfully.

'It was.' Von Karien began to pour himself another drink, and frowned at the last trickle of ale as it poured from the jug. There was barely enough in his tankard to cover the bottom of it. 'But it was the right thing to do.' He laughed harshly. 'Of course there were those who said I'd only denounced Manfred to get my hands on his inheritance, petty-minded maggots. I soon put a stop to that, though.'

'How?' Rudi asked, intrigued.

'I gave the whole thing over to the Church,' said von Karien. 'I didn't want the estates, or the mansion, or the money. Just thinking about owning anything my cousin had left made my skin crawl. Let it do some good for once, make restitution for the evil that the family had done.' He gestured around them again. 'This pest-hole is all that's left of the family fortune, and I'd have burned it to the ground by now if I didn't need a roof over my head.' He looked at Rudi appraisingly. 'Disappointed?'

'Not really.' Rudi thought about it, trying to be as honest as he could be. 'I came here looking for answers, not money or a title, and from what I've seen of Chaos, I wouldn't want either if they'd been touched by it.' He nodded at his bow and backpack, still lying beside the table. 'Besides, I'm a woodsman. It's all I know, apart from a few months of picking drunks out of the gutter in Marienburg. Whatever your friend has to say about my lineage, that's all I want to get back to: a hut in the forest where I can be left alone to live my life in peace.'

'Well said.' Von Karien was looking at him with a strange expression on his face. 'Not many people would have felt the same, I can promise you that.' He stood, a little more slowly. 'Is there an inn I can find you at tomorrow?' Rudi shook his head.

'I haven't found anywhere to stay yet,' he said. 'Could you recommend somewhere around here?' Von Karien laughed.

'Not to anyone I liked.' He turned, picking up a candle from the table. 'It doesn't matter. There are plenty of rooms I don't use. Some of them have beds in, I think.'

'Thank you,' Rudi said, still trying to assimilate the events of the evening. Von Karien was strange, it was true, but he seemed willing to at least entertain the possibility that Rudi was indeed his long-lost relative. Perhaps he was as pleased as Rudi had hoped he would be; to find some solace in what appeared to be a solitary and shunned existence. Despite himself, he yawned widely. 'That's very kind of you.'

'We'll talk more tomorrow,' von Karien said. He stood aside, and gestured to the doorway. 'Help yourself to a candle.' Rudi did so, picking up his pack and weapons with the other hand. As he passed von Karien, a new thought occurred to him.

'The missing boy,' he said, 'Manfred's son. What was his name?'

'Rudolph,' von Karien said. He glanced across at von Eckstein's letter, discarded among the remains of the meal they'd shared. 'But I'm sure you can't be surprised by that. It's often shortened to Rudi, isn't it?'

CHAPTER EIGHTEEN

RUDI WOKE SLOWLY the next morning, a little disorientated by the absence of the faint rocking motion that he'd become used to in his time aboard the *Reikmaiden*. A thin shaft of sunlight was forcing its way between the warped wooden shutters, leaking inwards to illuminate the room in muted tones of pale grey, and after a moment he remembered where he was: von Karien's house. Last night's conversation replayed itself in his mind as he struggled back to full wakefulness, and swung his legs over the side of the bed.

It seemed he had the answers he'd been so desperate to find at last. Unfortunately, they only appeared to confirm his worst fears. If he truly was Rudolph von Karien, then his legacy was a dark one indeed: the son of two heretics, dabblers in the darkest of arts, he could hardly expect Gerhard to stop his obsessive pursuit of him now. Just the knowledge, which he could no longer deny, that his adopted father had been a member of a Chaos cult back in Kohlstadt had been enough to keep the witch hunter on his trail, at least until their mutual confrontation with Magnus and his disease-riddled minions in the most blighted corner of Marienburg. If Gerhard ever learned the truth about his origins, Rudi was sure that he would redouble his efforts to track him down.

Pulling on his britches, he took stock of his situation. At least things weren't quite as bleak as they might be. He'd found shelter, and possibly an ally in Osric von Karien. His father's cousin was undeniably eccentric, but given his tragic history and the opprobrium that had overtaken the family name, that was hardly surprising. The authorities seemed to think that his probity was beyond doubt, at any rate, and that might be enough to shield him from the witch hunters too, if his strange relative could be persuaded to vouch for him.

Yawning, he filled the washbowl from the pitcher that von Karien had provided the evening before, and banished his whirling thoughts and the last vestiges of sleep in the welcome shock of cold water.

His host hadn't been exaggerating about the house having plenty of extra space, Rudi thought. The room he'd been given was evidently unused, at least in the normal course of events. Indeed, it was quite obvious even to a cursory glance that no one had set foot in it for months, if not years. A thick layer of dust covered everything, and he could clearly see his own footprints on the worn wooden floorboards.

The bed had been comfortable enough, though. The mattress smelled faintly damp and musty, it was true, and the straw within it had coagulated into hard lumps in several places, but to someone used to sleeping outdoors that had hardly been a problem. Bundled up in his travelling blanket, his head pillowed on his rucksack as usual, Rudi had slept far more soundly than he'd expected to. Up on the second floor the ever-present clamour of the city streets was muted to some extent, which had probably helped as well.

Buckling his sword belt on, Rudi made his way to the door. He hesitated at the threshold, glancing back at his bow and his pack, and then shrugged. They'd be safe enough, and he didn't see any reason to take them with him.

The corridor outside was shrouded in darkness, as it had been the night before when von Karien had shown him up to his room and bidden him goodnight, but enough light penetrated to reveal a little more of his surroundings. Several doors, all firmly closed, receded into the distance, the dust outside them undisturbed, except for the one immediately opposite his. Here the ubiquitous grey blanket was channelled with a thin, clear path, leading directly to it from the landing. Rudi didn't need to call his tracking skills into play to infer that this was von Karien's bedroom, chosen, he suspected, simply because it was the nearest one to the stairway. Unsure whether his host had risen yet he paused, just long enough to knock hesitantly on the thick wooden panel.

There was no reply, and he was just about to move on when something caught his eye. A single hair, stretched across the latch, practically invisible in the all-pervading gloom. Had it not been for his tracker's instincts, which had been trained to register such minute incongruities as a matter of course, he would never have noticed it.

Shrugging, he turned away. Evidently, Osric von Karien wasn't quite ready to give him the benefit of the doubt yet after all. Well, he could hardly blame the man for that.

The landing was just as small as he remembered from the previous night, although the tenuous daylight seeping into it did reveal one more detail that he'd overlooked on his way to bed. What he'd taken for a deep patch of shadow the evening before turned out to be a narrow flight of stairs, disappearing upwards towards the roof space. To his complete lack of surprise, though, no one seemed to have used it in a very long time.

'The servants' quarters,' von Karien said, appearing from the floor below, and immediately noticing the direction of his gaze. 'Currently unoccupied, of course.'

'Why "of course"?' Rudi asked.

Von Karien shrugged. 'Would you want to work for a man with my reputation and family name? Even around here there are precious few that desperate.' He turned, and began to descend the stairs again. 'I just came to see if you were awake. There's breakfast downstairs if you can stomach it.' Suddenly aware that he was hungry, Rudi followed.

'It does seem a little odd, though,' he said, as they passed through the first floor landing. A corridor led off the stairwell, just as it did upstairs, although here it evidently provided access to the house's suite of living rooms. To Rudi's complete lack of surprise the carpet of dust was almost undisturbed here too, although a few blurred footprints showed that von Karien was evidently in the habit of visiting one of them from time to time. 'The Graf von Karien doing his own cooking and laundry, just like anyone else.'

'Osric,' von Karien said. 'If you must call me something, call me that. I renounced the title when I gave up the estates, and I prefer not to use the family name if I can avoid it.' His voice mellowed a little. 'Even if your claim is substantiated, you might do better to stick with "Walder". I would in your position.'

'I'll bear that in mind,' Rudi said, following him down the final flight of stairs and into the kitchen. A pot of porridge was bubbling on the stove, and he sat gratefully at the table while von Karien ladled most of the contents into a couple of crude earthenware bowls and dropped them on the wooden surface between them. It was thick and lumpy. The nobleman was evidently as accomplished a maker of porridge as he was of stew. He sat down opposite Rudi, and spooned up a glutenous mouthful.

'Besides, I could hardly drag a valet around with me in the Chaos Wastes, could I? I had to fend for myself then, and I don't see any reason to break the habit now. Too hot for you?'

'No, it's fine.' Rudi took a cautious mouthful, and decided that it was no worse than he'd expected. He continued eating, grateful that at least it was warm and filling. 'So what do we do now? Go and look for this friend of yours?'

Von Karien nodded.

'I can leave word at his house that I need to talk to him, and if we're lucky, he might be at the temple today already.'

'The temple?' Rudi asked, trying to ignore a formless sense of apprehension at the words.

'All the records we'll need to consult are there,' said von Karien. 'They were removed from the estate when I handed everything over to the Church, and deposited in the archives.'

'Of course,' Rudi said, through a sticky mass of porridge. He cleared his throat. 'So what did they do with the place, anyway?' He had only the vaguest idea of what the ancestral estate had been like in any case, imagining something like von Eckstein's home, although perhaps a little more rural. 'Turn it into a temple?'

'In a manner of speaking,' von Karien said. He spooned up another mouthful of porridge. 'The house and grounds are a few miles outside the city, near the hamlet of Hammerhof. It used to be called Karien, of course, but none of the peasants liked living in a place tainted with the name of a heretic, and petitioned the Church for a more pious-sounding alternative when they took over as lords of the manor. You can hardly blame them for that.'

'No, I suppose not,' Rudi agreed. Von Karien dropped his spoon back into his bowl, and pushed it away.

'Anyhow, the house became a seminary.' Clearly noticing the expression of puzzlement on Rudi's face, he elaborated a little. 'Somewhere, initiates learn to become priests. Close enough to the city for the temple to keep an eye on them, far enough away for them to concentrate on their devotions without getting distracted.'

'I see.' Rudi nodded, giving up on the rest of the porridge, which was beginning to set hard inside his stomach by the feel of it. He stood, suffused with a sudden rush of nervous energy. 'Do you think the temple will be open yet?'

'It's always open,' von Karien said, with a trace of amusement. He stood, in a rather more leisurely manner. 'I suppose if you've had enough to eat we might as well go.'

AS THEY STEPPED out into the narrow street, Rudi was struck once again by the incessant noise and stench of the city. Inside the house he'd been insulated from the worst of it, but as von Karien slammed and locked the heavy door behind them, sound and odour alike rolled over him like a wave. The smell, at least, seemed a little more tolerable, even heady. As he inhaled it, he felt slightly giddy, as if he'd drunk a little too much alcohol, the sickly sweet stench of putrescence almost intoxicating. After a moment he rallied, putting the moment of dizziness down to the excitement of finally learning the truth about his identity. The noise was another matter entirely, a never-ending cacophony of raised voices echoing in the narrow gaps between buildings. Noticing his expression, von Karien smiled sardonically.

'You get used to it,' he said.

'If you say so,' Rudi replied, following the nobleman into the maelstrom of hurrying bodies. At first he was worried about losing his host in the ever-present throng, but von Karien's black cloak and hat stood out clearly among the crowd, and he was able to keep up with him easily. After a while he noticed that the swarm of people, although as thick as ever, seemed a little more permeable. Not only was he able to remain close to his companion, he was being jostled notice-ably less often than he had been the previous day.

Once he realised this, the reason became immedi-ately apparent. Everyone who noticed their approach did their best to get out of the way, looking at them as they did so with barely disguised hostility, if they bothered to try hiding their feelings at all. Some passers-by averted their gaze, as if even to look at them would bring down disaster, while others stared, almost mesmerised, like rabbits in front of a fox.

'There are some advantages to being a pariah,' von Karien said, reading Rudi's expression. 'I get where I'm going without hindrance, and no one's tried to pick my pocket in months.'

'Glad to hear it.' Rudi dodged around one of the ubiquitous halfling pie-sellers, alert to the dangers of an apparently random collision after his encounter with Peasemold and Ned in the Koenigsplatz the previous day, but this one appeared to be intent on nothing more nefarious than vend-ing his wares to an unsuspecting populace. 'Is this really the best way to the temple?' They'd only been walking for a handful of minutes, and already he was completely disorientated.

'More or less,' said von Karien. 'We need to see if Luther's at home first?'

'Of course,' Rudi said. The part of the city they'd entered seemed a little more salubrious than the quarter where von Karien lived, but the locals seemed just as eager to stay out of their way. He began to see a few more non-humans among them, halflings for the most part, but dwarfs and elves too. He even caught sight of the deceptively bloated-seeming bulk of an ogre mercenary, wading through the crowds like a sailor breasting the waves, a light snack of what looked like half a pig in his hand. 'Are we somewhere near the docks?'

'Good guess,' von Karien confirmed. 'Other side of the Talabec, though. This is where most of the burghers who do business there live: shipping agents, cargo brokers, second-rate lawyers, that kind of thing. Pretty much everyone around here is either going up, or going down. Not many stay in the neighbourhood for long.'

'What about your friend?' Rudi asked.

'He's an exception,' von Karien said shortly, leading the way onto a bridge, which was only distinguishable from the street leading up to it by a short length of balustrade between two of the buildings lining its edges. From the width and height of the piers, Rudi thought it must span the Reik itself, a guess confirmed by a passing glance over the low wall as he passed it. Shimmering water stretched away into the distance, crowded with boats of all kinds, and for a moment he felt a twinge of nostalgia for Marienburg.

Momentarily distracted by the sight, he failed to realise that von Karien had stopped outside the door of one of the houses on the southern span. By the time he'd noticed, and retraced his steps to rejoin him, the nobleman was already engrossed in conversation with a servant standing just inside the threshold.

'Very well.' Von Karien sounded resigned, and not particularly surprised. 'Perhaps you could ask him to join us at the temple archives as soon as he returns?'

'Of course, sir.' The servant nodded deferentially, although Rudi couldn't quite shake the feeling that such formal politeness was something of a charade. The man was stocky and muscular, with a faint tracery of scars across his face, and held himself like a fighter. His clothing was sober enough, though, and he had a small silver comet of Sigmar on a chain around his neck, similar to the one adorning the clasp of von Karien's cloak.

Rudi had come across plenty like him during his career as a watchman, and suspected that his true job was closer to bodyguard than domestic servant. It made sense, he supposed, a scholar was likely to have valuable books and artefacts in his home, and knowing that someone like this was taking care of the premises in his absence would no doubt ease his mind a great deal. Becoming aware of Rudi's scrutiny, the man closed the door with a final disdainful glance in his direction.

'We're in luck,' von Karien said, turning away and beginning to march southwards again. 'I wasn't sure he was back in Altdorf yet.' Rudi lengthened his stride to catch up.

'Where's he been?' he asked, more to make conversation than because he cared particularly.

'Sigmar alone knows,' von Karien said dryly, echoing Rudi's words of the previous evening. 'He comes and goes, whenever he hears about something somewhere that takes his interest. I suppose that's why he likes living near the docks.'

Rudi was forming a clearer picture of the man they were going to see. An itinerant scholar, willing to pursue his researches wherever they led; no wonder he needed a bodyguard.

Their first sight of the temple of Sigmar was so sudden, and so awe-inspiring, that Rudi stopped dead in his tracks, and simply stared. Only after two passing stonemasons, an obstreperous dwarf, and an apologetic young man in the robes of an initiate had bumped into him did he manage to start his legs moving again. It was only by sticking close to von Karien, whose aura of social exclusion seemed undiminished even this far from his home, was he able to avoid further collisions. Despite its vast size, the narrow streets and looming buildings had hidden the temple from view until they were almost on top of it.

The main building seemed to soar upwards ahead of them as if about to take flight, its stonework spotted with bird droppings, but still managing to look as if it was somehow ethereal, great buttresses taking the enormous weight of its bulk with unobtrusive elegance. Noticing his young companion's awe-struck expression, von Karien smiled with more warmth than Rudi had seen him display at any time since their initial meeting.

'They say the dwarfs had a hand in its construction. Looking at it, I can well believe it.'

'So can I,' Rudi said. It hardly seemed possible that human hands could have crafted stone so cunningly. The Imperial Palace, which stood facing the temple on the other side of the huge square dividing the two principal buildings of the capital, looked lumpy and ill-formed by comparison, although it was sumptuous enough by any reasonable standard, making the splendours of the staadholder's palace in Marienburg fade into insignificance.

'This way.' Von Karien led Rudi towards the temple, nodding in homage to the vast statue of Sigmar over the main doors, which stood open to admit a steady stream of visitors. Not until he noticed them was Rudi able to appreciate the truly titanic scale of the structure itself. The scurrying humans were reduced to the apparent size of halflings by the mighty portal, which loomed at least four times their height, and the statues of warriors flanking the doors glowered down at them like disapproving parents.

As they moved closer to the great slabs of finely carved wood, Rudi felt that he was about to be swallowed by some vast stone leviathan, and fought down a rising sense of irrational panic. His heartbeat thundered in his ears, and his footsteps stumbled.

'Are you all right?' von Karien asked, an expression of mild puzzlement on his face. Rudi nodded.

'I'm fine,' he said. 'I just felt a bit dizzy, trying to take it all in.' The same thing had happened outside the cathedral of Verena in Marienburg, he remembered. He should have learned his lesson, and tried to absorb the atmosphere of this building a little more cautiously. He took a deep breath, finding the ever-present stench of the streets curiously bracing. It was surprising what you could get used to, he supposed.

'I see.' Von Karien nodded, and started walking again, angling slightly away from the imposing wooden doors carved with the twin-tailed comet of the Empire's patron god. Feeling more or less recovered, Rudi trotted after him.

'Aren't we going inside?' he asked, trying to mask the flood of relief that he felt at the words. In the distance, the right-hand crossbar of the T-shaped building, which supposedly reproduced the exact proportions of Ghal-maraz, the legendary dwarf warhammer of Sigmar, began to grow a little clearer, and he became aware that the temple itself was surrounded by a cluster of smaller structures which he'd barely noticed, since his eye was naturally drawn to the stone behemoth that dominated the skyline.

Von Karien turned to look back at him. 'We're here to consult the records, not burn a bit of incense.' His expression softened. 'If you want to say a few prayers once we've concluded our business, I certainly wouldn't object. There's no finer place to do it in the whole of the Empire. Just being inside it is balm to the soul.'

'Let's hope we have the time,' said Rudi, trying to ignore the fresh spurt of panic that sparked somewhere in the back of his mind at the prospect. He forced it down angrily. The key to his identity, final confirmation or denial that he truly was the missing

von Karien heir, was within his grasp at last. This was
no time to be getting the jitters.

'This way.' Von Karien led the way between two of
the buildings on the fringes of the complex surrounding the temple, and once again Rudi was lost in a
labyrinth of stone. Here, though, the clamour of the
streets was absent, the purposeful figures hurrying or
loitering about their business moving quietly or con-
versing in hushed tones. Many of them wore the robes
of priests or initiates, the hammer of Sigmar around
their necks, although to his surprise he saw a few
green-robed acolytes of Taal and Rhya as well, and
once caught a glimpse of a white-robed priestess of
Shallya, talking earnestly to a couple of Sigmarites.

'The Empire needs all its gods,' von Karien reminded
him when he remarked on the fact. 'We do well to
remember that, and discuss the matters we all have in
common.'

'I suppose so,' Rudi said. A couple of armed guards
had been on duty at the gate they'd entered the warren of buildings by, and both had nodded affably at
von Karien as he'd walked through. Now, another
black-clad templar inclined his head as he hurried
past on some errand of his own.

'Osric, you're looking well.'

'Well enough.' Von Karien returned the greeting cordially.

'You know him?' Rudi asked, surprised. It seemed
that his companion was well thought of in some quarters, after all.

'I should do, he saved my life once.' Von Karien
shrugged. 'Mind you, I've returned the favour, so I

suppose we're even.' He led the way through a wrought iron gate into a small courtyard, where more of the soberly dressed guards were practising with swords and pole arms. 'If we cut through here we'll save a bit of time. The storerooms of the library are a bit out of the way.'

'Where are we?' Rudi asked, confused. Wherever it was, it seemed more like the watch barracks he'd lived at in Marienburg than anything to do with a temple.

'Templars' Court,' von Karien explained. Understanding at last, Rudi nodded. If von Karien did have any friends here, it made sense for them to be among the Church's elite warriors.

'I see. They must remember you helping them raid the family estate.' Von Karien laughed.

'I suppose a few of the older ones might, but most of them remember me because I'm the one who put them through eight kinds of hell to turn them into fitting instruments of Sigmar's vengeance on the unholy.' He led the way up a short flight of stairs, and the clang of sword against sword faded into the background. 'After that night, when I'd faced the taint of Chaos at the heart of my own family, I became a templar myself. I could hardly go back to the Panthers and pretend that nothing had happened.'

'And you've been one ever since,' Rudi concluded.

'I've served Sigmar, and fought the forces of Chaos as best I could.' Von Karien opened a small, undistinguished door with a key from a pocket somewhere beneath his cloak, and ushered Rudi through it. Once they were both inside, he locked it again, and returned the key to wherever it had come from. Rudi found himself in a narrow, windowless corridor, lit by oil lamps.

'Where are we?' he asked.

'One of the outlying annexes of the main library,' von Karien explained. 'Not everything is out on the main shelves. Most of the stuff in here is at least three hundred years old, and I don't suppose anyone's so much as glanced at it since it was brought down and forgotten about.'

'Someone must have done,' Rudi said, following the black-garbed man along the passageway, 'otherwise the lanterns wouldn't be alight.' Their footsteps echoed against the flagstones, and shadows flickered as the draft of their passing disturbed the flames in the lamps. A thought occurred to him. 'They must trust you well enough to give you your own key.'

'I'm not sure that the librarians know I have one,' von Karien admitted, leading the way into a book-lined room. A table, scarcely better cared for than the one in the nobleman's kitchen, stood in the centre, a scattering of chairs around it. More lamps burned, and the smell of combustion mingled with the acrid odour of old books and parchments. Shelves stood around the walls, some of them projecting out into the room to afford access from both sides, forming small enclosed areas of their own, and making it hard to tell just how big the chamber really was. 'Over the years, my colleagues and I have found it a useful place to meet, and discuss our more sensitive business.'

'What sort of business?' Rudi asked, trying to read the titles on the spines of the nearest books, but they were too encrusted with grime to be intelligible.

'Protecting the Empire from its enemies, of course.' Von Karien glanced at a sheaf of documents lying on the table. 'It seems we're in luck again. Someone's already here, and apparently working on our little problem.'

'They are?' Rudi felt a shiver of unease. 'Who?'

'Who do you think?' Von Karien raised his voice. 'Luther? Is that you?'

'Osric?' Someone moved behind one of the bookshelves, a black-clad silhouette coming slowly into view. Bleak blue eyes bored into Rudi from the centre of an all too familiar face, disfigured by a partially healed burn, but still unmistakable. 'I see I was right.'

'You were.' Von Karien nodded. 'He came running straight to me, just as you said he would.'

'You're working for Gerhard?' Rudi asked, aghast, and still struggling to grasp the magnitude of this latest betrayal. Von Karien shook his head impatiently.

'No, boy, with him. Who do you think burned your parents in the first place?'

CHAPTER NINETEEN

A TIDAL WAVE of anger burst over Rudi, the insensate desire to kill hammering in his veins. Before he was even aware of what he was doing, he drew his sword and leapt to attack.

'There's no need for this.' Gerhard's blade sprang from its scabbard, blocking the blow as he moved to evade it, but he held back from delivering the counter strike that Rudi had been expecting. As in their previous encounters, the witch hunter seemed content to fight defensively rather than going in for the kill. 'Put your sword down, and let's talk. There's a lot you need to know.'

'I've seen how you talk,' Rudi snarled, renewing the attack. 'I was there when you talked to Frau Katzenjammer, remember?'

'I told you, that was a regrettable necessity.' Gerhard parried his next attack, and stepped back to open the distance, hemming himself in between two of the projecting bookcases as he did so. 'There's so much at stake here.'

'So you say,' Rudi said, moving in to take advantage of his enemy's inability to evade. He cut at the witch hunter's head, intent on nothing more than spilling his blood, blind to every other consideration. His heartbeat thundered in his ears. Gerhard ducked in the nick of time, and Rudi's sword embedded itself in the wood of a bookshelf, the tip of it slicing into an incunabulum, raising a cloud of dust and scattering the pages as the age-rotted leather binding split. Rudi wrenched frantically at the weapon, trying to free it, but it was stuck fast in the age-darkened wood. Before he could recover the sword, Gerhard had taken full advantage of his loss of momentum, diving at his chest and grappling like a wrestler.

Rudi stumbled backwards, trying to shrug off the witch hunter's pinioning arms, and feeling a sudden shock of impact against his back. A moment later the unexpected blow was followed by agonising pain, searing up into his torso. Turning, he found von Karien behind him, a bloody knife in his left hand, and an expression of shock in his eyes.

'You…' Rudi tried to draw his own dagger, but Gerhard forestalled him, expertly shifting his grip to clamp a muscular hand around his wrist. The senior witch hunter glared at von Karien.

'Are you insane? You know what happens if he dies!'

'He just stumbled into me.' Von Karien dropped the red-stained dagger, which clattered loudly on the stone floor of the chamber. 'I only drew it in case I needed to parry.' His arm went around Rudi's shoulders, holding him up just as the young forester's knees gave way. Rudi tried to speak, but the taste of blood filled his mouth, and he hawked crimson phlegm onto the flagstones. The images of Bruno, and all the pirates and ruffians he'd killed since leaving Kohlstadt, rose up in his mind, taunting and vindictive. Was this how their last few moments had felt? His kinsman's voice held an edge of desperation. 'Is there anything we can do?'

'If Sigmar wills it,' Gerhard said calmly. He pulled one of a pair of thin leather gloves from his belt, and held it between his palms, murmuring a prayer beneath his breath.

Von Karien lowered Rudi to the cold stone floor as gently as he could, the chill seeming to seep upwards into his very bones as he did so. Rudi's vision began to blur, and something seemed to stir in the darkest depths of his soul. Despite the pain, he felt a sudden surge of malevolent triumph sweep through him, leaving him giddy and disorientated.

'Hurry.' Von Karien rolled Rudi over onto his side. 'He hasn't got long.'

Recalling the event afterwards, Rudi was never quite sure what actually happened next. The glove in Gerhard's hands seemed to dwindle and shrink, like dispersing smoke, and then it vanished, as if it had never been. Gerhard knelt, and pressed his hand to Rudi's back, right where the wound from von Karien's dagger had been inflicted.

A wave of pain surged through his body, spasming his muscles, and with a howl of agony the shadowy presence deep within him returned to wherever it had emerged from. Both witch hunters sighed with relief.

'Sigmar be praised,' von Karien said, making the sign of the hammer. Gerhard nodded.

'Indeed,' he concurred dryly. He shrugged. 'It seems I'll need another new pair of gloves.'

'A small price to pay,' von Karien said, and Gerhard nodded his agreement.

'Can you sit up?' he asked, supporting Rudi's shoulders again.

To his surprise, Rudi found that he could. The pain in his chest was gone, replaced by a numbing chill. He drew in a shaky breath, unimpeded by blood or phlegm.

'What did you just do?' he asked, curiosity driving out fear and anger, at least for the time being. Whatever his reasons, Gerhard had clearly just saved his life. Shaking the witch hunter's arm off, he staggered to his feet, leaning against the table for support. Von Karien retrieved his sword from the bookcase and his own dagger from the floor, placing both well out of reach, and moving to block the door. Gerhard pulled out a chair, and motioned to Rudi to sit.

'I prayed to Sigmar for aid,' he said. 'Sometimes he intercedes, if the cause is just.'

'It looked like sorcery to me,' Rudi said. If he still felt too weak to fight the man physically, he could always lash out with words. 'Shouldn't you run off and burn yourself?'

'There is absolutely nothing like sorcery in the blessings of the gods!' von Karien said angrily, 'and only a heretic would dare to suggest such a thing!' For a moment, Rudi thought his kinsman was about to strike him, and tensed for the blow, but to his surprise Gerhard intervened.

'It's a natural mistake to make,' he said evenly. 'Both magic and prayer can alter the fabric of the world. The difference is that a priest can only do so by the grace of the divine, while witches and sorcerers can change reality by the force of their own wills.'

'You've lost me.' Rudi sat down slowly, waiting for the strength to return to his body. There were two of them, it was true, but he'd fought against worse odds than that before. The real problem was the locked door behind him, but once he'd subdued his opponents, finding the key wouldn't present too big a problem, he was sure.

'Then I'll make it simple,' Gerhard said, sitting down opposite him. 'I healed you by calling on the power of Sigmar. Your friend the witch incinerates people by calling on the power of Chaos. That's the difference.'

'He's been consorting with witches?' von Karien asked, the expression of horror on his face echoed in the timbre of his voice. He looked at Rudi with obvious contempt. 'He's clearly been tainted beyond any possibility of redemption.' His expression became appraising. 'Is that why you went to the Bright College before coming to my house? Escorting your witch friend to be with her own kind?'

'There were reports of a disturbance outside the college gate last night,' Gerhard said thoughtfully. 'I take it that means her application was unsuccessful?'

'She's safe,' Rudi said, hoping the half-truth would serve to protect the girl. 'You'll never get your hands on her now.'

'I'll take that as a no,' Gerhard said levelly. 'If the Bright Order had taken her in, you wouldn't have been able to resist throwing that in our faces. Why did they reject her?'

'Because she was tainted, wasn't she?' von Karien put in. 'Her mother was a witch, and a worshipper of the Lord of Change. That's how she got her magical talent, straight from the Dark Powers.' Rudi wondered how much else Gerhard had told his friend of what he'd discovered in Kohlstadt and Marienburg.

'Rudi,' Gerhard leaned across the table, his voice calm and reasonable. 'Your loyalty is admirable, however misplaced, but surely you must realise how dangerous Hanna is? She's almost as dangerous as her mother.'

Rudi shook his head stubbornly, trying to forget the expression on Gerrit's face as he'd died, the burning silhouettes of Alwyn and Conrad, the indifference, even malevolence, Hanna had seemed to show every time she'd used her abilities to maim or kill since they'd fled from Marienburg.

'If she is, then who made her that way?' he shot back. 'You're the one who tried to kill her, just for being who she is. So far as I'm concerned, she's entitled to do whatever it takes to defend herself!'

'Where is she?' von Karien loomed over him, his face dark. 'We might need you alive, boy, but that doesn't have to mean whole.'

'Osric.' Gerhard made a dismissive gesture with his hand. 'We're getting away from the point here. The witch will keep for now, wherever she is. We have a far more pressing problem to deal with.'

'That's true.' Von Karien nodded reluctantly, and pulled up a chair of his own. 'I don't suppose she'll get far, with both the templars and the colleges after her, in any case.'

'She's safe!' Rudi insisted, 'with friends.' He glared at von Karien, 'You can keep on asking until you're blue in the face, but I don't know where. Greta said that was for the best, and I'm beginning to see why.'

'So her mother's here too.' Gerhard exchanged a glance with von Karien. 'They've probably taken refuge with the Silver Wheel, then. Perhaps you'd better start lifting a few stones when we've finished here, and see what crawls out.' Von Karien nodded.

'Perhaps I'd better,' he said. He glanced at Rudi. 'You think they're planning something to do with him?'

'It's possible,' Gerhard said. 'Greta Reifenstahl was living in the same village for years, undoubtedly keeping an eye on Magnus von Blackenburg and his cult. Now she's here in Altdorf, and reunited with her daughter, just when we've caught up with Rudi. That's a pretty big coincidence, and we know only too well that there's no such thing as coincidence where the Lord of Change is concerned.'

'Then we'd better finish this quickly,' von Karien said.

'Finish what?' Rudi asked impatiently.

'I'm afraid it's rather a long story,' Gerhard said, 'and much of it is inference and deduction, but it all goes back to the night we raided the von Karien estate, and found your father's cult enacting a hideous ritual.'

'I know about that,' Rudi said. 'Osric told me.'

'I told you some of it,' von Karien said. 'What I didn't mention before was that you were there. You were a part of it.'

'What do you mean, I was a part of it?' Rudi asked, apprehension and horror sweeping over him with renewed vigour. His months as a watchman had made him adept at detecting evasions and falsehoods, and both men spoke in the level tones of someone telling the absolute truth. All the thoughts he'd had of fighting his way free were gone. The only thing he wanted was to know the full story of his past, although his hands trembled with unease at the prospect. 'How could I have been?' An appalling possibility presented itself, as he recalled von Karien's words the previous night. 'You mean they were going to sacrifice me? My own parents?' His stomach twisted at the enormity of it, but to his vague relief von Karien's plaster-thick porridge seemed determined to remain where it was.

'Worse than that,' von Karien said heavily. Gerhard nodded.

'It took some time to deduce the nature of the ritual. It was one we'd never seen before, and the battle left few traces of what had been going on, but in the months that followed, as we combed through the papers your father had left, and interrogated the peripheral members of the cult we'd been able to track down, we began to find clues as to what he had hoped to achieve.'

'Which was what?' Rudi asked, his mouth dry. Gerhard was silent for a moment, clearly wondering how best to explain.

'What do you know of the nature of daemons?' he asked at last. Completely taken aback by the question, Rudi shrugged.

'Nothing at all,' he said. He looked from one witch hunter to another, and clearly this was the answer they'd been expecting. 'Well, only what everybody knows,' he added, trying to be helpful. 'They're powerful and nasty, and you don't want to meet one.'

'True enough,' Gerhard said, 'but what most people don't realise is that the most powerful tend to be servants of a particular one of the Dark Powers. Your parents were attempting to invoke a daemon prince of Nurgle, the Lord of Disease.'

'The same power that Magnus worshipped?' Rudi asked.

Gerhard nodded. 'Him and his cult, both in Kohlstadt and Marienburg, although the one in the city seems to have had another leader, at least in his absence.'

'The lawyer, van Crackenmeer?' Rudi asked.

'He's a plausible suspect. Why do you think that?' Gerhard asked.

'I found a letter from Magnus in his office,' Rudi explained, 'talking about me, and Greta Reifenstahl, and somebody's grandchildren. I'm not sure who the grandchildren were, though.'

'His fellow degenerates,' von Karien said, with manifest loathing. Rudi's confusion must have shown on his face, because he paused to explain. 'The Plague God's acolytes refer to him as Grandfather Nurgle. Presumably in an attempt to deny the truth of what they're worshipping by making it sound protective and benign.'

'I wanted to talk to van Crackenmeer to find out where Magnus was living,' Rudi explained, 'but by the time I got to his office, he was already dead.'

'I realised you hadn't killed him as soon as I saw the body. It was obviously the work of a mutant. If you'd discussed matters reasonably then, as I asked, instead of making a fight of it, I would have made that abundantly clear.'

'It was Hans Katzenjammer,' Rudi explained. There was no point in not being as honest as he could at this juncture, he thought. The witch hunters obviously knew more about what was going on than he did, and any information he was able to add to that would only enable them to explain things to him more clearly.

'Katzenjammer?' Gerhard looked surprised for the first time. 'Are you sure?'

'I'm a tracker,' Rudi reminded him, 'and I'd followed him through the woods, remember? The traces he left were pretty distinctive.' He hesitated, and then hurried on, reminding himself that there was no point in holding anything back. 'Besides, I'd already seen him in Marienburg. He was there with Greta. They attacked Magnus and his cultists.' He frowned, still trying to understand the bizarre confrontation that he'd witnessed. 'I still don't know what to make of it, to be honest. I got lost in the Doodkanal shortly after we arrived in the city, and I found this old warehouse on the waterfront. Magnus and his followers were there, chanting about a boat, and then Greta and Hans arrived and killed them all, or, most of them, anyhow. Magnus got away, and a few of the others I think.'

'A boat?' Von Karien looked confused. 'Are you sure?'

'Yes,' said Rudi. 'They kept saying, "Hail the vessel".' Another thought struck him. 'That's what they were chanting in the forest too, just before the beastmen attacked.'

'You were there as well?' Gerhard asked, his voice intent.

'I just stumbled into the clearing. I was looking for my father in the woods, and somehow I knew the right way to go. It was like that in the city too, when I found the warehouse. It just seemed right.'

'You were being summoned,' von Karien said. 'At least...' he hesitated, and glanced at Gerhard. 'The vessel was.'

'It can't have been,' Rudi told him. 'Kohlstad's miles from the Reik. There's nowhere a boat could dock anywhere near the place.' He glanced at Gerhard. 'You've been there, you must remember.'

'The main characteristic of daemons,' Gerhard said, 'and it's a fortunate one indeed, is that they're tied to the Realm of Chaos. Except for the most tainted of places, they can't remain in the mortal world for long, unless they possess a mortal host.'

'I see.' Rudi nodded, a tight knot of terror winding itself around his gut. The implications were obvious, but he still couldn't bring himself to face them. 'So this daemon my parents were invoking would have vanished again soon anyway.'

'Ordinarily, yes,' Gerhard nodded soberly, 'but it seems that your father had struck a bargain with a daemon prince. In exchange for power, and knowledge that only a madman would crave, he agreed to provide it with a host, a vessel.'

'His own son.' Von Karien's voice was so thick with disgust that it was barely recognisable. 'You.'

'That's impossible!' Rudi protested, more by reflex than because he believed it to be true. So much that had perplexed him now made a twisted kind of sense. 'If I was possessed, I'd know it, wouldn't I?'

'Not necessarily,' Gerhard said. 'It's quite common for the victims of possession to be unaware of the presence inside themselves.' He gazed levelly at Rudi. 'Have you ever woken somewhere with no memory of how you got there? Found periods of time missing from your recollection?'

'No.' Rudi shook his head, feeling the first faint stirrings of relief. 'Nothing like that.' He remembered something else. 'Besides, you interrupted the ritual, didn't you? It was never completed.'

'Exactly.' Von Karien nodded soberly. 'At the time, we thought that would be enough to thwart their fell design. It was only after we'd examined Manfred's papers that another, more disturbing possibility presented itself.'

'Which was?' Rudi asked, already dreading the answer. Gerhard went on, his pale blue eyes boring into him like an auger.

'That enough of the daemon's essence had already entered you for it to remain trapped there, in a dormant state. It's my belief that the ritual in the woods was intended to revive it, and complete the process.'

'That's ridiculous!' Rudi protested, uncomfortably sure that it wasn't.

Gerhard shook his head soberly.

'It's my belief that whoever removed you from the house sent you to Kohlstadt, perhaps by magical means, knowing that von Blackenburg would prepare the way to complete the pact. You said yourself that he'd had dealings with the von Karien family. Manfred must have been aware that he was a fellow cultist, at the very least.'

'Why would he wait so long?' Rudi asked, seizing on every objection he could think of to the chain of reasoning that Gerhard was laying out so patiently.

Von Karien shrugged. 'Partly because he needed to make extensive preparations,' he said. 'Incarnating and binding the daemon would require a great deal of power, and a full coven of worshippers.' Gerhard nodded his agreement.

'Not only that, some kinds of ritual magic are most potent at particular times. The Chaos moon was in exactly the same alignment that night as it had been when your parents first tried to summon the daemon. It wasn't until I examined the site of the ritual, and searched von Blackenburg's house, that I began to notice certain similarities with what I'd seen fifteen years before. I began to wonder if you might possibly be the missing vessel, and set out to find you. By then it was too late. You'd already fled.'

'Then if the beastmen hadn't attacked…' Rudi's voice trailed away, unwilling to complete the thought.

Gerhard nodded soberly. 'The daemon would have taken control of your body, consuming your soul in the process. As it was, it seems to have remained dormant, at least for the most part.'

'So that's why Magnus tried to kill me,' Rudi said. He felt numb, beyond all feeling. The magnitude of the concept was just too great to grasp. Gerhard nodded.

'He knew he'd lost. All he could do was free it, and allow it to wreak as much damage as possible.'

'So if I die,' Rudi said, looking from one witch hunter to the other, letting the idea sink in slowly, 'the daemon escapes.'

'That's right,' Gerhard said, 'and sooner or later, you will. Everyone does, and that leaves us with a considerable problem.'

CHAPTER TWENTY

'ANY NEWS?' RUDI asked hopefully. Gerhard shook his head, and pulled up a chair next to the fireplace, where a small fire sputtered fitfully. The room was a large, but bare, with tiny vertical slots in the stone for windows. Its contents numbered two hard chairs, a bed, and a rickety writing table.

'No progress at all.' Their regular evening conversation concluded, both sat staring at the dying flames, as if a solution to their terrible dilemma might somehow be found within them. The form of words might have changed from night to night, but the import of them hadn't, for the whole of the three weeks that Rudi had been staying in a secure room in the templar chapter house.

In all that time, he hadn't left the temple precincts once. He'd hardly even been allowed to set foot outside the room, and the bustle and squalor of the city surrounding them had faded to a distant memory. The predominant odours were of incense, wafting on the breeze from the scores of small shrines scattered around the sprawling site, and cooking, exuding from the refectory. That, at least, was some compensation for being kept under arrest, he thought, the viands provided by the temple authorities were of the finest quality, even his uneducated palate able to discern subtleties of flavour that he'd never considered possible before. All in all, he was better off now than he'd had any right to expect, especially given the way things had been at first.

When they'd left the library annexe, he'd tried to make a run for it, but still weak from the near-fatal stab wound and the after-effects of Gerhard's healing prayer, he'd stumbled within a handful of paces, and been mercilessly battered to the ground by the two witch hunters. By the time they'd finished with him, he'd been barely able to stand, let alone walk, and had acquired a grim understanding of what von Karien had meant by his assertion that needing him alive didn't have to mean whole.

Certain that he was in no fit state to resist any further, the two men had hoisted him up between them and dragged him away to a small, windowless room somewhere in the cellars of the chapter house.

How long he'd remained there, he had no idea. Day and night ceased to have any meaning, and the only relief from the stygian darkness surrounding him was the faint glow of torchlight from the corridor beyond as it leaked around the jamb of the ill-fitting door, accompanied by a draught that chilled him to the bone. What sleep he could get was fitful at best, interrupted periodically by the clatter of boots in the corridor outside, and intermittent bursts of agonised screaming, so muffled by the intervening walls that he couldn't tell whether they came from a man or a woman.

As if that hadn't been torment enough, his head ached constantly from the talisman that Gerhard had fused to his forehead, just as he'd done with Hanna the first time the fugitives had fallen into his hands, in order to keep the daemon within him bound even more tightly than it already was. He'd soon given up trying to touch the thing, every attempt resulting in a blinding stab of pure agony, and if it was possible, he found himself hating the witch hunter even more than he had done before. Not so much on his own behalf, but because of his renewed appreciation of how much Hanna had suffered during their months in Marienburg, while a similar abomination had been suppressing her magical abilities.

Somehow, the anger had given him the strength to endure his captivity, and the growing hunger pangs, which, by the time the door finally creaked open again, had grown even more painful than the ache in his head. Forewarned by the rattle of the key in the lock he'd clawed himself upright against the moisture-slick stone, determined not to show his captors the slightest sign of weakness.

'It's about time,' he'd snapped, blinking dazzled eyes at the silhouette filling the doorframe: Gerhard, of course. Of von Karien there'd been no sign, other than the distant screaming, some luckless member of the Silver Wheel, he assumed, or some even more luckless innocent mistaken for one. With an effort of will he ignored the sound, trying to sound confident. 'Get me some food, unless you want me to starve to death and let the daemon out.'

'That won't happen,' Gerhard said flatly. 'We'll keep you alive, you can be sure of that, and sooner or later you'll tell us where the witches are hiding.'

'Even if I knew, I wouldn't tell you,' Rudi said, not even trying to hide the sudden surge of joy he felt at the witch hunter's words. Hanna was still safe. With any luck, she and Greta had both left Altdorf days ago, and were now far beyond the templars' ability to find them. 'I wouldn't be so sure you can keep me alive, either.'

'Never make a threat you're not prepared to carry out,' Gerhard said, understanding his meaning at once. A thread of contempt entered his voice. 'You're not the kind to take your own life.'

'Are you sure?' Rudi locked his eyes on the witch hunter's, summoning up every iota of loathing and hatred that he could. 'What have I got left to lose? The joy of being buried alive down here, being threatened with torture? I'd rather die now, and leave you to deal with the daemon. If you really think you can.'

'In the precincts of the temple of Sigmar? The holiest site in the Empire?' Gerhard laughed curtly. 'Of course we could.'

'Then why haven't you?' Rudi challenged him. 'Just cut my throat, let it out, and exorcise the damn thing.' He took a tottering step towards the witch hunter, who was still standing barring the door. 'But you won't, will you? You're afraid you won't be able to handle it once it takes possession of my body.' He was standing nose to nose with the man in black, practically spitting in his face with the vehemence of his words. 'Come on, I'll make it easy for you.'

The knife in his boot had gone, confiscated after a brief search, along with the one from his belt, but that didn't matter. Gerhard kept a dagger concealed up his sleeve, and with one convulsive motion he snatched at the witch hunter's shirt, ripping the fabric. The blade flew reflexively into the witch hunter's hand, and he took a step back into the corridor outside, instinctively making room to use the weapon effectively. Rudi followed, pushing his chest against the point of the blade.

'Go on,' he challenged. 'Let it out. I dare you.' For a moment he feared he might have overplayed his hand, but Gerhard hesitated, and he knew he'd won his gamble. Turning abruptly, he shouldered past the man in black, and took a step towards the door leading to the yard outside. Then he turned, and glanced back. 'I want a meal, a wash, and a bed, in that order. Then we can talk.'

RATHER TO HIS surprise, his ultimatum had proven more successful than he'd expected. The quarters provided for him were a slight improvement on the dungeon he'd so briefly occupied, but despite their relative comfort he was still a prisoner, and the sense of enclosure the four walls created in him was stultifying. There was nothing to do, no one to speak to, and his body cried out for exercise. Most of his days were filled with reading, or practising the sword drills that Theo had shown him so long ago, with the aid of a pewter candlestick to simulate the weight of a weapon.

His only visitor was Gerhard, occasionally accompanied by von Karien. Monotonous as these conversations were, concerned solely with the progress that the witch hunters were failing to make in finding a way to rid him of the daemon, or trying to get him to reveal whatever he could remember that might help to find Hanna and Greta, he almost looked forward to them. Despite the veneer of politeness that both he and Gerhard tried hard to maintain, the simmering hostility between them was never far from the surface.

'Have you eaten yet?' Gerhard asked after a while, having failed yet again to trick Rudi into disclosing what he didn't know. Rudi shook his head.

'I'm not particularly hungry,' he said. Somehow the limitless supply of gruel and dry brown bread had blunted his appetite.

'I'm heading down to the refectory,' said Gerhard. 'If you'd care to join me.' Rudi hesitated for a moment before replying. No doubt an ulterior motive lurked behind the apparently casual invitation, Gerhard probably hoping he might let his guard down away from the room and let something slip that could be used against him. Then he shrugged.

'Might as well,' he agreed. 'I could do with the exercise.' Not that the few hundred yards they'd have to walk would stretch him at all, but it was better than nothing. In the three weeks he'd been here he'd only left the chapter house a handful of times, to pray in the temple, a concession that Gerhard could hardly refuse, and once to go to the temple library, to select a few books to while away the hours of his captivity. On every occasion, he'd been accompanied by a group of armed guards, and after the first visit to the archives he'd simply asked someone else to collect books on his behalf, finding their lurking presence among the bookshelves while he tried to make his selection intolerable. Rising, he reached for the thick woollen cloak that Gerhard had provided for him. 'I assume it's still cold outside?'

'It's stopped snowing, if that's what you mean,' Gerhard said, rising too.

Catching a glimpse of himself in the glazed window, rendered reflective by the darkness outside, Rudi was struck by how different he seemed. Gone were the battered clothes in which he'd fled across the Wasteland and up the Reik. He was dressed like a templar, all in black, his new cape fastened with a small silver hammer. He could almost have passed for one of his own guards, had it not been for the ugly weal of wax in the centre of his forehead, which continued to induce its faint, throbbing headache without respite.

When Gerhard had first given him the hooded cloak, he'd hesitated for a moment before putting it on, seized by an unaccountable nervousness at the sight of the hammer on the clasp. Then he'd donned it impatiently, aware that the unease was the daemon's, not his, and that he had nothing to fear from the holy symbol. Indeed, if anything, it seemed to strengthen his resistance to the daemonic parasite nestled against his soul.

Now he knew the reason for the panic attacks that had afflicted him whenever he'd tried to set foot on consecrated ground. He had ventured into the temple itself several times since his stay began, initially, simply to prove to himself that he could do it. The first time had taken a tremendous effort of will, he had to concede. He'd stood outside the great doors, sweating and shaking for what had felt like several minutes before he'd been able to force his trembling legs into motion, and he'd left after only the most cursory inspection of the wonders inside, but he'd felt a surge of triumph in the victory over the thing within him, and subsequent visits had been a great deal easier.

He'd become particularly fond of the tiny shrine to the dwarf gods, in one of the side chapels, although he couldn't have said why; perhaps because no one else ever seemed to go in there, and he was able to savour the solitude he'd grown to love in the woods around his home near Kohlstadt. Even his ever-present bodyguards would hang back outside, leaving him to his own company for a while, no doubt feeling that nothing much could happen to him in there.

'A little snow won't hurt you,' Rudi said, trying to keep the conversation light.

They left the chambers that Rudi had been given, and the pair of templar initiates who had been waiting outside the door fell into step behind them. After a pace or two, Gerhard turned, and dismissed them with a gesture.

'He should be safe enough with me,' he said, and the two young men disappeared back into the shadows from whence they'd come. They, or others like them, had been within arm's length of Rudi every time he left his room since he'd arrived, and their absence felt like a small liberation. Gerhard smiled thinly at Rudi. 'Perhaps that will sharpen your appetite,' he said.

'Perhaps it will.' Rudi pulled the hood of his cloak up over his face, concealing the wax stigma that marked him out as a heretic. He still didn't trust the witch hunter's intentions.

Despite Gerhard's assurances to the contrary, it seemed that the snow was beginning to fall again, a few desultory flakes drifting in the flickering light from the torches outside many of the buildings. A few spots along their route were illuminated by the clearer, steady light of lamps at the top of iron columns, like those that Rudi had been told were set to light the streets around the temple, the Imperial palace, and a few of the wealthier areas of the city. Passers-by were few, driven into the light and warmth by the onset of winter, although the snow that had already settled was trampled to slush by the evidence of their passing.

'I'm sure it's only a matter of time,' Rudi said, certain that they wouldn't be overheard in the maze of narrow passageways between the buildings. 'I won't die of old age for years yet, and you're bound to find an answer before then.'

'I wish I shared your confidence,' Gerhard said, as they stood aside to make way for a small procession of dignitaries following an icon of Sigmar into one of the innumerable subsidiary chapels scattered across the site, clustering around the temple like skiffs around a carrack. This one, Rudi vaguely remembered, had been endowed by the cordwainers' guild centuries before as a mark of gratitude for Sigmar's protection against the siege of the vampire counts. As the last of the celebrants vanished inside, sweeping the accumulating patina of snow from his shoulders, the witch hunter's voice rose again to a conversational level. 'We have to proceed as if time is of the essence.' He led the way up a narrow stone staircase, which seemed to lead directly to the refectory through the Scribes' Cloister. 'Suppose you slipped on a patch of ice this evening, and broke your neck? Accidents happen.'

'Then I suppose I'm lucky to have so many of your colleagues looking out for my welfare,' Rudi said sarcastically. He shrugged, brushing the melting snowflakes from his shoulders as they gained the shelter of the cloister. The patch of ground inside the main quadrangle was bare of anything, even footprints, save for the white-shrouded shape of a sundial, denuded of purpose by the fall of night.

'It's not a random accident I'm worried about,' Gerhard said. This was new, he'd never admitted to being apprehensive about anything before. Perhaps that was why he'd wanted to talk away from the chapter house, eliminating even the possibility of being overheard. 'We have reason to suspect that our enemies are drawing their plans against us. I'm far less concerned about the possibility of an accident than I am about a deliberate attempt on your life, or something even worse.'

'You mean Hanna, I suppose,' Rudi said.

Gerhard nodded. 'Her mother, too. No doubt she's been using this time to instruct the girl in still darker sorceries. She clearly has some long-term aim in view, involving you, or the taint of raw Chaos you carry. What that might be, however…'

Rudi felt his jaw tightening, and kept his voice level with an effort.

'You know what I think. I think they're both long gone, somewhere they'll be safe from murderous fanatics like you, and as soon as we get this abomination out of my head, I'll be gone too.' He looked at Gerhard challengingly. 'Unless you intend to kill me as soon as we safely can, just to be on the safe side.'

'It has crossed my mind,' Gerhard admitted, his voice still conversational, 'but that's a problem for another day.' He glanced across at Rudi, his expression neutral. 'After all, there's no guarantee that you'll survive whatever we have to do to destroy the daemon.'

'I see,' Rudi said, masking his anger as best he could. 'And if I do?'

Gerhard shrugged. 'That rather depends on how co-operative you are at the moment.' The refectory was growing nearer, and Rudi found that the combination of cooking smells and the keenness of the air had sharpened his appetite.

'I am co-operating,' Rudi said, pushing the heavy wooden door open. Warm, steamy air and the babble of conversation rolled out to meet them. 'I've told you all I know.'

'You've told me all you think you know,' Gerhard said, following him inside and doffing his hat. Rudi pulled the hood of his cloak a little lower over his forehead, hiding the brand of heresy as best he could. 'You, of all people, must understand what's at stake if we fail. Perhaps in a more relaxed environment you might be able to recall some new little details that can help us.'

So that was it. Gerhard was hoping he'd let his guard down after a breath of fresh air and a decent meal. Rudi nodded, as if considering it carefully.

'There are a couple of seats over there,' he said at last, indicating a gap in the long bench flanking one of the tables that stretched the length of the hall. Gerhard nodded.

'That should do,' he said evenly.

Discussing their real business during the meal would have been impossible, surrounded as they were by other ears. Since they had virtually nothing else in common, they fell back on discussing the books that Rudi had been reading.

Not unnaturally, the majority of the volumes the temple library contained had turned out to be theological material of a degree of abstruseness that was far beyond his understanding, but he'd discovered a shelf full of travellers' tales during his brief foray into the labyrinth of bookshelves, and had spent his days since then learning all that he could of the ways and peoples of the Empire, and the lands beyond its borders. For some reason books on Lustria held a particular fascination for him, and he wondered if that was because of the items he'd seen in the package that Shenk had brought up the Reik for von Eckstein.

'Possibly,' Gerhard conceded, polishing off the last of his veal. 'It's a fascinating place, they tell me.'

'It seems to fascinate the Amethyst College,' Rudi said. He'd already mentioned his encounter with Magister Hollobach in a previous conversation. Von Eckstein's letter of introduction was proof that he'd met the nobleman, and Gerhard had seemed as interested as von Karien in how they'd become acquainted and the nature of the package that Rudi had defended aboard the riverboat. Rudi had, however, glossed over Fritz's presence in Altdorf. Gerhard had ordered him burned once before, and would be certain to try and arrest the young bodyguard if he was reminded of his existence.

'I'm not surprised,' Gerhard said. 'The lizard folk would seem to have a long tradition of death magic.' He shrugged. 'I've no doubt that was why Magister Hollobach was so keen to get his hands on the bauble you described. I'm certain he was hoping to learn something of their methods.'

'I'm surprised you didn't rush off to confiscate that too,' Rudi said, as they approached the chapter house again. It was snowing in earnest, thick white flakes blurring the outlines of the buildings surrounding them, and no one else was abroad. The only sign of life that Rudi could detect was the sound of singing from the service in the cordwainers' chapel as they passed by it. 'I'm sure you think it's some artefact of Chaos, like everything else magical.'

'On the contrary,' Gerhard said. 'From what I've read on the subject, the lizard people are implacably opposed to Chaos in all its forms. If we could only reach some kind of accommodation with them, what formidable allies they would be.' He shrugged, with a trace of self-mockery. 'Other than being stuck on the other side of the world, of course.'

'That makes sense,' Rudi said, without thinking. 'When I saw the artefact, I felt panic-stricken, like the first time I tried to get into the temple. It must have been the daemon, recognising something belonging to an enemy.'

'That seems plausible,' Gerhard said. He stood aside, motioning Rudi up the staircase leading to his room. As always, the two young templars were standing outside the door, awaiting his return. Gerhard turned, ready to depart. 'I'll see you tomorrow.'

'Goodnight.' Rudi began to climb the stairs without a backward glance, angry for having given the witch hunter the satisfaction of seeing his stratagem rewarded. True, he hadn't made the connection between the Lustrian artefact and the daemon inside him before, and the new shred of information might prove useful in some way, but he felt as if he'd granted his enemy some kind of moral victory by sharing it.

'Excuse me, sir.' The senior of the two templars called after Gerhard. 'Master Walder has a visitor. He specifically said he wanted to see you both when you returned.'

'Did he indeed.' Gerhard hurried up the stairs after Rudi, just as the young forester pushed open his door, and followed him into the room.

'There you are.' Von Karien looked up from one of the chairs by the fireplace. He glanced from one of the men to the other, barely suppressed excitement threatening to break through a thin veneer of self-control. 'I think I've discovered a way to break our little deadlock.'

CHAPTER TWENTY-ONE

APART FROM THE presence of his kinsman, the room seemed exactly the same as when Rudi had left it. Ignoring Gerhard, who closed the door behind them, no doubt to prevent the ever-present guards from overhearing whatever secrets were about to be disclosed, he hurried forward with rising excitement, eager to hear what von Karien had to say.

'Well?' he asked impatiently. 'What have you discovered?' Von Karien stood, and walked across the room to the unused writing table, motioning the others to do the same. A scattering of papers lay across it, along with a large, open book, bound in decaying leather, its pages discoloured with age.

'You will recall,' von Karien said to Gerhard, 'that there are several references in my cousin's papers to certain passages in the *Fulvium Paginarum*.'

'The what?' Rudi interrupted.

'That.' Gerhard indicated the volume on the table, his face twisting with disgust. 'One of the most damnable texts on the art of Dark Magic in existence. Your father evidently used it to help him select the daemon that he thought was most likely to provide him with what he wanted, and to determine the correct ritual to summon it.' He turned to von Karien. 'This is hardly new, Osric. We knew about it fifteen years ago.'

'Precisely.' Von Karien nodded, apparently unconcerned by the implied rebuke. 'But fifteen years ago we didn't have our hands on the Vessel.' He glanced meaningfully at Rudi. 'His description of the Kohlstadt ritual was most illuminating. Look at this.' He indicated a passage in the book, and held one of the handwritten fragments up next to it. 'See the discrepancy?'

Rudi craned his neck to look, but to his intense frustration neither the sinister tome nor the notes his father had made were in a language he recognised. The words clearly had some arcane power, though. As he looked at them, he felt the thing in his mind begin to stir again, incongruous feelings of glee and exhilaration rising up in him, until a stab of incandescent agony shot through his head, making him reel.

'What's the matter?' Gerhard asked, holding out a hand to steady him as he swayed over the tabletop.

'Your damn talisman's giving the daemon a kick,' Rudi said, leaning back in his seat again, and taking a deep lungful of air. Gradually his sense of his own identity began to reassert itself, through the pounding

in his head. 'It seemed to recognise whatever that gib-
berish is, and was getting excited.'

'Was it indeed. Then it seems that Osric is on to
something, after all.' Gerhard returned his attention to
the book, and the fragments of paper, studying them
both intently. 'There do seem to be a few inconsisten-
cies,' he conceded.

'Precisely.' Von Karien nodded. 'At the time, there
was no need to make a line by line comparison. Manfred wasn't the first heretic to make use of this vile
tome, and he's unlikely to be the last. Merely knowing
that he had done so, and which rituals he had
employed, was sufficient for us to deduce what he had
hoped to accomplish. However, it occurred to me that
it might be worth examining these documents again,
in the light of the new information that Rudi was able
to supply. As so often in these cases, it seems, the daemon's in the detail.'

'Perhaps he just copied it down wrong,' Rudi suggested.

'Possible, but unlikely,' Gerhard said. He read a little
more, his expression growing more thoughtful by the
moment. 'It appears that he varied some of the elements of the ritual quite deliberately.'

'What elements?' Rudi asked. The two witch hunters
exchanged glances.

'The exact details are unimportant,' von Karien said at
last, 'but they appear to be the key to the soul-binding
process.' He looked at Gerhard again, a trifle
reproachfully. 'If we hadn't been spending so much
time trying to track down the witches, I would have
found this much earlier.'

'It's never wise to forget that we have more than one enemy,' Gerhard said.

'Well, we have managed to root out three covens while we were searching,' von Karien agreed, 'so it's hardly been a wasted effort. No doubt the papers and grimoires we've recovered will lead us to more heretics once we've had time to study them.'

'So what does all this mean, exactly?' Rudi asked, trying to understand what he was looking at. 'I can only read Reikspiel, remember?' The slightly peevish tone in which he spoke reminded him of the evening when he and Hanna had stumbled across the remains of the old elf watchtower, and her amused reaction to his naïve assumption that being able to read the common tongue of the Empire meant that she could read the inscriptions in archaic Eltharin just as easily.

'In simple terms?' Gerhard pointed to the age-yellowed book, and once again Rudi found his vision blurring until he turned his head away. The script on the page formed shapes that no human eye should be able to perceive, and seemed to squirm like maggots if he tried to look at it directly. 'This ritual is a conventional one, if such a word has any meaning applied to so monstrous an endeavour, intended to summon and bind this particular daemon in the usual way, allowing it to exist for only a limited time in our world.'

'Whereas these alterations,' von Karien added, 'appear designed to allow the daemon to manifest through a human host, and remain here indefinitely.'

'Through me, you mean.' Rudi felt a chill of pure horror ripple down his spine at the thought of it.

'That's right.' Von Karien nodded. 'And it would undoubtedly have done so, if it hadn't been for our timely intervention.'

'And Greta Reifenstahl's,' Rudi reminded him. 'The same thing would have happened in Kohlstadt if she hadn't sent the beastmen to disrupt the ritual there. It seems to me that you should be thanking her, not trying to track her down and burn her.'

'Indeed it would have done.' Gerhard nodded curtly, while von Karien's face curdled with barely suppressed anger. 'The question is, why did she act as she did, and why has she continued to take an interest in you ever since? No doubt it would amuse her to disrupt the machinations of a cult dedicated to her patron power's deadliest rival, but let's not forget that she serves the Lord of Change. There's a deeper and darker purpose to her intervention, which we've yet to discover, I have no doubt.'

'Well, unless she turns up again, we'll never know, will we?' Rudi said shortly.

'We haven't seen the last of her, or her daughter,' Gerhard replied. 'I'm quite certain of that. That is why we need to destroy the daemon as quickly as possible, before whatever she's planning can come to fruition.'

'This might just be the key to that.' Von Karien gestured to the fragments of manuscript. 'By understanding how the daemon was fused to your soul in the first place, we should be able to find a way of prising it loose.' This, Rudi had gathered at an early stage of his unwilling association with the witch hunters, was what had made a conventional exorcism problematic at best. The fusion was so strong that it would require an exceptionally powerful ritual to stand even a chance of success, and there was a substantial risk of obliterating his soul along with the daemon. Von Karien, he strongly suspected, was in favour of trying it anyway, if no other possibility presented itself soon.

'That sounds promising,' Rudi said cautiously. 'How soon can we begin?'

As THE FOLLOWING days dragged out into another fruitless week, and beyond, Rudi found himself alternating between hope and despair. The witch hunters were making slow progress, even with the full resources of the temple to draw on, spending hours closeted with librarians, scholars, and members of the clergy. On several occasions they consulted priests of Shallya and Morr as well as their Sigmarite brethren, although Rudi wasn't sure why he should be surprised by that. If any deities other than the protector of the Empire were taking an interest in the problem he presented, it would surely be those of healing and death.

'I'm glad to see you're exploring every option,' he said dryly one evening, when Gerhard paid his habitual visit. The cold was still bitter, although for once the cobbles outside his lodgings were clear of the carpet of snow that had covered them for most of the week, and the witch hunter took his accustomed seat in front of the fire gratefully.

'Of course we are.' Gerhard stretched his hands out towards the flames, smiling as if picturing a heretic writhing among them. 'The archivists of the temple of Morr have an unrivalled collection of texts concerning the separation of the mortal realm from what lies beyond, and are taking a keen interest in the matter at hand. Their assistance is proving most helpful.'

'What about the Amethyst College?' Rudi asked. 'Surely they'd be able to help too.' A faint frown appeared on Gerhard's face at the suggestion.

'We're not that desperate,' he said at last. 'Magic is born of Chaos, however vehemently the Magisters might wish to deny it. Using sorcery against itself is like trying to extinguish a fire with lamp oil.'

'You used a wizard before, though, didn't you?' Rudi said. 'Alwyn was a Grey mage, wasn't she?'

'She still is, so far as I'm aware.' Gerhard looked at Rudi levelly. 'Slip of the tongue? Or is there something else you know that I should be appraised of?'

'We met your hired muscle in Carroburg, on our way up the Reik,' Rudi said, trying to match the witch hunter's even tone. 'Alwyn tried to use magic against us, and Hanna retaliated. I don't know if she survived or not.'

'I see. And yet you still insist that the girl isn't dangerous.' To Rudi's surprise, a trace of amusement entered Gerhard's tone. 'They say love makes fools of us all. Let's hope that's the worst it can do to you.'

'I don't...' Rudi started to protest, but spluttered to a halt in the face of the witch hunter's obvious scepticism. He squirmed uncomfortably, unwilling to examine his feelings too closely, trying to ignore the growing suspicion that Gerhard was right after all. There was no denying that he was an astute judge of people, adept at ferreting out things they didn't want to admit, even to themselves. 'That's ridiculous. We're just friends, that's all.'

'I'm quite sure you are,' Gerhard said, clearly disbelieving him. Rudi felt his face colouring.

'Well, what if I do feel… more than that. It's not as
if I'm ever going to see her again, is it?' The thought
struck him as von Karien's dagger had done, with a
sharp stab of pain deep inside his chest. Gerhard nodded soberly.

'I sincerely hope that's true, but I doubt it.' His blue
eyes fixed on Rudi's, his level gaze adding weight to
his words. 'If I turn out to be right, be very wary. Your
feelings may betray you, and if that happens, the consequences will be most unpleasant.'

'I'll bear that in mind,' Rudi said sourly, trying to
ignore the sudden rush of exaltation that swept over
him at the thought of seeing Hanna again after all.
Perhaps they really would meet one another once this
insanity was behind him, and they could make a life
together somewhere the witch hunters would never
find them, beyond the Empire, the Border Princes
perhaps.

'I hope so.' Gerhard continued to stare at him, as if
able to read his thoughts. 'You can't trust her, whatever your heart tells you. Remember that.' He broke
his gaze after another moment of silence, and
resumed their conversation easily. 'As for the shadowmancer, I needed assistance, and she simply turned
out to be a part of the group I hired. At least the Grey
Order is renowned for their loyalty to the Empire,
which I suppose goes some way towards mitigating
the threat they represent to it by their very existence.'

'She saved your life,' Rudi pointed out. 'And by using
sorcery, too.'

'Indeed she did.' Gerhard looked uncomfortable for a moment. 'I'm not denying that, on the whole, the Orders of Magic are at least well-intentioned, and on occasion their abilities can prove beneficial in the short term. We'd have had a far harder time throwing Archaon's horde back last year without them, for instance. But in the longer term, every time one of them casts a spell it allows another minute trace of Chaos to seep into the real world, nibbling away at the roots of existence.'

'That's not how the colleges see it,' Rudi replied. Gerhard shook his head.

'No, I imagine not, but the point remains that we're not desperate enough to enlist their aid in this matter.' He sighed, as if being forced to confront an unpalatable truth. 'Not yet, anyway.'

THE MORE HE thought about that conversation afterwards, the more Rudi found himself wondering if the witch hunter had been right: had he really fallen in love with Hanna, and if so, when? Not in Kohlstadt, certainly, even if she had been the prettiest girl in the whole valley. They had cordially detested each other then, and had continued to irritate one another even after they'd been forced to flee the village together. At some point, however, on the long and dangerous journey to Marienburg, he'd begun to understand something of the complexity of her character, how hard it had been for her to conceal her gift, and how much she must have trusted him to risk revealing her secret.

Not that she'd had much choice, of course. They would have frozen to death if she hadn't kindled a fire the night they'd fallen from the riverboat and swum to the banks of the Reik. She'd revealed a lot more than her talent for wizardry, he thought, flushing at the memory, discarding her sodden clothes to keep warm.

Now that he was able to acknowledge his true feelings for the girl, he found himself returning to the images of firelight flickering across her skin, the shadows and highlights accentuating the curves of her body, the warm orange glow making a nimbus of gold around her head as it reflected from her hair with increasing frequency. He remembered the times they'd touched briefly, the warmth of her hand in his, the yielding softness of her in a fleeting embrace, and felt an absence and a yearning every time he thought of her, which was somehow both painful and exhilarating at the same time. He thought of her smile, and her knowing green eyes, and tried to imagine the softness of her lips against his.

'All right,' he muttered irritably to himself, after another fruitless attempt to fall asleep. His head was spinning with thoughts of Hanna, as it seemed to do almost every night, robbing him of rest, and despite the lateness of the hour he felt wide awake, almost feverish. 'You were right, you know-it-all bastard. I'm in love with her.' It was the first time he'd ever dared to voice the thought out loud, and he felt a sudden lightness in his chest as he did so. Saying it made it real, he thought. I love Hanna. So, what am I going to do about it? Nothing.

The surge of exhilaration deflated again, as abruptly as it had risen. He had no idea where she was, or what might be happening to her. Greta would keep her safe, he was sure of that, but all of a sudden he was desperate to see her again, and to hear the sound of her voice. Was there some way he might be able to get a message to her?

'Bad idea,' he told himself firmly. Even if he knew how to, he wouldn't dare. The witch hunters might find out, and if they did, and tracked her down... He shuddered at the thought. Besides, if Gerhard and von Karien hadn't been able to find a clue as to her whereabouts in all this time, what chance would he have of locating her all on his own?

'To hell with this.' He rose and dressed quickly. All of a sudden the room seemed unbearably cramped. He was a forester, for Taal's sake, he belonged in the open air, not festering away in a small stone box. He flung the cloak around his shoulders, and opened the door.

'Master Walder?' The two templars outside stared at him in vague surprise, their expectation of a long, dull watch while their charge slept abruptly swept aside. 'Is something wrong?'

'I need some fresh air,' Rudi said, biting down on the temptation to tell the earnest young man that there was more wrong than he could possibly imagine. 'I'm having trouble sleeping.'

The guard shrugged. 'Did you try counting sheep?' the other man suggested, sarcastically.

'I need to visit the temple,' said Rudi. 'Maybe some prayers will help settle my mind.'

Exchanging resigned looks, the two templars fell into step behind him. Though he'd never been to pray at this hour before, Rudi thought, they'd find the request a familiar enough one to grant without arguing or referring it to a higher authority, and at least he'd be able to spend a short time out of doors.

Outside, the air was sharp, biting into the exposed skin of his face, and Rudi raised the hood of his cloak as much for warmth as to hide the mark of heresy on his forehead. The young men a couple of paces behind him did likewise, and Rudi was sure he heard a couple of muttered curses as they followed his lead across the hoar-slick surface of the Templars' Court. It was bitterly cold, sharp points of frost glittering in the silver light of Mannslieb, which cast pale shadows on the whitened ground. The lamps and torches they passed, hissing slightly as a few stray snowflakes immolated themselves in the flickering flames, spilled warm orange light in thick sticky pools across the cobbles.

He entered the temple as he always did, through a back entrance normally reserved for members of the clergy, quelling the rising sense of panic from the daemon trapped inside him almost reflexively. It was strange how easy it had become to tell which emotions were his, and which belonged to the spiritual parasite embedded in his soul. A skill he wouldn't need for much longer, he sincerely hoped.

It was the first time he'd been inside the temple at night, and he was surprised by how different it felt. The high, airy vault was still as imposing as ever, the statues of Sigmar and his most faithful followers dominating the congregation from their niches as always, but the ceiling was hidden by shadows, and the vast stained glass windows were reduced to blank-faced mirrors by the darkness beyond.

The floor of the temple was brightly lit, however, hundreds of candles suffusing the great stone building with a welcoming warmth, which still attracted a size-able congregation despite the lateness of the hour. The midnight observances were long over, but many of the celebrants still lingered, contemplating the icons and statuary, or staying behind to continue their private devotions at the many side chapels in the cross of the great T, which mirrored the shape of Sigmar's hammer so exactly. As he wandered up the aisle Rudi found himself surrounded by one such group of worshippers, arguing amiably about the most recent theological controversy to grip the Church.

'I'm not saying that Valten necessarily was Sigmar Reborn, I'm just saying that even if he wasn't, he was definitely blessed, wasn't he? So it would be nice if they had a statue or an icon of him or something.' This was an argument that Rudi had heard all the sides of during his sojourn in the temple complex, second only in popularity to the question of whether or not the current Grand Theogonist should step aside in favour of his predecessor or have him burned as a daemon-possessed heretic, and he ignored the rest of the debate as he tried to make his way around the chattering pilgrims.

'Excuse me, sorry, coming through.' He sidestepped a middle-aged couple, arm in arm, but still bickering amiably about whether the blessed blacksmith mer-ited his own shrine, and collided with a young woman on the fringes of the group. Her face was shadowed by a warm woollen cloak, in anticipation of the bone-chilling cold outside. 'Pardon me.'

'That's all right.' To his surprise, the girl took hold of his arm. Looking straight at her in sudden perplexity, he saw inside her enveloping hood for the first time. Blonde hair framed a heart-shaped face, with a wide mouth, and green eyes that sparkled with mischief. His breath left his body, as if he'd been punched in the stomach.

'This way, quickly,' Hanna said, smiling at him, and drew him into the shadows beyond the candlelight. 'We haven't got much time.'

CHAPTER TWENTY-TWO

HIS HEART POUNDING wildly, Rudi glanced around for his escort, his sudden rush of joy and relief at finding Hanna again drowned out almost at once by his fears for her safety. If the templars realised who she was, she was as good as dead. Clearly sensing the reason for his agitation, Hanna smiled.

'If you're looking for your watchdogs, they're over there.' She pointed to the other side of the nave, where the two guardians assigned to him were ambling away after another young man in a templar cloak, his face concealed by the enveloping hood, just as Rudi's was. They'd evidently lost sight of their charge for a moment in the milling crowd of worshippers, and seeing someone of the same height and build, dressed in the same way, began to follow the wrong man by mistake. Rudi sighed with relief.

'Luckily for you,' he said. 'If they'd caught sight of you…' He didn't dare to complete the sentence, for fear of tempting fate.

'Well, they didn't.' Hanna grinned at him again. 'I thought you'd be a bit more pleased to see me.'

'I am pleased,' Rudi assured her fervently. The impulse to blurt out his newly admitted feelings for her was almost impossible to resist, but this was hardly the time, or the place. There could only be moments left before the templars discovered their mistake and returned to look for him. Hanna's expression softened a little as she gazed into his face, perhaps divining more of his meaning than he'd intended from the intensity of his voice.

'I'm glad. I've… missed you too,' she said. The pressure of her hand on his arm increased a little as she spoke, and something seemed to turn a somersault in the middle of Rudi's chest. Perhaps his feelings weren't entirely unreciprocated after all. The sudden rush of elation that followed the thought made him feel breathless and giddy.

'What are you doing here?' he asked urgently. Hanna had drawn him into the lee of the pedestal of one of the statues of heroes lining the nave, and they stood almost concealed by the shadow it cast, tucking themselves back into the space between the monument and the niche it occupied. No one around them seemed to have noticed their presence yet, perhaps Sigmar really was looking out for them, he thought.

'Waiting for you.' Hanna moved a little closer as she pushed him further into the concealing cleft, and Rudi became aware of a soft, yielding pressure against his chest. 'Something's going to happen soon, and I wanted to make sure you stay safe.'

'What kind of thing?' Rudi asked, a faint echo of Gerhard's warning floating to the surface of his mind despite himself.

'I'm not sure. Something to do with the daemon inside you, I think.' Hanna glanced at the talisman on his forehead, with a grimace of sympathy. 'I'll say one thing for Gerhard, he's certainly consistent.'

'Yes, he is.' Refusing to be distracted, Rudi returned to her previous remark. 'What do you know about the daemon?'

'Not a lot,' Hanna admitted. 'Mother was hoping to find a way of getting rid of it for you, but it looks as though you'll have to rely on your new friends instead.'

'They're not my friends,' Rudi said vehemently. Hanna grinned again.

'I'm delighted to hear it. But it's not like you to sit back and wait for someone else to solve your problems, especially someone like Gerhard.'

'I'm not!' Rudi protested, before the realisation dawned that that was precisely what he had been doing. 'Anyway, it's not as if I have a choice, is it?'

'You always have a choice,' Hanna said earnestly. 'You'll find a way. Trust me.'

'I… I suppose…' Rudi said, overwhelmed with the reality of her presence. The scent of her hair was in his nostrils, and despite himself he couldn't prevent his arms from rising to encircle her. To his delirious surprise, instead of pulling away, Hanna returned the embrace. Then, after a moment, she began to pull away, with palpable reluctance. 'I can't stay any longer, Rudi, it isn't safe for me here. I have to go now.'

'Wait!' One nagging question rose to the surface of his befuddled mind. 'How did you know I'd be here tonight?'

'The Changer maps everyone's path,' Hanna said, with a trace of amusement. 'Yours isn't so hard to follow.' She leaned in again, and kissed him lightly on the lips. Astonished, Rudi began to return the kiss, hungrily, but she pulled away. 'Our paths will cross again, you can be sure of that.'

His mind whirling, Rudi watched her slip away through the thinning congregation without a backward glance, lost within moments in the vast echoing space. Taking a deep breath he moved away from the shadowy niche, and made the sign of the hammer in front of the main altar. He'd hoped for a miracle without actually expecting one, and that seemed to be precisely what he'd been given.

Turning away from the sanctuary, he found himself looking into the relieved eyes of his guardians. Both looked a little breathless, but he affected not to have noticed their brief absence at all.

'Thank you for your patience,' he said, mildly surprised at how steady his voice sounded. 'I feel a little better now.' Although he doubted that he'd get much sleep tonight, after his unexpected encounter with Hanna. His visions of the girl were stronger and more vivid than ever.

'ARE YOU ALL right?' Gerhard asked the next evening, gazing at him quizzically. Rudi nodded. His sleepless night had been succeeded by a restless day, in which he'd eaten sparingly, and had finally grabbed a fitful nap in the middle of the afternoon.

'Apart from a daemon parasite sucking on my soul, you mean?' he asked sarcastically. Gerhard nodded.

'I take your point,' he said mildly, 'but these things take time. You know we're doing all we can to find a way of removing it.'

'That's just it,' Rudi said, pacing the room. '*You're* doing it, you and Osric. I'm just sitting here, day after day, waiting for something to happen, and it's driving me crazy!' His voice was rising, he realised. Now that he was giving vent to the frustration that had been boiling away inside him for so long, the relief seemed almost exquisite. 'I'm tired of carrying this abomination around in my head, I'm tired of being jerked about by Chaos-worshipping lunatics, and I'm tired of sitting on my hands waiting for someone else to sort it all out for me. I want to do something about it myself!'

'That's highly commendable,' Gerhard said levelly, 'but while you remain here, you're as safe as we can make you. We can't take the risk of letting you run around the streets, where the agents of Chaos would have an opportunity of striking at you again.'

'I know that,' Rudi said. 'I'm not asking you to let me go out looking for cultists. That's your job. I'd just like to do something to help speed things up, that's all. You said it yourself, the sooner we get rid of this thing inside me, the better.'

'That's true.' The witch hunter nodded judiciously. 'Did you have anything specific in mind?'

'I could help in the library,' Rudi said. 'I can read, at any rate, and I could hardly be safer anywhere else than in there. You heard Osric say that he would have found out about the ritual earlier if he'd had more time to spend checking the records.'

'That's true.' Gerhard nodded thoughtfully. 'But I'm afraid most of the books he's consulting aren't that easily read.'

'I noticed,' Rudi said dryly. 'But some of them are in Reikspiel, aren't they? I could look through those, at least.'

'I suppose you could.' Gerhard looked at him levelly. 'But it's highly unlikely that you'd find anything pertinent in any of those documents. Most grimoires are in arcane languages at best, and a few of the most likely sources are in no human tongue.'

'It's worth a try, though, isn't it?' Rudi asked. He looked challengingly at the witch hunter. 'I bet you don't even know for sure what you've got locked away down there.'

'That's true,' Gerhard conceded. 'Most of the books we've acquired over the centuries are there to be contained, rather than consulted. There are those who argue that they'd be better off burned and forgotten, but destroying the page doesn't destroy the knowledge written on it, and if others use such blasphemies against us, we can fight them more effectively if we know precisely what we're up against.'

'Exactly,' Rudi said, 'and even if there isn't much chance of me finding anything useful, at least I'd feel better for doing something.'

'Fair enough.' Gerhard nodded thoughtfully. 'The talisman should prevent the daemon from taking advantage of anything you come across. I'll get Osric to make the arrangements.'

THE FOLLOWING DAY, Rudi began his researches in the library, or to be more precise, in the outlying annexe that the witch hunters used for their clandestine meetings. Gerhard conducted him there shortly after dawn, and left him there under the watchful eyes of von Karien, his ever-present templar shadows left waiting outside the door. His kinsman expressed no surprise at his newly discovered enthusiasm for ferreting through the stacks of arcane tomes, merely glancing up from the volume he was perusing at the battered wooden table in the centre of the room as Gerhard ushered Rudi inside. Rudi glanced at it in passing, but the text was in Classical, the long-dead language used only by scholars, and found outside libraries almost nowhere but in the ruins left by those who had passed from the Old World long before Sigmar had reshaped it in the forge of his indomitable will.

'So, this was your own idea, was it?' von Karien asked, once his colleague had departed. Rudi nodded, taking the man's meaning. In his position, Rudi supposed, he would be wondering if the newly kindled desire to search through books of arcane lore was entirely innocent, or the result of Chaotic contamination from the daemon he carried within him; perhaps even at the instigation of the daemon itself.

'I think so,' he said, meeting the implied challenge to his motives head on. Von Karien nodded, curtly.

'I hope so. What changed your mind?'

'I'm not sure,' Rudi told him, somehow sure that sullen vagueness would seem more convincing than an elaborately-prepared lie about his conversation with Hanna. 'I just got sick and tired of waiting around for someone else to solve my problems for me, that's all.'

'I'm glad to hear it,' von Karien said. 'I haven't exactly been thrilled about wet-nursing you, either.' He gestured to the bookshelves behind them. 'I've had anything that seems even vaguely relevant brought in here, for my own researches.' Rudi turned his head to look in the direction the witch hunter had indicated. Several of the stacks had been cleared of the old books that he'd noticed the last time he'd been in the room, and replaced with bundles of paper and a handful of bound volumes. 'Most of the material in plain Reik-spiel is on the shelves in that corner. Interrogation transcripts, the grimoires we recovered from the witches and necromancers we came across looking for your friends, that kind of thing.' He shot an evaluating glance at Rudi. 'I hope you've got a strong stomach, boy.'

'Strong enough,' Rudi replied shortly. 'I'll start with the necromancers. They're supposed to know something about life and death.'

'They think they do,' von Karien said, with a trace of vindictive amusement, 'but they burn just as easily in the end.'

'Well they should know something about the soul too, shouldn't they?' Rudi replied shortly.

'I've never known one with anything worth the name left,' von Karien said, and returned to his own researches.

Despite his casual denial, Rudi found the material he began to read through that morning hard-going, the minds who'd produced it so clearly deranged that the insanity of its authors seemed to permeate the very pages it was written on. There was a palpable malevolence about much of it too, a positive glorying in death and destruction, which he found both distasteful and disturbing. Nevertheless, he persevered, reluctant to give in so easily and allow von Karien the satisfaction of having his opinion confirmed.

His dreams that night were dark and unnerving, so much so that he woke suddenly, his heart hammering, and he almost resolved to remain in his room the next morning and leave von Karien to his researches. Then he remembered Hanna's assertion that he wasn't the kind of person to let others solve his problems for him, and the idea of betraying her confidence in him was even more painful than that of facing another day subjected to the ravings of madmen. The thought of her calmed him at last, and he fell asleep again, the image of her face strong in his mind.

After that it became much easier to deal with the horrors he read, the thought of Hanna a potent antidote to the spiritual poison on the pages in front of him. On the third day he was astonished to discover what appeared to be the manuscript of a play, bundled up and sealed.

'This is by Detlef Sierck,' he said, bemused, glancing at the name on the title page. 'What's it doing in here?'

'Not being performed,' von Karien said. 'And it never will be again. Once, I gather, was more than enough.' Shrugging, Rudi returned it to the shelf. Fascinating as the chance to read a suppressed work by the Empire's greatest playwright would normally have been, it wouldn't help him to gain any insights into the problem that faced him at the moment. Forcing a space between two of the bound volumes on the shelf he'd been working along to make room for the folio, he found it obstructed by something behind them. Von Karien glanced up, leaning back in his chair to peer around the shelf at him. 'What's the matter?'

'There's something jammed in behind here,' Rudi said. He pulled a couple of the larger volumes off the shelf and fished around behind them, eventually producing a small book. It was bound in plain leather, worn with age, and with what looked like water stains marring its surface. Its pages were wrinkled with damp, and smelled faintly of mildew. Evidently it had spent a good deal of time out of doors, or perhaps in a decaying building somewhere, becoming gradually exposed to the elements as the structure around it crumbled away. He'd seen a couple like it already, although neither had been in quite such poor condition. 'It's just another diary by the look of it. It must have fallen down the back there when this lot was put on the shelves.'

He returned to the table and opened it at random, half expecting the words to wriggle away from his eyes as they had done when he'd glanced at the *Fulvium Paginarum*. They didn't. Instead, they remained fixed on the page, faint, crabbed handwriting, the words blurred a little where the ink had seeped into the dampened paper, but still perfectly legible.

…this day did I again encounter the beastmen, escaping barely by means of concealment within a tree of alder, due to the clamour of their coming. Of the yrbes I obtained I anticipate much, and hope not to venture within the wood again for considerable time…

The Reikspiel was somewhat archaic, but still easy to understand. Rudi stared at the page, wondering who had written it, and why.

That question at least was easily answered. He flicked back through the leaves until he found the first.

Being a chronicle of my researches into the mystical realm, begun this day the third of Sigmarzeit in the 1832nd year of the Empire, set down for the guidance of others, by Theodoric of Ostermark.

Rudi felt the hairs on the back of his neck begin to prickle. This document predated the founding of the Colleges of Magic by almost five hundred years, and the destruction of the fabled lost city, which had once been the capital of its author's home province, by more than a century and a half. Perhaps this Theodoric, whoever he had been, really had stumbled across a crucial piece of knowledge lost to future generations.

The more he read, the more he began to realise that this was nothing like the deluded and blasphemous ravings he'd been plodding through so wearily before. Though most of Theodoric's notes concerned matters that Rudi knew nothing about, the man seemed to have been rational and cautious, building methodically on his earlier discoveries, and putting such arcane lore as he was able to glean from other sources to the test wherever possible. In the cases where it wasn't, because to do so seemed too dangerous or the collaboration of other spell casters was required, the sage of Ostermark had merely recorded what he'd heard or read, with such observations as had evidently seemed pertinent at the time, and moved on to more readily verifiable researches.

It was one such passage, about halfway through the book, which arrested his attention. By this time, Rudi had been reading for several hours, and his eyes were blurring with fatigue.

…it is said that the True Essences may be conjoined by means of such a ritual, as was once used by the shamans of the Old Way to commune with the spirits of beasts, although great care must be exercised lest the souls thus conjoined be intermingled too greatly for their subsequent dissolution…

For a moment, the words hung before him, their meaning obscured by the fog of exhaustion that had descended inexorably upon him as the day wore on, but as they penetrated his fatigue-dulled synapses a flood of familiar panic shook his body. Trembling so violently that he almost dropped the book, he took a deep breath and fought for calm. Whatever these notes might mean, the daemon inside him was clearly terrified of their implications. Rudi gave a feral smile.

'Got you,' he told the thing, savouring the prospect of imminent victory. He took a deep breath, stilling the hammering of his heart, and looked up at the witch hunter sitting opposite. 'Osric. I think this may be it.'

CHAPTER TWENTY-THREE

'YOU'RE SURE THIS is genuine?' Gerhard asked. Von Karien nodded, the flickering of firelight in the grate of Rudi's chamber in the Templars' Court deepening the shadows around his face, and imparting an uncharacteristic glow to his normally pale features.

'It certainly appears to be. It's old without a doubt, and the text is a close match for the known fragments.'

'The known fragments of what?' Rudi asked, and Gerhard glanced in his direction.

'Theodoric's manuscript. It's been copied many times over the centuries, no doubt being pared down to just the passages that the transcriber understood in the process, until little remained in circulation but a

handful of spells, passed from witch to witch.' Von
Karien nodded again.

'That's all I'd assumed it was, when we recovered it
from one of the Silver Wheel covens we raided last
month. I never thought to look at it more closely. If
Rudi hadn't found it when he did, we might never
have realised it was the original.'

'Or at least a full copy,' Gerhard said. He frowned,
looking troubled. 'This ritual seems like a promising
place to start, but it also confirms what we most
feared. Greta Reifenstahl, or her associates, are definitely planning something.'

'Then we need to act quickly,' von Karien urged.
'Having the book in our hands should spike their
guns nicely, at any rate.'

'Unless they've already copied the parts they need,'
Gerhard pointed out.

'All the more reason to get on with things,' Rudi
said, remembering Hanna's whispered words in the
temple. The others were only speculating, but he knew
for certain that Greta was planning something dangerous. Or had Hanna really meant to warn him
about the witch hunters? Perhaps he should stall for
time, and attempt to delay their attempt until the sorceress had been able to carry out her plan after all...
His head hummed with confusion, made all the
worse by his ever-present headache.

'I agree,' Gerhard said, taking matters out of his
hands once again. 'Whether or not the Silver Wheel
intended to use this ritual to liberate the daemon, we
can use the same method to destroy it.' A thin smile
appeared on his face, matching von Karien's. 'I have to

admit, there's a certain amount of satisfaction to be had from turning our enemies' own weapons against them.'

AFTER THAT, EVENTS seemed to move with bewildering rapidity. Clerics of increasing seniority came and went, poring over the battered book, and scribbling copious notes of their own, while the witch hunters held hushed and urgent meetings from which Rudi was pointedly excluded. Once again, he was gripped by the sensation of being thrust to the periphery of events, but this time the sense of frustration he'd felt before was absent. Hanna had promised that they'd meet again, and although he'd failed to catch sight of her on any of his subsequent visits to the temple, he continued to find the thought of her hovering presence reassuring.

So it was with a surprising degree of calm that he listened to Gerhard a couple of evenings later, while the man in black outlined the plan they were to follow.

'I can't deny that it's going to be tricky,' the witch hunter said, sipping a mug of mulled wine as he watched the snowflakes flicker past Rudi's window.

Winter had gripped the Imperial capital in earnest, and the temple precincts were becoming overrun with the desperate destitute, hoping to find some measure of warmth and comfort in the home of the Empire's patron god. The temple itself was more crowded than ever, the queues for alms only kept sullenly restive by the conspicuous presence of heavily armed templars, and on a couple of his forays to pray there Rudi had stumbled over beggars who had somehow managed to make their way out of the public areas and into the warren of byways connecting the peripheral buildings. What had happened to them, he had no idea. They were removed by the guards, he supposed, or had possibly frozen to death trying to find the way out again.

'I hardly expected it to be easy,' Rudi countered, 'otherwise we'd have done it by now.' And he would have been off in search of Hanna.

'True,' Gerhard said, and sipped at the warming drink, 'but at least we know what we're doing now.'

'Which is what?' Rudi sipped at his own drink, feeling the welcome sensation of warmth washing through his body as it drifted down into his stomach. 'I'm only the vessel, don't forget. Nobody tells me anything.'

'How very remiss of us,' Gerhard said dryly. He sat down, in his accustomed chair in front of the fire, stretching his legs towards the flames. 'I'm sure the daemon inside you would like to know how we intend to destroy it almost as much as you do.' The calm confidence in the witch hunter's voice sparked a flood of conflicting feelings within Rudi: a fierce elation, which he recognised as his own, and raw unreasoning hatred from that abominable other that shared his skin. He fought down the interloper's emotions almost reflexively, and nodded.

'I take your point,' he said, more calmly than he would have thought possible. 'So what can you tell me?' Gerhard looked at him thoughtfully.

'Only that it appears to be possible,' he said. 'The ritual you found so fortuitously in that book should enable us to separate your soul from the essence of the daemon. After that, a conventional service of exorcism should be sufficient to banish it back to whatever hell it came from in the first place.'

'I see,' Rudi said, feeling the first faint stirrings of apprehension, although whether they were his or the daemon's he couldn't, for once, be certain. 'And how soon do we try this?'

Gerhard smiled at him, in the bleakly humourless fashion that Rudi had grown all too familiar with since their fateful meeting little more than half a year ago.

'Tonight,' he said simply.

To Rudi's surprise, after leaving his room the witch hunter led him away from the familiar path towards the temple, disappearing instead down a small side passage that he had always vaguely assumed led to a cellar or storage room somewhere. The snow was falling thickly around them, and even the sporadic gleams of lamplight from the windows they passed, or the flickering torches in their wall brackets, revealed little of their surroundings. Muffled inside his hooded cloak, for which he was more than grateful, Rudi glanced around in an effort to orientate himself.

'Where are we going?' he asked, completely lost.

Gerhard shrugged, an indistinct shape in the darkness ahead of him. 'To one of the subsidiary chapels. You didn't think we were going to use the temple itself for this, did you?'

'Of course not.' Rudi hadn't actually considered the matter before, but now he came to think about it, it did seem pretty obvious. The ceremony, or whatever else Gerhard had in mind, would have to be held somewhere private and out of the way, far from prying eyes, especially if something went wrong and the daemon escaped after all... The shudder that rippled though him at that thought came from more than just the cold.

'In here.' Gerhard led the way through another door, larger and more ornate than most of those that Rudi had seen around the complex, but before he could fully assimilate the details of it the heavy wooden portal had slammed shut behind him, sucking him down into a welcome haven of warmth and light.

At first, Rudi was simply too busy doffing his cloak and savouring the cessation of the bone-chilling cold to fully take in his surroundings. When he eventually did so, he was unable to suppress a gasp of astonishment.

The room was huge and circular, and dominated by an altar to Sigmar at its exact centre. The carving and workmanship of the shrine was exquisite, easily the equal of anything he had seen in the temple itself. Even this paled into insignificance compared to the magnificence of the walls enfolding the small but grim-faced congregation, however.

Every square inch of them was covered in a finely detailed mosaic, depicting men and dwarfs of breathtaking nobility in savage conflict with the most bestial orcs imaginable, and after a moment Rudi recognised the scene as the Battle of Black Fire Pass. The only figure missing seemed to be that of Sigmar, and as he approached the altar, turning to take in every detail of the amazing panorama surrounding him, he discovered the reason for that. The god himself, still then in his mortal form, was behind him, standing guard over the entrance to this staggering sanctuary. At the sight of the incarnate deity Rudi felt the hideous presence within him quail, and his confidence grew.

His gaze travelled upwards, drinking in the ornamentation of the dome, which rose from the walls around them to enclose the whole space in a magnificently airy fashion. The mosaics continued without a break, chronicling the rest of the mortal life of Sigmar, culminating in the great twin-tailed comet that blazed across the centre of the dome. The whole space beneath it was lit by gently swinging lamps, depending from chains fixed into the ceiling so cunningly that their very presence seemed a part of the overall design, like stars surrounding and illuminating the comet itself.

'Awe-inspiring, isn't it?' Gerhard asked quietly. Rudi nodded.

'I never knew anything like this existed,' he said. 'Not even in…' He broke off, suddenly sure of where they were, but not quite able to believe it. 'This is the Sun Chapel, isn't it?'

'That's right.' Gerhard nodded. 'One of the most holy places in the whole of the Empire.' Looking around, his jaw slack, Rudi didn't feel too inclined to disagree. The gold-plated exterior dome, which gave the building its name, housed the private chapel of the Grand Theogonist himself, and few others were ever granted the privilege of entering it. If the Church of Sigmar could be said to have a single spiritual centre it was undeniably here, where the man who led it came to commune with the Empire's patron deity in person. The main temple, sanctified as it was, would merely follow the spiritual path that began here, at the altar in the centre of the room.

'Is the Grand Theogonist going to perform the ritual himself?' Rudi asked, his voice trembling a little despite his best efforts to prevent it. Gerhard shook his head.

'He has other matters to deal with.' The tone of his voice was enough to imply that in the witch hunter's opinion there were none that couldn't have been delegated with a little more willingness to make the effort. 'And if things were to go wrong…' He shrugged. 'Another difficult succession would hardly be in anyone's interests at the moment.' Again, it was quite evident from his tone that Gerhard had little time for the internal politics of the Church.

'He has, however, pronounced his blessing on our efforts here this evening,' a new voice chimed in. Rudi took the proffered hand of a chubby little man in clerical robes more by reflex than design, and shook it automatically. 'For that, we should at least be duly grateful.'

'Perhaps you'll thank him for us when you see him,' Gerhard said, his due gratitude sounding distinctly muted.

'I'm Lector Markzell,' the man said, introducing himself to Rudi as if they'd met purely by chance at some kind of social function. Only his old watchman's instincts enabled Rudi to spot the undercurrent of nervousness beneath the podgy clergyman's veneer of relaxed affability.

'Rudi Walder,' Rudi said, as if Markzell hadn't already known precisely who he was, and the lector nodded. Despite his air of evident good living his handshake had been firm and purposeful, and Rudi wondered how many people had made the fatal mistake of underestimating him over the years.

'Herr Gerhard has explained what we're about to do?' Markzell asked. Rudi nodded.

'In principle,' he said.

'Good, then we might as well get started.' Markzell stepped back a pace and turned, gesturing to the rest of the people present. Rudi expected him to attract their attention by calling out, or clapping his hands perhaps, but such was the force of the stout little priest's personality that everyone fell silent at once, and began to take up what were clearly prearranged positions around the room. Markzell turned back to Rudi. 'If you would care to make yourself as comfortable as you can on the steps of the altar? Anywhere you like, it shouldn't matter.'

'Right.' Rudi turned to follow the lector's instructions, and found Gerhard barring his way. He was about to push past, when, to his surprise, the witch hunter took him by the arm.

'Sigmar bless and keep you, Rudi,' he said quietly. By the time Rudi had got over his astonishment enough to respond, Gerhard had already turned away and gone to join the pair of templars flanking the ornately carved door of the shrine.

Perhaps it was because of this that Rudi sat where he did, facing the giant icon of Sigmar himself, the stern visage of the god gazing down at him from his vantage

point over the portal. Or perhaps he would have done
so anyway, drawing comfort from the deity's protection. In either case, it was a decision that was to save
his life before the hour was out.

CHAPTER TWENTY-FOUR

ONCE THE RITUAL actually began, Rudi thought, it seemed oddly anti-climactic. Eight priests spaced themselves in a perfect circle around the altar, midway between the shrine and the walls, at the cardinal points of the compass and equidistantly between them, chanting sonorous phrases which Rudi couldn't understand but which seemed to resonate deep inside his bones. Markzell bustled about at the altar, sometimes chanting in counterpoint to the others, and at other times doing mysterious things with incense burners or drizzling uncomfortable doses of sanctified oil over Rudi's head. Gerhard and his templars continued to stand before the doors, their expressions either intent or indifferent, it was hard to be sure.

For a long time, it seemed, nothing was happening, and Rudi began to find the warmth and the chanting

soporific. His vision began to blur, the encircling line
of clerics and the inspiring mosaics beyond them rippling as if through a summer heat haze. He blinked,
trying to clear his eyes, and as he did so he realised
with a sudden shock that Markzell and the altar were
still perfectly in focus. Something was happening to
the air itself, the power of the ritual sealing the altar
off from the room beyond. Inside him, the daemon
stirred, and a howl of impotent rage burst from his
throat.

'Good! Fight it Rudi, fight it!' Gerhard's voice came
as if from a long way away, forcing itself through the
thickening air between them. Markzell was chanting
again, facing the shrine, his voice deepening, and
beads of sweat beginning to settle in the folds around
his jowls. Without pausing for breath, he lifted a silver
hammer from the surface of the altar and turned, suddenly, bringing it down in one smooth motion
towards Rudi.

Taken completely by surprise, Rudi tried to parry the
blow with his forearm, rising to his feet as he did so,
but for once, his fighter's reflexes seemed to have
deserted him. He stumbled, his muscles cramping
painfully, and Markzell's silver hammer came down
upon his head.

Agony greater than anything he had ever
experienced roared through his body like a tidal bore,
reducing the world to a white-hot core of pain that
seemed to go on forever. Deep inside him something
seemed to tear, and as the onslaught of anguish
diminished, he became aware of his surroundings
again. Rolling over on the chill marble floor, he

staggered to his feet and looked around, dazed and confused.

Markzell was still standing by the altar, the silver hammer in his hand, and Rudi took up a street brawler's guard position as best he could on trembling legs, ready for another attack. It never came; the priest's attention was on something else, something that was inside the circle of curdled air with them. Rudi felt his stomach begin to lurch, and mastered it with an almost superhuman effort, grateful that he'd eaten lightly that evening.

A bloated mass of putrescence, nearly twice the height of a man, was oozing out of the air to take physical form before the altar, the stench of it almost beyond endurance. Arms and legs bulged obscenely from the sack of decay that caricatured the shape of a body, through which pus and rotting flesh seeped from a thousand gaping wounds. Loops of intestine, shining with mucus, twitched and writhed like sinuous creepers of putrescence. A cloud of buzzing flies circled endlessly around the mass of corruption, the noise they made drilling into Rudi's temples like an augur.

The tearing sensation inside him was diminishing, and he began to realise that the less he could feel of the daemon's presence, the more solid it appeared to be. Carried away by anger and loathing, he staggered forwards, seizing a candlestick from the altar to strike at the thing.

'Wait!' Gerhard's voice echoed thinly through the mystical barrier, and the incessant whining of the insects. 'If the connection isn't completely severed...'

He never completed the warning, as the door behind
him banged open to admit a blast of frigid air, a flurry
of snow, and a trio of ragged figures bundled up
against the freezing night outside.

For a moment Rudi assumed they were beggars from
the city, lost like the ones he'd seen before, but that
impression only lasted seconds. With a gleeful howl,
the largest of the intruders ripped away his concealing
rags to reveal a well-remembered enemy.

Without further warning, the mutant form of Hans
Katzenjammer leapt into the attack, his talons
extended to rake at the torso of the nearest chanting
priest. For a moment Rudi thought the man was
surely dead, but Gerhard was faster, his sword leaping
from its scabbard to deflect the blow. The blade met
the ridge of bone along Hans's forearm, swinging him
around to meet this new threat, and the cleric continued to chant, his voice faltering for a moment, but
picking up the rhythm again with barely a pause.

'You dare to pollute this holy place with your presence?' Gerhard's voice was thick with outrage as he
pressed his attack, and the two templars circled, striking at the mutant's thick armoured torso with their
own blades. Several of the hits were striking home,
but Hans's skin seemed to have thickened to the con-
sistency of leather, and the blows that landed
appeared to be having little effect. His three eyes
blinked lazily, and he laughed as they fell on Rudi.

'You're next, Walder, as soon as I've finished with
these fools.' The words seemed to come even more
painfully than Rudi remembered, as if he was losing
the ability to use human speech at all. 'We don't need

you any more, and you're mine.' He felled one of the
templars with a vicious backhanded swipe, which
threw the man against the wall. A splash of blood
marred the exquisite mosaic behind him as he slithered to the floor.

'I dare anything,' a cool feminine voice responded to
the witch hunter's challenge. 'The filth daemon is
mine to destroy, not yours. The Changer wills it, and
thus it must be.' The second figure walked calmly forwards, raising a hand, and the hood fell back from her
face. For a moment, Rudi's heart skipped at the sight
of a familiar mane of blonde hair, and then his eyes
fell on the pair of horns protruding through it.

'Blasphemy!' The surviving templar dashed forwards to challenge Greta Reifenstahl, aiming a cut at
her head with his sword. 'This is Sigmar's domain!'

'Not for much longer.' The horned sorceress evaded
the strike easily, extending her hand as if to push the
man away. He staggered backwards, screaming, as his
flesh seemed to flow and melt, twisting into unnatural
shapes. His sword clattered to the floor as the arm
wielding it sprouted feathers and lost its fingers,
becoming something akin to a bird's wing.

'Sigmar take your soul!' Gerhard evaded another
swipe from Hans's taloned hands, and took the head
off his luckless comrade with a single swing of his
sword. Rudi couldn't be sure, but he thought he saw
something like gratitude in the templar's ruined face
as his corpse crumpled to the floor, fountaining
blood.

'How very noble.' Greta turned towards the nearest
chanting cleric. 'Are you going to save me the trouble

of killing all these fools?' Rudi felt a spasm of insensate hatred for the sorceress, but a surprisingly muted one, and at the same time, the putrid daemon roared a challenge. The two of them must still be linked, he thought, but only barely. The mountain of filth charged towards Greta, but recoiled on the brink of touching the encircling barrier of shimmering air.

'Defend yourselves!' Markzell called to his brethren. He turned to Rudi. 'The daemon is ours. We must destroy it ourselves. If the witch does–' He had no time to continue his explanation, as, baulked of its intended target, the daemon turned towards them instead, lashing out with a huge, festering limb. The lector leapt to one side with surprising agility for a man of his bulk, and the impact of the huge fist against the floor sent splinters of marble spinning through the air. Rudi felt his cheek sting from a sudden sharp blow, and a slow trickle of blood began to make its way down the side of his face.

'What do I do?' Rudi turned to the priest for guidance, but Markzell had stumbled into the altar, striking his head, and was stirring feebly on the floor, trying to rise. The young forester was on his own, at least for the next few minutes.

For an instant, he quailed at the magnitude of the challenge before him. How could he possibly fight an abomination like this unaided? Then he rallied with a rush of fierce determination. He'd been fighting the daemon all his life, albeit unknowingly, and it hadn't beaten him yet. With a desperate scream of 'For Sigmar!' he leapt forwards, striking at it with all the strength he could muster.

It was like hitting a sack full of dung. The base of the candlestick slid smoothly through the putrid flesh, leaving a long, stinking gash, from which fluids, rank with corruption, spurted. It didn't seem to disconcert the monster in the slightest though. To Rudi's horrified astonishment, it laughed, a long, thick sticky bubbling of amusement, like gas rising through a festering cesspool.

'Such spirit, little fleshling,' it gurgled delightedly. 'What a tasty morsel your soul will make for our grandfather. Embrace his blessings, for they come to all, whether they will it or nay.'

'A mere sideshow,' Greta said, flinging a ball of sizzling flame at the nearest priest with a flick of her wrist. It burst, engulfing the man, who staggered back, screaming. Within seconds, he had been reduced to a small pile of ashes, marring the pristine marble floor of the chapel. 'Change is the essence of Chaos, in all its infinite variety. Corruption is only a tiny part of that, presided over by a weakling of a god.' She strode forwards, the barrier of rippling air in front of her abruptly dissolved by the death of the priest, and flung a stream of arcane fire at the daemon.

'Kill the witch!' Gerhard bellowed, ducking under Hans's latest attack, and laying open a wound across the mutant's belly, which barely slowed him. The daemon howled as rainbow flames engulfed it, and Rudi felt a faint echo of its suffering in the hollow space in the centre of his being, which it had occupied for so long.

'Don't you know any other songs?' the third figure asked, a familiar edge of sarcasm dripping from every syllable. Hanna strode unhurriedly into the middle of the melee, a nimbus of raw, red fire rippling into existence in front of her. Rudi stood, dumbfounded, suddenly paralysed by indecision again. 'Hello, Rudi.' She smiled warmly at him. 'Ready to go?'

'Go where?' he asked.

'Wherever you like,' said Hanna. 'It's almost over. As soon as that thing's dead, you're free.' The echo of the daemon's terror quivered inside him, and at last he understood.

'She's really killing it, isn't she? Not just banishing it back to the Realm of Chaos like Markzell's trying to do.'

'That's right.' Hanna flung the fireball she'd conjured into existence at another of the priests, but instead of striking and immolating him, it fizzled and went out. A moue of disappointment crossed the girl's face for a moment, to be replaced by one of alarm as the cleric responded with a short prayer, and a streak of golden fire shot through the space between them. Hanna cried out as it struck home, scorching through the concealing cloak she wore, and staggered.

'Hanna!' Concerned for her safety, Rudi took a step forwards, and then hesitated. Everywhere he looked, there was nothing but confusion. Gerhard and Hans were still exchanging blows, neither apparently able to gain the upper hand, and the daemon was still shrieking, engulfed in mystical flames that flickered and danced like Rhya's Veil, the mysterious polychromatic lights that occasionally appeared in the night time skies of the northlands. Markzell was still groaning, trying to regain his feet, and the other priests, far from running in panic after the gruesome deaths of their comrades, as Rudi had expected, were coming together, a common expression of grim resolution on their faces.

His decision made, Rudi took Hanna by the arm. Whatever else happened, he had to get her to safety.

'Rudi!' Gerhard ducked a slash from Hans's talons, which tore a small hailstorm of multicoloured tiles from the wall. 'Don't let her kill it!' To Rudi's astonishment there was a clear edge of panic in the witch hunter's voice, something he'd never expected to hear there. He hesitated again, wondering why the man was suddenly so frightened, and what he should do for the best.

'Help me, Rudi.' Hanna turned a pale face to his, and staggered against him.

'What happens if it dies?' Rudi asked, reaching out an arm to support her. The priests were muttering among themselves again, and more bright streaks of light, like miniature comets, were hurtling across the room. Some struck Hans, making him stagger, while the rest expended themselves against a sudden flare of yellow flame that sprang up to surround Greta. Only his proximity to the girl, Rudi assumed, prevented Hanna from being a target as well. 'Tell me!'

'What does it matter?' Hanna asked, leaning in towards him. Once again, Rudi felt the strength of his love for her warring against his rational mind. 'When it's gone, you're free. We can go wherever you like, make a real life together.'

'What happens?' Rudi insisted. The backwash of agony from the dying daemon was diminishing, becoming barely perceptible. The point would become moot in a matter of moments anyway. Hanna sighed, and looked up at him, her eyes alight with a disturbing joy that he'd never seen there before.

'Isn't it obvious? We'll have sacrificed a daemon here, in the name of Tzeentch! You can't imagine the power that will unleash. This place will become his, along with everything it touches!'

'The Church of Sigmar. The Empire itself.' Rudi staggered back, releasing her, the enormity of the idea almost too huge to grasp. 'You're delivering it all into the hands of Chaos!' Hanna straightened, apparently no longer needing his support to stand.

'That's right. So you might as well be on the winning side. After all, you made it possible.' She smiled, with the same expression of disdainful amusement that he remembered so well from Kohlstadt. 'It's not as if there's anything you can do to stop it.'

His mind spinning, Rudi glanced around the chapel, hoping to find some form of inspiration. The daemon had stopped howling, and was whimpering, making a sound like thick sludge trickling down a faraway drain. It seemed smaller, diminished, dwindling away even as he watched. Hans was staggering, his armour-like skin pockmarked from the impact of the priests' miraculous fire, and Gerhard was pressing him hard, his sword a blur of motion in the light from the swinging lamps. Greta remained invulnerable behind her curtain of shimmering yellow flame. It seemed that Hanna was right. There was nothing he could do, and no one he could call upon for help.

Then his eyes fell on the huge icon of Sigmar, protector of the Empire, and a new sense of resolve flooded through him. Almost as if the idea had come from somewhere outside himself, he suddenly knew what he had to do. Quickly, before his courage failed him, he felt for the last fading vestiges of his connection to the dying daemon.

'Hurry,' he thought, hoping the link still functioned both ways, and that the crippled abomination was still whole enough to respond, 'while there's still time!'

Suddenly the thing vanished, disappearing from the mortal world again in a single burst of imploding air. Greta staggered, as if she'd been struck, and the nimbus of flames surrounding her abruptly went out.

'What happened?' She turned to glare at Rudi, her face a mask of perplexity and horror. 'What in the name of all change have you done?'

'What I had to.' Rudi staggered, reaching out to the altar for support. He could barely believe it himself.

'In here we swear by Sigmar, witch.' Markzell had regained his feet at last, suffused by an aura of power that made the hairs on the back of Rudi's neck stir. His voice had become deeper, more resonant, echoing from the apex of the dome. 'And his will is absolute!'

'Hans! Save Hanna!' Greta shouted, and the mutant broke off his battle with the witch hunter at once, sprinting across the violated chapel to scoop up the girl in his inhumanly strong arms.

'Put me down! Mother!' Hanna began to protest as the mutant turned for the door, evading a final thrust from Gerhard's blade as he did so. Greta began to turn, clearly intent on following them, and then the world seemed to explode.

'This desecration is ended!' Markzell bellowed, and the chapel became filled with silver flames, rippling outwards from the lector, and from the altar at which he stood. Hans, a screaming, squirming Hanna still struggling in his arms, barely made it out of the door in time, howling as his heel was caught in the wash of cleansing fire, and was instantly seared to the bone.

Rudi cringed, anticipating an agonising death, but the flames flickered around him without burning, seeming cool and soothing to the touch. Their radiance filled the chapel, and as they washed over him, he felt a deep sense of calm. Almost without realising it, his eyes were drawn to the titanic figure of Sigmar, who seemed to be gazing back at him with an expression of compassionate reassurance.

The priests, too, were looking at the icon of their god with awestruck reverence. Gerhard had fallen to his knees, an expression of peace and joy on his face, completely at odds with what Rudi thought he knew of the man's bleak and unyielding personality. Although he couldn't be sure, as he strained his eyes to see through the flickering luminescence surrounding him, he thought he could see the figures of the immolated priest and the mutated templar as well, restored to their former selves, standing with their comrades for a moment or two, before vanishing entirely in a soundless burst of light.

An agonised scream, which seemed to go on forever, wrenched his attention back to his surroundings from the vision of blissful peace he'd been gifted with. Unlike everyone else in the chapel, Greta wasn't being protected from the full effect of the affronted god's wrath. The fire was consuming her, from the inside out, burning cold through her eyes and mouth in streamers of blue-white flame. As Rudi watched, she dwindled, like melting candle wax, hissing and falling to the floor, where, in a handful of seconds, she was consumed utterly, vanishing as if she had never been.

A moment later the mystical fire began to diminish, and the chapel began to take on its everyday appearance. It was still as magnificent as it had always been, but somehow, Rudi knew, it would always seem pale and tawdry now, to those few who had been here tonight and seen it touched by the hand of Sigmar himself. He could think of no other explanation for what had happened. Markzell took a deep, shaky breath, clearly profoundly moved.

'What happened?' The templar who Hans had struck down, and who Rudi had assumed to be mortally wounded, was stirring and climbing to his feet, an expression of bewilderment in his eyes. The mosaic behind him was clean and unmarred. As he looked around the chapel, Rudi suddenly realised that all the damage inflicted in the battle had disappeared, along with the bodies of the fallen, leaving not a trace of the momentous events that had transpired here. 'I thought I saw...' he shook his head, bemused.

'You saw a miracle,' Gerhard said, trying hard to regain his usual composure. He looked across at Markzell. 'Is it done?'

'No.' Markzell shook his head. 'I never got to complete the separation, let alone the banishment. The daemon just vanished.'

'Then what happened to it?' Gerhard demanded. Rudi looked at him wearily.

'It's back where it started,' he said, trying to ignore the flare of malicious amusement in the old familiar corner of his being where the parasite dwelt. 'Inside me.' He met the witch hunter's uncomprehending stare with blank resignation. 'I had to take it back. It was the only way to prevent...' His voice trailed away. The consequences of not having done so would have been unthinkable, and he still didn't dare to contemplate them. Gerhard nodded soberly.

'Thank Sigmar you did,' he said.

'Can we attempt the ritual again?' Markzell asked. Gerhard shook his head, working out the full implications of this final twist of fate in his mind.

'I don't think that's possible,' he replied bleakly.

CHAPTER TWENTY-FIVE

'SO THE BOOK was a trap,' von Karien said, his voice bleaker than the snowstorm that continued to flurry around their heads as they plodded wearily back to Rudi's lodgings. Every templar in the complex had turned out to hunt for Hanna and Hans, the moment the alarm had been raised, and von Karien had headed straight for the Sun Chapel to find out for himself exactly what had been going on. Gerhard nodded his head in agreement, coming to the end of a terse summary of the apocalyptic events of barely an hour before.

'Obviously we were meant to find it, and make use of the ritual it contained. Allowing the daemon to manifest on consecrated ground weakened the aura of sanctity enough for the witch to enter the chapel and invoke the power of her own blasphemous god, even in a place blessed by Sigmar, himself. If we hadn't pre-pared the way for her, she would never have been able to cross the threshold.'

'Then it's all my fault,' Rudi said, his heart colder than the flensing wind that tugged eagerly at his cloak. 'If I hadn't insisted on reading those papers, none of this would have happened.'

'It would have been brought to our attention some other way,' von Karien said shortly. 'You can be sure of that. If they were willing to sacrifice a dozen of their own people just to make sure the damned book fell into our hands, they wouldn't have just left it to chance that we'd find what we were looking for in there.'

'One of the cultists we brought in with it would have been told just enough to point us in the right direc-tion after sufficient persuasion,' said Gerhard. 'All you did was bring things to a head a few days earlier than they would have otherwise.'

'What exactly would have happened if she'd man-aged to kill the daemon?' Rudi asked, still trying to comprehend the enormity of what Greta had hoped to achieve. Like everyone else in the Empire, he'd heard whispers about the malign influence of Chaos all his life, and his recent first-hand dealings with its agents had opened his eyes to the reality of the threat it represented, but its true magnitude seemed too great for the human mind to grasp. 'I know it had something to do with desecrating the chapel, but I don't see how that would have tainted the whole Empire.' Or perhaps he didn't want to see it, he told himself bleakly, still clinging to some vestige of hope that Hanna hadn't fully understood what it was that she'd been helping to bring about.

'The chapel would have been re-consecrated to her own dark deity,' Gerhard said, 'and the taint would have spread from there to the rest of the Church. If she'd succeeded, every prayer to Sigmar in Altdorf and beyond would have been twisted to further the power of Tzeentch. At least for a time, until the True God reclaimed his own.' How long that would have been, Rudi had no idea, and he suspected that Gerhard didn't either, but even a handful of minutes would have been enough to wreak untold spiritual corruption throughout the Old World.

'Then we should give thanks that Rudi had the presence of mind to realise what had to be done, and the courage to go through with it.' Von Karien looked at Rudi with a respect he'd never shown before, 'Few men would have, I'm sure.'

'I had a little help from Sigmar,' Rudi said, feeling uncomfortable with the witch hunter's unaccustomed approval.

'That's true enough,' Gerhard said. He looked at Rudi, an expression curiously akin to confusion flickering across his face behind the obscuring curtain of snow. Rudi had clearly been touched by Sigmar, aided directly by the god whose temple he served, which meant that according to everything he believed in, the young man couldn't be a heretic after all. On the other hand, he continued to harbour a daemon within him, one that would become immensely powerful the moment he died, which meant that he was still a walking embodiment of Chaos.

Rudi had little sympathy to spare for the witch hunter's crisis of confidence. He too was being torn apart by conflicting emotions. The magnitude of Hanna's betrayal was only just beginning to sink in, but that hadn't diminished the yearning he still felt to be with her. Somehow, that had become mingled with anger and bitterness, so that he was no longer sure where love and loathing blurred into one another. Sometimes he thought that she must still be an innocent dupe of the Dark Powers, just as he had been, and at others that she'd been a party to this monstrous conspiracy from the beginning, even before they'd left Kohlstadt together. He'd probably never know the whole truth, the point at which her Chaotic heritage had finally overwhelmed her, and whether she'd fought against it to the last, or chosen to embrace it willingly in the end.

'I take it there's no point in attempting the ritual again?' von Karien asked, narrowing his eyes against the flurrying snow.

'None at all,' Gerhard said. 'Rudi accepted the daemon willingly this time, rather than being an innocent victim. The bond between them is indissoluble.'

'Perhaps that's just as well,' Rudi said, trying to put a brave face on the unalterable. 'We can't trust a thing in that damned book. Even if we tried, Sigmar alone knows what else we might be stirring up that we weren't ready for.'

Despite all he could do to prevent them, his thoughts kept returning to Hanna. How could he have been so blind? Gerhard had been right, his feelings

had betrayed him. Damn it, he'd known her mother
was a Chaos cultist when they'd gone off together;
how could he have been so stupid as to trust her?

It was because he loved her. *Had* loved her, he corrected himself hastily. Now he felt... He didn't know
what he felt. The image of her laughing face floated
across his mind, and suddenly all his old feelings were
back, as fresh as they had been when he'd first
acknowledged them. Then they were swept away by a
fierce, passionate anger, and he wanted nothing more
than to see her burn as she deserved, the treacherous,
conniving witch.

He breathed the freezing air deeply, grateful for the
distraction it afforded. Snow still lay thickly around
the temple complex, rutted to slush by the passage of
innumerable feet along the most frequently used
byways, which were now becoming resurfaced with
irregularly indented ice as the mess refroze. Rudi and
the witch hunters placed their feet carefully, keeping
their balance easily with the confidence of experienced fighters.

Preoccupied with his whirling thoughts, he barely
noticed a small group of cloaked and cowled figures
approaching them from the direction of the temple.
Like everyone else they'd seen that evening they were
heavily muffled against the cold, and their gait
seemed a little unsteady as they slipped and slithered
on the rutted ice.

As they got closer, Rudi heard them muttering
among themselves: just another group of clerics on
their way to a service somewhere, murmuring prayers
as they went. He relaxed again, only then becoming

aware that his hand was groping for the hilt of the sword that no longer hung at his belt, impelled perhaps by the memory of the disguised interlopers who had disrupted the ceremony in the Sun Chapel.

It was at that point that he became aware of the words the little group was chanting, and without any conscious thought he leapt into the attack.

'Hail the vessel! Hail the vessel!' The phrase was unmistakable, the very chant that he'd heard from Magnus's band of cultists in Kohlstadt and Marienburg.

'Rudi! What in the name of Sigmar–' Gerhard began, but his protest died away, his weapon leaping into his hand. Rudi's first punch had dislodged the hood of the leading cultist, and the face revealed left his true allegiance in no doubt at all, as its owner reeled back into a pool of flaring torchlight. Thick black blood welled stickily from a nose, mashed back into a visage ravaged by disease, pustules blooming across swollen and febrile cheeks.

'Templars! To arms!' Gerhard bellowed, moving up to stand shoulder to shoulder with Rudi, and deflecting a downward blow from a rusted knife blade as he did so. He caught the luckless cultist on the backswing, hewing through his or her windpipe, the body so swollen with corruption as to completely obscure its sex. Von Karien barged Rudi aside, stepping in to impale the man he'd punched on the point of his own sword, and the mutant monstrosity folded, gurgling.

Despite the witch hunters' attempts to keep him out of the fight, Rudi found himself facing another of the shrouded figures. He parried another knife thrust easily with his forearm, seizing his assailant's billowing cloak and pulling the cultist sharply forward. Off balance, the madman lost his footing on the treacherous cobbles and fell heavily at Rudi's feet. Rudi stamped down hard on the creature's neck, hearing a *crack!* like a dried twig snapping, and the follower of Chaos spasmed under his boot sole.

'Rudi! Keep back!' Gerhard roared a warning, his blade flashing in the torchlight as it reaped its crimson harvest of Chaos-worshippers. Von Karien ran another would-be assassin through, and suddenly the narrow passageway was quiet and still, save for the groans of the dying.

Gerhard sheathed his sword as a group of templars hurried up to them, their own weapons drawn.

'See if there are any survivors in a fit state to put to the question,' he ordered, 'and burn the rest of this offal at once.' He turned to Rudi, his face concerned. 'You're bleeding. Are you all right?'

'I'm fine,' Rudi assured him. 'It's just a scratch.' The tip of the cultist's dagger must have caught his sleeve as he parried it. 'Look, it's barely broken the skin.'

He smiled as he spoke, holding up his forearm to the light of a hissing torch in a nearby sconce. The exercise had left him feeling comfortably warm, despite the freezing temperature. If anything, it had felt good to be facing a simple, uncomplicated threat again.

'Nevertheless, let's get you back inside,' Gerhard said. He glanced at von Karien. 'Can you tidy up here?'

'No problem,' von Karien assured him, taking charge of the party of templars with easy authority.

'I'm all right,' Rudi insisted, following Gerhard up the stairs to his room. Though the fire was unlit, it still felt warmer here than outside. He discarded the heavy cloak with a feeling of relief. The faint scratch along his forearm was barely visible, and he cleaned it in the bowl on his washstand as he spoke. 'I'll need a new shirt, though.'

'That can be arranged.' Gerhard headed towards the door. 'But first things first. I'll get a healer to look at your arm. There's always the risk of infection.'

'If you must.' Rudi listened to the witch hunter's feet clatter down the stairwell. True, when he died the daemon would get loose, taking possession of his body in the process, but there was no reason to suppose that he wouldn't live to a ripe old age first, particularly with one of the most powerful institutions in the Empire taking an obsessive interest in his welfare.

Of course, that was simply postponing the problem, and from the daemon's perspective a few more decades here or there, before taking physical form and wreaking untold havoc across the face of the Old World, was probably no more than a minor inconvenience. There would be plenty of time to find an answer before then, and he would, he vowed. Whatever it took, he would send the daemon back to hell, and prevent the foul legacy of his parents from polluting the lands of the Empire.

There was no sign of Gerhard returning, and no point in going to bed until he did.

Stifling a yawn, he picked up the book that he'd been halfway through on the night he'd persuaded the witch hunter to let him wade through the material recovered from the cults they'd raided, inadvertently springing Greta's trap in the process. Since then all he'd read had been the ravings of madmen, and the chance to lose himself for a while in the fanciful tales of faraway lands that he'd become so fond of held out the promise of an hour or two of welcome relief from the thoughts that continued to torment him. Opening the book at the scrap of paper he'd used to mark his place, he continued to read.

Of all the marvels which the continent of Lustria has to show, the greatest must surely be the vast temples and dwelling houses of the lizard folk, which continue to stand from time immemorial, despite the encroachments of the jungles which surround them. Though many have lain abandoned for so long that the time since last a footfall echoed among them would seem vast even to the elf or dwarf kinds, a wise traveller would do well to avoid entering such places: for the scaled ones still account them sacred, and pursue such trespassers as they become aware of without pity or respite.

Rudi nodded. He'd read similar warnings in other accounts of journeys through the New World, and had heard as much at first hand from von Eckstein, the afternoon the nobleman had shown him and Hanna the artefacts he'd obtained from that far distant continent. Along with that thought, the memory of the strange disc of polished stone and the bundle of knotted cords floated to the surface of his mind, and there was something else, too. He'd felt a flare of irrational panic at the time, he remembered, merely puzzling

then: one of the flashes of inappropriate emotion that
he'd felt from time to time, which had come and gone
so capriciously. With hindsight, and his newfound
ability to distinguish his own feelings from those of
the daemonic parasite within him, it had obviously
been the daemon that had reacted so strongly to the
peculiar objects. He'd even mentioned as much to
Gerhard.

A new hope began to rise within him. It was a long
shot, of course, but perhaps, just possibly, the Lustrian
artefacts might provide the answer they were looking
for. If the daemon had been so afraid of them, there
must surely be a reason.

The room felt hotter than ever, and he swallowed,
suddenly aware of a raging thirst. He stood, the
book falling unheeded to the floor, and took a step
towards the ewer of tepid water sitting on a table by
the door. His head reeled, and his footsteps stumbled. Raising a hand to brush the thin sheen of
sweat from his forehead, he caught sight of the
scratch on his arm. It was livid now, puckering up
from the skin like the weal of a lash, and a thin,
pale fluid was beginning to weep from it. A roar of
vindictive triumph echoed around the inside of his
skull.

'Rut you, pusbag. I'm not dying yet!' Summoning
up the last vestiges of his strength, he pulled the door
open, and staggered across the threshold.

'What's wrong?' The nearest guard caught him as he
fell, a note of panic entering the man's voice. Somewhere in the distance, Rudi heard the sound of
running feet hurrying up the stairs.

'Tell Gerhard... Hurry...' he managed to gasp, and then the world disappeared into a maelstrom of swirling grey.

CHAPTER TWENTY-SIX

TIME PASSED IN an indeterminate blur as Rudi drifted in and out of dreams that seemed as real, or intangible, as the events going on around him. Now and again, in his more lucid moments, he became aware that he was surrounded by activity, voices droning in prayer or conversation, only to segue seamlessly into the realm of febrile imaginings.

Finally he woke normally, stirring in his bed to find daylight leaking in through the window, and levered himself up on his elbows, panting with the effort of attempting to sit upright.

'Good, you're awake.' Gerhard was looking at him narrowly, relief and concern mingled on his face. 'Here, drink this.' He handed Rudi a goblet full of some herbal infusion that smelled foul and tasted worse, although once it was down, Rudi felt a little more energy flickering through his body.

'What happened?' He tried to swing his legs over the side of the bed, and the room seemed to rock around him, almost as if he was back aboard the *Reikmaiden*. After a moment, the solid walls seemed to steady themselves. 'Have I been ill?' It was possible, he supposed, although he'd never known a day's sickness in his life.

'You were poisoned.' Gerhard looked at him soberly. 'The blades of the scum who attacked you were coated in venom, a foul concoction that even the best apothecaries in the city have been unable to fully identify.' He shrugged. 'They've been treating you with antidotes for the components they have been able to isolate, however, and I've been praying for your recovery.' Remembering how Gerhard's intercession had healed his knife wound, Rudi found that more comforting than anything the apothecaries might have done.

'Thank you.' He swung his feet to the floor, relieved to find that his legs, though weak, would still take his weight. 'How long have I been asleep for?'

'Eleven days,' Gerhard said, and Rudi felt his head spinning again. With an effort he forced himself to breathe deeply, and his hammering heartbeat began to slow down. 'Fortunately you were able to take a little broth, so there was no danger of you starving to death. Nevertheless, it's been an anxious time.'

'I can believe it.' Rudi looked around the familiar room, finding that fresh sigils and holy symbols had been chalked on the window and door, and that a circle had been inscribed on the floor around the bed.

The implication was obvious, fearing for his life, and uncertain that the talisman on his forehead would be enough, Gerhard had made whatever preparations he could to contain the daemon in case he died and released it. This, above all, brought home to him how much danger he had been in, and how narrow the margin was by which he'd been able to cling to life.

Gerhard looked as if he was about to say something else, but before he could do so, the door opened to admit von Karien. His kinsman glanced in Rudi's direction with an unmistakable air of relief, and then returned his attention to Gerhard.

'Your guest's here.' A troubled expression crossed his face. 'Are you absolutely sure about this?'

'No, of course I'm not.' Gerhard shook his head. 'But we're out of options. If it's a choice between the possibility of long-term damage and the certainty of imminent catastrophe, then that's hardly a choice at all.'

'I suppose not,' von Karien said, although he sounded far from happy. He turned to go. 'I'll show him in.'

'Thank you.' Gerhard watched him leave the room, an expression of resignation flickering over his usually impassive visage. Rudi was beginning to pick up on the man's moods more readily now, a result he supposed, of their enforced association. He was beginning to understand a little more about what drove the witch hunter, and the terrible price that would have to be paid if he ever failed in his duty, but that didn't mean he had to like the man, or approve of his brutal methods.

'Did any of them talk?' he asked, recalling the last order that Gerhard had given the templars before they'd returned to his room together. Taken by surprise at the question, Gerhard shook his head.

'None of them were in any fit state to,' he said, 'but we're certain of who they were in any case.'

'The remains of my father's cabal,' Rudi said, having come to the same conclusion.

'That's right,' the witch hunter said. 'We knew someone must have survived the raid on the family estate, your disappearance made that obvious. They must have gone to ground after that, waiting for a chance to complete their foul design. Your arrival in Altdorf conveniently gave them that.'

'Well, it's like you told Osric,' Rudi said, 'we should have remembered that we were dealing with more than one enemy.'

'Indeed we should.' Gerhard nodded soberly. 'And we should have tightened security immediately after the incident in the Sun Chapel, instead of devoting all our resources to hunting the witch that got away. If one group of heretics could get in undetected...'

'It would never have worked,' von Karien assured him, reappearing at the door. 'The only way to secure a place like this is to keep the populace out of it entirely, and what use is a temple without worshippers?'

'Very little, I would imagine,' a dry voice behind him commented, and von Karien stood aside to allow the other man into the room. The voice had sounded vaguely familiar, but it was only as he took in the purple robes and the cadaverous face above them that Rudi recognised its owner.

'Magister Hollobach,' he said, failing to mask his astonishment, 'what are you doing here?' The Amethyst mage looked at Gerhard, and then back to Rudi.

'You haven't been told?' he asked, a carefully modulated tone of surprise entering his voice.

'He's only just regained consciousness. There hasn't been time to explain,' said Gerhard.

'I see.' The pale eyes took on an enquiring look. 'Then perhaps it's time our young friend here became acquainted with the facts.'

'What facts?' Rudi asked, somehow sure he didn't really want to know. He looked challengingly at Gerhard. 'You said that consulting the colleges was out of the question.'

'I'm hardly ecstatic at the prospect of working with the witch hunters myself,' Hollobach said, 'but our mutual friend has impressed upon me the absolute necessity of our co-operation in this matter.'

'Mutual friend?' Rudi asked, perplexed. His head was spinning again, and he felt simultaneously hungry and nauseated by the thought of food.

'Von Eckstein. He has the artefact we need,' said von Karien.

'The Lustrian stone?' Rudi asked, taking his best guess. Hollobach nodded. 'I thought he was giving it to your college for study.'

'It's not quite as simple as that,' Hollobach said. 'As you've probably gathered, Graf von Eckstein trades influence and favours – all for the good of the Empire, of course. From his point of view, the Lustrian talisman is just a small part of a much bigger picture. He needs it to impress potential investors, and the interests of the colleges must be traded off against that. I have access to the item in question only under such conditions as he cares to set.'

'When I explained to him why we need it, he insisted that Magister Hollobach be involved,' von Karien said, with evident resentment. The magician nodded again.

'The progress I've made in decoding the quipu makes that unavoidable,' he said, with the barest trace of smugness. 'It would have taken you weeks to translate it yourselves, even with the aid of my notes. Time, I may remind you, which we do not have.'

'What's a quipu?' Rudi asked, trying to understand. He had a vague memory of having come across the word before, in one of the books he'd read, but his sluggish mind refused to disgorge the information he wanted. With shaking hands, he poured himself a drink from a ewer standing on a nearby table. Gerhard watched the liquid slopping in the cup with evident concern.

'The lizard priests encode information in cords, by means of a series of knots. Each one has a precise meaning,' Hollobach explained. 'The quipu, which accompanies the Lustrian talisman, explains what it is, and how it should be employed.' A trace of animation entered his voice. 'It's quite fascinating. It seems the talisman can be used in a ritual to bind the soul irremovably to the body.'

'You mean you can make me immortal?' Rudi asked, astounded. If that happened, the daemon would never be able to escape and take possession of his physical shell. Hollobach shook his head.

'Not exactly, no. It's more a question of anchoring the soul to the mortal plane than prolonging life as we'd normally think of such a thing.'

'That sounds like necromancy!' Rudi said in horror, the blood draining from his face as he recalled some of the obscene ravings he'd read in the collection of papers that he'd waded through.

Von Karien nodded his vigorous agreement.

'Exactly. The darkest of dark magic; the idea's unthinkable!'

'Believe me, if this was anything remotely like necromancy I'd have no part of it,' Hollobach said vehemently. 'Such things are a perversion of natural law, which my order regards with absolute abhorrence. This is different.' He coughed gently. 'You would simply be suspended between this life and Morr's realm, a part of both, but fully in neither.'

'A ghost, you mean?' Rudi asked, even more confused. In his weakened state it was hard to be sure whether the spasms of fear and horror that continued to shake him were his own or the daemon's: probably both, he thought ironically.

'Not a ghost,' Hollobach said. 'Your spirit wouldn't be free to wander. The whole point of this ritual is to keep it confined to your physical form.'

'It's the only way, Rudi,' Gerhard said. 'If we do this, the daemon can never manifest itself, because your spirit can never leave your body to make room for it.'

'You mean I'd be trapped inside a rotting cadaver for eternity?' Rudi asked, an abyss of terror opening up beneath his feet at the prospect. 'Aware of what was happening the whole time?'

'Not exactly for eternity,' Hollobach said, in the tones of a man who cared more about reassurance than accuracy. 'The mage priests of the reptile folk who've undergone this process have apparently endured for several thousand years, but their bodies have been mummified to preserve them. Yours would simply crumble to dust in a few centuries, and by that point there would be nothing left for the daemon to possess. Presumably when that happens you'd be able to complete your journey to Morr's realm, and the daemon would simply destabilise.'

'If there was any part of me left by then,' Rudi pointed out.

Hollobach shrugged.

'That's a considerable risk, of course. There's no denying that you'd be trapped for hundreds of years with a daemon entangled in your soul; hardly a prospect to take lightly.'

'Well, thank you for explaining it to me so clearly,' Rudi said. He took another gulp of the water, which for some reason did little to quench his thirst. He glanced at Gerhard. 'And thank you for taking my suggestion seriously after all. It seems we'll just have to keep looking for an answer.'

'I'm afraid it's not that easy,' Gerhard said heavily. 'We've run out of time to look for one.'

'Run out of time?' Rudi looked from one face to another, all three men clearly hoping one of the others would explain. 'What do you mean?'

'You're dying, Rudi,' Gerhard explained, after the silence had lengthened uncomfortably. 'The antitoxins were only partially effective, and even healing prayers can only reverse so much of the damage that the poisons left behind in your system are doing. Every major organ in your body is breaking down, quickly and irreversibly.'

'How long have I got?' Rudi asked numbly, ignoring the howl of triumph from the oubliette in his psyche where the abomination inside him dwelt.

'The rate of deterioration is accelerating,' von Karien said. 'Our best guess is four or five days, a week at the outside.'

'Then let's do it,' Rudi said, 'as soon as we can.' A strange sense of calm had descended on him. Events were moving beyond his control again, but he could at least decide his ultimate fate. The daemon's euphoria evaporated almost as quickly as it had erupted, to be replaced by the familiar surge of thwarted rage. Rudi ignored it, as he had done so often before.

'That's a brave decision, Rudi.' Gerhard nodded, relief evident in his eyes. He turned to Hollobach. 'Where do you want to carry out the ritual? We could probably find somewhere in the temple precincts.'

The Amethyst mage shook his head dubiously.

'Remaining here on consecrated ground would give us more protection, there's no doubt about that, but if something was to go wrong, and the daemon escaped after all, there's a whole city full of souls out there for it to harvest. I'd advise moving out to a rural shrine, where fewer innocents are at risk.'

'Hammerhof,' Rudi said slowly. Von Karien glanced at him sharply, and then nodded.

'The perfect place,' he agreed. 'It's consecrated ground, and it's miles from anywhere.' He shrugged. 'And I can't deny there's a pleasing symmetry about it.'

'I know.' Rudi nodded, shivering, and pulled the counterpane up around his shoulders. 'It all started there – it's only right that it should finish there, too.'

CHAPTER TWENTY-SEVEN

TWO DAYS LATER they left the temple precincts just after dawn, in a coach surrounded by templar outriders, and Rudi watched the dismal city streets jolting past beyond the window in a desultory fashion. He'd insisted on climbing aboard by himself, shrugging aside Gerhard's offer of a helping hand with a pettishness that vaguely surprised him.

'I'm dying, not an invalid,' he'd snapped, clambering up the steps with more effort than he would have believed possible, and dropping onto the hard leather seat with a sigh of relief. The cold winter air had invigorated him a little, and enough of it seeped around the pane of glass that he now leaned against to keep his head clear, but the biting chill seemed to be settling into his bones, a constant presence, and he shivered uncontrollably most of the time. He pulled the thin travelling rug that Gerhard had handed to him around himself, grateful for its presence.

He'd brought very little with him, even less than he'd left Kohlstadt with so many months before. There didn't seem to be any point in burdening himself with possessions now, not even a change of clothes. By this time tomorrow, he'd have no need of anything. Before leaving his room in the Templars' Court for the last time Rudi had dumped the rest of his worldly belongings, a pitifully small collection, on the bed and contemplated them.

'I suppose Osric should have these,' he'd told Gerhard before turning towards the door, the last remnants of his former life already forgotten. For a moment he'd considered bequeathing something to Fritz, who, if not exactly a friend, had certainly become a companion on his adventures, despite the mutual loathing they'd had for one another back in their home village. But so far as he knew, Gerhard was still unaware of the young man's presence in Altdorf, and it might not be prudent to draw his attention to the fact. The last time the witch hunter had laid eyes on Fritz, he'd ordered his execution as a heretic for attempting to conceal his brother's mutations.

Rudi sighed heavily, misting the glass for a moment. The streets of the capital city were just as crowded as he remembered them, despite the ravages of winter, and the omnipresent stench, which he'd almost forgotten about in the incense-scented cloisters of the temple, wound its way in through the gaps in the coachwork along with a myriad of freezing draughts.

All those people, he thought, going about their lives, far from the remnants of Archaon's armies and the havoc they'd wrought in the north, blissfully unaware of the fact that Chaos was here too, gnawing away at the foundations of their safe and secure little world. He shuddered again, not entirely from the cold, and watched street traders and burghers, fishwives and mercenaries, servants in livery and beggars in rags, and envied them all their ignorance. Some glanced at the coach as it passed, but most ignored it, wrapped up in their own petty concerns.

Well, if his sacrifice was to be the price of all those lives continuing to potter along in peaceful obscurity, oblivious to the threat all around them, then perhaps it was worth it after all. He'd known what the stakes were in the abstract, but seeing all these people, flesh and blood human beings, made it seem real. For the first time, he began to understand that this really was about more than the struggle between himself and the daemon inside him, and that its final defeat wasn't just a matter of personal pride.

'Feeling tired?' von Karien asked. The two witch hunters were sitting on the bench seat opposite.

'No more than usual.' He continued to stare out of the window. So many faces, and none of them the one he suddenly realised that he'd hoped against all rational expectation to see. There were plenty of young women about, many of them blonde, but Hanna, naturally, was nowhere in sight.

That was probably just as well too, he thought. It wasn't as if he knew what he'd do if he did catch a glimpse of her. Smile and wave, or cry *'Witch!'* like the lynch mob in Kohlstadt had done, and watch while the templars rode her down? Once again his warring emotions contended briefly, before subsiding quietly into apathy. None of it seemed to matter any more. Their paths had diverged again, as he'd always known they would in the end, and by some twist of fate they'd ended up on different sides in a battle that neither of them could ultimately win.

He jerked back to wakefulness, suddenly aware that he'd been dozing. They'd passed beyond the city gates, journeying through a bleak winter landscape, the fields and occasional patches of woodland muffled beneath a blanket of snow. For the most part it seemed undisturbed, apart from the ribbon of rutted slush marking the approximate limits of the road they followed, although the crisp white surface was mottled here and there with traces of the small animals that continued to eke out a living in the harsh winter conditions. Even from within the jolting coach Rudi could recognise rabbit tracks, and the marks left by scavenging birds, and felt his spirits lifting. This was where he belonged, he thought, out here in the countryside, as far as possible from the thronging hives of humanity where he'd spent so much of the past year.

He glanced back, seeing the long, low bulk of the city wall receding into the distance.

'How much longer?' he asked. Von Karien shrugged, looking a little uncomfortable, and Rudi felt an unexpected pang of sympathy. No doubt his kinsman was recalling the last time he'd been to the old family estates, fifteen years before, and had devoutly wished never to return.

'An hour or two, it depends on the road.' Rudi nodded, as the coach shuddered against a particularly deep rut. The ground was frozen solid, which at least meant they wouldn't be bogged down in the mud as they would have been in the spring or autumn, but the icy conditions would be treacherous, and the coachman would have to drive cautiously.

'How's Hollobach getting there?' he asked, suddenly aware that the three of them were alone in the carriage. He'd been expecting the magister to join them for the journey, but they'd evidently bypassed the Amethyst College completely. It wasn't all that surprising, now that he came to think about it. The simmering animosity between the wizard and the witch hunters had been all too evident at their previous meeting, and it was hard to tell which of them most disliked having to work with the other.

'I've no idea,' Gerhard said, managing to imply that such a state of affairs suited him fine. With nothing much else to say, Rudi returned his attention to the bleak winter landscape.

RUDI HADN'T BEEN quite sure what he expected to find in Hammerhof, but the large, sprawling manor house still managed to surprise him. They'd come to it through the hamlet, a small cluster of homes and businesses that barely merited so grandiose a title as 'village', and he'd anticipated something on a similarly modest scale. Instead, as the carriage rounded a small copse of snow-shrouded trees, he found himself looking at a mansion, which seemed at first to rival the scale of von Eckstein's town house in Altdorf.

'Impressive,' he said. He looked across at von Karien. 'I'd no idea you'd given up so much.'

'It was tainted,' von Karien said shortly, 'as I told you. I wanted no part of the place, and I still don't.'

'I'm sure the use the Church has been able to put it to has more than redressed the balance,' Rudi said. The patch of woodland was disappearing behind a wrought iron gate in which the symbols of the hammer and the twin-tailed comet were intricately intertwined, and he gave the copse a last, regretful look as his view of it was finally cut off by a high brick wall. He could picture the quiet and solitude within the glade, and felt it calling to him, a final lingering reminder of his old life. The gatekeeper, an elderly priest bundled up in a thick cape against the cold, clanged the portal closed behind the coach and scurried gratefully back to the warmth of his gatehouse.

'I hope so,' von Karien said.

The main driveway swept up to the front of the house, which seemed to be flanked by the same jumble of outbuildings that graced von Eckstein's estate. This was the main entrance, Rudi reminded himself, and had been laid out with the intention of impressing visitors, but it was hard not to feel awed by the place. After everything he'd heard from Gerhard and von Karien, he'd been expecting there to be some brooding reminder of the manse's sinister history in the very atmosphere surrounding them, but the only ambience he could discern as he disembarked painfully from the coach was one of cheerful activity. Initiates and clergy were hurrying from building to building, discussing matters of doctrine, devotional

art, or the latest plays on the stages of Altdorf as they
went, while servants moved about quietly in the background, unobtrusively catering to their more worldly
needs in order that they might turn their minds more
readily to higher things. Many of the outbuildings
appeared to have been converted to scholarly uses,
and it didn't take Rudi long to pick out a chapel and
a library. Most of the main rooms of the house, he
assumed, were used for study or accommodation.

This guess was confirmed as soon as he crossed the
threshold, finding himself in a high, wide entrance
hall, flagged in marble. Twin staircases rose in an elegant curve at the far end, giving access to the upper
floors, and a statue in the same material, depicting
Sigmar leaning on his fabled warhammer, loomed
over everything, its head level with the second storey
landing.

'Ah, you're here at last.' Magister Hollobach emerged
from a drawing room on one side of the hall, his footsteps echoing on the pale, milky stone. The neutral
surroundings seemed to emphasise his lack of
colouration, making him fade into the background,
so that his vivid purple robe struck the senses with
even greater force. 'We arrived some time ago.'

'We?' von Karien asked, with manifest suspicion, casting around for a glimpse of other wizards. 'I thought you
were to be the sole representative of your Order.'

'I am.' Hollobach looked at the witch hunter with
amused disdain. 'I was referring to von Eckstein's
emissaries. You didn't think he'd let me remove the
talisman from the safety of the college without sending someone along to keep an eye on it, did you?'

'No, not really,' Gerhard admitted. He glanced at the oak-panelled door from which the magister had emerged. Hollobach had left it open, and Rudi caught a glimpse of a fire beyond it, and a scattering of comfortable chairs. Some of them seemed to be occupied, although he couldn't tell by whom. Hollobach noticed the direction of his gaze.

'Do you want to rest, or take some refreshment, before we begin?'

'What's the point?' Rudi asked. Resting wouldn't relieve the aching in his bones, he knew, and the thought of food or drink merely nauseated him. 'Let's get this done.' The daemon inside him was thrashing in panic, wave upon wave of thwarted rage battering against his own resolve, but instead of wavering, Rudi found that he was taking fresh heart from it. His life was all but over whatever he did, and by Sigmar he was going to make his death mean something. He glanced at the two witch hunters. 'Unless you'd like to take advantage of the offer, of course.'

'We can wait,' Gerhard said. He and von Karien had shared a simple meal of bread and cheese in the coach, although Rudi hadn't been able to stomach the thought of eating anything himself.

'Then we might as well get started,' Hollobach agreed. 'I'll get the talisman.' He disappeared into the drawing room again.

'Where are we going to do this?' Rudi asked. 'The chapel?' Von Karien shook his head.

'I've exchanged letters with the abbot about this, and we've agreed that the old lodge would be the best place. The cellars are still intact, and we can seal them up again afterwards. Apart from us, no one will ever know you're down there.'

'The old lodge,' Rudi echoed, feeling a faint sense of foreboding at the words. 'Where's that?'

'Out in the grounds, away from the house,' von Karien said. He hesitated. 'It's where Manfred and Gertrude conducted their blasphemous rites.'

'It was properly blessed and sanctified when the Church took the place over, of course,' Gerhard said, no doubt anticipating some objection on Rudi's part, 'so there's no danger of the daemon drawing any power from some lingering taint.'

'But it's where it was summoned,' Rudi said. Once again he was overwhelmed by a sense of inevitability. Subconsciously, he supposed, he must have been expecting this from the moment he'd suggested returning to the estate in the first place. 'Completing the circle.' He took a moment to savour the irony, goading the struggling daemon within him. It would spend centuries trapped immobile in the very spot where it had hoped to gain limitless freedom to rampage across the mortal world. He shrugged. 'That seems fitting.'

'I'm glad you approve,' von Karien said. Footsteps rang on the marble floor, and the three of them turned to face Hollobach, who was returning with the first of his travelling companions. A woman was with him, wearing britches and a travelling cloak, striking red hair falling down around her shoulders.

'Rudi.' Mathilde looked at him, an expression of shocked pity on her face. Hollobach had undoubtedly told her what they were doing there, but being brought face-to-face with it was evidently proving more of a shock than she'd anticipated. It was the first time that Rudi had ever seen her lost for words, her habitual air of breezy self-confidence momentarily absent, and he found that more disturbing than he could have put into words. He noticed the new ring on her left hand.

'Hello Mathilde. Sorry I missed the wedding.' He felt the pity in her eyes like a punch in the face, and tried to inject a little spontaneity into his rictus grin. 'Something came up.'

'We heard.' Mathilde turned her head, glancing back through the drawing room door. 'Just how long does it take you to finish a drink anyway?'

'Sorry, my love.' Fritz appeared, wiping his mouth on the sleeve of his shirt. 'Sigmar's teeth, Rudi, you look awful.'

'You don't look so bad yourself,' Rudi said. If anything, he found the lad's habitual lack of tact refreshingly honest. Fritz seemed about to return the pleasantry when he glanced past Rudi to his companions, and the expression of amiable idiocy on his face turned to one of murderous fury. His sword hissed from its scabbard as he registered Gerhard's presence for the first time.

'You murdering scum, you killed my mother!'

'Surrender or die, heretic!' Gerhard drew his own blade, and squared up to face him.

'If you want him, you'll have to go through me.' Mathilde drew steel too, and stood shoulder to shoulder with her husband.

'You see how the taint of heresy spreads?' Gerhard asked Rudi, facing them both with easy confidence, and moving into the attack.

CHAPTER TWENTY-EIGHT

'ARE YOU INSANE?' Despite his frailty, Rudi lunged forwards to stand between the putative combatants.
'We're here to prevent a daemon getting loose, not
squabble among ourselves!' He seized Gerhard's
sword arm in a grip a kitten could have broken, but to
his relief the witch hunter refrained from shrugging
him off. Gradually Gerhard began to relax, but he still
kept his sword up.

'Easy for you to say,' Fritz snarled. 'It wasn't your
mother he killed, was it?'

'Actually he did,' Rudi snapped back. 'He burned her
as a witch fifteen years ago, my father too.'

'And you're willing to go along with this maniac?'
Mathilde asked, incredulous.

'Well yes, I am,' Rudi said, wondering if he could get
everyone to put their weapons away before the strain

of channelling his anger caused him to collapse. Another headache thundered behind the talisman fused to his forehead, and he used the pain, fighting to keep his thoughts focused. 'For one thing they both deserved it, and for another, if I don't then thousands of innocent people are going to die. So let's stop this stupidity right now, and go and save the Empire while it's still here to save, all right?' He swayed on his feet, and grabbed at von Karien for support. To his vague surprise he found the gesture hadn't been entirely theatrical.

'Eminently practical advice,' Hollobach said dryly. He turned a scornful gaze on the pair of witch hunters. 'Unless you'd rather waste precious time executing the trusted agents of one of the most influential men in the Empire on a whim? The consequences of that for your order would be... interesting.' The prospect seemed to amuse him. For some reason, Rudi suspected, the mage's derision was the deciding factor for Gerhard.

'We'll settle this later,' the witch hunter said shortly, sheathing his sword. A moment later Mathilde followed suit, scowling.

'Fine by me, but if anyone calls me a heretic again I'll let my sword do the talking.' She nudged Fritz, who finally put his own blade away, with a truculent expression that suddenly reminded Rudi of the taciturn bully the young man used to be.

'All right. What she said.' He glared at Gerhard. 'And as soon as the daemon's dead, you're following it to hell.' He rubbed his arm absently where Mathilde had punched it. 'Why did you do that?'

'Don't pick a fight unless you're ordered to,' Mathilde said. 'It's not what we're paid for.'

'Your husband harboured a mutant, madam.' Gerhard had obviously noticed the matching rings the couple now wore. 'That's an act of heresy, pure and simple.'

To his evident surprise, Mathilde laughed.

'You've just described Fritz in a nutshell: pure and simple. He'd be the first to admit he's not the sharpest arrow in the quiver; he just wanted to help his brother, that's all.'

'Besides,' Rudi put in, 'you told me you killed Frau Katzenjammer in case the taint had spread, and it obviously didn't. Fritz hasn't mutated at all, has he?'

'Damn right.' Mathilde nodded, grinning in a self-satisfied manner. 'Believe me, I'd have noticed.'

'I'll bear that in mind,' the witch hunter said sourly, 'but Rudi's right. This is not the time to debate the matter.'

'Fine. Then let's get on with it before I drop dead and the daemon gets loose, shall we?' Rudi said, turning towards the panelled oak entrance door, still leaning on von Karien for support. Everyone fell in behind him, their minds finally back on the business at hand. Only Fritz continued to glower at Gerhard, clearly unwilling to let his personal vendetta go, and Rudi could hardly blame him for that.

'Osric,' he said, 'you know the way. Where's this old lodge?'

'Some way from the house, I'm afraid,' von Karien said, leading the way out into the snow-covered grounds. Away from the cluster of buildings the footing became treacherous, the snow ankle-deep, and Rudi stumbled frequently, grateful for his kinsman's supporting arm. He breathed the cold air deeply into his lungs, revelling in the sense of openness and space after being so long surrounded by buildings and people. In the distance, beyond the wall, a flock of birds burst into flight, rising from the patch of woodland he'd noticed before.

'Someone's been this way ahead of us,' he said, noticing the faint indentations in the snow where later falls had settled in the prints left by other feet. There were several sets of tracks, apparently heading out in the direction they were following, and then returning towards the house. Von Karien nodded.

'The abbot sent some of the ground staff out to open the cellars up for us. They've been sealed for a long time.'

'That was a good idea,' Rudi said dryly, panting a little with the exertion of walking. 'I'm not really up for swinging a pick myself.'

'It's not much further,' von Karien reassured him, as Rudi's feet slithered on a patch of ice beneath the snow, and he stumbled, almost falling. The witch hunter pointed to a low mound in the blanket of whiteness, and squinting his eyes against the glare of reflected sunlight, Rudi was just able to make out the shrouded remains of tumbled walls, grey stone blackened by the traces of a long-dead fire.

'I see your methods haven't changed much in the last fifteen years,' he said to Gerhard, and Fritz's expression darkened even more, if that was possible.

'Simple, but effective,' Gerhard said.

The ruins afforded some shelter from the wind at least, and Rudi leaned against a segment of wall, looking out over the grounds while he recovered his breath. The wind felt good against his face, ruffling his hair, and it occurred to him with a pang of regret that this would be the last time he'd ever experience the sensation of standing in the open air.

'Where is the cellar?' Hollobach asked, glancing around the ruins.

Von Karien pointed. 'Over there.' He led the way towards a corner between two interior walls, reduced to about waist height. A mound of rubble, lightly dusted with fresh snow, stood in the angle of the tumbled partitions, and he bent down to brush a layer of white powder from a couple of planks covering a ragged hole in the floor. As Rudi turned his head to follow his progress, the westering sun struck shadows and highlights from the undulating blanket of snow smothering the gardens.

'That's a fair-sized hole,' Fritz commented. 'Must have taken them quite a while.'

'It looks like they had some help with it,' Rudi said, gesturing to the marks only he could see. 'There's another set of tracks coming in on the other side.' Part of him marvelled that he was still capable of holding a casual conversation, this close to a living death. The thought of what was to come, bricked up immobile in impenetrable darkness while his body rotted away around him, rose up suddenly in a paroxysm of suffocating panic, and he fought it away with an effort of will stronger than he would have believed possible. He'd made his choice, and he'd stick with it. He'd vowed to do whatever it took to frustrate his family's twisted plans, and that was an end of the matter. In the meantime he'd take whatever pleasures life still had to offer, however small and fleeting they might be.

'Estate workers, probably,' von Karien said. Before he could say any more a mound of snow on the far side of the wall erupted, revealing a snarling mass of muscle and hair.

'Beastmen!' Rudi yelled, his astonishment giving way to the reflexive urge to defend himself. He reached for his sword instinctively, finding nothing there, and fell back against the crumbling brickwork, panting with the effort. Warned by his shout, von Karien ducked a vicious blow from a large-bladed axe, and drew his own weapon.

'Defend yourselves!' Gerhard yelled unnecessarily, as more of the grotesque fusions of animal and man burst from their concealing cocoons of snow. Fritz and Mathilde moved back-to-back, while Hollobach muttered something. A moment later a scythe of glowing blue flame materialised in his hands, and he struck out at a howling creature with goat-like horns and a second, fang-filled mouth in the centre of its forehead. The creature came apart in the middle as the mystical weapon struck home, the crude club it wielded clattering to the rubble-strewn floor. 'Protect Rudi!'

His head spinning, Rudi tried to make sense of the ambush. The creature that had attacked Hollobach was undoubtedly dead, but there were four more of the things charging home against them, bloodlust shining in their misshapen eyes. The hulking bull-headed creature that had challenged von Karien closed in on the witch hunter, who parried its second strike skilfully, and opened up a slash across its belly with his sword as he riposted. Far from discouraging it, however, this only enraged the monster, and it struck out savagely again. Von Karien leapt back, barely avoiding its axe.

Two of the others converged on Gerhard, who gave ground grimly, his blade flickering as it parried attack after attack, until Hollobach stepped in, his shimmering scythe taking the hand of one of the beastmen off at the wrist as it swung an ugly, spike-studded club at the witch hunter's head. The ram-headed creature bleated in fury and turned on the mage, drawing a dagger from its belt as it did so, and flying at him, trying to strike under his guard. Hollobach stepped backwards to avoid it, slipping on the carpet of snow as his foot found an obstruction under the muffling blanket, and fell, his head striking one of the protruding pieces of rubble. The mystical weapon vanished, and the beastman hurdled the body of the fallen mage to lunge at Mathilde, who deflected the clumsy thrust easily, and stabbed it through the heart. The creature fell, its knife dropping from nerveless fingers to skitter along the frozen ground.

The fourth figure howled with glee as it leapt the wall and closed in on the woman, slashing down with talon-tipped fingers, and with a thrill of horror Rudi realised that this was no beastman after all, but the mutated form of Hans Katzenjammer. Mathilde ducked, just in time, and countered, her sword rebounding harmlessly from the ridge of bone along Hans's forearm.

'Rudi.' He turned, feeling a light touch on his shoulder. Hanna stood there, smiling, and for a moment, he felt all his old affection for her rushing back. The pressure of her hand increased a little, as she tried to urge him into motion. 'Come with me. We don't have much time.'

'Time for what?' In the periphery of his vision, the battle continued. Blood fountained as the bull-headed monster struck von Karien in the arm, driving him to the ground, and the blood-stained axe rose to administer the *coup de grâce*. Hollobach rose to his knees, his purple robes sodden and grubby, an expression of grim resolution on his face. Gerhard continued to engage the second beastman that had attacked him, but it moved like quicksilver, striking and slashing with the sword in its hand and the sting in the long, curving tail that rose up over its shoulder. Most of the creatures had mutations as well as the bestial appearance of their kind, Rudi realised, which probably wasn't all that surprising given the allegiance they seemed to owe to the Lord of Change. Mathilde fell too, struck down by Hans. Bellowing with laughter, the mutant prepared to finish her.

'We have to kill the daemon inside you,' Hanna said. Her arm slid around Rudi's shoulders, supporting him, trying to lead him away. 'Quickly, while the others keep these fools off our backs.'

'You can't,' Rudi said. 'It's too late.' His head reeled with the desire to help his friends, but he was too weak to move, and Hanna's close physical proximity was as heady as it had always been.

'Of course I can.' The strange stone she'd taken from the skaven was glowing again, Rudi realised, channelling her power as he'd seen it do before. Hanna glanced up, as if noticing something barely significant for the first time. 'There's just a little something I need to do first.'

Before he could intervene or protest, a seething ball of hellish red flame burst into existence in front of her, and streaked through the air towards Gerhard. He saw it coming, and tried to move aside, but it burst against his right arm, searing the flesh, and burning through to the bone beneath. Screaming, the witch hunter fell, his sword dropping to the ground beside him, and rolled, steam hissing from the site of the wound. The beastman lunged down, striking with its sting, and Gerhard jerked, spasming as the venom it carried began to course through his veins.

'Stop it!' Hanna shrieked, her face suddenly dissolving into a mask of petulant fury. 'He's mine!' The mutated beastman turned, an almost human expression of astonishment flickering across its muzzle, just before another ball of crimson fire burst against its chest. 'I told you, he's mine!' Turning away from the shrieking creature, whose fur was completely ablaze, she smiled at Rudi again, as if nothing untoward had happened at all. 'No one ever listens,' she said, as if it was merely a minor annoyance.

'I'm listening,' Rudi said. Hollobach was on his feet again, his lips moving, and the bull-headed creature froze in the act of bringing its axe down on von

Karien's prostrate form. The witch hunter rallied, striking upwards with his sword, and penetrating the creature's chest. With a bellow of agony its eyes rolled upwards and it toppled slowly to the snow.

'Leave her alone!' Fritz yelled, leaping in to stand between his wife and what had once been his brother. A viciously-taloned hand rose to swat him out of the way, and then a spark of recognition seemed to flicker in the trio of eyes, and a bellow of inhuman laughter echoed around the ruins.

'Growing a backbone, Fritzie? Out of my way, or I'll finish you too, as soon as I've done for your slut.'

'I won't let you hurt her!' Fritz took up a guard position, his sword steady. 'My mother's dead because of you! You're not taking anyone else I love!'

'Love?' the mutant laughed again, the harsh gutturals of his voice all but unintelligible. 'You've never loved anyone. Poor little tag-along Fritzie, never had any friends, never did anything I wouldn't do first. You were pathetic then, and you're pathetic now.' The gigantic hand rose, swatting Fritz aside as if he was a fly.

'As soon as I kill the daemon, you'll be free,' Hanna said, dragging Rudi's attention back to her. 'Then we can be together for always, just like you want. I know that's what you want.' She smiled, coquettishly. It should have been enticing, Rudi thought, but somehow the effect was grotesque, as if she was playing a part that she didn't quite understand. 'We can do this.' She kissed him, long and slow, and Rudi felt his senses reeling. 'And more, much more.'

'I'm sorry,' Rudi said, slumping against her. 'I can't move. I'm so weak.' He buckled at the knees.

'Come on, hurry.' Hanna seemed to have forgotten her attempt to seduce him already. 'I can help you.'

'Thank you.' Rudi straightened, putting an arm around her shoulder for support. Von Karien was struggling to his feet, blood pouring from the gash in his arm, while Gerhard still lay prostrate on the ground next to the noisily expiring beastman that Hanna had struck down in a moment of anger.

Hollobach was stumbling towards Hans, his lips moving in some arcane incantation, but his intervention was to prove unnecessary. Fritz dodged his brother's blow at the last moment, and struck, aiming the point of his sword straight at the third eye in the middle of Hans's forehead. The mutant's neck snapped straight, with a howl of agony, and he fell to his knees, rancid ichor seeping from the wound.

'You little...' the words died away in a rattling gasp, and an expression of petulant astonishment crossed his face. Powerful claws flexed against the frozen ground, trying to find a purchase. 'I'll kill...'

'No. I will.' With a surge of anger-fuelled strength, Fritz thrust the blade in up to the hilt, the tip of it bursting from the back of his brother's skull. The mutant's arms flailed for a moment, trying to find a target, and then the light went out in his remaining eyes, and he toppled to the ground.

'Some honeymoon this is turning out to be,' Mathilde grumbled, scrambling unsteadily to her feet. She kissed Fritz. 'Thanks.'

Leaning into Hanna for support, trying to ignore the intoxicating effect of the yielding warmth of her body against his, Rudi slipped the point of the dagger he'd plucked from the concealed sheath in her bodice through the thong supporting the skaven stone around the girl's neck. He cut the cord in one swift movement, snatching the little leather bag with his other hand, and throwing it as far as he could. Hanna screamed with anger, rounding on him and pushing him to the ground.

Rudi fell heavily, feeling the breath being driven from his body as he watched the girl sprinting after the talisman. He tried to rise, but the toxins in his system were doing their baleful work, their effects intensified by the physical exertion, and he couldn't find the strength.

'Stop her!' he shouted. 'Don't let her pick it up!'

His warning was unnecessary. Perceiving the danger, perhaps through some arcane attunement to the magical world, Hollobach was already running towards the strange stone that the girl had carried for so long. Hanna was younger and fitter, however, making a desperate dive for it before the magister was anywhere within reach.

'Sorry.' Mathilde tackled her, driving her to the ground, and the Amethyst mage bent down to pluck the little bag from the tips of her scrabbling fingers. 'Stuff like that's better left to proper wizards.'

'I'll kill you!' Hanna tried to throw Mathilde off, but the older woman was an experienced professional fighter, and held on to her easily.

'Need a hand, Rudi?' Fritz leaned down, proffering assistance. Rudi seized him gratefully by the wrist, and was pulled awkwardly to his feet.

'Thanks,' he said. He glanced at the two wounded witch hunters. 'You'd better help Osric and Gerhard.'

'This one's beyond help,' Fritz said, stepping over Gerhard with barely a glance. The animosity he clearly still felt for the man might have been affecting his judgement, but Rudi found it hard to disagree. Gerhard's face was pale, and his breathing laboured. The witch hunter reached out to take Rudi by the ankle as he passed.

'Hurry,' he breathed.

'We will,' Rudi assured him. Fritz was binding up the gash in von Karien's arm with a surprising degree of skill, but without much enthusiasm.

'What is that thing anyway?' Mathilde asked, looking at the little leather pouch curiously, ignoring both the squirming and the stream of invective beneath her. Hollobach tipped the stone out into the palm of his hand.

'I've never seen anything like it,' he admitted at last.

'I think it stores magic, somehow,' Rudi said. 'It drained the energy away when Gerhard's talisman prevented Hanna from casting spells, and she seems a lot more powerful when she's got it with her.'

'Of course.' Von Karien nodded. 'That's how she hoped to sacrifice the daemon, by drawing power from the stone. It wouldn't have had the catastrophic effect polluting the temple in Altdorf would have done, but it would have tainted the ministry of all the souls who trained for the priesthood here.'

'You know nothing,' Hanna said, scornfully. 'You think you do, but you're just insects. I'll kill you all.'

'You talk a good fight, I'll say that for you,' Mathilde said cheerfully, hacking off a strip of Hanna's skirt with her dagger, and expertly tying her hands with it.

Hanna struggled to her feet, glaring at everyone in turn, her eyes finally coming to rest on Rudi.

'You idiot,' she said, her voice dripping with contempt. 'You could have had everything you wanted; a long life, free of that filth inside you, and me.'

'If it's any consolation, it was tempting,' Rudi said, 'but the price was too high. My soul's my own, and I'm keeping it.'

'Want to bet?' Hanna asked, her voice becoming suffused with the gleeful malevolence he'd noticed before when the destructive side of her powers had overwhelmed her. 'I don't need the stone to cast spells, remember?'

Rudi flinched back as another ball of hellish red flame burst into existence in front of her. Then, to his relieved astonishment, fizzled and went out, vanishing as if it had never been.

'I'm afraid you do,' Hollobach said. 'Consecrated ground, remember? Chaos magic won't work here without something to boost its potency.'

'No!' Hanna's air of self-confidence began to crumble. She glared at Rudi. 'This is all your fault! My mother's dead because of you!' Her eyes began to fill with tears, and a howl of grief and loss escaped her. 'And now they're going to burn me, and I'll die screaming, and it's *all your fault!* I *hate* you! I'm *glad* you're going to suffer forever. *I hate you!*' The last few words were barely coherent, a raw, primal scream of anguish that made the hairs rise on the back of Rudi's neck. Then the girl's knees gave way under the pressure of her emotions, and she fell heavily to the ground, bawling and raving, calling down every curse she could think of on her captors. From this angle something seemed odd about the fall of her hair, and with a prickle of apprehension he realised that the buds of two small horns were beginning to grow through it.

'They're not going to burn you,' Rudi said, as calmly as he could. 'I promised you that when we left Kohlstadt, and that's one promise I can still keep.' With more strength than he knew he still possessed, he struck down with the dagger in his hand, clean through the vertebrae at the top of her neck, as quickly and neatly as dispatching a rabbit. Hanna's body jerked and spasmed, falling suddenly to the ground, a flickering of something that might have been astonishment and gratitude in her eyes for a moment, before the deep emerald green of them clouded forever.

'Talking of burning,' Fritz said, a challenging edge to his voice. Von Karien shook his head.

'You've proven to me where you stand,' he said. He turned to Gerhard, whose breathing had become so shallow that it was almost impossible to tell that some faint spark of life still lingered. 'Luther might disagree, but it's my decision, and so long as you serve the Empire faithfully you'll have nothing to fear from me or my order.'

'Is there anything at all you can do for him?' Rudi asked Hollobach. He supposed he ought to feel something after Hanna's death, but he had no energy left for emotions, and there would be time enough to consider everything later. For a moment he quailed anew at the thought of the eternity of suffering that lay ahead, and then he steeled himself again. He'd made his choice, and he knew now that he'd lost Hanna a long time ago, if he'd ever even had her in the first place, which he doubted. The mage shook his head.

'I can ease his passing,' he said gravely, 'but that's all.' Gerhard stirred, shaking his head feebly.

'No magic,' he whispered.

'It's your choice, of course.' Hollobach nodded to Fritz. 'Do you wish to intervene?'

'No,' Fritz said shortly, turning away, 'let him suffer.'

'We'll finish it,' Rudi promised the dying witch hunter. Gerhard nodded once, and tried to say something, and then the breath rattled in his throat and his body convulsed. A few flakes of snow drifted down from the leaden sky, settling across the still face and unblinking eyes.

Rudi turned away, remaining upright and unsupported purely by willpower. There wouldn't be a better time, he thought. All the instincts of a lifetime spent outdoors told him that the first flurry of snow was only the precursor of a much heavier fall. By the time his companions had bricked up the cellar and returned to the mansion, there would be no trace of their handiwork visible until the spring, by which time the new mortar would have weathered to the point where it would be almost indistinguishable from the old. No one else would ever know he was there, entombed in his own private hell, fighting an eternal battle to preserve the Empire from the ravages of the daemon within him. He staggered, feeling the toxins in his body doing their baleful work. He was almost out of time.

He took a step towards the dark hole in the floor of the derelict building, savouring the sight of the last sunset he'd ever know.

'Let's get this done,' he said simply, and went to meet his destiny.

ABOUT THE AUTHOR

Sandy Mitchell is a pseudonym of Alex Stewart, who has been working as a freelance writer for the last couple of decades. He has written science fiction and fantasy in both personae, as well as television scripts, magazine articles, comics, and gaming material. His television credits include the high tech espionage series *Bugs*, for which, as Sandy, he also wrote one of the novelisations.

Apart from both miniatures and roleplaying gaming his hobbies include the martial arts of Aikido and Iaido, rifle shooting, and playing the guitar badly.

WARHAMMER
FANTASY ROLEPLAY

Enter a grim world of perilous adventure!

It is a dark time in the Old World. The Empire of man is assaulted from all sides by war-hungry orcs. Dwarfs fight a desperate battle against goblins and foul skaven. And from the teeming cities of the Empire to the dark ruins of forgotten centuries, an evil power is stirring. The servants of Chaos rise and plot to bring about the end of the world and the victory of their Dark Gods.

Warhammer Fantasy Roleplay is a game in which players take on the roles of brave adventurers, taking up arms against the approaching evil. The rulebook contains all you need to begin exploring this world of dark adventure.

The fate of the Old World is in your hands!

Visit us at www.blackindustries.com